*On a ship that's made of paper
I would sail the seven seas*

"Just to Be with You"
Bernard Roth

A Ship
Made of
Paper

Daniel and Hampton were paired by chance and against their wishes. They were not friends—Hampton did not particularly like Daniel, and Daniel had every reason to avoid being alone with Hampton. But Daniel's girlfriend or partner or whatever he was supposed to call her, Kate, Kate went home to relieve the baby-sitter who was minding her daughter, and Hampton's wife, there was no ambiguity there, his wife, Iris, with whom Daniel was fiercely in love, had gone home to look after their son. Daniel and Hampton stayed behind to search for a blind girl, a heartsick and self-destructive blind girl who had run away from today's cocktail party, either to get lost or to be found, no one was sure.

The searchers, fourteen in all, were each given a Roman candle—whoever found the lost girl was to fire the rocket into the sky, so the others would know—and each of the pairs was assigned a section of the property in which to look for Marie.

"Looks like you and me," Daniel said to Hampton, because he had to say something.

Hampton barely responded and he continued to only minimally acknowledge Daniel's nervous chatter as they walked away from the mansion through an untended expanse of wild grass that soon led into a dense wood of pine, locust, maple, and oak. Aside from the contrast of their color—Daniel was white, Hampton black—the two men were remarkably similar in appearance. They were both in their mid-thirties, an inch or so over six feet tall, broad-shouldered, reasonably fit. They were even dressed similarly, in khaki pants, white shirts, and blue blazers, *though Daniel's jacket was purchased at Macy's, and Hampton's had been sewn specially for him by a Chinese tailor in the city.*

Two years after he was kicked down the stairs of his apartment building in New York City, which shattered his wrist, chipped his front tooth, and, as he himself put it, broke his heart, Daniel Emerson is back in his hometown, driving Ruby, his girlfriend's four-year-old daughter, to her day care center, called My Little Wooden Shoe. The drive is ten or fifteen minutes, depending on the weather, and though Daniel is not Ruby's father, nor her stepfather, it usually falls to him to take the little girl in. Daniel cannot understand how she can so willingly and unfailingly absent herself from the beginnings of her daughter's day; Ruby's mother, Kate Ellis, cannot bear to rise early in the morning, nor can she bear the thought of having to deal with Melody, or Tammy, Keith, Tamara, Griffin, Elijah, Avery, Stephanie, Joel, Tess, Chantal, Dylan, or any of the other Wooden Shoers, not to mention their fathers and their mothers, a few of whom Daniel knew thirty-two years ago in this very town, when he was Ruby's age.

It's fine with Daniel. He welcomes the chance to do fatherly things with the little girl, and those ten morning minutes with dear little four-year-old Ruby, with her deep soulful eyes, and the wondrous things she sees with them, and her deep soulful voice, and the precious though not entirely memorable things she says with it, and the smell of baby shampoo and breakfast cereal filling the car, that little shimmering capsule of time is like listening to cello music in the morning, or watching birds in a flutter of industry building a nest, it simply reminds you that even if God is dead, or never existed in the first place, there is, nevertheless, something tender at the center of creation, some meaning, some purpose and poetry. He believes in parental love with the fervency of a man who himself was not loved, and those ten minutes with Ruby every weekday morning, before he drops her off at My Little Wooden Shoe and then drives over to his office, where he runs a poorly paying, uneventful country law practice, in the fairly uneventful town of Leyden, one hundred miles north of New York City, those six hundred sweet seconds are his form of worship, and the temperamental eight-year-old black Saab is his church.

Or was, actually, because, unfortunately, this is no longer the case. The drive is still ten minutes, Ruby is still snugly strapped in her child safety seat in the back of the car, her sturdy little body encased in lilac overalls, her short-fingered, square hands holding a box of raisins and a box of grape juice, and today she is commenting on the familiar landmarks they pass—the big kids' school, the abandoned apple orchard where the wizened old trees wreathed in autumn morning mist are so scarily bent, the big yellow farmhouse where there is always some sort of yard sale, the massive pasture where every July the county fair assembles, with its cows and snow cones, Ferris wheels and freaks—but today it is all Daniel can do to pay the slightest bit of attention to Ruby, because his mind is seized, possessed, and utterly filled by one repeating question: *Will Iris be there?*

Daniel has been carrying the unwieldy weight of this desire for months now, and so far his behavior has been impeccable. When it comes to Iris the rules he has made for himself are simple: look but don't touch, long for but don't have, think but don't say. All he wants to do is be in the same room with her, see what she is wearing, see by her eyes if she has slept well, exchange a few words, make her smile, hear her say his name.

Until recently, it was a matter of chance whether their paths would cross. Iris's deliveries and pickups of Nelson were helter-skelter, one day she'd have him there at eight o'clock, and the next at nine-thirty—it all depended on her class schedule at Marlowe College, where she was a graduate student, as well as Nelson's morning moods, which were unpredictable. But now, suddenly, she is exactly on Daniel's schedule most days, her Volvo station wagon pulls into the day care center's parking lot at virtually the same time as his. He wonders if it's deliberate on her part. He has reached the point of thinking so often of her, of so often going out of his way to pass her house, of looking for her wherever he goes, that it's become difficult for him to believe that Iris is not thinking, at least some of the time, of him.

Daniel pulls into My Little Wooden Shoe's parking lot and sees her car, already in its customary spot, directly facing the playground, with its redwood climbing structures, sandbox, and swings. He is so glad to know that she's here that he laughs.

"What's so funny?" Ruby asks, as he unsnaps her from her car seat, lifts her up. Her questions are blunt; he guesses one day she'll be a tough customer.

"Nothing."

"Then why are you laughing?" She smiles. Her milk teeth are tinged brown: as a baby she was sometimes allowed to fall asleep with a bottle of juice in her crib and the sugar wore away her enamel. Now the dentist says the best thing to do is just let them fall out. Yet the brown, lusterless teeth—along with her slight stoutness, and her ruddy complexion— make her look poor and rural, like a child in the background of a Brueghel painting.

"Just crazy thoughts," Daniel says. "How about you? Any crazy thoughts lately?"

"I want to go to Nelson's house after day care."

"That's not a very crazy thought."

She thinks about this for a moment. "I want to sleep over."

"You never know," Daniel says. He swoops her up into his arms, turns her upside down. She clutches her knapsack, afraid that her snack and box of juice will slip out. Daniel restrains himself from suggesting to Ruby: *Ask him, ask Nelson if you can spend the night.*

Today, Iris is wearing plaid cotton pants that are a little too short for her and a bulky green sweater that is a little too large. Her clothes are rarely beautiful, and it has often struck Daniel that Iris herself may have no idea that she is lovely to look at. Her dark hair is cut short, she wears no makeup, no jewelry, everything about her says, *I'm plain, don't bother looking at me.* Maybe he has drifted into the periphery of her life because somehow in the grand design of things—and this private, pulverizing love he feels makes him believe in grand designs—he is the man who must awaken her to her own beauty. Is there some casual, defused way he can say to her: *Do you have an idea how lovely you are?*

He wants to hold her in the moonlight. He wants to stroke her shoulder until she is fast asleep.

She is crouched next to Nelson, whispering something in his ear. He loves seeing her with her son, the intimacy of it pierces him. She seems a perfect mother: calm, present, able to adore without consuming. Nelson is a handsome boy, strong, bigger than most of the children in the day care, several shades lighter than his mother. There is something regal and disdainful in him. He has the air of someone forced to live around people who don't understand the full extent of his excellence. He nods impatiently as his mother speaks to him, and when his eyes light upon Ruby he bolts and the two children greet each other wildly, almost in a burlesque of happiness, holding hands, jumping up and down. Iris heaves a sigh and stands up, shakes her head.

"Sorry about that," Daniel says.

"Those two," says Iris.

"It looked like you were giving him some last-minute instructions," Daniel says.

Iris looks around to make certain she will not be overheard. "There was a note in his cubby from Linda. It seems he hit one of the other children yesterday."

"Oh well, these teachers have a way of catastrophizing everything."

"I just don't want the one African-American child in the whole school to be the one committing little acts of violence."

She never refers to race around him, and Daniel wonders if her saying this now is a way of inviting him in, or pushing him back.

"Do you have time for a cup of coffee or something?" he asks her.

She looks at her watch. "I've got a meeting with my thesis advisor in half an hour."

"That's nothing compared to the tight schedule of an unsuccessful, small-town lawyer," he says.

"Where would be fast?" Iris says.

"The Koffee Kup. The coffee's so bad they spell it with a K. And the lighting is so bad, it's impossible to sit there longer than fifteen minutes. I'll race you there."

———

He drives behind her, not wanting to risk letting her out of his sight, and feeling the juvenile, slightly demented thrill of looking at the back of her head, her hands on the steering wheel. A Marlowe College sticker is on her rear window. The sight of it ignites a little fizz of pity and tenderness in him—at thirty-three, she's new to Marlowe's graduate program, and her fixing that sticker to her car connotes some desire for definition, a will to belong, or so it seems to him. She maintains the exact thirty-five-mile-per-hour speed limit all the way to Leyden's miniature Broadway, and when she pulls into a parking spot in front of the diner she uses her turn signal. Such devotion to the rules, such commitment to the principles of highway safety—it would be ludicrous to believe that a woman like her could ever entertain the possibility of some sexual adventure, of entering into the grim geometry of infidelity.

He is astonished by his own ardor. He is like a man who suddenly discovers he can sing, who one day opens his mouth in the shower and music bursts out of him, each note dipped in gold. But the timing is wrong. He is thirty-six years old, he has commitments, and until now he gave no more credence to the transforming, commanding power of love than he did to the myth of Atlantis. Yet this desire, this overwhelming need to look at Iris—who he is convinced is not only beautiful but beautiful in a way that only he can fully appreciate, a beauty somehow designed especially for his eyes—is something he has allowed himself to succumb to. What harm, really, can it do?

Daniel wants to do no harm, nor does he want any harm to come to him. In fact, he has moved back to Leyden, home of his bucolic, mediocre childhood, leaving a prosperous career back in New York City, largely because he had lived for months with the fear that either one or several African-Americans were going to beat him within an inch of his life, or perhaps go that extra inch and kill him. It was not an idle, racist fantasy; he had been told flat out that his time was near. He had unsuccessfully defended a black man accused of dealing drugs, and on the day of the sentencing, a short, mild-looking black man in a blue suit, a white turtleneck, and a diamond earring whispered to Daniel, "Keep your eyes open. You know what I'm saying?" Within a week, Daniel's own dread had wound itself around him so tightly that he couldn't see a person of color—a cleaning woman, a bus driver, acrobats and break-dancers in Washington Square Park, a bunch of high school kids horsing around on the subway platform—without thinking that this one, or that one, might be an emissary from his furious client. "I'm afraid of black people," he finally said to Kate. It was the most shaming thing he had ever told another person. He felt like an insect, a fool. Kate, for her part, was entirely sympathetic. *And to think you defended that fucking idiot for free,* she kept on saying. Did anything she said make him feel better? He can no longer remember. He spent another two months crossing the street to get away from suspicious-looking blacks, spending a fortune in cab fares, exhausting himself with gasps and double takes, feeling weak and loathsome, and they caught up with him anyhow.

Daniel and Iris walk into the Koffee Kup together. Of the three breakfast spots in Leyden, this is the oldest, and the core clientele are natives of Leyden. It's a simple, sparsely decorated storefront, with a high ceiling and overhead fans, a row of dark wooden booths, a long Formica counter, and a scattering of tables up front. The women who run it—country women with checkered domestic lives and a penchant for teasing and wisecracks—open for business at six in the morning, when the truckers, contractors, and farmworkers gather for ham and eggs. Now that Leyden is changing, with more and more city people moving in, there are fancier and, to be honest about it, better places to have breakfast, but Daniel still frequents the Double K, where his parents took him for his first restaurant meal. He holds the door open for Iris, knowing there will surely be people here whom he knows, people to whom he will have to nod, or greet, or perhaps even speak with. Kate, however, will certainly not be among them. It is not yet nine o'clock and she is probably still sleeping, or if she is awake she isn't out of bed yet. She is probably pouring herself a cup of Viennese roast from the thermos he always places at her bedside before leaving with Ruby in the morning.

Daniel and Iris sit at a table near the front window. The youngest of the Koffee Kup waitresses, ponytailed and pierced Becky, brings Daniel a coffee and a glass of water, which is what she always does as soon as he sits down. She brings nothing for Iris and seems, in fact, not to register her presence.

"I think we're going to need another coffee here, Becky," Daniel says. Becky looks momentarily confused, and then she turns and looks at Iris as if seeing her for the first time.

"Oh, sorry," she says, her voice flat.

"Do you have decaf?" Iris says brightly, smiling. She has a space between her front teeth.

"Do you want decaf?" Becky asks. She heaves a sigh.

"That would be great," Iris says to Becky.

What Daniel does not see: Iris's foot is tapping nervously. The waitress's slight stubbornness about the decaf is potential trouble. All Iris wants is for it to go unnoticed; the small rudeness is the sort of thing that her husband would be fuming about, if he were here right now. He's thin-skinned, his radar for slights is always on, always scanning the social horizon for incoming missiles. Iris has sat with him in innumerable restaurants while he has glared at the waitress, gestured impatiently at the waiter, sent back the soup, sent back the fish, asked to speak to the manager, and let it be known with a few choice words that he was no one to be trifled with. And it's not just in restaurants that this highly tuned sensitivity to insult turns what Iris always hopes will be a simple outing into a kind of despairing war against prejudice. At a Yankees game when the usher asks a second time to check his tickets, in the first-class cabin on a flight to Hawaii when the stewardess forgets to bring him an extra pillow and then tells him there are no more macadamia nuts, at the

Jaguar dealership where the salesman will not let them take the car out for a test drive without xeroxing his license and taking an imprint of his American Express card.

"I guess they're brewing up a fresh pot of the decaf," Daniel says. "Are you going to have time?"

They talk about the children, and Daniel feels the minutes ticking away; it's like feeling himself bleed to death. He wonders, wildly, if Iris remembers that he is not really Ruby's father. How can he bring that up without it seeming small-minded? Iris's coffee has still not arrived, and she checks her watch, looks quickly over her shoulder at Becky, who is at the far end of the counter leisurely chatting to an old man in a tractor cap and suspenders.

"I'm having such a hard time in school," Iris says. "And I can't be late for this meeting with my advisor. He already thinks I'm a flake."

"He can't think that."

"I'm getting my doctorate in American Studies, and I can't even figure out my thesis. I keep changing it. The thing is, I really want to get my degree, but another part of me would be happy to stay in school forever. It's so much fun, and it's not like I've got to put bread on my family table."

"When I first met you, you were thinking about Thurgood Marshall."

"That was my husband's idea. Marshall was sort of a friend of his family. Well, there have been many changes of topic since then. God. All this time off from school, all this marriage and motherhood, it's sort of gummed up my brain. I'm in a state of constant confusion."

"I never liked school," Daniel says, though it's not true. He's not sure why he said it.

"I like school. I just don't like my brain right now." Her laugh is soft, heartrending. She pushes the sleeves of her sweater up, showing her articulated forearms, dark and hairless. "I better get out of here," she says.

"This is ridiculous. You didn't even get your coffee."

"It's no big deal." Her heart is racing; how long will it take him to figure out that the waitress is deliberately not serving her? "Anyhow, you said the coffee's not very good here."

"Well, at least drink the water, the water's excellent."

Outside, they linger for a moment. "Becky was weird in there," Daniel says.

"Becky?" Iris can feel it coming; he is going to declare himself outraged on her behalf. He is going to be her prince in shining liberal armor.

"Yes, our waitress," he says. He feels a quickening, he has found a way to say what he has wanted to say for so long. "The thing about Becky is she's weird around beautiful women." There. It's said. He makes a helpless gesture, as if he were tossing up his life, seeing where it would land. He doesn't dare look at her. "Because you are. So extraordinarily beautiful."

"Oh." She says it as if he were a child who has come up with something adorable. "Well, thanks."

"I still owe you a cup of coffee," he says. "How about tomorrow?"

"Tomorrow's Saturday," she says.

He watches her as she hurries toward her car. Her generous bottom, her funny little run. The sky is dark blue and the autumn sun is warm and steady, as if promising that winter will never arrive. A slow breeze moves down the street, carrying the perfume of the slowly dying leaves, a nearby field's last mowing, the river. What can the world do to you with its beauty? Can it lift you up on its shoulders, as if you were a hero, can it whoopsie-daisy you up into its arms as if you were a child? Can it goad your timid heart, urge you on to finally seize what you most shamefully desire? Yes, yes, all that and more. The world can crush you with its beauty.

———

Back in the city, Daniel's firm had offices that took three floors in a stylish Art Deco building on Lexington Avenue, with astrological mosaics in the lobby, and arte moderne numerals over the filigreed brass elevator doors. But here in Leyden his place of work is as humble as his practice, two rooms in a wood-framed building near the center of town. It's an ungraceful, stolid sort of building, the architectural equivalent of a schoolmarm, a nun, a maiden aunt; it once had been, in fact, a boardinghouse, from 1925 to 1960, owned by two musical, free-thinking

German sisters, and run exclusively for local unmarried women—genteel shop-women, schoolteachers, and a woman named Marjorie Ingersoll, who had a small private income that she supplemented by giving painting and drawing lessons, and whose cheerful landscapes, with their agitated skies and roller coaster hills and valleys, are still displayed along the stairways and in the hallways. Now, the house has been turned into an office complex, where Daniel rents a two-room suite, where century-old locust trees scrape their branches against the windows at the wind's slightest provocation. Eight hundred and fifty dollars a month, which back in the city would get him thirty square feet in Staten Island.

Daniel climbs the back stairs to the second floor, so lost in thought as he replays and what-ifs this morning's meeting with Iris that he forgets today's first appointment will be with his parents, who have announced that they wish to review their last will and testament. Daniel is not their lawyer; the meager bits of legal business they have generated throughout their adult lives have been handled by one of the town's old-timers, Owen Fitzsimmons, an ectoplasmic old sort with funereal eyes and icy hands. Fitzsimmons was a longtime chiropractic patient of Daniel's father's, and while Mrs. Fitzsimmons was alive, the two couples took golfing vacations together to Phoenix and San Diego, formed a wine-tasting club that was quite a success in Leyden in the late 1970s, and one summer traveled together to Scotland and Ireland, where they stayed in castles, golfed, and came back home percolating with plans to retire and expatriate to what they continually referred to as "the British Isles." When his parents called for an appointment, Daniel had wondered if there'd been some falling-out with Fitzsimmons, though that seemed to him unlikely. Daniel found Fitzsimmons both vain and dour, a chilly man in a worn blue blazer with some mysterious crest over the pocket. But then Daniel's parents—Carl and Julia Emerson—were no less dour, and even shared with Fitzsimmons whatever circulatory difficulty it is that prevents one's hands, fingers, and particularly fingertips from getting the blood flow necessary to keep them at a mammalian temperature. Because their work entailed touching people, both of them were continually blowing on their hands to try to warm them.

Daniel's secretary is named Sheila Alvarez. She is a stout, round-faced woman. She wraps her dark braids so they sit like a woven basket on top of her head, and she wears complicated necklaces with tiny stones, bits of seashell, and pantheistic amulets. The least alluring of three daughters, she is one of those women who get stuck with the task of caring for aging, suffering parents, and when they died she was all alone in the world, and too emotionally spent to do anything about it. She has a far-flung network of women friends, with whom she is continually on the phone. She is, however, unfailingly efficient, and since getting ill last winter, when Daniel not only protected her job during a long convalescence but also paid for the hospital charges that the insurance company didn't cover, she is fiercely loyal to Daniel, protective and vigilant, as if the office were under continual attack, or threat of attack, though, of course, it is not: it's just a humdrum rural practice, with one criminal case for every ten real estate closings, and even the criminal cases rarely come to trial.

This practice barely affords him a decent living—in fact, he's not really clearing much more than he pays Sheila—and it is as close to his former, sleek professional life as a campfire is to a blast furnace, and sometimes it is remarkable to Daniel not only that he has chosen this quiet, country life but that he finds it so agreeable. True, leaving New York was more like fleeing New York, but he could have chosen someplace with more people, better cases, more money to be made. Yet here he is, right back in Leyden, which, for years, every time he left it—during prep school, college, law school, after holidays, summers, the funeral of an old grade school buddy—he always assumed he was seeing it for the very last time. Kate, upon agreeing to move to Leyden with him, sensed that Daniel wanted to be near his aging parents, and, despite her misgivings, she didn't see how she could prevent him from fulfilling his filial duties. Though every story he ever told her about his parents made them seem as if they were monsters of reserve, two towering touch-me-nots who treated Daniel as if he were not so much their son as their charge, one of those boys from a nineteenth-century novel, a boisterous nephew left behind by a floozy sister, an orphan whose parents have disappeared under mysterious circumstances in India, a little human mess it had fallen to them to mop up.

Sheila hangs up the phone as Daniel closes the outer door of his office behind him. She is quick to end what was obviously a personal call, but her smile is warm and unrepentant.

"Everything okay here?" he asks.

She puts a short, bejeweled finger over her peachy lips, and then quickly scrawls a note to him on a yellow Post-it. "Your parents are waiting for you inside," it says.

In truth, he has forgotten they were coming, and he *does* feel a little dismayed, but he exaggerates his feelings to amuse Sheila—his face a stark, staring mask of mock horror. He crumples the note, his eyes dart back and forth, as if he were about to bolt. *What am I going to do?* His lips soundlessly form the words. His hand goes to his throat. Sheila laughs, also soundlessly, and then she leans back in her high-tech swiveling office chair, and the contraption tilts back so abruptly that it seems as if she is going to tip over, which elicits a scream of shock and delight from her.

Great, Daniel mimes to her, and then he strolls into his inner office, where Carl and Julia are seated on the sofa, but leaning forward, their heads tilted, looks of concern on their faces.

"What was that scream?" Daniel's father asks.

"Sheila," Daniel says. "Tipping over." He greets his parents with affection, which he presents to them mildly, delicately, with the kind of reserve you expect in a funeral home or in an intensive care unit. He kisses his mother gently on the cheek, shakes his father's hand while keeping his own eyes down. He sits at his desk, runs his hands over its clear, waxed surface.

"So what's the problem with your wills?" Daniel asks, wanting to take charge of the conversation. The last thing he wants to do is to answer their bread-and-butter inquiries about Kate and Ruby, neither of whom they have bothered to try to know very well, but whom they would be likely to ask after, for the sake of form.

Carl and Julia exchange nervous looks, openly, as if they are communicating over a client who is facedown on the chiropractic table. Daniel, for his part, pretends not to notice. When he was young, he was curious to discover what lay behind his parents' ceaseless secrecy and reserve, what horrible little habits they might conceal, what gooey sexual secrets, what hidden morsels of biography. Maybe they carried some deep malice, perhaps they weren't really married, perhaps he was adopted, maybe his father was a quack, maybe his mother ended every evening in bed sniffing at a rag drenched in ether, and just maybe they were from outer space. It's puzzling to him how his curiosity has persisted, but now he fears that if they were ever to suddenly confide in him he might want to clap his hands over his ears. It's too late for that. His effort has been to make peace with the people who raised him, the creaky couple who always winced if he raised his voice, the punctual pair who had a clock in every room and who marked the passing of the hours with their sighs, their meals, their TV programs. If they were to show him something different now, it would upset that peace, the treaty would be nullified, he would have to start to try to understand them, and he did not care to.

Somehow, in their little exchange of glances, it is decided that Carl will present the problem to Daniel. "We've made some changes in our will," he says, in his calm, authoritative voice. "And Owen strongly advised us to go over them with you."

"Okay," Daniel says, stretching the word out. He is looking closely at his father, imagining himself looking like him in forty years. Worse things could happen. Carl is fit, leaner than Daniel is now. His blue eyes are sharp beneath spiky, emphatic eyebrows. There is something strange in the intensity of his father's gaze. When he looks you in the eye it doesn't feel like frankness, it feels like aggression. His hair is still dark and abundant, his posture a living advertisement for his particular branch of the medical arts. He looks scrubbed, well rested, prosperous—pleased with life, and pleased with himself. Julia, however, is starting to age rapidly. She has become frail, a little trembly, and her once imperious features look surprised by her own onrushing mortality.

"Well," Carl continues, "as you know, in the past three or four years your mother and I have become much more involved in the Windsor County Raptor Center, over in Bailey Point."

"No," Daniel says. "As a matter of fact, I didn't know." Raptor Center? And then it hits him: his father's eyes are those of a hawk, an eagle, a falcon.

"Yes, you did," Julia says, a little accusingly. "Don't you recall my showing you pictures of your father and me at the center? Father had a falcon on his arm?" Her throat seems as if it were irritated by the work of talking, and she coughs into her hand.

"You know me, Mom. I have a terrible memory. But I do know the place. An old friend of mine from fifth grade runs it."

"Lionel Sanderson," Carl says, with a smile.

"Right," says Daniel. "How is he?"

"Overworked, but what dedicated man is not?"

"He remembers you, of course," Julia adds. "He often recalls the nice afternoons after school at our house."

Daniel is both stunned and amused by the untruthfulness of this. First of all, he and Lionel were never close friends and did not spend their time after school in each other's company. And secondly, *no one* came to the Emerson house after school, or on weekends, or during the summer, or any time at all, except to quickly call for Daniel and be on their way. His parents found the racket and clutter of boys unbearable. The house itself was a meticulous and unfriendly place, and the pictures on the walls were of skulls and spinal cords, giving the place a kind of permanent Halloween ambiance—a chilling, childless Halloween. But Daniel knows better than to challenge their take on the past—he has tried it before when other inconsistencies have arisen, and it has caused hard feelings.

"Well, it's not that we have any plans to be kicking the bucket," Carl says, "but we wanted you to know that we've decided to leave the bulk of our estate to the Raptor Center. Right now, the whole operation is squeezed onto twenty-five acres, and there's not a building on the property that doesn't need some major repair. What they would like to do—"

"Need to do," Julia says.

"Is double the acreage, and create facilities that can safely house fifty birds."

"I see," Daniel says. He senses the injury of what is being said, but he can't feel it. It's like cutting your thumb with a fine blade and seeing the little crease in the skin but not yet the blood. "Well, that sounds good. Raptors."

"What we wanted to avoid at all costs," Julia says, "is having you learn about this after we're gone. And then feeling that we've done this *against* you somehow."

"Because nothing could be further from the truth," Carl adds.

"Yes," Daniel says. "Well. Raptors. You're not planning some early departure scenario, are you?" He sees the confusion on their faces, clarifies. "You know, ending it all. Suicide." He raises his voice on that word, startles himself.

"Absolutely not," says Carl.

"But we're not getting any younger," Julia says. "Dan, let's concentrate on what is important here. If your father and I thought you needed money, then of course we would have left every penny we have to you. But here you are." She makes an encompassing gesture, indicating his office, the Moroccan carpet on the floor, the glassed-in bookshelves, the antique oak file cabinets. "The Raptor Center is barely making it."

"We're assuming you must have salted away a pretty penny from that job in New York—or else why would you have retired from it?"

He'll let that pass. "I just never knew you two were so involved with birds of prey," he says.

"It's recent," says Carl. "We don't want this to cause any hard feelings. Your mother and I have been talking this over for months, and that's the most important thing, that there be no hard feelings. This is in no way meant to indicate what our feelings are for you, Dan. You're our son."

"Our only son," says Julia. "Our only offspring. Our only family."

"Are we talking about every penny you have?" asks Daniel.

"And the house," says Carl.

"Not the contents, however," Julia says, prodding Carl with one finger.

I couldn't care less, Daniel thinks. Yet the affront of this is unmistakable. *I'm read out of their will? Why are they trying to punish me? Did I miss a Sunday dinner? Did I fail to rake their leaves, clean their gutters, haul their empties to the recycling center?* And then, in an instant, a huge and unhappy thought presents itself to him: *I came back here to be near them.* And, in the next instant, the thought is gone.

Carl has opened his briefcase and produced a manila folder containing Polaroids of the various pieces of furniture and works of art Carl and Julia have deemed the most valuable of their possessions. The grandfather clock, with its long, tarnished pendulum, which Daniel was always forbidden to touch, the spindly nesting table, which he was also not allowed to touch, the blue willow setting for twelve, also out of bounds, the purple and red Persian rug, which he was allowed to walk across, but only without shoes, the antique hat rack upon which Daniel was never permitted to hang his hat—parenthood came late to the Emersons, and when Daniel was born, they did not childproof their house, they houseproofed their child.

"Whenever you see something you really and truly want," Julia says, "just turn the picture over and put your name on it."

"I don't really see the purpose of this," Daniel says.

"We wanted you to have first choice," says Julia.

"First choice over whom? You don't have any other children. Do you think the birds are going to want your china cabinet?"

Again, Carl and Julia trade worried glances, gesture back and forth, as if they are alone.

"This is exactly why we wanted to get this done when all three of us could sit calmly together and hash it out," Carl says. "We don't want any misunderstandings."

"The thing is, I don't want your money. I make a decent living—I *am* charging you for this appointment, by the way." Daniel laughs but is not surprised when his parents don't join in. Once, about twenty-five years ago, he made his mother laugh at a knock-knock joke, but he hasn't been able to get so much as a chuckle out of either of them since.

"But you see?" says Julia. "That was exactly our thinking."

"You're doing fine," says Carl. "You always have. From the very beginning. I hope you realize what a blessing it was for your mother and I to have a son whom we trusted, who did the right things, who kept out of trouble, and who was never a danger to himself or to others. Believe me. You may think of your mother and me as living in a bell jar, but we see what other people have gone through with their children. Drugs and homosexuality being just the most lurid examples. The great luxury you afforded us was that we never needed to doubt your basic stability. It was such a relief to know that no matter what, you were always going to be just fine. Your head was always screwed on right."

"Well, that's really incredibly moving, Dad," Daniel says, gathering up the photographs, closing the folder, handing it back to his father. "Maybe you better hang on to these, okay? Who knows? I might disappoint you after all, and you wouldn't want any of this fine furniture falling into the wrong hands."

———

Throughout that day he taps his feet beneath his desk while he pretends to listen to clients, and then in court he keeps one hand clenched in his pocket while he enters a plea of not guilty in a criminal mischief case. Thoughts of Iris have completely eclipsed any reflections he might have had over being cut out of his parents' will. All he can think of is getting out of his office and driving past her house. He likes to see where she lives, the house, its reality pleases him. There is something at once sacred and pornographic, knowing she is in there. Today is Friday, a particularly important day to drive by. It is the day that Hampton, her husband, returns from the city for his weekend at home. The sunset looks like melted vermilion, the houses and trees are drawn in black ink. He navigates his car down Juniper Street, listening to Dinah Washington sing "What a Difference a Day Makes" on the car stereo, and it strikes him that all his life he has been in love with black women—Dinah Washington, Billie Holiday, Irma Thomas, Ivie Anderson, Ella Fitzgerald, Ma Rainey, Bessie Smith.

Juniper Street is only four blocks long, lined on both sides by single-family houses, some with a will toward grandness, others compact Dutch dollhouses, tight little structures painted brown or yellow, with churchy windows and bronze plaques over the doorway announcing the year of their construction. As he rolls closer to Iris's house, he turns off the music, slows to practically a stop. Her house is white clapboard, with a small porch, red shutters, a quartet of maple trees on the front lawn. The windows are dark, they hold a faint reflection of the sunset. Iris's car is not in the driveway, and Daniel, no stranger to her comings and go-ings, in fact having more knowledge of them than he would ever admit to anyone else, realizes she has left for the train station to pick up Hampton, whose train is coming in at 6:05. Daniel can hardly bear to think of this—imagining her on the platform peering into the windows of the train as it pulls in, trying to see if it's him, or him, or him, and then there he is, the conquering hero, home from a week of shuffling expensive paper, with his Hugo Boss suit and shaved head, his Mark Cross leather satchel, his Burberry raincoat draped over his shoulders like a cape, here comes the Count of Venture Capital, and now the inevitable kiss, the child between them, symbol of their unbreakable bond, the little wink over Nelson's head, a promise of a fuller, more intimate reunion later on: by now Daniel's mind is a scorpion stinging itself to death.

He resists speeding over to the train station and instead drives home, out six miles east of town to Red Schoolhouse Road. It's Kate's house, her down payment, but surely his half of the monthly mortgage entitles him to feelings of ownership. It is a two-hundred-and-fifty-year-old farmhouse, calm and elegant like Kate herself, with French doors, an immense fireplace, ten acres, the remains of a barn. The dark gray night has healed over the gash of the sunset; a wind is coming off the river. When he pulls into the driveway, he sees an old winter-ravaged Dodge parked next to Kate's impeccable Toyota, and when he lets himself in he sees Ruby in the living room, sitting on the sofa with her baby-sitter.

"Look, Daniel! I have a baby-sitter!" Ruby cries out, with incongru-ous elation.

The sitter is a high school girl named Mercy. Daniel figures Ruby's joy must mean she has extracted a promise from Mercy to let her watch TV. He chats with the two girls for a minute, and then goes upstairs to find out where he is going tonight, since as far as he knew there was no plan in place.

He finds Kate in their bedroom, a dark-green room with odd angles, wide plank floors, a Persian rug. She is putting on lipstick and keeping an eye on the portable TV, which has become indispensable to her. The sound is off and she continually checks the set—sometimes in the mirror, sometimes turning around to face it—in order to see if there's anything on the news about O. J. Simpson, who for the past several months has been on trial for the murder of his ex-wife.

"Any news?" asks Daniel, just to be polite.

"Nothing, same old, same old."

"What if he's innocent, Kate?"

"Yeah, right."

"You got a sitter for Ruby?"

"You said you wished we went out more. So. Presto! We're going out."

"Great. Where we going?"

"Iris Davenport called this afternoon." She glances at Daniel to see his reaction in the mirror. Nothing. She's impressed. He's standing up well to this. "She was trying to arrange something or other for the children. I'm sort of surprised she didn't arrange it with you, that seems to be the way these things get done around here. But, anyhow, she mentioned that she and her husband were going to a concert tonight and the next thing I knew I had volunteered us to go along with them." She turns toward Daniel, puts her hand against her throat. "Is that all right? And dinner after?"

"I thought you don't like eating with strangers," Daniel says, struggling to keep it casual. "I thought you don't like watching them put food in their mouths."

Kate's attention is momentarily seized by something on the TV screen, but it's another black athlete, walking over a pulsating green landscape of little hills with a golf club over his shoulder. Tiger Woods.

How can there be no O. J. news today? Like millions of others, Kate has become obsessed with the case—with not only the defendant but the lawyers, the judge, the DNA experts. Stalled on her novel, unable to touch it, often unable even to think about it, she has become facile as a journalist and lately she's been writing about the case, and since the jury is sequestered and she is not being paid for her objectivity, she has been having no trouble in clamoring for Simpson's conviction.

"I thought you'd be happy I made these plans," Kate says. "You mention her constantly. I figured it was time we got to know them, another couple, like actual grown-ups."

"I mention her constantly?"

"I don't know, probably not. I'm not trying to give you a hard time. I'm trying to make you happy." With rich, shining brown hair, smooth skin, and the scent of perfume on her, she glides to Daniel's side. She would like to put her arms around him, but it might seem she was forcing the issue.

"You do *like* them, don't you?" she asks. A surviving bit of her old southern accent stretches the "i" in "like."

"I don't really know him."

"Do you like her?"

"Iris?"

She gives him a look. Of course Iris, who else are they talking about?

"Yes," he says. "Sure. Why not? She's Ruby's best friend's mother. That's got to be worth something. And she's nice. She's funny."

"Tell me something funny she's said. It'll whet my appetite for an evening of unbridled hilarity."

"Okay." He takes a deep breath. "Last spring—"

"Last spring? You have to go *that* far back in time?"

"Actually, it was the summer. She got a mosquito bite, and I guess she was scratching it and scratching it." His eyes shift away from Kate's; he realizes he is talking himself into a hole. "And she turned the bite into a sore, you know how that happens. And so she took a pen and wrote 'ouch ouch ouch ouch' in a circle all around the bite."

"That's it? She wrote ouch on her arm?"

"You know what, Kate? I think we should call them and say we can't make it."

She wouldn't mind doing just that, but she's already set her course. "Nonsense," she says. She holds her pearls out to him and he comes behind her to fasten them. In her scoop-necked dress, Kate's collarbones look as sturdy as handlebars.

"You look nice," Daniel says. He seems to mean it. He even touches her hair. "You look beautiful."

She cannot fully believe that Daniel has embarked on some flirtation. It contradicts not only her trust in him but her sense of him. She met him when she was sick to death of eccentric, neurotic men. She had a year-old baby and a busted-up marriage, a successful novel and a contract for a second, and all she wanted from a man was clarity, kindness, and dependability. She distrusted despair, had an aversion to any kind of domestic drama. Daniel back then had been a lawyer in the firm that represented Kate's publishing house and he, too, was recently out of a shabby affair, this one with a woman who turned out to have a hair-trigger temper and a penchant for violence. Kate and Daniel used to joke with each other about being the last normal people on earth, and the joke turned into a kind of emotional contract; they were promising each other affection with tranquility, a life of measured gestures, respect for boundaries. It would be a levelheaded alliance; they would be Swiss bankers of the heart.

"I can't believe you did this, put this . . . this evening together," he is saying.

She watches his face, carefully. Despite her belief that he would never actually have an affair, he seems to be a man who wants to take a journey. He hasn't booked passage, he doesn't have a ticket, he doesn't have the guts. Kate is certain that he has not betrayed her. It hasn't gone that far, not yet. It's still an affair of the mind. He thinks a love affair will rescue him. From what? Yet in a way, that no-idea-what's-wrong sort of life might be exactly what he wants to be rescued from. Kate feels curious but removed. She has decided to let it play out.

She would like to take a closer look at Iris. Lately, he has been mentioning her, telling stories that have no point except to give him an occasion to say "Iris." Kate, thus far, fails to see the appeal. Iris is ten pounds too thin, fidgety, psychologically evasive but physically a little *too* present, with a cat-on-a-hot-tin-roof quality to her, a woman used to being sought after, loved, but not really satisfied, used to adulation, a daddy's girl, perhaps.

Of course, her blackness is a part of what draws Daniel to her, Kate is certain of this. All those blues records, all that soul music, and even gospel music, the man listens to Sam Cooke singing about Jesus and gets tears in his eyes, though he himself has no more belief in Christ than he has in the Easter bunny. He must have been preparing himself for this all along. Getting the soundtrack down for his big movie spectacular. The story of his life taking shape, the story of himself as a great romantic hero, crossing the color line. How passé! How pathetic! As if getting involved with an African-American could be the solution to his problems. As if it would give him something to believe in. The poor little unloved son suddenly draping himself in three hundred years of another people's history, the invisible man taking shape beneath the swaddling of black bandages.

"Do I have time for a shower?" Daniel asks.

———

The night is chilly. A stiff westerly wind blows through the trees and black clouds are snapping at the moon. A steady procession of concert-goers march into St. John's, where tonight the Leyden Musical Society is performing the *Messiah*. To Kate, even after three years in Leyden, it's a procession of strangers, but Daniel knows most of the crowd by name. She watches him waving, smiling at whoever makes eye contact. She is often exhausted by his outwardness. His smile can grate on her as if it were a cough. Kate realizes that in the vast literature of wifely complaints this doesn't register with great intensity, but Daniel smiles too easily and she doesn't care for it. The man smiles while he sleeps.

Yet even as he smiles, he's craning his neck, on the lookout for Iris and Hampton. Kate doesn't mean to think in racial terms, but it seems to her that black people are always running late. Maybe it's a bit of aggression toward whites, maybe with each other they're as punctual as the six o'clock news. She watches Daniel, swiveling his head around like an adulterous owl.

"Daniel?" She pats him on the arm. "You look a little crazy."

"I do?" He blinks, as if just awakened. And then they see them, moving quickly along Manchester Avenue, hurrying, arm in arm.

"Hello!" Daniel calls out, eagerly raising his hand as if he were a schoolboy with the right answer. Iris is wearing a gray overcoat, black pants, boots, a kind of African hat. Everything seems a couple sizes too large, she is like some goofy kid wearing her mother's clothes. Not so with the husband. Hampton—his skin pale toffee, his emanation of coiled energy, his aura of wealth—is wearing a sumptuous, practically edible-looking cashmere coat, a paisley silk scarf with tassels. He has those round little glasses, steel framed, gentle, scholarly, that Kate identifies as deliberately reassuring, nonsexual, a little eunuchy, really, the signifying eyewear of the black professional.

Daniel kisses Iris's cheek, and Hampton, seeing this, plants a quick kiss on Kate, with all the tenderness of a clerk stamping a bill paid.

The four of them make their way into the church. St. John's is for Leyden's upper-class Episcopalians, and for those who like to pray with their betters. It's chilly, Spartan, like a lodge high in the Austrian Alps. All that woodwork, the fresh white flowers, and the Episcopalian flag that reminds her of the Red Cross. She and Daniel, and then Iris and Hampton, find places in a back pew. The orchestra is already tuning up as they arrange themselves. Daniel and Iris seem to be intent on not making the slightest eye contact.

Kate tries to keep her attention riveted upon the orchestra and the chorus throughout the concert. The conductor is Ethan Greenblatt, president of Marlowe College, a handsome young academic superstar with an explosion of curly hair and a fussy bow tie. He is pushing the musicians through the piece at breakneck speed, as if afraid of detaining the audience past its attention span. But from time to time, Kate must glance at Daniel. His eyes are closed, but she's sure he's awake. Hampton takes Iris's hand, brings it to his lips, while she stares intently ahead. And then, Kate sees Daniel glancing at Iris. Their eyes meet for a moment, but it has the impact of cymbals crashing. It is a shocking, agitating thing to see. It's like being in a store with someone and watching them steal something.

Afterward, the four of them walk to the George Washington Inn, where Iris has made dinner reservations. The Inn is redolent with Colonial history—low, beamed ceilings, wormy old tavern tables, an immense blackened fireplace. A high school girl serves them a basket of rolls, then comes back to fill their water glasses. She pours Hampton's last and accidentally fills it to the very top; in fact, a little of it laps onto the table. "Oops," she says, but Hampton looks away. His jaw is suddenly rigid. Iris touches his knee, pats it, as if to calm him down. With her other hand, she is dabbing the little dime-sized puddle with her napkin.

A moment later, a waiter appears to take their drink orders. Daniel and Kate are used to this waiter, middle-aged, vain, and formal. Hampton, however, sees the waiter's extreme tact as an extension of the busgirl's spilling his water, and he orders a vodka martini in a surly voice. "Use Absolut," he says. "I'll know if the bartender uses the house brand."

Iris looks down at her lap; when she raises her gaze again she sees Daniel is looking at her, smiling. It startles her into smiling back. The two of them seem so happy to be gazing at each other, and Kate feels like Princess Kitty standing at the edge of the room and noticing the joy that floods their faces when Vronsky's and Anna Karenina's eyes meet. Kate wonders exactly how far along these two really are. Is it too late to stop them?

"So, Hampton," Kate says, "tell me. I hear all about Iris from Daniel, but nothing about you. You're in the city most of the time?"

"I come up here on the weekend," Hampton says. "During the workweek, I stay at the apartment where we used to live before Iris got into Marlowe."

"It's a beautiful apartment," Iris says. She glances at Hampton, who smiles at her.

"So what keeps you down in the city all week?" Kate asks.

"I'm co–managing director of the Atlantic Fund," Hampton says.

"He's an investment banker," Iris says, in the same anxious-to-please tone in which she said their apartment was beautiful. To Kate, Iris sounds like a woman whose husband has complained about how she treats him in public.

"The Atlantic Fund provides capital to African-American business," Hampton says. "It's sometimes difficult for black-owned businesses to get what they need from the white banking structure." He cranes his neck, looks for the waiter. "Just like it's hard to get a white waiter to bring you a drink." He breathes out so hard his cheeks puff for a moment. "I've never come here, and now I know why."

"Have we really been waiting that long?" asks Kate. "It seems like we just sat down." She looks to Daniel for confirmation, but all Daniel can manage is a shrug. He is on a plane and he has just heard something in the pitch of the engine's roar that makes him feel the flight is doomed.

"God, that music was so wonderful," Iris says.

"The first time I heard Handel's *Messiah,* I was four years old," Hampton says, his eyes on Kate. "My grandmother was in a chorus that performed it for Richard Nixon, at the White House." This comment is in keeping with remarks he's been making since they left the church. Already they'd heard references to his grandfather's Harvard roommate, his great-grandfather's Presbyterian mission in the Congo, his mother's spending five thousand dollars on haute couture in Paris when she was eleven years old, his aunt Dorothy's short engagement to Colin Powell, the suspicious fire at the Welles vacation compound on Martha's Vineyard. He boasts about his lineage in a way that Kate thinks would simply not be allowed from a white person.

"Thurgood Marshall was a friend of the family and he was there, too, of course. Unfortunately, he fell asleep after ten minutes. Gramma said they all sang extra loud to cover Justice Marshall's snoring."

Kate wonders if Hampton is trying to put Daniel on alert. He, too, must sense what's happening. She has to admit that she is enjoying this foursome more than she'd dared hope. It captures her imagination in some creepy, achey way, like sucking on a tooth that's just starting to die.

"Is this the same grandmother who played the cello?" she asks. *Maybe if you thought a little less about your grandmother's pedigree and a little more about your wife, she wouldn't be squirming in her chair and eyeing my boyfriend.*

"No, the cellist was Abigail Welles, of Boston, my father's mother. The singing grandma was Lucille Cox, of Atlanta, on my mother's side."

"I have many Coxes in my family," Kate says. "On my mother's side, many of them from Georgia, too."

There is a brief silence, and then Kate says what she guesses must be passing through everyone's mind. "Of course, there's a chance that one of *my* Coxes held one of your Coxes in slavery."

"In that case," says Daniel, lifting his wine glass, "dinner's on us."

For the first time that evening, Hampton smiles. Beaming, his face grows younger. His teeth are large, even, and very white, and he casts his eye downward, as if the moment's pleasure makes him shy. Kate can imagine the moment when Iris first saw that smile, how it must have drawn her in and made her want to fathom the secret cave of self that was his smile's source.

"Hampton," Kate says. "That's an interesting name."

"My family's full of Hamptons," he says. "We come from Hampton, Virginia. A few of us attended Hampton University, back when it was Hampton Normal and Agriculture Institute."

"Hampton Hawes," says Daniel.

"What?" says Hampton.

"He's a jazz piano player, West Coast."

"Daniel knows everything about jazz," says Kate. "And blues, and rhythm and blues."

The waitress arrives and presents them with yellowfin tuna, coq au vin, filet mignon, risotto funghi. "Look," says Iris, "everything looks so good!"

"Is that tuna?" Hampton asks, peering at Iris's plate.

Every marriage, Kate thinks, seems to have one person wanting what's on the other's plate.

Iris smiles, but she doesn't look pleased. "Do you want some?"

"Okay, a taste." He watches while she cuts her sesame-encrusted tuna in half and then transports it carefully to his plate, next to his charbroiled slab of steak and French fries and homemade coleslaw. He doesn't offer her so much as a morsel of his food.

"Iris doesn't share my interest in family traditions," Hampton says, cutting into his steak.

"All I ever said is that sometimes they can be a little limiting," says Iris, trying not to plead, but Kate can tell she would like to. "In America you can make your own history."

"Dream on, my sweet," says Hampton.

"All right, then I will. And in the meantime, can we just relax and enjoy being alive?"

"So you work on Wall Street?" Kate asks.

"Does that surprise you?" asks Hampton. "That I'm an investment banker?"

"Yes," she says, "I thought maybe you were a tap dancer."

Hampton smiles, points his finger at Kate. "That's funny," he says, instead of laughing.

"I wrote a piece last year about the stock exchange," Kate says. "I love all those men crawling over each other and shouting out numbers as if their lives were hanging by a thread. And then the final bell rings and everyone cheers and goes out for drinks. I loved the whole thing, including the bell and the drinks."

"That's not what I do. But I'd like to read your article."

"Oh no, please, no. The only way I can churn that crap out is to tell myself that absolutely no one will ever set eyes on it." She catches the waitress's eye and gestures with a twirl of the finger: more drinks over here. "It's just to pay the bills. And wrap fish."

"Do you mostly write about financial topics?" Hampton asks.

"What I'm supposed to be doing is working on my next novel, but that's been the case for quite a while. So in the meanwhile, editors call me up and I give them whatever they want. It's amazing how easily the stuff comes when you don't really have your heart in it. Right now, I'm doing a piece about the O. J. trial and about this woman artist calling herself Ingrid Newport."

"What kind of artist is she?" Hampton asks.

"She's sewn up her vagina," Kate says. She can practically *hear* Daniel's heart sinking. He worries about her when she drinks. And then he does something that strikes her as *intolerable*. He actually looks over at Iris and shrugs.

"They keep on assigning me these sexual mutilation pieces," Kate says. "It's becoming sort of my specialty. My little calling card." Is this putting Iris in her place? Kate has no idea. Iris may be one of those rare monsters: a person of unshakable sexual confidence. "I tell them, 'Hey guys, how about a piece about the reemergence of the lobotomy as an accepted psychiatric practice,' but, no, they say, 'What we really want is fifeen hundred words on Peter Peterson, that guy in Dover, Delaware, who crucified his own penis.' They all tell me I write so well about gender issues, by which they really mean sex. I guess I should be pleased. No one ever said I did anything well when it came to sex." Kate laughs. "But now I'm getting a lot of O. J. assignments, so that's good. Have you all been following the case?"

No one's taking the bait on that one. Getting this crowd to talk about O. J. would be like trying to convince them to take off their clothes right there in the restaurant. Kate feels sour and self-righteous, the way you do when you seem to be the only person willing to face something ugly.

Iris's eyes are locked on her meal. She seems to be hurrying to finish it before Hampton tucks into it again. Kate watches her hands as they delicately maneuver her knife and fork. She finds her cute but hardly irresistible. Lean body, broad shoulders, big behind. Kate feels sorry for black people with freckles, it's like they're getting the worst of both worlds.

"You know what we should have done?" says Daniel, his voice bright silver. "Kept the kids together, with just one baby-sitter."

"Wasn't I lucky to have found someone like Daniel?" Kate announces. "When my marriage broke up and I was left with my kid, I thought I'd be alone forever. But Daniel's a better parent than I am." She waits for Daniel to contradict her, but he doesn't. "Well, maybe not *better,* but he is so good to Ruby."

"She's a great kid," Daniel says softly.

"She is," says Iris.

"And she so loves Nelson," Daniel says. His face colors, and he looks to Kate for relief. "Doesn't she? How many times has she talked about him? Right?"

"Kids can fall in love," Kate says. "In fact, in childhood, we may be at our highest capacity to just go head over heels for another person. I was in love with a little boy when I was five years old. A little black boy with the perfect little black boy name: Leroy. Leroy Sinclair." She signals the waiter for more wine. In for a penny. "His mother cleaned the little medical arts building where my father had his office. He was a real butterball, Leroy. Just as fat as a tick, but with the most charming, lazy smile, a real summer-on-the-Mississippi smile. He wore overalls and high-topped sneakers. His mother had to take him to work and apparently she fed that poor boy sweets all through the day to keep him quiet. I used to go to Daddy's office every Saturday and Mrs. Sinclair—"

"You called her Mrs. Sinclair?" Hampton asks.

"Not at the time. We called her Irma. She weighed two pounds, shoes and all."

"Poor Leroy," says Iris.

"I used to read to Leroy. I was precocious. I'd bring a book every Saturday and read to him while Daddy worked in his office, two hours of paperwork, nine-thirty to eleven-forty-five, every Saturday, to the minute. I used to read Leroy these bedtime books, right there in the middle of the day, sitting on the inside staircase of this little medical arts building out on Calhoun Boulevard. And Leroy had all this candy his mother gave him, stuffed in his pockets, little red-and-white mints, butterscotch sucking candies, all fancy wrapped . . ."

"She probably took them from one of the houses she cleaned during the week," Iris says.

"Yes, I suppose she did. Stolen sweets. What could be better?" She narrows her eyes, lets Iris draw her own damn conclusions. "I read him *Goodnight, Moon,* and he put his head right in my lap and closed his eyes and I patted and rocked him and he pretended to fall asleep. And when I was finished with whatever I was reading, I kissed the palm of my hand and pressed it against his cheek, over and over, hand to my lips, hand to his cheek. And I remember thinking: I love Leroy. I love Leroy Sinclair. And just saying those words put me into a kind of hypnotic trance."

The high school girl has cleared the plates away. The waiter hovers over to the side, waiting for a break in the conversation.

"And then one day I saw my father talking to Mrs. Sinclair," Kate is saying, "and I knew she would never be allowed to bring Leroy to work with her again. And I was right. The next time I saw him, maybe two years later, he was on his way to his school and I was with a couple of my silly, awful little girlfriends from Beaumont Country Day School, and I called to him across the street—Hey, Leroy—and he just looked at me as if I was the most ridiculous thing he had ever seen, and he didn't say a word. But whose fault was it? We were both caught in something so large, and so terrible. His people came over in chains and my people sat on the porch sipping gin. Something that begins that badly can never end well . . ."

Kate looks around the table, smiling.

"How about you, Hampton?" she says. "Did you ever fall in love with someone not of your race?" If he finds this offensive he gives no indication—but Kate quickly looks away from him, throws her slightly bleary gaze first at Iris, and finally at Daniel. "Anyone?"

Once they were in the woods, the remains of the afternoon light seemed to shrink away. The shadows of the trees—a shocking number of which had fallen over to the ground from the weight of last month's sudden snowstorm—seemed to pile on top of each other, one shadow over the next, building a wall of darkness. Once, there had been paths through the woods, made by the herds of deer, or left over from the old days when there had been enough money to maintain and even man-icure the Richmond holdings. But the October storm had dropped thousands of trees and the paths were somewhere beneath them, invisible now. Daniel and Hampton could not take two steps without having to scramble over the canopy of a fallen tree, or climb over a trunk, or a crisscross of trunks, slippery with rot. And where there weren't fallen trees there were thorny blackberry vines that furled out across the forest floor like a sharp, punishing fog.

The evening was not a success. After Kate's story about Leroy, the si-lences became prolonged. When Kate ordered an after-dinner co-gnac, neither Iris nor Hampton ordered anything, putting Daniel in the position of having to order a cognac for himself, which he feared might create the impression that he and Kate were both heavy drinkers. As soon as Kate drained her snifter, Hampton announced that they had promised their baby-sitter an early night, and it was over.

In the car, Daniel and Kate do not speak. Daniel has the car's cassette player tuned low. Etta James singing "Love's Been Rough on Me," then Buddy Guy doing "Hold That Plane." When Albert King's "I Found Love in the Welfare Line" comes on, Kate rouses herself out of her torpor and hits the off button. "No singing Negroes, please."

"Fine. Whatever you like."

"Are you feeling like Herman Melville, darling?" Kate asks, her breath rich and fermented.

"Am I?"

" 'In the soul of a man there is one insular Tahiti, full of peace and joy, but encompassed by all the horror of the half-lived life.' Did you have a little peek at Tahiti and now you have to go home to your half-lived life?"

Daniel remains silent. He doesn't want to argue with Kate, doesn't want to spar with her, to feel the flick and jab of her. He is content to be driving and thinking about the various little gestures Iris made during the dinner. He thinks about what she ate. He thinks about how she had refolded her napkin at the end of the meal and placed it next to her plate, good as new. He thinks about her expression as she listened to the others speak, a quality of appreciation and grace, as if her mind lapped up information like a cat with a bowl of milk. He thinks about how she continually turned her wedding ring around her finger, as if it might be impeding the flow of her blood. She had been wearing that perfume that he had come to associate with her—Chanel No. 19. A few weeks ago, in the city, he had gone to Saks and sniffed thirty tester bottles before finding which fragrance was hers, and then he bought a small bottle and kept it in his desk at the office. *May I help you? May I help you?* The clerks on the main floor had kept trying to make themselves available to him. But they couldn't help him; nobody could.

"Feel my forehead," Kate says. "I think I have a fever."

He touches her with his fingertips and then the palm of his hand. A jolt of remembered love goes through him. The car drifts left, the tires bite at the gravel at the side of the road. "You're warm."

"I'm dying."

She closes her eyes and their silence reasserts itself.

"Did you have an okay time tonight?" Daniel asks. As his sense of guilt increases, his tolerance for silence decreases. He knows he's just blathering, but she did seem to like Hampton. She who likes no one.

"Not really. It felt like work."

"You seemed to be enjoying yourself," he says. "You and Hampton—"

"Fuck me and Hampton," Kate says, and turns her face away from him, as the two-lane blacktop turns into a narrower dirt road that leads to their secluded old house. They drive past a neighbor's rolling fields, a pond ringed by weeping willows. A pebble driveway leads from the road to their house, and as the stones crunch beneath the tires, Kate opens her eyes. Their car's headlights shine on the red wreck of the baby-sitter's car.

"I hope Mercy treats children better than she treats her car," Daniel says. He turns off the engine; the lighted windows in their front rooms shimmer before them.

"Why did you tell that story about that little boy?" he asks her.

Kate sits up, rubs her eyes with the heels of her hands. "Did you like that story?"

"I never heard of Leroy before. I thought I knew about every boy who ever passed through your life."

"I think what I was saying was Leroy and I could never be friends."

"Why? Because he was black and you were white?" Despite everything, he allows himself to feel indignant. He thinks Kate's white southern girlhood is asserting itself in a highly unpleasant way.

"Be glad I didn't tell the story of why we left New York City, how you were scared to death of every black person you saw."

"Why would you ever say anything like that?"

"Because it's true, you were."

"My life was threatened. And the people who made the threat were black. I overreacted, I admit it."

"You were scared to death."

"Let's just drop it," Daniel says. "I'm over it." He opens the door to get out, but Kate catches him by the arm.

"If it's any consolation to you, the marriage won't last."

"What marriage?"

"Iris and Hampton's. He's on edge all the time, looking for little slights against his dignity. She wants to live in a world where a little spilled water is just an accident, not an incident."

Inside, Mercy Crane is on the phone, which she hangs up without a word of good-bye as soon as Kate and Daniel come in.

Kate goes up to check on Ruby. Daniel pays Mercy and locks the door. He goes back into the living room to gather up the half-eaten bowl of ramen noodles and the can of Sprite she has left behind. He sees something poking out between the sofa cushions—a half-full pack of Camel Lights, with a book of matches squeezed beneath the cellophane. He tosses them onto the table, hoping for Mercy's sake her parents don't smell the smoke in her hair. Her father's a cop and her mother teaches at a Christian elementary school; both are known to be strict and unforgiving.

After clearing Mercy's little mess, he falls back onto the sofa and lights one of her cigarettes. When he moved in with Kate, she asked him not to smoke around the baby, and he went with the program and quit altogether. But now he would like to taste tobacco and inhales deeply, blows a smoke ring, and watches it make its way like a jellyfish through a shaft of lamplight. Then he hears Kate's footsteps coming down the stairs.

"I don't have a temperature," she announces. She's already in her nightgown.

"You're probably just tired. You should go to bed. I'll bring you up some orange juice."

"You're smoking?" she asks. "You're actually smoking in the house?"

Just then, the doorbell rings. Daniel flicks the cigarette into the fireplace and goes toward the door, his heart racing, as if this might really be Iris. Kate stops midway down the staircase. Daniel shrugs at her and opens the door.

"My car won't start, Mr. Emerson," says Mercy.

"Oh no, poor you!" His voice is booming, as would be expected in a man who has just, against all odds, been offered a means of escape. "I'll drive you home." He realizes how eager this sounds, and so he adds, "I'm just no good at automobile repair. If it doesn't involve a gas can or a jumper cable, it's out of my league."

"I could stay here, if that would be easier," she says. Her voice is plaintive. "I could sleep on the couch. If you wanted, I could make Ruby breakfast in the morning and you and Kate could sleep late."

"It's okay," he says. "It's really okay."

For the first couple minutes of the drive back to town, Daniel and Mercy don't exchange a word. Daniel rolls the window down. There's a faint smell of skunk in the air.

"I'm really sorry about the car," Mercy says.

"I hope you can get it running again."

"My brother's home from the Army. He can fix it, for sure. Is it okay if we come over in the morning?"

"Of course." He slows down. There are dark, luminous eyes peering from beneath the trees at the side of the road. Deer. You never know if they'll come leaping into the path of your car.

"Both my brothers are in the Army," says Mercy.

"So, are you the youngest in the family?"

"Yeah." She sighs, fidgets in her seat. He can tell: she is getting ready to ask a question. She circles it like one of the deer tramping down the tall grass. "What rights does a teenager have?" she says.

"About what?"

"What if a teenager wanted to move out or something? Do you ever do that? As a lawyer? Sheri Nack said I should ask you."

"Does Sheri want to leave home?" Sheri is a doughy, dog-collared girl who looked after Ruby a couple of times—until Kate started noticing liquor was disappearing.

"Not really."

"But you do."

"Yeah."

They are almost in town now. The houses are closer together. A gas station. A plant nursery. The Riverside Convalescent Home. A little empty vine-covered cottage that once was a real estate office—Farms and Fantasies—run by a guy from Yonkers who turned out to be a drug dealer. And then, the blinking yellow light that hangs on a low drooping cable a few hundred yards from the village itself. A soft rain is falling and the wind is picking up, swinging the yellow light back and forth like a lantern held in the hand of a night watchman.

"There are lawyers who specialize in family law," Daniel says.

"I don't know any lawyers, except you."

"What is it you want, Mercy?"

"I want to move out."

"How old are you?"

"Seventeen. I've got to get out of there, Mr. Emerson. I've got to get away from them. Maybe get my own place. Maybe I could be a nanny or something."

"Seventeen's a little young. Can't you wait a year?"

"A *year?*" The cold light of the streetlamps leaps in and out of the car, flashing on her face, with its furious, hopeless expression.

Before he can think of what to tell her, they arrive at her house. It's a small yellow one-story house, with a steep set of wooden stairs leading to the front door. The porch light is on and two moths fly around and around it, as if swirling around a drain of light.

"Are you all right, Mercy? Are you going to be okay?"

"I'm all right."

"Are you safe?"

"I'm okay."

"If you want to come in to my office, and talk about it, you can—anytime. You don't need an appointment, it doesn't have to be a big deal. You can just come in and we can talk."

"Is there any kind of law for me?"

"There's something called the Emancipated Minor Act."

She's silent for the moment. Daniel has for the most part suppressed his own adolescence, and he finds it difficult to project himself into what exactly it feels like to be Mercy's age, to be in that jumble of misery and helplessness, hormonal energy and sheer lassitude.

"There's case law," he says, "in which the court has required parents to pay for rent and food for emancipated minors."

"You mean they'd have to pay for me even if I moved out?"

"It's not really my specialty. I'd have to look it up."

"I guess I'd feel really guilty," she says, smiling for the first time.

"Guilty? Why?"

"Well, they're my parents. I don't want to hurt them." But the smile remains.

"You don't have anything to feel guilty about. You have a right to make yourself happy. You're not obliged to stay where you're miserable. Nobody does."

She nods quickly. She's heard enough. She opens the door on her side. The light comes on in the car and she glances back at Daniel. "Thanks, Mr. Emerson," she says, "really, thank you." And then, right before she slips out of the car she puts her arms around him and touches her forehead against his chest.

Daniel waits until she is safely in her house, though he wonders if her house is really safe. She opens the front door and waves good-bye, and a moment later the door is closed and the porch light goes off and every window in her house is opaque.

He backs away from Mercy's house and onto Culbertson Street, the beams of his headlights filled with fluttering moths. He turns on the radio, as if the voice of reason might be broadcasting from somewhere on the dial, but there are only love songs, urging him on.

He tries to pretend to himself that he has no idea where he is going next. But after a minute or two, he must admit that he's heading toward Juniper Street, where Iris lives. All he wants is to look at her house—once—and then he'll be able to return to his own, he'll be able to walk up the stairs to the second floor, tiptoe into the bedroom, disrobe, slip into bed next to Kate, close his eyes.

A few moments later, he's in front of Iris's house. The Volvo station wagon is in the driveway; every window in the house is slate black. It means they are asleep. In bed. Together. Daniel's hands tense, he lowers his head until his forehead touches the steering wheel. *Go home,* he says to himself.

Yet a competing inner voice also weighs in on the matter, a sterner, hungrier, more focused self that he has somehow managed to keep at bay for his entire life, and this voice wordlessly wonders: *All around you life seethes, grasps, conquers, and here you are, thirty feet from what you desire most and all you can do is quake, all you can think about is Go home.*

He pulls away. He switches on the radio. Van Morrison singing "Here Comes the Night."

Upstairs, in bed, Hampton sleeps in his customary pose of noble death: flat on his back, his legs straight, his toes up, his arms folded across his chest, his fingertips resting on his shoulders, his face waxy and unmoving, his breath so silent and slow that sometimes it seems not to exist.

He dreams of the train. He is getting on in New York, at Pennsylvania Station, presumably on his way up to Leyden. The Amtrak conductor who directs him onto one of the cars looks familiar, a white guy, the guy who is always on Chambers Street selling souvlakis and hot sausages from his steam cart. Here you go, Mr. Davis, the conductor says, gesturing to an open door. Steam pours up from the tracks, onto the platform. Hampton walks through the steam and steps on the train, and he wonders why the man has called him Mr. Davis. Has he mixed him up with somebody else, or is that just the conductor's idea of a black name?

In the dream, Hampton is wearing a Hugo Boss pin-striped suit, a Burberry raincoat, with the lining, a scarf, gloves. The train is hot. Everyone else is dressed for summer; most of them seem to know each other. Perhaps they are some club on their way to a lake somewhere. He is sweating. He feels sweat in his eyes, feels it rolling down his ribs. Oh my God, he thinks, and presses his elbows in, as if his armpits were the source of the most terrible stench. He scans the aisle for an empty seat. And he notices a few rows to the rear a couple of black men, real backcountry, old school all the way, one dressed in overalls, the other in a yellow velvet double-breasted suit and a purple shirt. They are passing a bottle of beer back and forth and laughing at the tops of their voices. Hampton does not even want to make eye contact with them, but they make it impossible for him to ignore them. *Hey, man, come on over,* says the one in the velvet suit, and Hampton has no choice but to march over to them and say, *You're not just representing yourself on this train, you know.* And as soon as he says this, he notices his mother, sitting primly on the other side of the aisle, with her hands folded onto her lap. She purses her lips and nods, as if to commend his job well done.

Next thing, the train has started and he is sitting beside a white woman, who seems to have moved as far from him as the seat will allow. She leans against the window as if the train has taken a sharp turn. He continues to keep his elbows pressed against his ribs. He thinks, *I wish they'd turn the air conditioning on,* but not only is the air conditioning not working but the reading lights are sputtering off and on. He looks out the window. They have left the tunnel. The late afternoon clouds lie along the horizon like broken stones, red, orange, dark blue. The river is dark lavender, the prow of a rusting tanker parts the waters in a long luminous chevron. *Beautiful, beautiful,* he thinks. And then he says to the white woman, *My stop is an hour and a half from here.* She smiles at him gratefully, she knows he is trying to reassure her. *I'm just going to close my eyes for a few minutes,* he says. She looks at him, and then shakes her head. Is she warning him not to?

And then he sees Iris. Like everyone else, she is dressed for warm weather. She is wearing a sleeveless blouse, shorts, sandals. She is walking right past him, carrying a bottle of club soda and a bag of pretzels from the refreshment bar. Somehow, he knows he must not say anything to her. She sits in a seat three or four rows back. She is traveling with a white man, who looks familiar. He takes the bag of pretzels from her, tears them open, but before either of them can eat one of them they begin to kiss, passionately. First one long kiss and then another and now the white guy is practically climbing on top of her. Desperate, Hampton turns to the woman next to him. *Get a load of that,* he says to her. And as soon as he says this to her, she claws at his face with her long fingernails.

He awakens, frantic with confusion and anxiety. He is not used to nightmares; normally, he isn't even aware of his dreams. It takes him a moment to realize that he is safe, at home. He props himself up on his elbow to guard against falling back to sleep—that world, that terrible dream world of the train is still there, waiting for him to tumble back in. He forces his eyes open, looks to Iris's side of the bed. It's empty, the sheet in her space is cool. He is about to call out to her but then he sees her, standing at the window. She is wearing a baggy pair of men's boxer shorts and a once-red T-shirt from which most of the color has been bleached.

There is a glow out there, rising up from the headlights of a car.

"Iris?" says Hampton.

She turns quickly. "You're awake," she says.

The light in the window is caught in the back of her hair. He can't make out her features, but he senses from her voice and posture that he has interrupted her, or startled her. "Who's out there?" he asks her.

"No one." She turns, looks out again, as if to check her own story. "No one."

"I just had a nightmare," he says, reaching his hand out to her, beckoning her to bed. He knows that he should not be so commanding—Iris has even told him as much—but the gestures of the favorite son, the always-sought-after man, come from the deepest part of him. To change these things would be like changing his voice, it would take constant vigilance. She finds him arrogant, but he doesn't feel arrogant. It just seems to him that his being found attractive is a part of the natural order of things, and when Iris resists him, or is slow to respond, it irritates him, not because he is a potentate and she is his lowly subject, but simply because a mistake is being made.

The sight of those long, outstretched fingers illuminates Iris's nervous system with a rage that ignites like flash powder. She wonders if she ought to hold her ground or go to him. Sometimes she has the energy to resist him, but each time she does she enters into the conflict with the knowledge that it will extend through the night.

Hampton switches on his reading light. His cranberry-colored pajamas are streaked with night sweats. He sits up straighter, arranges his pillows, and then reextends his reach for her.

"Are you okay?" she asks.

He pats the sheet on her side of the bed, indicating where he wants her to be. Sometimes she thinks about the men who have wanted to go to bed with her and whom she refused, the good men, handsome, clever, large-hearted men, and how strange it is that life would deliver her to this point: treated like a little dog who is being beckoned to hop up onto the sofa.

Okay, if that's how he wants it. She bounds across the room, leaps onto the bed, falls forward onto her hands and knees, facing him. Then, completing her private joke, she lets her tongue hang out and she pants.

He counters with excruciatingly contrived tenderness. He strokes the side of her face. "We have to sleep," he whispers.

This is night language, code; somewhere in the blind, improvised journey of marriage, sleep has come to mean sex. It has come to mean let me lose myself within you, let me begin the fall into the silent heart of the night between your legs. "Are you tired?" has become an invitation to make love; a loud yawn and a voluptuous stretch of the arms are supposed to function the way once upon a time his coming behind her and pressing his lips against the nape of her neck did.

She continues to pant like a dog, until his frightened, confused expression is replaced by a frown. She takes her place beside him. She lies flat, she feels her blood racing around and around, as if looking for a way to leave her body. Each time it makes its orbit around her, she feels warmer and warmer.

"I can hardly wait for you to finish your thesis and for us all to move back to New York," Hampton says. This is meant to be a kind of sweet talk, signifying that he misses her, that he cannot carry much further the burden of their weekly separations. But Iris knows what he is *really* saying: I hated those people tonight.

"I'm sorry it's taking so long," she says. She's tempted to go back to pretending to be a dog, but she thinks better of it. She feels his long, hard fingers closing around her hand. He lifts her right hand and very carefully, emphatically, ceremoniously places it on his penis, and then he presses down on the back of his hand and lifts his hips up, as if responding to her, though he is only responding to himself.

She pulls her hand away from him—but before he can complain, she rolls over, drapes her leg over him. Lifting herself up on her elbow, she looks down at him and says, "Pretend you're raping me."

"What?"

"Don't hit me or anything, but rape me, really really rape me, tear my clothes off and force yourself into me."

"Are you serious?"

She nods yes.

"Iris," he says, in a fatherly, admonishing tone. But her request has already had its effect on him. His hardness feels urgent, brutal. He grips the band of her shorts, gives it a tug, waits to see what she will do.

Iris rolls onto her back, she lifts her chin, closes her eyes. She is about to be erased, obliterated, but on her own terms.

"Who should I be when I do this?" he asks. His throat is dry, his voice has a small fissure running through it.

She feels herself softening at her center, the way a peach will if someone has dug their thumb in, softening, beginning to rot. "You're just you and I'm me," she says.

"This is strange," he says.

"Shhh," she answers. "Come on. It's all right."

She has a sense of him as completely under her command. She is controlling the situation, him, the night belongs to her at last. But then he surprises her. He tugs her boxers down, fast, with something expert and irrefutable in his movement—just one long pull and they are around her knees. And then before she can even take a breath he turns her over swiftly and a little cruelly, and then the weight of him on top of her presses her nose and mouth into the mattress and all she can think is, *Jesus, he is really going to do this to me.*

———

Daniel comes home, closes the door quietly behind him, and tiptoes with exaggerated care across a minefield of squeaking floorboards. He is like the henpecked hubby in a cartoon, sneaking back home after a night's carousing. He sits on the steps, takes off his shoes, and ascends to the second floor in his stockinged feet.

Knowing it will only increase his agitation, in some hapless way courting the self-torture, he looks in on Ruby. His love for Kate's child has taken on the harrowing qualities of a crime in the planning stage. She is the night watchman in a store he is going to rob, she is going to be in harm's way. He has a dream of his own happiness, and if he is lucky enough to one day attain it, bold enough to seize it, man enough to keep it, that joy will be paid for, at least in part, in Ruby's tears.

Her bedroom is so dark he cannot see her, but he hears her slow breathing. He feels a kind of thud in the center of his consciousness, as if he has just knocked something down to the carpet in the dark.

As he feared, Kate is waiting for him, fiercely awake. Her pillows are stacked up to support her back and she rests her head against the wall, exactly in the center of the bedposts. She has wrapped her arms around her chest and she flutters her fingers on her upper arms. Instinctually, his eyes scan her bedside table: a stack of books, a little tape recorder for the taking of her own dictation, a little blue Chinese bowl holding a United Airlines sleep mask and foam rubber earplugs, and——what he was looking for and what gives him the sour pleasure of a hypothesis confirmed——a bottle of zinfandel, in which she has made quite a dent.

"I'm sorry," she says.

"For what?"

"For giving you a hard time, in the car." It seems she means to be somehow repentant, but her words are delivered with a little tremor of sarcasm on the edge, though he is not sure who is being mocked—he for being so touchy, or she for behaving badly?

"It's all right," he says. "It's fine."

"I had no right."

"It's okay. It's just . . . you know. Talk." He feels as if he is evading her conversation, she is the bull and he is the matador.

"I would like to apologize," she says, her eyes narrowing. "And I would like you to accept my apology."

"You did nothing and said nothing that needs an apology."

She shakes her head, amazed at the depths of his treachery.

"You won't even give me that?" she asks.

"I wouldn't know what I was giving. I really have no idea what this conversation is about."

She takes a deep breath, pours herself a little more wine, a scientifically minute portion that splashes at the bottom of her tall glass. "Daniel, I have this terrible feeling about you. No, sorry, not about you. Sorry. But about what's happening to you."

"It's late," he says. "I've had a long day, we both have. Tomorrow's Saturday, we can talk tomorrow." He has peeled off his socks and now he is stepping out of his trousers. For a brief moment he has allowed himself to wonder what it would feel like if he were getting undressed to get into bed with Iris Davenport, and now that the thought has presented itself he cannot get rid of it. It just flies around and around within him, like a bird that can't find the window that let it into the house.

"It's already tomorrow and I want to talk now. It's no big deal, I just want to ask you a question. Is that all right? One teeny-tiny question? Or maybe not teeny-tiny, maybe more medium-sized."

"You're sort of loaded, Kate."

She doesn't mind his saying this. "Do you believe in love?"

"I don't know. No. Yes. I don't even know what you mean."

"O. J. believed in love. Even though he's lying about killing his wife, in his heart he knows he did it, and he might even think he did it for love."

"I don't believe in killing, if that's what you mean."

"You know," Kate says, pouring herself more wine, less judiciously this time, "people think that *love* is what's best in each of us, our capacity to *love,* our need for *love.* They think love is like God, and they worship their own feelings of love, which is really just narcissism masquerading as spirituality. You understand? If we say that God is love, then we can say that love is God, and that gives us the right to all these chaotic, needy, lusting, insane feelings inside of ourselves. We can call it *love,* and from there it's just a hop, skip, and a jump to calling it God. But here's a thought. What if God isn't love? And love isn't God? What if all those emotions we call love turn out to be what's really worst in us, what if it's all the firings of the foulest, most primitive part of the back brain, what if it's just as savage and selfish as rage or greed or lust?"

"I don't know, Kate. It sounds sort of counterintuitive."

"Intuition? What is that? We intuit what we want to intuit. We never intuit things that are against our interests and desires. Maybe intuition is just one of the many ways we have of elevating desire, making it something mystical rather than base. Did you ever think of that?"

"No."

"Love has become some insane substitute for religion, I think that's what's happened. And in this country it's pounded in on us at all times, every radio station, every TV station, all the magazines, all the ads, everywhere, it's like living in a theocracy, it's like living in Jordan and people are shouting out lines from the Koran from the top of every mosque. Love, love, love, but what they're really saying is: Take what you want and the hell with everything else. We've even changed the Bible to go along with this new religion. When I was a kid, people used to read Paul's letter to the Corinthians as being about charity—it used to be faith, hope, and charity, remember charity? the humility of that?—but now they've changed the translation and it's not charity at all, it's love. Big old encompassing love, spreading all over everything like swamp gas. Love is like a crystal ball, you gaze into its cracked heart and you see what you want to see. It's really scary. It feels like the whole culture has gone insane."

Daniel is sure that the best thing would be to remain silent, he has recited to himself his own domestic Miranda rights, but he cannot resist saying, "I haven't gone insane, Kate, if that's what you're implying."

"I know you haven't, and I don't think you will. I really feel as if I've found a kindred spirit in you. And this isn't intuition, or some mystical crapola about our being cosmic twins, or that it was written in the stars, because, let's face it, that's not how life is, life's a bunch of accidents, senseless. We improvise, we keep it together. But with you, it's more. It feels nice. And that's why if I were a betting woman, I'd put my money on us. I think we'll always be together."

He's silent. Surely she doesn't expect him to comment on this.

"We may have our hard times," Kate says, "and we may have to take breaks from each other, maybe long breaks. But I don't think we'll ever be free of each other. And not because we're the most romantic couple in the world, or anything like that. It's a mysterious connection, a fucking mystery . . ." She laughs. "Or a not-fucking mystery, or maybe a fucking-once-in-a-while mystery. Who knows? But I was sure of it from the first time I met you, I just never told you."

She's silent and Daniel realizes he must say something. "Really?"

"Yes. I thought to myself, I'm never going to get away from this guy."

"Did you want to?"

"And then I thought, And he's never going to get away from me." She rolls away from him but then slides over, pressing her hindquarters against his hip. "And I feel even stronger about it now. I just feel so grateful. I've got you, and Ruby, and my talent, and what's left of my looks." She presses herself harder against him. "I know what you're thinking. She's drunk, she's drunk. Once again. But I'm not. I was, maybe. Back at the restaurant, with those terrible people. But I'm sober now, and meaning every word. I couldn't get drunk if I tried."

"Have you been trying?" Daniel asks.

He regrets saying it. It sounds so put-upon, so long-suffering. But the words are out, there's no way to take them back. He waits for her reply, already devising how he will defend himself. But the plans aren't necessary. He has not hurt her feelings, he has not irritated her. She is breathing deeply, and a few moments later her breaths deepen with a little aural fringe of snore.

Outside, an owl screeches in triumph. From farther away comes the manic whoop of coyotes. The colder it gets outside the more the creatures of the night seem to celebrate their catches, the triumph of having survived another season. The world belongs to those who can satisfy their hunger. The rest are food. Even the stars in the sky shine out the story of their own survival.

They had no idea where they were going. They walked. The crunch of their foot-
steps. The cries of invisible birds. Daniel cupped his hands around his mouth and
called Marie's name, silencing the birds. The noise of their footsteps on the brittle
layer of dried leaves that covered the forest floor was like a saw going tirelessly
back and forth.

They walked up a hill, zigzagging around fallen trees and swirls of bramble.
Daniel walked in front. He looked over his shoulder. Hampton was having a hard
time keeping his balance.

"I'm ruining these shoes," Hampton said. He leaned against a partially fallen
cherry tree and looked at the sole of his English cordovan. The leather was shiny,
rosy and moist, like a human tongue.

The next morning, Daniel takes Ruby with him to a new bakery in the village, where he plies her with chocolate croissants and chocolate milk. Daniel recalls Iris having mentioned this place—chrome and glass, with a sort of 1940s feel, overpriced, but with comfortable, long-legged chairs lined up facing the huge window overlooking Broadway—and he sits there with Ruby, ostensibly reading the paper and drinking espresso, but in reality watching for Iris or her car. After an hour of this maddening activity, during which he is unable to read more than a few headlines, and the coffee tastes like scorched ink, he takes Ruby back home with a cup of latte and a cranberry muffin for Kate, who, to his surprise, is awake and dressed when they return.

"Where was everybody?" she asks.

"Breakfast," he says, handing her the takeout bag.

"What did people eat in pre-muffin America?" Kate asks, peering into the bag. She notices Ruby, whose mouth is ringed with chocolate and whose T-shirt is spotted with it. Kate looks questioningly at Daniel.

"That's what happens to little girls whose mothers sleep late," he says, surprising himself with the bite of his own voice.

"I want to play with Nelson," Ruby says.

It seems strange to Daniel: as his heart swells from the added freight of love and desire, it becomes in its fullness less and less substantial, until it is like a feather in a stiff wind, unpredictably blowing this way and that, spiraling up, plunging down, rocketing sideways at the slightest provocation—the lucky-sounding ring of the phone, the melancholy shift of the afternoon light, the hum of an oncoming car. He has resisted all morning the treacherous impulse to plant in Ruby the idea that she and Nelson get together today, but now, God bless her, she has come up with the idea all on her own, and his spirits soar.

"I don't think so," Kate says. "Nelson's father is home and that's their private time over at Nelson's house."

Ruby looks at Kate, squinting, wringing her little hands, as she tries to think of some counterargument to this. But the combination of Kate's professional needs and temperament has made the concept of "private time" sacred. Still, Ruby cannot hide her disappointment, and she even manages to enter into a brief, unsuccessful negotiation, during which Daniel stands transfixed, unable to shake the feeling that his happiness hangs in the balance.

In the end, Kate prevails. Not only can Ruby not go to Nelson's house, but Nelson cannot come to hers. And when Ruby counters with all she has left—"Then I'm going to be so bored"—Kate says that maybe they can all go to Lubochevsky Farms, where the enterprising owners have devised a way to get tourists and even some of the locals to pay for the privilege of harvesting the annual raspberry and apple crops. Daniel is taken aback by Kate's suggestion. He cannot imagine her climbing the rickety stepladders, filling the flimsy baskets with apples, enduring the sunlight and the hefty autumnal bees. And then what? Eat the apples? In three years of knowing her he has never seen her take a bite of an apple. No. There is only one explanation. She is concocting this little outing as a way of roping him in, and when Daniel realizes this he reacts like someone jumping away from an onrushing car.

"I have to go to the office," he says. He feels the desperation of a gambler: if he can just sit at the table, then maybe he can catch a card.

"On a Saturday?"

"Sorry. It happens." He is experiencing that bicameral lunacy of a man with a secret life; he is talking to Kate, making his excuses, arranging his features in a way that would suggest regret. He is already gone.

"I need to work, too," she says. "I've got two O. J. articles going, and both are due."

"What is with you and that case? I thought you were a novelist."

"He butchered his wife and might end up walking. I know we like to cheer for the African-American side, but there is a question of justice at stake. I'm sure even Iris Davenport would agree with that."

It is unnerving to hear her say Iris's name, and he shifts his eyes, afraid for a moment that he might give himself away, though he is beginning to wonder if there is much secrecy to his secret life. He might be no better hidden than an ostrich with its head in the sand and fat feathered ass in the air.

"Why don't we split the day, then?" he says. "All I need is two or three hours. I can take them now or I can take them in the afternoon. Or I can take them at night, for that matter." It really doesn't matter. All he needs is to get out of this house for a couple of hours. But as soon as that thought crosses his mind, it is replaced by a second, more urgent idea. He should go first, then Kate could work in the afternoon, and then he could take more time away in the evening. That way he could have as many as six hours. To do what? That part hasn't been worked out yet. To cruise by Iris's house? To patrol the village in search of her car? To sit at his desk dialing and redialing her number?

"All right," Kate says, her voice measured, a little cool. "Then you go first." He knows she is onto him. He can feel the pressure of her intelligence and her deep common sense. He feels like a half-wit miscreant tracked by a master sleuth.

His sense of impending exposure quickens his pace, and in minutes he is out of the house, in his car, and on his way to somewhere or other. From the house on Willow Lane to his office in the middle of town is a ten-minute drive and one that could, without any loss of travel efficiency, bring him past Iris's house, if he should choose to take that route, which he does.

The Saturday has turned warm; it's already October, winter is next. Daniel drives past the familiar landmarks of his childhood. Putnam Lake, with little puckers of silvery light caught in its waves, ringed by tall blue spruce; Livingston High School, surrounded by cornfields, its asphalt parking lot in the process of receiving freshly painted yellow lines; the infamous ranch house where his old friend Richard Taylor lived with his drunken parents, where you could walk right in without knocking, where there was no housekeeping, no food, no supervision, where the lamps did not have shades, and where Daniel drank his first whiskey when he was eleven years old, smoked his first joint at twelve, and, that same year, got into a ferocious fist fight with Richard's deaf older cousin. The Taylor place was one of a dozen houses around Leyden where Daniel spent his time after school, where he slept on weekends, where he hid like a little desperado. In those grim but somehow fondly remembered childhood days—when he was his own man, needed by no one, responsible to no one, when the unanimous possession of his self was a pleasure that outflanked every deprivation and annoyance—he would rather have been anywhere in the known world than in his own home. He would rather have slept in school than in his parents' house.

His parents were latecomers to parenthood, vegetarians, Congregationalists, campers, tall gray people with solitary tastes for reading, hiking, and the brewing of homemade beer. They were in their forties when Daniel was born, and by the time he was a teenager they were nearly sixty, their habits thoroughly calcified. The foods they liked, the Mozart that soothed them, their ten o'clock bedtime and their six-forty-five rising, their hour-long ablutions, their Canadian Air Force exercises, their aversion to moving air (no air conditioners, no fans), their daily porch sweeping, their dishes, cups, and silverware cleaned in kettles of boiling water—these were the things that Julia and Carl Emerson revered. These were, in their minds, the cornerstones not only of civilization but of sanity; without them they would be plunged into madness.

When Daniel entered their lives they taught him not to touch the vases, which antique carpets to avoid, which lamps were safe to use. He was not to run, jump, or shout. He was not to play the stereo console in their parlor, nor was he to use the electric typewriter, the adding machine, the juicer, the blender, either of the vacuum cleaners, or the electric toothbrushes. Above all, the back half of the house was off-limits; this was where the Emersons saw their patients. Here was the waiting room with its intriguing collection of offbeat magazines—from *Prevention* to *The Saturday Review*—the dark walnut apothecary case filled with amber bottles of vitamins, the vanilla plastic skeleton hanging from a hook, and the his and hers chiropractic tables—neither of them ever worked on someone of the opposite sex. Here came everyone from beefy back-strained farmers to neurasthenic housewives, here backs were cracked, hips were realigned, toes were pulled, fingers were popped, heads were yanked suddenly to the left or right, moans were moaned, and for some reason that Daniel never could fathom, people returned again and again.

Daniel continues his drive along the outskirts of the village. There are tourists in town today—the weekend, the splendid color change, when the maples turn to flame and the oak leaves are the color of honey. It strikes him as funny that the town has become a tourist destination; he cannot imagine how the day-trippers pass the time. There are jokey

T-shirts for sale that say Paris London Tokyo Leyden. There are home-made jellies to be purchased. But the bagels here aren't as good as in the city, and the same goes for the breads, the pies, the croissants. Shoes, slacks, dresses, hats—all are cheaper and better in New York. The restaurants are merely adequate. The antique stores have been shopped clean and now sell items from the 1970s. Still, every weekend, except for the long dead of winter, there are at least a hundred new arrivals, parading up and down the two-block commercial center, with an ice cream cone in one hand and a T-shirt in the other, glancing shyly at the locals and de-lighting when someone nods back or says hello.

Not far from the high school is the town cemetery, where the head-stones are thin as place mats and worn smooth and illegible over time. It was to this graveyard, in the company of all that Colonial dust and the ceaseless squirrels, that Daniel used to go when there was no one left to visit and it was still too early to go home. With the marker of one of the Stuyvesants to support his back, Daniel read the books of his youth—Salinger, Heller, Baldwin—and, in his thirteenth year, before his parents released him from their benign bondage and sent him off to a third-tier prep school in New Hampshire, it was here that he wrote poetry for the first and only time in his life.

They were not great poems or even good poems, they were not by most standards really poems at all. They were poetry as he understood it, the poetry of which he was capable, and they ran through the changes of longing and desolation, seduction and heartbreak, trust and betrayal like a hamster on a wheel, celebrating lips he had never kissed, eyes into which he had never gazed, caresses he had yet to enjoy. They were for Baby, they were for Darlin', they were for Janey, though he knew no one by that name, they were for Suzie, and though he did happen to know a Suzie, he did not love or even like her. In each of these poems, Daniel was alone, carrying within him a heart that ticked like a bomb. A great many of them began: *And I walk* . . . One went *And I walk through this night / with only one light / and that's my heart, darlin', burning for you.* Another: *And I walk and I walk and I walk and I walk / And wherever I go I'm looking for you.*

But who was this "you"? She did not exist. There were girls in his daily world whom he liked and who seemed to like him, but they could not be fit into the staggering, narcoticized world of his desire, the atmosphere was not conducive, it made them shrivel and die. And then, one day, the longing was gone. He cannot remember a precipitating event. It just happened, like the day he suddenly stopped believing in fairies and ghosts, or the day the notion of Santa Claus was abruptly ridiculous. Weeks went by without him writing in his notebook of love poems, and then it struck him that if anyone ever came upon those verses the humiliation would not be survivable, and he brought them down to the river, thinking of making a ceremony of their disposal, a kind of burial at sea, but in order to get to the river he had to trespass across one of the immense riverfront estates and by the time he was at the water's edge he heard the rumble of a caretaker's truck, surely on the way to roust him out, and he ended up tossing the notebook into the water wildly and running.

Now, as he makes a couple of left-hand turns that bring him ever closer to Iris's house, he is remembering those mawkish scribblings for the first time in twenty years.

Side-arming that notebook into the river did not mean that from then on he lived in some anguished exile from romance; he was not like a priest who loses his faith and then becomes a drunk or a fornicator. He did not feel bitterness, he did not feel any loss. He simply knew better and it was over. Those feelings were like his milk teeth; his bite was sturdier after that. And in place of all that inchoate desire, he went on to other pursuits: public service, respectability, sex, money. His brief childish dream of love was over, and he went on. He had relationships. He had *a life,* by which people seemed to mean a certain accumulation of days and experience, all mortared into some kind of shapeless shape by an adult gravitas. He went on to prep school, on to college, on to law school, on to a year traveling on the cheap in Europe, on to a year in Mississippi working for a civil rights lawyer, on to Minneapolis for more public service, where he lived with the daughter of a blind Norwegian piano tuner, a large, brown-haired girl with creamy skin and enormous eyes, who seemed to him like an old-fashioned dessert, the kind they serve you when you're too sated to eat another bite, and on to New York, to Kate and Ruby, and on and on and on—but had he been walking an ellipse all that time? Because here he was again, not exactly at the spot at which he had written those rhymes twenty years ago, but certainly within shouting distance of it. Around and around he'd gone, and now it seemed to all be coming to this: that phantom female, that ghostly girl, Darlin', Baby, all those creatures of his longing, all those spirits of love and desire whom he thought he had exorcised with the power of plain old common sense, put in their place at the back of the class by irony, experience, and practicality, they had survived after all, they had not been cast out, they had merely shrunk back, they had hibernated, and now they are awake, they are swirling around and around, and they have fused into a single woman.

Juniper Street. The fashion of the playful flag has arrived. On Iris's block Daniel counts eleven flags displayed over the entrances, and of these only two are the stars and stripes. The other households seem to be pledging their allegiance to countries of the imagination. Flags here depict a crow perched on a pumpkin, Dorothy and the Tin Man, a cobalt heaven riveted with silver stars, a golden retriever, a pair of ballet slippers. It's after ten on a pretty morning but no one is on the street, a fact for which Daniel is grateful, since he is now driving so slowly that he may as well be parked in the middle of the road.

Iris's Volvo is no longer in their driveway and his mind races as he tries to assign meaning to this fact. One thing he knows for sure: it means they are no longer in bed together—at least one of them is out of the house. Perhaps Iris has gone to run some errands, in which case Daniel might run into her if he drives quickly over to Broadway. Or maybe she's gone to the campus, or across the river to one of the malls. Or maybe it's Hampton who's gone, in which case Iris is right there in the house. He reminds himself not to suddenly introduce a new aspect to the plan; he told himself that all he would do is drive by her house and move on. Now he is casting about for reasons he might knock on her door, and he forces himself to ignore every spontaneous scenario and to stick with the original plan.

He has seen the house. Enough. Maybe he will return in an hour or so to see if the car has returned. Maybe there will be other signs of life, little changes, clues from which he can concoct a plausible narrative of their day. He steps on the gas pedal, bringing the speed of his car up to fifteen, but as he pulls away from the house he is gripped by the idea that Iris is in there, and that all that separates them is fifteen paces and a knock on the door. And though he has promised himself no unplanned actions, he does add one thing to today's reconnaissance. He dials her number on his cell phone. Yet on the first ring, he feels an overpowering sense of creepiness and remorse, and he pushes his thumb against the end call button on his phone with such force that he almost veers into a parked car—an old Mercedes with a bumper sticker that says COMMIT RANDOM ACTS OF IRRATIONAL KINDNESS.

Because he told Kate he was going to do some work, Daniel heads toward his office, for the tiny squirt of moral salve it might afford him, though not before driving down Broadway one last time and looking for Iris's car. He pretends not to see everyone who waves hello to him, and he thinks to himself that if he had remembered more clearly all the waving or howdy-doing that goes on in Leyden, he would never have moved back here. Yet to not have moved back here is now unthinkable, a speculation that leads to an infinity of emptiness, like imagining not having been born. The equation is simple. No Leyden = No Iris. Of course, there are a million details of life and circumstance that had to fall into place to bring him to the spot in which he now finds himself. But in the end it seems to Daniel to come to this: if he hadn't lost that case back in the city, if he hadn't been kicked down the stairs by those three thugs, with their huge hands and reddish eyes, if he hadn't developed the humiliating, excoriating fear of every dark-skinned stranger he saw on the street, then none of this would be happening.

He wonders what Iris will think of the story of his flight from New York. He wonders if he will ever need to tell her. He nervously imagines how it will sound to African-American ears—the panicky white boy packing his bags, quitting his practice, heading for the cornfields and the pastures and the perfect white village with his southern girlfriend and her porcelain daughter in tow. Surely this will have a meaning to Iris somewhat different from the meanings to which he is accustomed, and for no other reason than she is black. He is getting way ahead of himself, but he can't help it. He remembers Kate's remark about Leroy from the night before: *His people came over in chains and mine sat on the porch sipping gin. Something that begins that badly can never end well.* So will that be the contest? History in one corner and Love in the other? Fine. Ring the bell. Let the fight begin. *Love,* he thinks, *will bring history to its knees.*

———

At last, it is Monday, and Daniel is in court, standing in front of Judge Hoffstetter. On one side of Daniel stands Rebecca Stefanelli, who most people know by her nickname, Lulu. She is a five-times-divorced, hard-living woman in her early forties, with red hair and a tentative, defensive smile on her face, the smile of a woman who has had a number of unkind remarks made at her expense, and who would rather appear in on the joke than be its unwitting target. On the other side of Daniel stands James Schmidt, a muscular, scrubbed widower who runs a little lawn mower and chain saw repair business out of his garage; Rebecca and James had a brief, more or less geographically determined fling a couple of years ago and relations between them have been stormy ever since. Standing next to Schmidt is a barrel-chested, white-haired, flush-faced old lawyer named Montgomery Paisley, in semiretirement but still making a handsome living representing the company that sold Schmidt his home insurance. Though summer is long past, Paisley is wearing a blue-and-white seersucker suit and light brown shoes.

Rebecca is suing Schmidt for failure to keep his section of the public sidewalk clear of ice. She slipped and fell in front of Schmidt's house last March, sustaining a concussion, and she claims to have been suffering from debilitating headaches ever since.

Judge Hoffstetter is manifest in his dislike of Lulu Stefanelli. "Miss Stefanelli," he says, "I'll thank you not to wear sunglasses in my courtroom."

"Your Honor," Daniel is quick to say, "my client is wearing dark glasses on the advice of her physician, as a way of warding off headaches."

"This is not a sunny room, Mr. Emerson. Please instruct your client to remove her sunglasses."

It's outrageous to Daniel that Hoffstetter is harassing Lulu about her glasses. Hoffstetter used to be a state patrolman in Windsor County; in fact, it was he who gave Daniel his first and only speeding ticket, twenty years ago, when Daniel was seventeen. In those days, Hoffstetter was a hard, fit man, with an accusatory, military bearing, and he was never without his mirrored sunglasses. Now, however, the judge is fleshy; his eyebrows are a thick tangle of silver wire above his professorial half-glasses, his long, porous nose is a ruin of self-indulgence.

Hoffstetter is silent. He leans back in his creaking chair, taps his fingertips together. He peers at Daniel as if he's about to cite him for contempt. But then he sits forward, claps his hands together.

"Okay, you two, chambers."

"What's he doing?" Rebecca Stefanelli whispers to Daniel. Her breath has a warm vermouth quality to it and Daniel can only hope Hoffstetter hasn't gotten a whiff of it.

"Don't worry," Daniel says. And when she looks at him questioningly, he adds, "We're right and they're wrong and that still means something."

Montgomery Paisley is fastening the clasp of his enormous old briefcase; he looks as if he's carrying the folders for every case he's ever tried. He hoists it up and, with his free arm, gestures gallantly for Daniel to go first.

Judge Hoffstetter's chambers are really just one room, which he has turned into the Judge Hoffstetter Historical Museum, with pictures of himself on every wall, depicting the highlights of his life, from high school baseball, to his induction into the state police, to his marriage to Sally Manzardo and their fifteenth wedding anniversary in Barbados, to his late-in-life graduation from Fordham Law School and becoming a county judge.

Hoffstetter sits heavily behind his desk, opens the top drawer and pulls out a cigarette and a little battery-operated fan, to dispel the smoke.

"You've got no case, Mr. Emerson," he says.

"Do you mind if I sit?" says Paisley.

"You do whatever you want, Monty. You're walking out of here a winner."

"That's highly improper, Your Honor," Daniel says.

"Counselor, Mr. Paisley has three statements from Leyden Hospital emergency room staff, all of them stating that when your client came in after having suffered a head injury in front of Schmidt's house she was drunk as a skunk."

This is not the first time Daniel is hearing this. The whole thrust of his case is to dispel the allegations of Stefanelli's drunkenness.

"Your Honor, the salient fact of this case is not my client's score on a Breathalyzer test, or the alcohol level in her bloodstream—though no such tests were given to her and the allegations of her being under the influence of alcohol are completely without proof. The salient fact is that Mr. Schmidt failed—and, in fact, refused—to remove the snow and ice in front of his house, thereby creating a hazard. Anyone could have fallen on that treacherous piece of pavement."

"But no one did, Daniel," Hoffstetter says, smiling. "No one but your booze hound of a client."

"Your Honor, I really must object—"

"Don't bother." Hoffstetter sighs, shakes his head, and continues. "I must say, Mr. Emerson, I never thought I'd see you in my court arguing a case of such little merit. Why did you go to the trouble of getting such a prestigious education if all you're going to do is practice law of the lowest common denominator?"

Is that what this is going to be about? wonders Daniel. *That I went to Columbia and Hoffstetter did law at proletarian Fordham?* Yet there is something weirdly sincere in the judge's question and it finds its way through Daniel's customary defenses. He is capable of feeling a bit of chagrin over some of the cases he handles, though, frankly, Lulu Stefanelli's fall is, he thinks, a decent case, unlike a couple of the divorces he's worked on, or the estate work he's done for a few of the local pashas.

Yet, like many lawyers, Daniel looks back at his beginnings and feels that he has fallen more than a little short of his initial goals. In law school, Daniel envisioned himself practicing some kind of public service law, though exactly what kind constantly shifted. Children's rights. Civil rights. Environmental law. Something that could make the world a little better. And in order to practice that sort of law he had to be in a major city, New York, Washington. His first job out of law school was with the doomed Lawyers' Immigrant Defense Society, which lost its funding six months later. From there he went to a private law firm, with its share of corporate clients but with a reputation for doing interesting pro bono work—one of the partners had a son in prison in Malaysia on trumped-up drug charges and it resulted in the inflammation of the entire firm's conscience.

"My client deserves some consideration here, Your Honor," Daniel says softly, indicating with his tone that he's ready to deal. Lulu would be happy with Schmidt's insurance company covering her emergency room bills and maybe coming up with ten or fifteen grand for her pain and suffering.

"All this for a few measly bucks?" Hoffstetter shakes his head. "How the mighty have fallen."

Paisley speaks from the depths of his chair. "We're willing to pay her initial medical costs, Judge."

"Let's not encourage her, Monty. She'll be throwing herself in front of cars and diving into empty swimming pools if we go along with her little scheme here."

"Your Honor—"

"Mr. Emerson, I really did expect better things from you."

But Daniel persists. He knows he's getting whipsawed by Paisley and Hoffstetter, but in a few minutes he's able to go back to the courtroom and tell Rebecca Stefanelli that the other side is willing to settle for medical expenses plus ten thousand dollars, and she is so thrilled that she hugs him excitedly and kisses him first on the ear and then on the eye. And a few minutes after that, he's in his car, driving through a cold, pelting rain, on his way north to Leyden, for his next appointment. The mountains on the west side of the river are obscured by mist. A stiff wind comes from the northwest; the trees barely sway, they just bend and stay that way.

Daniel is on his way to his office, where he needs to gather some papers before going to his next appointment. He stops at a gas station a couple miles outside of Leyden. It's an Exxon station that used to be run by the father of one of Daniel's boyhood friends and is now owned by a couple of Egyptian brothers. He pumps a tank of gas into his car and then goes in to get a cup of coffee and a shrink-wrapped bagel. The rain lashes the windows of the station. There is a display of heavily scented carved wooden red roses, drenched in some artificial, vaguely roselike scent; the smell mingles with the smells of the coffee machine, the wax on the linoleum floor, and the residual aroma of gasoline. Both of the brothers are behind the counter, heavy men in their thirties, with rough skin, dark, wavy hair, and short-sleeved shirts.

Even when his friend's father owned this station, it was one of the few spots in the area where boys and men could find pornographic magazines. In the past, the magazines had names like *Chic,* and *Cheri.* Now, the magazines are not only more numerous, but their names are more overt, even a little nutty. *Juggs,* and *Beaver,* are next to *Ass Time* and *Pink and Tight.* And though there are precious few black people who live in Leyden, this store stocks a wide range of African-American porn magazines.

Daniel has been eyeing the black porn covers for quite some time, though he has yet to muster the courage to even browse through what's inside. But today, after getting his coffee and choosing his bagel, he saunters over to the magazine rack. He imagines the Egyptians will be watching him, but it's something he can live with.

Big Black Butt, Brown Sugar, Black Booty . . . There is something about the stridency of these titles that strikes a reluctantly responsive chord in Daniel. He picks up one of the more benign titles—*Sugar Mama*—and opens it up.

He has never slept with a black woman, never seen a black woman undressed. In high school in the hills of New Hampshire, he had a crush on a black girl named Carol Johns. They kissed, she pressed her hand against the fly of his jeans. But when he tried to touch her breasts, she moved away and said, "Uh-uh," and then the next day her brother, an ambitious, bespectacled kid in a blazer, hit Daniel full force in the back of the head with his algebra book.

The women inside the magazine have *noms de porn,* like Afreaka, Supremacy, Kenya, and Downtown Sugar Brown. Afreaka is photographed pulling herself open like someone showing an empty wallet. Downtown Sugar Brown has shaved, moist armpit skin that looks like cracked leather, long aqua fingernails, and a barbered crotch greased along the labia. She has hardworking hands, with dark, bunched skin at the knuckles, a faded butterfly tattoo on her shoulder, long, pendulous breasts, with lusterless coronas. The stretch marks around her hips are like fork marks in brown butter. Daniel feels vaguely sick, reduced, helpless, yet in communion with some reptile self that has been waiting for him. He turns the page and Downtown Sugar Brown is joined by another woman—Cydney. They are on their hands and knees on an unmade bed, their long tongues touching.

Suddenly, a hand grabs his shoulder; he feels the scrape of chin whiskers against his ear, and his head fills with the hoarse, aggressive whisper of his assailant. "Whatcha got there, you horny sonofabitch? Going for the dark side?"

It's Derek Pabst, one of the four cops on the Leyden Police Department. Derek and Daniel have been friends since the first grade. Derek was a sturdy kid with an oversized head and the defiant, wayward grin of a boy with a great many siblings and overworked parents. He never did his homework, he rarely passed a test, yet the teachers quietly promoted him at the end of every year, with the tacit understanding that his life was hard and that school was finally so unimportant to him that they should all be grateful he was attending at all. He had a wild streak that mesmerized Daniel. Through the course of their boyhood, through school days and summers, they were each other's constant companions. They climbed trees, forded rivers, shot guns, kissed girls. As far as Derek was concerned, they were to this day best friends, though the persistence of their friendship has largely been Derek's doing. When Daniel was sent off to boarding school, Derek wrote him letters and hitchhiked the hundred miles to sleep on the floor of Daniel's dormitory room. When Daniel finally moved back to Leyden, Derek was there to meet the van, with a picnic cooler full of beer, another filled with sandwiches, and three of his own children to help unpack the truck.

Feeling exposed and ridiculous, Daniel puts the magazine back in the rack and goes to the counter to pay for the gasoline, the coffee, and the bagel. "Will zat be ull?" the Egyptian asks, as if challenging Daniel to purchase one of the magazines.

"That's it for me," says Daniel, forcing his voice to sound cheerful.

"How are you, Eddie?" Derek asks. He slaps a five-dollar bill onto the counter. "Let me have a pack of Camel Lights." He accepts the pack of cigarettes, the few pieces of change. Eddie acts frightened of Derek, displaying the almost ritualized respect of a man who has been warned.

Derek eagerly tears the pack open, lights up. "Since Stephanie got the new furniture delivered, she won't let me smoke in the house," he says, smoke streaming out of his large, dark nostrils.

Daniel and Derek stand beneath the eaves of the gas station and watch the pelting rain.

"How's Stephanie doing?" Daniel asks.

"She's okay. She says she's going to give Kate a call, put together a dinner or something."

Daniel's heart sinks. He knows Kate will decline Stephanie's invitation, he only hopes she does it without being too blunt. Hurting Stephanie's feelings will only hurt Derek's.

"The kids could play, too," Derek adds. He takes another long drag of his cigarette. "How's Kate doing?"

"Hanging in there."

"You really scored on that one," Derek says. "She's a great lady. She's so pretty, and so fucking smart. You know what I like about her? Her laugh. She's got a great laugh. I look for that, you know. It's a sign."

Daniel raises his to-go cup, shrugs. "I'm sort of running late." It sounds too abrupt to Daniel, and so he extends the excuse. "I'm going over to Eight Chimneys, finally getting to wet my beak in some of that river gentry cash-o-rama." He grins, rubs his thumb against his first two fingers.

But Derek, fully aware that money doesn't mean very much to Daniel, acts as if Daniel hasn't said a thing. "I had a runaway kid this morning," Derek says. "At large and dangerous. I picked him up at the train station."

"Whose kid?"

"One of the boys from Star of Bethlehem. I swear, the people running that place don't have the slightest fucking idea what they're doing. They keep trying to *respect* those boys, or *rehabilitate* them, and meanwhile it's a fucking jungle, with some of the worst juvenile offenders in the state, with nothing to keep them in but a couple of counselors and an electric fence." He looks at Daniel, trying to gauge the level of agreement or disagreement. "These are the 'boys' that made you decide to get your white liberal ass out of the city and come back home. The kid I picked up? First of all, his mother, who was probably twelve or something when she had him, names him Bruce, probably after some Bruce Lee movie, and then, just to be Ebonic and make sure he never learns how to spell, she spells it B-r-e-w-s-e."

"Since when do you care so much about spelling?"

"I learned how to spell. You used to cram it into my head before spelling tests."

"I don't remember it doing all that much good. Anyhow, spelling's just custom. African-Americans are making their own customs."

"Yeah, well this kid makes a *lot* of his own customs. Like the custom of capping the first motherfucker who stands between him and a new pair of Nikes."

There's a sourness in Derek's voice, a disdain, which Daniel believes is an occupational hazard for cops, like squinting for a jeweler, or grisly jokes for a surgeon, but there's an element of racial scorn that Daniel can't recall ever having heard from Derek before. Is it because he caught

Daniel looking at the African-American porn magazines? Or does Derek somehow sense that Daniel has fallen in love with a black woman? Did Daniel ever, in some swoon of nostalgia for their old boyhood closeness, talk to Derek about Iris?

Derek draws on his cigarette and pulls the smoke deep into his lungs—he smoked marijuana before cigarettes and it shows. When he finally exhales, very little of the smoke comes back out.

"What about tonight?" he asks Daniel. "Want to get a bite to eat or something?"

"I don't know, Derek. It's really hard to get Kate to go out, you know that." And, for all Daniel knows, Derek may sense that Kate finds him dull company and that Stephanie is a sort of paradigm for suburban futility, with her mall bangs and turquoise spandex tights, her exhausting cheerfulness—Kate calls her the last of the Stepford Wives.

"I was thinking just you and me, Danny," Derek says. His face colors and Daniel realizes with a helpless lurch that his old friend feels embarrassed asking him to sit down and share a meal. But the embarrassment, rather than make Derek shrink back, somehow propels him forward. He has nothing more to lose. "I really would like that," he says. "We—"

"No, that would be great," Daniel says, not being able to bear the awkwardness a moment longer. "I'll just make sure nothing's pending at home. I'll call you around six, six-thirty." Who knows? They might go to a restaurant and end up accidentally seeing Iris. Wouldn't that be something?

Derek flicks his Camel Light into the rain. "How cool is it that you moved back here?" he says, grinning, shaking his head. His cruiser is parked next to Daniel's car, blue lights slowly revolving, and every car that passes on the highway slows down at the sight of it. He has left the window open and the sound of his radio can be heard. The dispatcher's voice, static moving through it like whitewater. Daniel cannot understand a word, and Derek seems not even to hear it.

"How's Mercy Crane working out?" he asks.

"She's great. Thanks for putting us in touch with her."

"She used to baby-sit for Chelsea." He clasps his hands behind his back and stretches extravagantly. "She's really something."

"Mercy?"

"Real strict parents, though. Especially Jeff. He's nuts, you gotta watch out for him. He's the kind of cop that gives cops a bad name."

"She likes movies. I always try and rent something interesting for her to watch."

"Oh yeah, she likes movies. And music, and just laughing her ass off. She's an amazing girl. And sexy, don't you think? Not that I would ever do anything, but God, she is so fucking hot, those big eyes and those little spindly wrists and always wearing just enough perfume to let you know she knows exactly what you're thinking." He claps Daniel on the back. "All right, buddy, go back in there and do your business, I'm out of here."

"Me, too."

"Yeah? What about your magazines?"

"Just looking."

"I didn't mean to bust you, Danny. Feel free. Our age, a nice jerk-off helps keep the lid on. Though I could never, not with a black lady. It just doesn't do it for me."

"I'll call you tonight, then," Daniel says.

"Okay, good. I really need to talk to you."

"Is everything okay, Derek?"

Derek looks at him as if he were insane. "Of course not," he says, and then laughs. Daniel stands there and watches Derek get into his cruiser and drive away. He gets into his own car and drives into Leyden, through the rain that is now just beginning to include a few intermittent streaks of snow, loose skeins of white woven into the gray of the day.

Daniel arrives at his office building, swings around back, where there is parking for tenants and clients only. The first thing he sees is a green Volvo station wagon, with the license plate WDC785.

Iris.

What's she doing here? It's unlikely she is doing business at Software

Solutions, and the financial planner is in Austria for the month. She must be here to see the child psychologist, Warren Maltby, an exceptionally small man, with tar-black hair. The thought of Iris up there, with Nelson or without him, strikes Daniel with sudden force. What could the trouble be? Were they taking him to a shrink because he supposedly hit a kid at day care? Daniel sensed that Nelson is one of the teachers' favorites— with his clean cubby, princely table manners, perfect diction, and startling beauty. Ruby has actually enjoyed a rise in status since becoming Nelson's best friend. Like the homecoming queen on the arm of the school's football hero.

By now he has wandered over to Iris's Volvo and peers into it. The baby seat is strapped into an otherwise empty and immaculate backseat. The family dog, an elderly Australian shepherd named Scarecrow, sleeps deeply in the way back, her eyelids trembling while she dreams. Daniel raps a knuckle against the side window and Scarecrow opens one reddened eye. "Hi, Crow," he says, currying the dog's favor. Then he looks into the front of the car. In the passenger seat is a stack of books with library markings on their spines. On top of the books is a spiral notebook, opened to a page of her handwriting, black flowing letters, old-fashioned in their shapeliness. Through the glare and his reflection, he reads, *Harlem Ren. economic engine B. intell. repudiate Marx 19% unem. extend. fam "A safety net made not of government giveaways and fashioned by would-be social engineers, but consisting of a weave of family structure, rural communalism and Christianity."* And then he opens the door and picks up the notebook. He riffles through the pages like a spy, and then, miraculously, and terribly, he sees, on an otherwise blank page, his initials. *DE,* written small, in the center of the page, the exact center, with a circle drawn around them. His heart accelerates as if he has suddenly sprouted wings and begun to fly.

But he doesn't have a chance to obsess, not just then. He turns around to see her walking across the parking lot. She is alone, not a hundred feet away. It's always so startling to see her, like spotting a celebrity. She seems to float toward him.

"I thought your lights were on," he says, dropping her notebook and swinging the door shut. It closes with a sturdy Swedish finality that he hopes will prevent her from asking any questions.

"You're all dressed up," she says.

Daniel touches the knot of his tie. "I was in court."

"Did you win?"

"That's the thing about court, you rarely win and you rarely lose."

"I once thought I was going to be a lawyer," Iris says. "My dad always said I should be one, but just because I argued over everything, you know that way slightly spoiled kids do. I thought I could talk him into anything."

The thought of her as a child both stuns and provokes Daniel, imagining her that way, in that distant world.

She senses his mind is elsewhere and moves her face a little closer to his.

"Is that why you wanted to be a lawyer?" she asks.

"I never argued with my parents, I was too afraid of them. I thought they'd fire me."

"I like to think of people when they were little kids. You must have been one of those heartbreaking little kids, with a serious face and secretive, really secretive. The kind of kid that a mother sort of has to spy on to figure out what's really going on." Distress courses across her eyes, like speeded-up film of clouds moving through the sky. Daniel guesses she is thinking about Nelson.

"That was fun Friday night," she says. Her voice rises with what seems like forced gaiety.

"My office is here," Daniel says, gesturing toward the building.

"I know," says Iris. She opens her oversized purse and pokes around for her car keys, finds them. "I knocked on your door on my way out."

"You did?"

"I guess you were down here."

"Yes, I was." A little more explanation seems called for. "I'm on my way to see a client . . . but I started looking at the snow. Early for snow, isn't it?"

She gets into her car, turns on the engine. The windshield wipers cut protractors into the fuzzy coating of snow. While Daniel watches her Volvo backing up, he thinks: *She knocked on my door.*

[4]

They reached the top of the small hill they'd been climbing, but the sight lines were no better than below. The only sky they could see was directly above them, gray, going black.

"What do you think?" said Daniel.

"I think we're lost," Hampton said, shaking his head.

"Next they'll be sending a search party after us," Daniel said. He noticed something on the ground and peered more closely at it. A dead coyote like a flat gray shadow. Sometimes at night, he and Kate could hear coyotes in the distance, a pack whipping themselves up into a frenzy of howls and yips, but this desiccated pelt, eyeless, tongueless, was the closest he had come to actually seeing one. He wondered what had killed it.

"What do you have there?" Hampton asked.

"The animal formerly known as coyote," Daniel said.

Breaking off a low, bare branch from a dead hemlock, Daniel poked the coyote's remains. Curious, Hampton stood next to him, frowning. A puff of colorless dust rose up. The world seemed inhospitable—but, of course, it wasn't: they were just in the part of it that wasn't made for them. Here, it was for deer, foxes, raccoons, birds and mice and hard-shelled insects, fish, toads, sloths, maggots. Hampton stepped back and covered his mouth and nose with his hand, as if breathing in the little puff that had arisen from the coyote would imperil him. Iris had often bemoaned her husband's fastidiousness, his loathing of mess, his fear of germs. He had turned their *water heater up and now the water came out scalding, hot enough to kill most household bacteria. There were pump-and-squirt bottles of antibacterial soap next to every sink in the house; if Iris had a cold, Hampton slept in the guest room, and if Nelson had so much as a sniffle, Hampton would eschew kissing the little boy good night, he would literally shake hands with him instead and then, within minutes, he'd be squirting that bright emerald-green soap into his palm, scrubbing up a lather, and then rinsing in steaming water.*

Ferguson Richmond watches the rain from the front of his immense, crumbling house, reclined on an old cane chair, with his work boots propped up on the porch railing. He comes from a long line of privileged men and there is nothing he can do to obscure that fact, though it seems he is engaged in a perpetual project of self-effacement. He is careless about his appearance. He barbers his own hair, ekes out twenty shaves from his disposable razor, and wears large black-framed glasses from the hardware store, which are held together with electrical tape. Today, he is dressed like a garage mechanic, in grease-stained khaki trousers and a shapeless green shirt that had once belonged to a Texaco attendant named Oscar. In a family of oversized men and strapping women—large-headed people, with broad, bullying shoulders—Richmond is the runt. He is five feet eight inches, with skinny legs and delicate hands, and he is steadfastly uninterested in all sports and games. He neither boxes, nor climbs, nor kayaks, nor shoots; his passions are for strong coffee and old farm machinery. All the same, there is something confident and authoritative in his manner. His light blue eyes have that arrogant flicker that comes from a genetic memory of luxury and power; they are rooms that had been emptied and scrubbed after a legendary party.

Eight Chimneys is a huge derelict holding, encompassing over a thousand acres on both sides of a three-mile curve of blacktop. There is disorder everywhere, from disintegrating stone gates overgrown with vines and capped by headless lions, to its unmown fields in which are hidden rusted threshers, ancient, abandoned tractors, and dead deer.

Some people wonder if Ferguson realizes that his once proud ancestral mansion is a wreck, a pile of weather-beaten stone and crumbling plaster. He is painfully aware of his house's derelict condition. Five- and ten-acre parcels could be put on the market and they'd surely be snapped up by builders, and investors, but the full reach and grandeur of Eight Chimneys had not been diminished by even a solitary acre since it had first been granted to the Richmonds by King George, and, like generations of his ancestors, Ferguson felt that his dignity, his manhood, his respectability, and his place in history were all dependent upon keeping the property intact. Unfortunately, if he doesn't do something soon to shore things up, the house might be lost forever. But how could he ever get enough money to put it right again?

He hardly cares about money, except how it might intrude on his right to reside at Eight Chimneys. Though his brothers, Bronson and Karl, and his sister, Mary, all own shares of the estate, each with a wing of the house, where they come and go unannounced and even invite friends to stay—none of them choose to live there. In fact, they have established their lives in St. Croix, Santa Barbara, and Nairobi, and they return only for the occasional holiday or funeral, at which time they heap scorn and mockery upon Ferguson for how he's letting the place go.

But now he has an idea, suggested by a lovely, surprisingly clever blind girl named Marie Thorne, who has been back at Eight Chimneys for the past year and with whom he is having the most exciting and pleasurable love affair of his forty-two years on earth. Marie wants to turn a portion of Eight Chimneys into a museum. Result? Taxes slashed, plus extensive renovations at the public's expense. The taxpayers will foot the bill, and what a sweet thought that is. Foot the bill, foot the bill, there are times when Ferguson literally cannot stop saying it to himself. It's his new mantra, which is what he said to his spiritually promiscuous wife. *Foot the bill om shanti shanti*. There are, of course, details to be worked out, proposals to be written in the strange language of such things, public support to be marshalled, legislators to be brought on board—and that is what today's meeting with Daniel is, a beginning, a first step in that direction.

But suddenly Ferguson finds himself staring at something he has never seen before in October. He shifts his weight, the front legs of his chair bang down onto the planks of the porch, and he stands straight up. The rain is turning to snow! Thick, heavy snow. At least a month too early. His father once told him about an early October snow and the destruction it wrought. On this property alone, thousands of trees were lost. Nature's design is for the snows to come after the leaves are off the trees. That way, the snow falls to the ground. But if the leaves are still on the branches, the snow catches in the canopies, until the branches cannot bear the extra weight, and then that's it, the trees succumb, they bend so far in one direction or another that their roots come right out of the soil, or else they snap in two, like old cigars.

Ferguson stands transfixed as the snow drifts over everything. In less than an hour, there is no green, no red, no brown, no gold: every tree is white, and every inch of open land is white, too. The snow is wet, porous; it lies in the field like that foam they spray on runways after a crash. This is very, very bad, Ferguson thinks. Yet he's smiling. He feels a kind of delight in the imminence of trouble, a morbid receptivity to disaster. Good, he thinks, good, let it all come down.

Moments later, Ferguson's wife, Susan, appears on the porch. Ferguson dresses like a handyman, but Susan favors capes, and at least two pounds of jewelry. She's a large-boned, voluptuous woman, full of enthusiasm and temper. With erupting, abundant black hair and fierce green eyes, she's the sort of woman who frightens children. She and Ferguson have been married for twelve years. They are second cousins on their mothers' sides, but whatever genetic risk that poses is a moot point. They have no offspring.

"The electricity just went off," Susan announces. "And once again we are plunged into shit."

Fuck yourself, I wish your head would explode, get out of my life, thinks Ferguson. *Let me sleep with Marie unmolested, spare me your pedestrian, boring guilt trips, get out get out . . .*

"I don't know why we don't have a generator," Susan adds.

"I'm working on it," says Ferguson. "Sit down, Susan. Look at all this snow. You may never see anything like this again. We are really in for it. This happened before, in 1934, and it was a complete disaster."

"I was hoping to bathe," Susan says. "And I was also hoping to make some progress in organizing the library." Eight Chimneys' state of disrepair has come to irritate Susan, and, lately, imposing some order on it has become a virtual obsession. She simply cannot take it any longer. What had once seemed like a charming, funky casualness, a kind of stylish nose-thumbing at all of those blue bloods who once occupied these rooms, now strikes her as a kind of hell, an inferno of shattered sconces, peeling wallpaper, cracked plaster, stained ceilings, threadbare carpets, broken windows, knobless doors, perilous staircases, inexplicable drafts, grotesque armoires, and heirloom furniture theoretically worth hundreds of thousands of dollars but in reality worth nothing because no one in his right mind would ever want it.

"I don't want you to organize the library," Ferguson says. "I need to go through everything first."

"What is it exactly that you want to 'go through'?"

"There's a lot to go through."

"And in the meanwhile, the disorder is intolerable."

"You should work on your tolerance, then, Susan. It's a brand-new world, nothing is ever going to be the way we want it. We have to adapt, we have to grow, learn, change. Haven't any of your spiritual advisors told you this?"

Susan can no longer tell if Ferguson is speaking his mind or trying to make her lose hers. He likes to play devil's advocate, which she thinks is the most corrupt, exhausting parody of real conversation.

"Who are you waiting for anyhow?" she asks him. "You've been out here for an hour."

"Dan Emerson. He's going to give us advice about making Eight Chimneys a historic site, and maybe even a museum."

"Oh yes, Marie's bright idea." She looks out at the snow. "He's probably not coming."

"He'll be here. A man like Dan Emerson isn't going to be pushed around by a few snowflakes. He's high energy all the way. And I don't think he's averse to developing some river clientele."

"Oh, no one gives a hoot about river people anymore."

"But I don't think he knows that. He was raised in our great collective shadow."

Susan sticks her hand out over the porch railing, the snow melts in her dark, henna-streaked palm. "Maybe the roads are already closed. We can never be sure what's happening out in the world. We're stuck away like lunatics in this place."

"I'm working on it, Susan. Anyhow, look who's here." He points toward the west, where a line of cedars stand like exclamation points. A car is coming toward the house, snow spraying from beneath the tires.

A few minutes later, Ferguson, Susan, and Daniel go into the library, where Marie Thorne awaits them. Serene and delicate, she stares sightlessly out the window. She has luminous long hair, practically to her narrow little waist, the hair of a woman not fully in the world. She has been blind since birth.

Daniel has heard about what is going on between Ferguson and Marie—people in Windsor County gossip about the local gentry as if they are royalty, or movie stars. Marie is the daughter of Skip Thorne, a former caretaker at Eight Chimneys, and she was raised right there on the estate. Ferguson has a reputation of being especially drawn to young girls, and it's also been said that he'd found Marie attractive even when she was eight years old.

She turns when they come in. She has been looking forward to this meeting. Her plan to save Eight Chimneys is her gift to Ferguson; she hopes it will put them on equal footing and allow them one day to have a life together. She is dressed for business, in an oatmeal-colored tweed suit and a strand of pearls.

"I'm here with Daniel Emerson," Ferguson says. "The lawyer?" His voice booms without effort, it seems like an unwelcome miracle of acoustics, he opens his mouth and a shout emerges.

"Mr. Emerson." Marie extends her hand and strides across the library to greet Daniel. She moves easily through rooms she has known her whole life.

"So you want to turn this place into a museum?" Daniel says, as soon as they are seated at the library table.

"Not all of it!" Susan says, with some alarm. "Not the whole house."

"We're thinking of just the main floor and the cellar," says Ferguson. "And maybe some of the land, the property right around the house."

"And a swath going down to the river," adds Marie.

"A swath?" says Susan. The word feels vulgar, like "hopefully," or "be that as it may."

"Let me give you a little background," Ferguson says. "You need to understand why we're considering . . ."

Susan rises to light the stubs of candles in various holders around the room. With unconscious frugality, she tries to light them all with one match. Suddenly the green shaded lamp on the desk flickers on, and a moment after that comes the whine of the water pump down below in the cellar coming back to life.

But the respite is momentary. The lamp goes dark again and the pump is still. Ferguson laughs his strange, grating laugh. "It's a mess, the electric company around here," says Ferguson. "And it was from the outset. Our uncle used to be on the board of directors of Windsor Power. Clare Richmond. People thought he was a woman. In fact, at one point I had an Uncle Clare and an Aunt Michael. Do you remember Aunt Michael?" he says to Susan.

Susan doesn't like to dwell on the fact that she and her husband are related, however distantly, and she ignores his question. "You can't cut out a swath of land, it doesn't make any sense."

The snow-filled windows are darkening, and the sudden sound of a splitting tree is like the deadly bark of a rifle. Ferguson returns to the subject of the museum. He makes something of a show of telling Daniel about the financial pressures facing Eight Chimneys. Good professional manners dictate that Daniel take this to be shocking, distressing news, though everyone in the area is fully aware of the perpetual peril in which the Richmond estate operates, and even if Daniel weren't privy to the local gossip, one look at the place would tell him all he needed to know.

"If we can't figure out this money business fairly soon," Ferguson says, "this property might very well fall into the hands of developers and end up as Eight Chimneys Estates, or be turned into a rest home, or a mental hospital."

"Some people think it already *is* a mental hospital," Susan can't keep herself from saying.

"Something you said makes me curious," Daniel says. "You said you wanted to use the main floor and the cellar."

"Oh, the cellar!" says Marie. She has turned her eyes toward Daniel. They are bright and somehow thick, like the inside of oyster shells. "That's one of the most important parts. Do you know the Underground Railroad?"

"Yes, sure."

"Well, as you know, it wasn't really a railroad, it was really a whole lot of hiding places. Like a system of them. And the cellar here was part of it. There are these secret rooms and passageways. Slaves, mostly from Georgia, they were kept there."

"We're so lucky to have Marie, aren't we?" says Susan, turning around. The corners of her mouth are turned down and her wide-set eyes blaze with anger. "Not only does she come to us with all her knowledge of arts administration, but she knows history, too."

"They're for storage now," Marie says, unfazed. "But we're going to clean them out and make them like before. You can go down there, if you want. You can still feel the spirits of the escaped slaves."

In unison, the four of them turn to a clatter of noise coming from the hall, and a moment later the library door swings open and two men walk in, one of them middle-aged, with a warm, beatific smile, a down vest, and a maroon beret sparkling with snow. He cradles in his arms several brightly printed Tibetan silk ceremonial flags. The other man is tall, angular, with long, black hair grown past his shoulders and a patch over his eye; he carries a large wooden box filled with fireworks.

"I'm sorry," the smaller man says, in a low, Spanish-accented voice, "we knocked and there was no answer."

"Oh, Ramon!" Susan says, springing up from her chair. "I didn't realize you were bringing all this over today."

"Tomorrow I go to Bogotá, and then to Buenos Aires."

"There's more outside in the truck," the taller man says. "We better hurry."

Susan accepts kisses from Ramon on both cheeks, and then peers into the crate filled with Catherine wheels, Roman candles, gigantic orange sparklers. "Come on, Ferguson," she says. "Help us unload this, please, before it's all spoiled. Let's get it off the truck and into the ballroom."

"The ballroom?" Ferguson says. "What's it going to do in there? What is this stuff anyhow?"

"It's for a purification ceremony two weeks from yesterday. We've got a van filled with monks coming up for it."

Ferguson reluctantly rises. "I'm surprised at you, Ramon. I thought you were a good Catholic."

"I sit at the feet of anyone with wisdom," Ramon says, beaming.

"If we don't do this soon, it's not going to happen," the tall man says.

"Please, Ferguson, let's hurry," Susan says. For a moment, it seems she is going to clap her hands, but she instead reaches out to him imploringly. "Marie can tell Mr. Emerson everything he needs to know, and what she forgets we can fill in when we get back."

When the Richmonds and the two men leave the library—their footsteps soon disappear into the dank, porous silence of the house—Daniel and Marie sit silently in the flickering gloom for a few moments. Daniel glances at Marie, afraid that she might sense it if he simply stared at her. She sits silently, her fragile hands folded. She has a prominent forehead, which, combined with her pale skin and dark hair, gives her the appearance of someone temperamental, a worrier, a sufferer, someone who is capable of lashing out. She breathes in; the nostrils of her long, stern nose practically close, and then she exhales and sits deeper in her chair, lets her head fall against the cracked leather back.

"It's so sad when love dies," she says.

"Yes, it is," Daniel says.

"This used to be a very happy house," she says.

"Ferguson's pretty excited about this idea of yours," Daniel says.

"My father loved this house, and everything connected to it."

"I met your father a couple of times," Daniel says. Marie has no noticeable reaction to this; perhaps she, like the masters of the house, believes that everyone in Leyden knows her and her family in some way. "He saw my father a couple of times. He came to the house."

"Who's your father?"

"Dr. Emerson. He's a chiropractor."

"My father had terrible back problems all his life," Marie says. The sound of a tree breaking nearby resounds like a cannon shot, making Daniel jump in his seat but leaving Marie unmoved. "I remember him talking about Dr. Emerson. He liked him, he thought he was good."

"I'm glad my father could help."

"Is he still alive, your father?"

"Yes."

"Does he ever work on you?"

"Oh no, never. I was always sort of physically afraid of my father. The thought of him cracking my back, or yanking my head and cracking my neck—I could never put myself in that sort of position. He'd put me on that table of his, I might never get up." Daniel means this to be amusing, but Marie frowns and nods her head.

She gets up and glides to the tall windows. She places her palm against the darkening glass and then presses her cold hand onto her cheeks. Daniel sees that she is flushed; beads of sweat have formed along her hairline.

"Everyone in this town talks about Ferguson and me, don't they," Marie says, turning toward the window again. She presses her other hand against the pane, then touches her forehead, her throat.

"People like to gossip, Marie. I don't pay much attention to what they say."

When she turns again, Daniel sees that a solitary thread of blood has crawled out of her right nostril and is making its way through the pale down of her upper lip.

"You're bleeding, Marie," he says. He feels in his pockets for a handkerchief, but all he comes up with is the plastic wrap from this morning's gas station bagel, the touch of which triggers a startling flash of memory: those magazines. He is beginning to understand the unbridled nature of desire when it is confined to the realm of make-believe, how without the reality of an actual person in its path, it races headlong, blind and frothing.

Marie seems not to have heard him. "I don't care what people say. Something amazing has happened between Ferguson and me. And that's all there is to it. If people are upset, then they'll just have to deal with it."

"Marie . . ."

"I'm telling you this because I want you to be careful with Susan. She once loved this place, but not now, not anymore, and she never loved Ferguson. And she'll do anything to wreck what we're trying to do, she'd rather Ferguson lose the house and everything else—which would kill him. This is his habitat. He can't live anywhere else. It's pretty funny, when you think about it, she's into all these world religions, the Muslim, the Buddhist, the goddess, the meditation, the drumming, the spinning around in circles, but she's cruel and she's selfish, she can't stand the idea that other people might find happiness." At last, the trickle of blood reaches her lip and she tastes it. She gasps and her fingers go to her lip and then her nose. "Blood," she says. She has smeared the blood over her upper lip.

"I don't have a handkerchief or a Kleenex or anything."

"If you could go to the kitchen." She has seated herself and tilts her head back.

"Where's the kitchen?"

"Walk out the nearest door, which will put you in the portrait gallery, go through the double doors, turn right, go to the end of the hall, and there it is."

The portrait gallery is barely lit by the anemic pearl light coming in through three adjoining sets of French windows. Here, paintings and drawings of the Richmonds and the various families related to them by marriage have been hung on the blue plaster walls with such economy of space that the frames touch, though here and there appears an 18 x 24 sun-bleached blank, where a portrait has been removed and sold at auction.

Daniel hurries through the double doors and into a long hallway, which is lit by a few bare bulbs. As the electric power continues to come and go, they flicker off and on, as if a child were playing with the switch. A small South American man in his twenties, wearing a serape and a fedora, and with a crow perched on his shoulder, leans against the wall, pulling a nail out of his sneaker sole with a pliers. He gives no indication of noticing Daniel, who rushes past him to the kitchen, a dismal, catastrophically disorganized room, where Ferguson and Susan are in the midst of a bitter argument.

"I didn't hear you say anything, Susan," Ferguson is saying.

"You were deliberately ignoring me," she answers. "You love to negate me."

"You're insane, Susan."

Daniel has entered the kitchen and there is no backing out. He stands next to the old eight-burner stove, every burner of which holds a cast-iron kettle or skillet. Herbs that were hung to dry from the overhead beams have long ago turned gray and powdery. The double sink is filled with two towers of dirty dishes; a calico cat with a rawhide collar swats at the drops of water that swell and then fall from the silver faucet. Ferguson and Susan have turned to face him.

"I'm sorry," Daniel says. "I need a paper towel or something."

"What for?" demands Susan.

"Marie has a bloody nose."

Susan's laugh is surprisingly throaty and warm. "Did you hit her?"

"We don't carry paper towels here," says Ferguson. He pulls a not very fresh-looking handkerchief from his back pocket, and as he is handing it to Daniel the lights cut off and then come back on—it seems as if someone were shaking the room—and then they go off again and that's it. They are not in total darkness but in a deep opaque grayness, as if they have been woven into the fabric of a sweater.

"Hurry, Ferguson," says Susan. "Run. She needs you."

"I need *her*, Susan. That's the mess we're in, and if you won't see that, you won't see anything."

Daniel feels like a servant in front of whom the lord and lady of the house think nothing of undressing. Clutching Richmond's handkerchief, he backs out of the kitchen, but before he is out, the door swings open and the two men who delivered the Tibetan flags and fireworks come in.

"Everything's put away," says the older of the two. He uses his beret to dry his forehead.

"Before the snow gets worse," says the younger. "I never seen anything like this."

"Thank you, Ramon," Susan says pleasantly. "You're an angel."

"I'm working on it," Ramon says, smiling. "May I ask you? Who is the young man with the crow on his shoulder?"

"He's our friend from Slovenia," says Ferguson. "He lives in Albany. He came down from Troy in July to work on the roof of the piggery, and for some reason he hasn't left yet. He found that crow near the river and he's made something of a pet of it."

"I'm going to see to this," Daniel says, backing out of the kitchen. He is seized by anxiety, thinking that if he doesn't leave in the next minute, then he could be facing impassable roads and a long entrapment in Eight Chimneys. As he makes his way down the hall, he notices a door to the outside is open. It is not the door he came in through, but finding this way out is irresistible to him, and rather than deliver Ferguson's handkerchief to Marie, he stuffs it in his pocket and heads out of the house.

He finds himself on a semicircular stone porch, a repository for busted-up furniture. He can't tell what direction he's facing; the world is chaos. He looks up at the sky, at the deluge of snow floating down. He opens his arms wide. He wants to shout out her name. Her name is her body, her scent, the shadow she casts upon the world. The violence and unexpectedness of this weather leads him not to the actual belief that the world is in a state of emergency and that everything now is suddenly permitted, but to something close to it, something that suggests what that would feel like. He walks carefully down the stairs, snow seeping through his shoes. Then he walks around the house until he finds his car, which in the half hour he has been here has accumulated a five-inch coating of wet, heavy snow.

He must dig around in his trunk to find the scraper and brush to clear his windshield, and once that is done he has no idea where the road is. He looks for the tracks left by the men who delivered the flags and rockets, but the tracks have already been filled. He drives the mile and a half slowly, slipping in the wet snow, having no idea if he is driving on pavement or grass.

He calls his office from the car. The answering machine comes on, but with a new outgoing message left by Sheila Alvarez. "This is the office of Daniel Emerson. We have closed early because of the snow. And Mr. Emerson, Kate called to say that the day care center has closed and Ruby went home with Iris Davenport, and if you can make it over there would you please pick her up. Everyone else, leave a message after the beep."

5

An immense oak tree lay on the ground a few feet from where they stood. Hampton rested his foot on it and then shouted Marie's name as loudly as he could. The veins on his neck swelled; Daniel had a sense of what it would be like to deal with Hampton's temper, about which he had heard a great deal from Iris. Like many men with clear goals, Hampton was impatient, quick to anger. Hampton shouted again. If Marie were nearby she might have cowered from the furious sound of his call. Daniel sighed, folded his arms over his chest.

I t was snowing and it was snowing and it was going to snow some more. A truck bearing the sign WIDE LOAD and carrying behind it a tan-and-brown modular home that was being delivered to a hillside already filled with similar ready-made houses lost traction on the main road about a quarter mile south of Leyden, jackknifing into the northbound lane and colliding with an oncoming U-Haul truck, which was being driven up from the city by a young couple who had just bought a little weekend house and were bringing up their sofa, chairs, tables, lamps, bed, pots, pans, silverware, mystery novels, cross-country skis, aquarium, and paintings. Firemen, police, and paramedics struggled to the scene—many had difficulty driving there—and once the wreckage was cleared away and the victims transported—the truck driver to Leyden

Hospital, the couple from the city to the morgue at the south end of the county—they were called to another highway disaster, and then another.

Six miles north, on the same road, a trucker on his way down from the Adirondacks, carrying twelve tons of freshly harvested hemlock, slammed on his brakes to avoid a collision with a Chevrolet driven by an old man who was moving no more than ten miles per hour. The trucker avoided rear-ending the old man, but the suddenness of the stop created a lurching backward and then forward motion in the logs, and, though they had been secured by braids of heavy chains, two of the smaller trees broke entirely loose and shot out over the back of the truck as if out of a catapult. One of them flew over the roof of the Toyota behind the truck, hit the pavement, and bounced off the road, entering the woods end over end. The other log, however, went straight through the Toyota's windshield, like a giant leg stomping through a thin sheet of ice, crushing the driver and sending the car killingly out of control, directly into another Toyota, a blue one, in the northbound lane.

An old silver van, with a high rounded roof and oddly diminutive tires, flipped over on a sharp, slushy curve on Frankenberg Road. The van was carrying two chestnut-and-white racehorses down from Canada to a horse farm in Leyden. The horses, a gelding and a mare, were both in canvas harnesses, which were strapped to the sides of the van to keep the horses in place during their three-hundred-mile journey. When the van overturned, the canvas did not tear and both horses dangled upside down, whinnying in terror, their pink, powerful tongues wagging back and forth, their chin whiskers soaked in thick white foam. The woman who owned the horses and the man who was their trainer staggered around on the side of the road, banged and bleeding, feeling lucky to be alive. But then, as the van began to smoke, and then to burn, they realized that the miracle of their survival would be forever compromised by having to spend the rest of their lives remembering the crescendo of cries and then the even more terrible silence as their horses were immolated.

At the Bridgeview Convalescent Home the loss of electricity would have normally switched on the auxiliary generator, but last winter's power failures had used up all of the generator's fuel and no one had thought to gas it up—winter was still a couple of months away. The lights went dull, then dark, like dying eyes. Clocks stopped. Those nurses who were generally irritable became more irritable. Those patients who were generally confused became more confused. The bedridden propped themselves up on bony elbows and looked around for some explanation. The patients who were chronically complaining shook their fists, spit on the floor, told the staff off. The fearful became terrified—the booming death of all those trees, the TVs with their gray blank screens standing in their corners like uncarved gravestones.

In a Victorian house out on Ploughman's Lane was a facility for teenage boys who had tangled with the law and been ordered there by juvenile courts ranging from the Bronx to Buffalo. It was now called Star of Beth-lehem and it was run by Catholic Charities. In deference to the people of Leyden, there were never fewer than four guards on duty, hulking, quiet men who patrolled the halls and the grounds in lace-up paratrooper boots and black turtleneck shirts, carrying black rubber batons. The doors were always locked and the windows were locked, too; the fence that sur-rounded its ten rolling acres was electrified. Shortly after the power failed, the staff herded the boys into their rooms. The staff at Star of Bethlehem were, for the most part, men who themselves had had tough dealings with the law in their youth, who seemed to operate under the principle that if they could put their lives on track, then these boys could learn to live right, too. They were usually rough, and with the power out they pushed and prodded the boys into their rooms, as if some gross breach of disci-pline had already been committed. It was a total lockdown.

The boys went docilely, confused by the gathering darkness, the moaning winds, and the distant sounds of cracking trees. Once they were in their rooms, they watched through barred windows as the snow brought down one tree after another. Star of Bethlehem's auxiliary power supply was already in operation: the Honda generator was pump-ing out enough power to light the lights and keep the boiler running. But it was unlikely that the generator was sending power out to the electric fence hundreds of feet away. A couple of the boys picked up a bed and smashed the metal frame through the windowpane—the electric alarms were silent, dead, useless. Then six of the eight boys in the room pulled mattresses off their beds, and wrapping their arms around them, holding them fast, as if they were warm, soft sleds, they dove out of the second-story windows and out into the pearl-white snow. The mattresses landed with thuds ten feet below and the boys left them behind as they scrambled up and slid down the hill, toward the powerless fence and the icy woods beyond.

6

Discouraged, exhausted, Hampton sat on the fallen tree—and immediately sprang
up again. He had sat upon the Roman candle in his back pocket and it had split
in two. He quickly pulled it out, with frantic gestures, as if it might explode, and
tossed the top half of the candy-striped cardboard tubing as far from him as he
could. "Oh no," he said.

  Now his back pocket was filled with the Roman candle's black powder, a mix-
ture of saltpeter, sulfur, arsenic, and strontium. If I kick him in the ass, he might
explode, thought Daniel. He had a comic vision of Hampton blasting off, sailing
high above the tree line, stars, pound signs, and exclamation points streaming out
behind him.

It takes Daniel nearly half an hour to drive the five miles between Eight
Chimneys and Iris's house on Juniper Street. Some roads are already
closed, and on others the traffic barely crawls. He is listening to a mix
tape he made—Don Covay, Marvin Gaye, Ray Charles, Irma Thomas. He
curses the storm, the roads, the other drivers, and imagines himself
making love to Iris. He thinks about her voice, the slightly spoiled,
slightly shy, and always shifting quality of it. He is envious of not only
Hampton but her fellow students, the library staff, the 7-Eleven clerks,
the shopkeepers up and down Leyden's miniature Broadway, a man

named Timmy Krauss, who mows her lawn, the tellers at Leyden Savings Bank, even Nelson.

He pulls into the driveway behind Iris's car. A branch from one of the four maples on her front lawn, as long and thick as a stallion's hindquarters, has snapped off from the weight of the snow and it sticks like a spear into the ground. Daniel looks up. The downward rush of the snowflakes, unusually large, looks like the blur of the stars when a spaceship accelerates into warp speed. He hears the creaking wooden sound of a window opening.

"Let yourself in, okay?" It's Iris from the second story. She has stuck her head out the window and her short black hair whitens instantly. "I'm up here with the kids." Her voice rings out in the silent world.

He steps into her entrance hall and peels off his gloves, feels the melting snow trickling down his back. There are raucous screams of crazy excitement coming from Ruby, who is beside herself with joy to be in Nelson's house. He hears Iris moderating.

Because the pickups and deliveries of Ruby generally fall to Daniel, he has been to this house ten or fifteen times, but each time Iris has Ruby dressed and ready to go upon his arrival. Nevertheless, in those moments of polite exchange, he has breathed in the smells of her domesticity— the aromas of whatever meal was being prepared, the smell of a newly painted room, of eucalyptus stalks stuck into a beaded glass vase that stood upon an end table in the living room, just visible from where he usually stood. He has taken in everything there was to see in the foyer itself: the blue-and-silver-striped wallpaper, the illustrative hooked rug (streetlamp, horse and buggy), the tiger maple table near the door, with its resident wicker basket filled with junk mail, the occasional stray mitten, and the curling cash register tape from the supermarket. From this he learned that her purchases included such items as Playtex tampons, and Dry Idea deodorant, Marcal bathroom tissues, Sominex sleeping pills, Tom's Natur-Mint mouthwash, Revlon emery boards, Tylenol PM.

Outside: the crack of falling trees. For a moment it seems the electric power will go out here, too.

Iris comes downstairs, beckons him in. She has taken off her shoes; her socks are bright electric blue. She wears a loose-fitting yellow sweater, jeans. She is a woman at home, she has put the world behind her.

"Are the kids okay?" Daniel asks.

"Ruby's amazing. She's got such compassion and wisdom in her eyes. I love looking at her."

Daniel feels unaccountably moved by this. It seems somehow more tender and appreciative than anything Kate has ever said. Kate loves Ruby, of course she does, but she has no patience for motherhood. Its unending quality confounds and irritates her. Kate longs for privacy, for uninterrupted mornings, for what she calls her Dream Time.

"Have you ever been to Ruby Falls?" Iris asks.

"No, where is it?"

"In Tennessee, outside Chattanooga. It's an underground waterfall, the biggest in the world, and it's red. Well, they might just shine red lights on it to make it look that way. I was ten years old when my family went there. I mostly remember how hot it was outside and how cool it was in that cave, and that everyone on the tour was white, but they were super nice to us."

"How wonderfully civil of them," Daniel says.

"I wasn't really used to seeing white folks, not then. I was so nervous." She sighs, closing the subject. Then: "I'm going to have some tea. Do you want some?"

He remembers the appearance of tea on one of her IGA receipts: Celestial Seasonings Almond Sunset and Celestial Seasonings Emperor's Choice.

"Sure." He is still in the foyer, stomping loose the snow that was jammed into the waffle sole of his shoes. "Tea would be great. Do you have like an almond tea or something?"

"As a matter of fact, I do," says Iris.

The dog comes in. Daniel crouches down to let Scarecrow sniff his hand. She has no tail but moves her rump back and forth to signal her acceptance of him. He strokes her lightly on the top of her head and she makes a low groan of pleasure.

"This dog is Jesus," he says, glancing up at Iris. He turns back toward Scarecrow. "Are you Jesus?"

"Don't answer that, Scarecrow," Iris says.

It strikes him with the force of revelation that this is the most fun he has ever had, ever, in all his life, this is the pinnacle, the greatest happiness he has ever known, right there, asking the dog if she is Jesus, and Iris telling the dog not to answer.

They walk across the living room, with its bay windows, dark mahogany molding, a white marble mantel over the fireplace. On the north side of the room, French doors lead to the dining room; on the south, a newly hung door leads to the kitchen. Daniel stops at the rack of compact discs to see what music she listens to and feels a rush of confusion, disappointment as he reads: Fleetwood Mac, Tony Bennett, Boyz 2 Men, Aaron Copland.

"I can't believe you like almond-flavored tea," she says to Daniel as they enter her kitchen. "To me, it tastes like arsenic or something. What is it, a guy thing? It's the only tea my husband will drink."

———

Iris cannot bear chaos. Beyond the rituals and reassurances of daily life lies danger. Go off the road—danger. Swim in the dark—tragedy. Those people in London all huddled in the subway stop while the bombs dropped? She would never have been able to do it. She'd hang herself first. Life without its presumption of reasonable safety—intolerable.

She is aware of a slow, engulfing terror growing within her. She has been holding her panic in check for a couple of hours now, telling herself that the storm and all those exploding trees are part of Nature, and she is fully capable of taking it in stride. But she cannot take it in stride, she cannot even *stride,* she feels trapped, waiting for something terrible to happen. And knowing that it's all in her head doesn't make it better; in fact, it makes matters worse—how do you hide from your own mind?

Night has come. It seems to be snowing harder now than it was an hour ago. The daytime sky was just running out of snow when the night sky rolled into place with a fresh supply. There is no fear that is not worse in the darkness.

Daniel. It astonishes her how closely he listens to her, how he leans toward her when she speaks and nods his head, yes, like the ladies in her grandmother's church, the Amen choir, in front of whom you could sing, or cry, and never feel the slightest shame. He seems to remember everything she has ever said to him, starting with their first hello. Like most married people, she is used to being heard only by half, and has even gotten used to being ignored. Daniel not only listens, he seems to possess, to embrace the things she says to him. Six months ago, she said she had decided her thesis dissertation would be on some aspect of Parchman Farm, and today, sitting in her kitchen, with the candles in their holders and a box of Ohio blue tips at the ready, she learns that Daniel has read *Worse Than Slavery,* one of the best books about Parchman. It initially gives her a guilty, embarrassed feeling because she's moved on from Parchman, it just didn't feel right—she might, in fact, have abandoned it later the same day she'd mentioned it to Daniel. She has been having a difficult time settling on a thesis; jumping from one possible topic to the next has been the source of no small number of nasty remarks from Hampton, who wants her to get her Ph.D. and move back to the city. But Daniel doesn't mind when she softly confesses that she has left Parchman behind.

"I switched to the music," she says. "I couldn't read about all the beatings, it was ruining my life."

"The music?" Daniel says excitedly.

"People survived, they made songs, it's very rich material."

He gets up from his seat at her kitchen table, suddenly full of animation. "I've got just the thing for you! Do you have a tape player in here?"

She points to a boom box on the kitchen counter.

"I'll be right back," he says. He goes out to the car to retrieve a tape from the glove compartment. He is unjacketed; wet clumps of snow slither down his back as he paws through lumpy old maps and a dozen cassette boxes, most of them empty, until he finds what he is after, one of the Alan Lomax Southern Journey compilations. It's not the one he was hoping to find—he wanted the field recordings of prison songs—but this one will have to do. "Sheep, Sheep, Don'tcha Know the Road." He shakes the box and hears the rattle of the tape within. *Thank God.* On his way back to the house, another limb snaps off the maple tree in her front yard and it comes hurtling down, plunging into the ground not ten feet from him. *Thanks again, God.*

Inside, he plays her "You Got Dimples in Your Jaw," sung by a man named Willie Jones. Daniel stands near the tape player and does his best not to dance along with the music, knowing it will make him appear foolish, but the music is so sexy and good, it's hard to stay still, with his arms folded professorially over his chest. The song is a paean to the beauty of the singer's girlfriend, especially her dimples. "I love the way you walk, I'm crazy about the way you walk, I got my eyes on you. You got dimples in your jaw. You my babe. Got my eyes on you."

When the song ends, Daniel pushes the stop button and releases a deep, satisfied sigh. "It gives you such insight, I think. It's a love song to a woman whose physical being has been devalued by racism, slavery, poverty, and this guy's saying to her: I see you, I notice every little thing about you, and it makes me so happy. It's sexuality subverting the whole system of slavery."

"You think so?"

"John Lee Hooker made it a semi-pop hit, for this little outfit in Chicago called Vee-Jay records, in 1950-something." He knows that it was in 1956, but he decides at the last instant to be imprecise, not wanting to seem like one of those geeks who memorize music trivia.

"I've heard of him. My uncle Randall used to have his records. He used to wear a turban or something? A cape?"

She must be thinking of Screaming Jay Hawkins, Daniel thinks. "Maybe," he says, not wishing to embarrass her. "I'm not sure." His fingers graze the controls of the boom box. "Do you want to hear another? There's this fantastic version of 'The Prayer Wheel,' by the Bring Light Quartet."

"Well, the truth is, I'm not doing the music thing. I had to let that one go, too."

He decides not to ask her why; surely she's had enough questions about that. "Have you decided on a new topic?" he asks her.

"I'm not sure. American Studies, you know. Lot of choices. The thing is . . ." She stops, lowers her eyes. Daniel looks at her. He feels it would be permissible to reach across the table and touch her.

"The thing is," says Iris, lifting her gaze. Her eyes are clear, with little flecks of amber in them. "All my topics have been African-American, and I think that's why I haven't been able to stick with them." She takes a deep breath. "I'm really getting *tired* of being African-American. I always thought of myself as just me. I know that sounds sort of weak, and when a *sister* says it, people think she's trying to get out of something, or she's like a traitor or something. But that's not it, not for me. I'm just exhausted by it, it's so much *work* being black. And no days off, either. And the pay stinks. But what am I going to do? It's my life. But I don't think I want to make it my academic life, too. Maybe I'll write about Eisenhower or *I Love Lucy,* or something. Something white, or better yet something that doesn't even have a color, if there is anything like that. I wouldn't mind being in school forever. I love learning. I realize it's not the most highly regarded occupation in our society, I realize you're nothing in America unless you're making money, but learning stuff makes me really happy. It's like being beautifully and luxuriously filled with all the knowledge there ever was."

"They've got a lot of old Lucy tapes at the video store, if you're really interested."

Outside, the trees continue to explode beneath the weight of the snow. It sounds like a long, nasty war is being fought.

"It breaks my heart to listen to all those dying trees," Iris says.

"It's a nightmare," he says softly.

"If only the snow had waited. I love the snow. But the leaves . . ."

"If it wasn't for the leaves, the snow would just fall right through the branches and not touch a thing."

"Everything's timing," she says. "The most wonderful thing at the wrong time? Disaster."

"But you never know," he says.

"Until it's too late," Iris says. "I'm afraid of things that can't be taken back. That's another reason I keep changing my thesis. I just don't want to create a document that says, This is what I know, this is who I am. I really admire your . . . what do you like to call her? Your . . ." She smiles. "Lady?"

"Kate."

"Well, I really admire Kate for just writing it down, sending it out, and getting on with it."

"The thing she most cares about—her novel—she can't write that." He feels his stomach turn over. "I better call her, actually. She'll be wondering where Ruby is."

Iris brings him the phone. She can hear Kate's hello clear across the kitchen, powerful voice, formidable, not someone you'd want to cross.

"Ruby and I are at Nelson's house," Daniel says. Oh, Iris thinks, *Nelson's* house. She turns slightly in her chair, not wanting to see what he looks like when he's being so devious and clever. "I think we better let things settle down before we try to make it home."

"I don't think the snow ever *will* stop," says Kate. She is in her study, facing her desk, where there sits an old Smith Corona manual typewriter and a dozen candles of different sizes, their flames dancing in the draft, an ecclesiastical whiff of paraffin in the air. "And when it does, it's going to take a lot more than the little men in their trucks to get things going again. The trees! They're everywhere and each one of them is going to have to be sawed up and dragged away. How about where you are?"

"It's pretty bad."

"Do they have electricity?"

"Yes, for the time being."

"Oh, you're lucky. That means you have heat, too. And water."

"For now."

"I don't blame you for wanting to stay there. Is the husband there?" But before he can answer, she blows right past it. "You know what I wish? That there was a radio in this place I could listen to."

"The one in Ruby's room runs on batteries," Daniel says.

"Ruby's room? She has a radio in there?"

"Yes, the red one. My First Sony, or something like that. You'll see it."

"I just want a way to tune in some news and keep track of the storm."

"I put fresh batteries in it a couple days ago," Daniel says.

"Oh, you're so good," says Kate. A little lurch in her voice. And then something being poured. He realizes she's getting loaded. Hard to remember, but there was a time when he liked her drinking, liked the freewheeling, southern bad girl aspect of her, the nocturnal romance of it. Those drunken nights were the occasions of their most uninhibited sex. Sweaty, a little mean. It was like screwing an escapee. The concentration was all on Kate. What would she like, what could she take? Her body arching and jerking as if she were being electrocuted. Enthralling, those nights, some strange combination of honeymoon and porn flick. Nasty and private and never spoken of afterward. But even then he felt those moments weren't quite valid, like those sports statistics that go into the record book with little asterisks after them, indicating a shortened season or a muddy track.

"Kate's out of her mind with happiness," he says to Iris, giving the phone back to her.

Another tree explodes, this one, from the sound of it, just a few feet from the house.

"Every tree that's falling took so long to grow," Iris says. There will be no more talk of Kate. "Some of them a hundred years."

"Maybe even more."

"I can't stand to hear them dying like this. It's like witnessing hunters shooting a herd of elephants."

"That's what I was thinking," says Daniel. "The elephants. It's what I was going to say. But don't worry. It'll be all right."

"You're the type who thinks *everything's* going to turn out all fine and dandy."

"How do you know that?"

"Aren't you?"

"Maybe I'm a bit of an optimist."

"I think you are."

"Could be that it's sort of . . . a white thing?" Daniel asks.

"Well, it sure ain't no black thing, honey child." Iris laughs, a little surprised at herself.

"Do you miss being around black people?" he asks her—much to his own surprise.

"What makes you think I'm not around black people?"

"There's not many around, not here."

"True. And here is where I am. I like it here, and, frankly, it's hard to find a really nice place that also has a lot of African-American families. I like to ski, and sail, and take walks in the woods. I like having a garden and I'm in a really good program at Marlowe. Anyhow, I've come a long way from that cave at Ruby Falls. I'm used to being in a white world."

Scarecrow totters into the kitchen and goes straight to Daniel's side, leans against him and groans softly, with deep canine contentment.

"What do you want, Scarecrow?" Daniel says. "Why are you looking at me? Because I said you look like Jesus?"

"Let me ask you something," Iris says. "Why did you say that?"

"About the dog being Jesus? I don't know. She seems very deep. Did it offend you?"

"I had the same thought. Just yesterday. It seemed sort of nutty and now you're saying the same thing today."

"That is strange. Is Jesus a big thing in your life?"

"Not too big. I think we're alone. There's no one to forgive us or punish us or help us in our hour of need, and I think nearly everybody deep down knows that. When I was an undergraduate, I took a course called 'Death and Dying.' "

"You did?"

"Oh yes, I've always been very interested in death. Anyhow, as part of my course work I volunteered in a hospice and I got to know quite a few people who were dying, mostly of cancer. My supervisor told me we weren't supposed to push any sort of religious ideas on the people we talked to, but it was all right to subtly, in some general way, offer them the comfort of faith, maybe mentioning heaven and meeting up with loved ones, that kind of thing. But you know what I noticed? The closer dying people got to the end, the more they knew that there was nothing next. The knowledge was in their bodies, they knew that was all, there was no heaven, no God, just blood and bones and pain and then silence. You could see this knowledge in their eyes. Even the ones who had been religious all their lives, and the ones who just were so scared they were willing to believe in heaven at the last minute, desperate for something to hold on to, to ward off the fear, you could even see it in their eyes—God was an idea, it was something out there, far far away, it was a story people told, a beautiful story, or a dumb story, but it was in the province of the living, and these dying bodies didn't have time for it anymore, they were too busy dying, the work of it. Even if they were praying out loud, holding on to the rosaries, calling on Jesus, be with me, Jesus, be with me, their bodies knew, there was a final knowledge right in their cells that it was all over."

"I saw you going to church in July. I was driving past St. Christopher's and I saw your car turning in."

"I go to church three times a year, on Christmas and Easter, and in July, around the Fourth. My baby brother, Leonard, drowned on the Fourth of July when he was six years old. I light a candle for him and I pray and I cry, but I don't even know why I do it."

"There's not too many places where you can go and have those feelings."

"Do you have a place?"

"The movies. Sometimes I cut out of work and go across the river to one of the mall movies. I sit there in the middle of the afternoon with a box of popcorn and some M&Ms, and kind of cry a little. It's totally pathetic and what's really pathetic is you're not even the first person I've told this to. I tell it to everyone."

"Maybe you want people to know you're lonely."

"You think that's what it is?"

"It must be strange for people to think of you that way, lonely."

"I know, I know. Because I'm such a cheerful presence."

"Well, you are. And—"

"I know," Daniel says. "Everybody likes me."

"It's good that people like you. I like you."

"Good. I like you, too."

"I know."

"Well, that's settled, anyhow."

"Can we be honest here?"

"We can try. It's not that easy."

"I just think we can be honest, that's all, I mean: why not? Maybe this is Armageddon."

"The snowstorm?"

"It's something," says Iris. "It's an occasion. We hardly ever get to say what we mean to say. That's why people who have crises in their lives, real ones, huge ones, they turn out to be more honest."

"Okay, some people have the Battle of Algiers, we've got the snowstorm. Anyhow, I think I know what you're going to say."

"What am I going to say?"

"You're going to say, 'I know you like me and I also have become increasingly aware that you stare at me and you seem unduly excited whenever we happen to meet.' "

"That's right," says Iris. "Except for 'unduly.' I wasn't going to use that word."

"So you don't think it's unduly."

"Maybe it is. I wasn't going to put it like that."

"How were you going to put it?"

"I was going to say you've been looking at me in a way that makes me uncomfortable."

"I'm sorry. I don't want you to feel uncomfortable."

"It *used* to make me uncomfortable. Now it doesn't. Now I like it."

"I think I might be having a heart attack."

"Look, please, don't make more out of this than what it's meant to be. I shouldn't have said anything. I'm indulging myself. Taking a little time off from reality."

"This is reality."

"It's just that the past couple months, since Nelson and Ruby have gotten to be such buddies, and you and I cross paths fairly frequently, it's been this little secret pleasure in my life. It's like a river under the road. Let's talk about something else."

"Do you have anything to drink?"

"More tea?"

"The tea is not good. The tea was a mistake. Something stronger?"

"Bourbon okay? I'll have one, too."

At home, Daniel is the designated driver, with or without an automobile. He has made it his job to not drink and through his example to somehow discourage drinking. This course of action, or inaction, has never met with the slightest success, but he cleaves to it nevertheless, limiting his consumption of alcohol to a glass or two of wine with dinner once or twice a week. Now, he sits in Iris's kitchen, watching her reach up to a high cabinet to retrieve a bottle of Jack Daniel's, watching her muscles move beneath her clothes—and he thinks: *What if this were really my life? What if I could spend a part of every day watching her? What if it were easy? What if I come behind her, put my arms around her, kiss her long bare neck, cup my hands over her breasts, push my groin against her awe-inspiring ass? Could I tolerate living with such happiness?*

She pours their drinks, they hold their glasses up and then move them very slowly together until they touch.

Iris is hoping a drink will soothe her nerves—the intense labor of appearing calm is wearing her out. And a drink might loosen up both of them, could even throw up a little makeshift bridge between them. Earlier, with Ruby in tow, knowing that Daniel would be coming to her house, Iris had felt that here, now, was the logical and perfect time to finally make something out of those months of flirtatious glances. It seemed, then, that all she had to do was to let him know she had seen them all, felt his eyes on her, heard what he did not say. All she had to tell him was that she is caught up in a marriage that has turned out to be a mistake. It would be simple, a simple thing to do. She does not worry about being attractive to him. He has already made all of that clear: she has never felt so desired.

But now she realizes that it will not be that easy, will not be easy at all.

Yet the giddiness of all this cannot altogether obscure her prescient view of the misery she would cause if she reached across the table and touched Daniel's soft, lank hair. It finally takes so little, a kiss, and now she's thinking about it, imagining it.

There's music from the second floor. The kids are listening to the Village People singing "YMCA."

"Nelson!" Iris turns, looks up at the ceiling. "Turn it down."

"How did that ever become a children's song?" Daniel asks. He's still making small talk, wanting only to keep her attention and to make sure there are no silences. "It's so completely West Village, cruising Christopher Street, 1978. It's strange the way the culture absorbs things and makes whatever use of them."

She refills their glasses, very judiciously, as if this were a familiar ritual.

Suddenly, there's a thud right above them, unnerving in its suddenness and force. Daniel's response is instant. Out of his seat, out of the kitchen, up the stairs, taking them two at a time. Iris follows. They both hear Ruby's plaintive little cry. Iris has a sinking feeling.

They reach the children. Daniel, wisely, has slowed himself down, trying not to add his alarm to the volatile mix. Ruby is just picking herself up. Her swollen blue eyes glitter with unshed tears and her face is scarlet. Without a word, she stretches her arms out toward Daniel. He lifts her up; her knees grip his rib cage, she wraps her arms around him, notches her head into the space between his neck and shoulder. Iris realizes her hands are clenched into fists; she forces herself to relax them.

"What's wrong, Ruby?" Daniel asks.

Nelson is simply standing there, his arms folded over his chest, his body rigid beneath his cargo pants and sweatshirt, a look of stony defiance on his face.

"She's all right," he says insistently. "She's not hurt."

The room in which they've been playing has a wide plank floor and a large circular orange-and-blue rug. The walls are decorated with travel posters from Bermuda and Denmark. The ceiling is slanted, the windows small, low—an adult would have to get down on her knees to see out of them. The sense of order in that room is fierce. The shelves and cubbies are filled with action figures, cars and trucks, books, tapes, CDs, dolls, paints, blocks, and Legos, all neatly kept.

"Nelson pushed me down," Ruby whispers.

"Oh Nelson, Nelson," Iris says. "Why do you do these things?" She tries to take his arm but he yanks it out of her reach. "Is she all right?" Iris asks Daniel.

"She's fine," he says. "Aren't you, honey?"

Ruby presses her face harder against Daniel and vehemently shakes her head no.

"What happened here, Nelson?" Iris says. She reaches for him and this time he cannot escape.

"Nothing." His eyes are mutinous and self-righteous.

"How did it happen that Ruby fell down?" Iris says.

"Kids fall all the time," Daniel says, stroking Ruby's head.

"I'm waiting for an answer, Nelson," Iris says. "How did she fall down? Did you push her?"

Nelson continues to glare at his mother, and Iris suddenly turns her attention toward Ruby. "Are you all right, Ruby?"

"I'm fine," Ruby says. She starts to squirm and Daniel sets her down. Her face is no longer flushed, and now without its wrapping of color they can see a pale little lump on her forehead.

"Oh Nelson," says Iris.

"I didn't do anything!" Nelson cries. "She was trying to kiss me!"

"I was not!" Ruby practically bellows.

"Ruby is a guest in our home, Nelson. You know what the tradition is." Nelson lowers his eyes.

"Are you two going to be okay?" Daniel says. "Or are you going to continue acting like children?"

He wants peace, at any price. He wants Iris to be put at ease, and he wants to be able to go back to the kitchen with her. He signals for them to leave—a little flick of the eyes, they are that much in synch—and they both back out of the playroom.

In the kitchen, they take their places at the table again. Outside: the crack of falling trees. Again, it seems they are going to lose electric power. Darkness stutters but does not yet pronounce itself.

"Nelson can sometimes be a little rough," Iris says.

"Really? He always seems so mild and considerate."

"He is, I really believe he is. But there are times . . . His father is teaching him how to box, it's the worst thing he could do. As soon as he gets off the train Friday night Nelson comes running up to him and Hamp gets into a crouch, like it's round one. That can't be good. Nelson needs to be gentled down, not . . ."

But wherever this line of conversation is heading, it's stopped by the huge groaning snap of another falling tree and then the flickering of the lights.

Iris whimpers, covers her eyes.

"Are you all right?" Daniel asks.

"It kills me. It's like watching your relatives die."

He looks at her, amazed. Everything she says makes her more imperative. "I better get Ruby ready and get out of here," he says. "While we still can."

"You really think it's safe?" Iris says, her voice showing alarm.

"Then what am I going to do?" he says.

"What can you do?"

Iris takes a small sip of the bourbon. It tastes suddenly chemical. And she doesn't want to get drunk. But she *could* use a little pat on the behind, like the in-flight trainers give the paratroopers. She is amazed by her own rectitude. Frankness is one of her qualities. Or *was*. Six years of Hampton have worn down her confidence. The peculiar degradation of living with a man who won't say so but who *thinks* she is not smart enough for him. It used to be easy with men—just something she could do, like swimming, or being able to sing. It had little to do with beauty, or even sex, it was an affinity, an unconscious knowledge of what they were thinking, what they wanted. She was raised with four brothers, and their fifty friends. Yet here, with Daniel, she cannot get it started. She takes a deep breath, pushes herself forward.

"I liked the way you jumped up when you heard your kid fall," she says.

"Jumping up when I hear a loud noise is one of my talents."

"I'm serious. Last summer, Nelson was in the backyard playing with his tricycle. He had it upside down and he was spinning the front wheel around and around and throwing little stones into the spokes. He said it was his popcorn machine."

"I used to do that, the exact same thing."

"Then somehow he got his fingers caught in the spokes. He was fine, but it hurt and he let out a yell. Hampton was just getting out of a bath, he's got this Saturday ritual."

Daniel envisions him, prone in the tub, his head tilted back and resting on a terry cloth square that had been folded with Japanese precision, his eyes closed, his cock floating on the soapy surface of the water, pushing through the bubbles like a crocodile through lily pads.

"And he just stood there," Iris is saying. "He heard Nellie screaming. I was in bed, I was sick, and I was calling out to him. He started down the stairs, but when he was halfway down he stopped, turned around, went *back* to the bathroom, and got his robe. His kid was screaming and he went back for his robe."

Daniel doesn't know what he can possibly say. She is comparing Hampton unfavorably to him, she is offering herself to him, she is saying she is unhappy.

"It just seems to me," Iris says, "that with your kid screaming the first thing you do is get to the kid, not run in the opposite direction. I got out of bed—"

"With your robe on?"

"Are you trying to annoy me?"

"No, amuse."

"It really appalled me. I felt something . . ." She is going to say either "close" or "die," but she says neither. Instead, she asks Daniel, "You wouldn't have done that, would you? Stopped for your robe with Ruby crying out in the yard."

He shakes his head No. Then, smiling, "But I'm sort of an exhibitionist."

She usually laughs when Daniel jokes, now it seems as if he is scrambling to put some distance between them, backing out of the whole thing. *Chicken,* she thinks. She only wants to go forward. And if he takes another step back, then she will have to take another step forward.

"You'd think Hampton would be an exhibitionist, too. He's so proud of *who* he is. Family and all that terrible stuff."

"I'm not really an exhibitionist," Daniel says.

"I know."

"And I don't have much of a family. Two parents who were too old for the job and sort of gave up on it, no brothers or sisters."

"Well, to Hampton, family's everything. His family, that is. You got a taste of that, didn't you?"

"It wasn't so bad."

"It wears on you. Those people, maybe you have to be black to really be angry with them. But it's that bunch of Neee-groes who look down on everyone else in the community." She points to herself.

"You?"

"First of all," she explains, "too dark. Second, bad hair."

"You have wonderful hair," Daniel says.

"You don't know anything about my hair," she says, laughing. "I can't stand when people talk about my hair, especially . . . Anyhow, my family wasn't part of their crowd. Hampton's people are really amazingly provincial. They're all intertwined with each other, mixed up in each other's business. My folks had enough money, that wasn't really a problem. I mean I wasn't from the projects or anything. My father's a hospital administrator, my mother taught kindergarten, before arthritis hit her. But I didn't belong to any of the right clubs. I was *not* a Girl Friend or a Jack and Jill. I didn't know shit about Oak Bluffs or Sag Harbor. I think one of the things Hamp liked about me was I wasn't perfect in the eyes of his family. I was his little rebellion. A dark-skinned girl, with rude politics. But . . . you know. The rebellion runs its little course and slowly but surely he turns into all those people who he swore he'd never be like. He really and truly wishes I was lighter, and I think he feels the same way about Nelson. And the really strange part of it is Hampton is obsessed with being black, he's black twenty-four hours a day, it's all he thinks about. He sort of dislikes white people, but at the same time he's like most of us: He really wants white people to like *him*. And that, by the way, is the dirty little secret of the Africans in America. We really want y'all to like us."

The electricity cuts out for about the time of a long blink, the world disappears, then shakes itself back into existence. When the lights come back, the digital clock on the stove flashes 12:00 over and over. Daniel and Iris sit across from each other, silent, waiting to see what will happen next. And then a few moments later, the lights go out, and this time they don't come back on. This time it's for good, they both can feel it. The children cry out upstairs, with more delight than alarm.

"I love you," Daniel says in the darkness.

7

Suddenly, in the distance was a pop, and then a plume of iridescent smoke rose above the trees, a vivid tear in the dark silken sky.

"Someone's got her," Daniel said. "I just saw a flare."

Hampton looked up. Only a small circle of sky was visible through the trees. "What was a damn blind girl doing out here? Even with eyes you can't make your way."

"She was raised here," Daniel said. "Her father was the caretaker. She came back to look after him when he got sick. Smiley."

"Smiley? What do you mean?"

"That's what everyone called him. I used to see him in town when I was a kid."

Hampton shook his head. "These people, they're living in another century. They got their old family retainers, their fox-hunting clubs, their ice boats, they play tennis with these tiny little wooden racquets, and New Year's Eve they put on the rusty tuxedos their grandfathers used to wear."

"Just a small percentage," Daniel said. "They can be pretty absurd, but it's okay, if you have a sense of humor about it."

"That was the first thing Iris ever said about you, how you have this terrific sense of humor."

"Class clown," said Daniel. "In my case, middle class."

In the city, Hampton comes home to what used to be his and Iris's apartment and which is now his alone. It's four rooms in a high-rise down on Jane Street, in the Village. On a block of picturesque town houses, most of them over 150 years old, the building is a twenty-five-story eyesore, but the saving grace is that once Hampton is inside he doesn't have to see it, all he looks out on are tree-lined streets, and pastel blue, pink, gray, and cream brick Federal town houses, with their tiny backyards and steep tiled roofs and the crooked old chimneys right out of *Mary Poppins*.

He's taken the subway home, the most efficient way uptown after work. A taxi from Wall Street to Jane Street would take an hour, whereas the subway gets him there in ten minutes. And the cost is a token, not the fourteen to twenty dollars a crawling, ticking taxi would cost. Hampton is becoming more and more careful about spending money. This creeping fiscal conservatism has nothing to do with how much he's making, because he's making more money than ever before, and it has nothing to do with rising expenses, because his expenses are stable. It just seems that the older he gets, the more watchful he becomes about his expenditures. He is still a long way from the miserly habits of his grandfather—who, according to family lore, held on to a dollar until the eagle grinned—and he will always disapprove of how his haughty, judging, acid-tongued mother would say things like "That Negro spends money like a nigger." But lately it seems to Hampton a breach of taste to squander money. When shopping, he counts his change carefully, increasingly certain he is about to be cheated. On the train up to Leyden he looks with contempt at the passengers who have paid nearly double to ride in that dopey Amtrak Business Class. For what? A bottle of Saratoga water and the mandarin delight of sitting in a seat that is exactly like every other seat on the train, except that the upholstery is blue rather than red. Yet even carefully monitoring his own expenditures leaves Hampton unsoothed and insecure. He worries over his investments, suffers the manic fluctuations of the NASDAQ, the slow attrition of some poorly chosen mutual funds. But even more than he worries about the stock market, Hampton worries about Iris's management of their household accounts. In his view, she remains a child with money, without impulse control, with no sense of sobriety, or planning, or self-denial. Sometimes in the middle of the day, like one of those mothers you read about who are suddenly certain that their son has just fallen on some battlefield halfway around the world, Hampton will look up from his work and practically *feel* Iris making some ill-advised purchase, an antique rug, a digital camera that will never be used, a half gallon of organic milk at twice the price of regular milk, a full tank of premium gasoline, even though he has told her over and over that a friend who covers petrochemicals has assured him that the so-called high-grade gas doesn't extend the life of your car's engine by so much as an hour, nor does it protect the environment.

He is sitting in the L-shaped dining room, with its narrow window looking out onto Hudson Street. Rain is falling in sheets, it's loud enough to drown out the usual sound of traffic, the taxis bumping over the cobblestone street. He flips through today's mail—statements from Smith Barney and Citibank, two phone bills, a Con Ed bill, requests to subscribe to magazines, buy golf clubs, upgrade home security, vacation in Portugal, switch credit cards, purchase vitamins, support the United Negro College Fund, and, on the bottom of the pile, an actual *letter,* with his name and address written in ink.

Eagerly he opens the envelope. The letter is from his old friend Brenda Morrison, now Morrison-Rosemont, sent from Atlanta, where she and her husband, Clarence, are doctors—he's an allergist and Brenda's a pediatrician. The letter is written on Brenda's professional stationery, at the top of which the first and last letters of her name seem to be toppling over, held upright only through the efforts of two hardworking teddy bears. She has sent along a snapshot, and Hampton notes that Brenda's weight gain continues unabated. She is now two hundred pounds, with two chins and working on a third. Hampton has known Brenda since they were children and she was a wild and bony thing, with scouring-pad hair and furious eyes, and enough of a survival sense to work her way into the Welles family fabric, first as Hampton's sister's best friend, and then as a kind of honorary Welles—Hampton's parents ended up sending Brenda to college. In the snapshot, she sits next to Clarence, with his prim little mustache, good-natured smile, his baby-blue turtleneck, and, on either side of them, golden retrievers, Martha and Ticonderoga, mother and son. The Post-it on the back of the picture explains: *Ti was the runt of Martha's litter and we just didn't have the heart to give him away. But now he's nearly eighteen months and he still acts like he's a baby. Except he think's I'm his mommy.*

Hampton finds himself staring at the note. He is stuck on the fact that she has spelled "thinks" with an apostrophe. A sharp twist of racial impatience goes through him, about how his people have had three hundred years to learn the language and here they are still misspelling the easy words. *Dear Hampton!*

Hampton looks up from the letter. Why in the world would she put an exclamation point after his name?

How are you? You wanted us to send you some material pertaining to Clarence and my idea for a business—helping patients collect what is due to them from their insurance companies. Well, we've been hard at work on a prospectus, and if I do say so myself what we've come up with is pretty damn impressive! Unfortunately, the computer design company we entrusted with our work was in the process of moving. I'm sure you would have advised me against doing business with family, but Clarence's nephew is really amazing with computers and graphics and that whole world I feel so uncomfortable with. Unfortunately, he's pretty disorganized. I think he's ADD or something, he just races from one thing to the next. I guess a lot of creative types have that problem. All this is to say, our work got lost in the shuffle. Clarence's nephew was really upset and we all spent a whole weekend looking everywhere for the stuff. It was really heartbreaking and quite a pain in the butt, and it'll set us back a couple of weeks. In the meanwhile, I didn't want you to think I'd forgotten about you or this project. We'd still love to get this thing up and running and you are still our favorite investment banker. (All right, you're the ONLY investment banker we know, but even if we knew others you'd still be our favorite!)

Amateur hour. Does she really expect him to raise money for her lit‐
tle cottage industry? Hampton senses her nervousness coming right
through her handwriting. Just as he could once detect the hesitations, the
soul-stammers of desire back in the days of courting and conquering
women, so now, too, in these moneyed days of his early middle age, can
Hampton radar out the slightest tremor of anxiety before someone de‐
livers a pitch. That this fumble for poise should come from Brenda is sad,
in a way—she's like family and she doesn't even need the money. But it
also gives him the grim, burnt comfort of thriving in a world that is, for
the most part, brutal and uninhabitable. He spends the best part of
nearly every day surrounded by people who make money, only money,
not houses, or soup, not steel, not songs, only money, and who quite
openly will do anything for financial gain, anything legal, and a few things
a little less than legal, too. But Hampton's proximity to this school of
sharks is more than physical, he has made an *alliance* with these squan‐
dered souls, these are his people, his teammates, and among them he
feels the pride of the damned. His friends are the guys who will fly
halfway around the world to convince someone to take a quarter of a
percent less on a deal. Everyone else is a civilian, all those fruits and
dreamers who do not live and die by that ceaseless stream of fractions
and deals that is the secret life of the world, that reality inside reality, the
molten core of profit and loss that burns at the center of history and
which everything else—temples, stadiums, concert halls, *everything*—
has been built to hide.

Clarence and I hope to be up in New York for a Conference of African‐
American Physicians Meeting from December 2–5. Clarence calls it the
Funference of African-American Positions. We'd love it if you could join
us for dinner or a show or anything on any of those days. If you could talk
Iris into coming into Manhattan then we could make it a foursome. I
hope you can tear her away from her school work. Maybe she can give us
that Harlem Renaissance tour she's been promising. Is her thesis still on
the Harlem Renaissance—or has she changed her mind?

Hampton stops reading. The rain continues to lash at the windows. Thunder booms like an avalanche of boulders. He knew Brenda couldn't get through a letter without a dig at Iris. Brenda couldn't possibly care what Iris is doing to fulfill the requirements of her Ph.D. What's Brenda, with her intellectual curiosity measuring something like 2 on the intellectual Richter scale, planning to do? Go to some college library and read Iris's monograph?

Yet. His heart feels queer, as if it is suddenly circulating blood that is a little oily and a little cold. Hampton is vulnerable to the suggestion that Iris might not be in possession of a first-class mind. There is a vagueness to her, a lack of precision. Sometimes, he thinks this is a result of her profoundly feminine nature, yet in his line of work he meets dozens of women whose minds are scientific, logical, calculating, aggressive. Iris's is not. Both she and Hampton have been explaining her long career in graduate school to themselves and to the world at large as somehow a result of an excess of intellectual curiosity, an unwillingness to be pigeonholed, and the demands of motherhood, and Hampton is perfectly willing to stay within the confines of this official explanation. What he is not willing to say, except to himself, is that Iris is still in grad school, and no closer to the end than she had been last year, or the year before, or the year before that, because she is simply too confused to complete her work; that, in other words, the machinery of her mind is not quite up to the task. Did he consider her his *inferior*? No, not necessarily—in fact, not at all. She is a little abstract. Yet she is perceptive, she can see right through him to his tender, undefended deeper nature. She is the center of his emotional life. Sex with her has more than once moved him to tears. She slows him down in ways he needs slowing down, helps him to see the fragile, transitory beauty of the world. He has sat with her in their house in Leyden, on the floor in front of the fireplace, in complete silence, watching the fire for an hour, two hours, enjoying a stillness and simplicity he could never have imagined without her. No, these are not the gifts of a second-rate mind, yet, sad to say, he has to admit they are not the characteristics of a mind on its way to academic achievement, either.

Hampton places Brenda's letter and picture back into the envelope. It occurs to him that Brenda might be the stupid one. True, she somehow made it through medical school—but in pediatrics, often considered the bottom of the medical barrel.

He stares at the rain and then thinks if the weather is this bad in the city it's probably worse up north. It gives him a reason to call Iris. He leans back in his Eames chair, dials the number with the same hand with which he holds the phone, his fingers moving as if he were playing the accordion.

On the sixth ring, Nelson answers. "Hello?" he cries, his voice vehement and obviously unnerved, yet distant, too. He's speaking into the wrong end of the phone.

"Hey, Nels, it's me." Hampton must speak loudly to be heard.

"We don't have any lights," Nelson says.

"Turn the phone around, Nels. You're talking in the wrong end."

"We do not have lights," Nelson repeats, after turning the phone around. "Ruby is kissing me." His pronunciation and rhythm are robotic, every syllable separate, patterned after a Saturday cartoon android.

Ruby?

"Where are you, son?"

"We are in the playroom."

"Where's your mother?" As soon as he asks, Iris picks up the extension. "Hello?"

Nelson hangs up the upstairs phone, hard.

"Iris, it's me."

"Hampton!" She sounds just the slightest bit startled.

"What's happening?" he says. Those were the first two words he ever said to her, uttered in what seems now a distant, sunlit country. Atlanta 1991. Iris had been sitting in a cruddy fifties theme restaurant called Blueberry Hill, with an economics professor who was her boyfriend for twenty minutes or so, they were quarreling, he grabbed her wrist, she yelped as if branded, a sugar shaker slid from the Formica table, she had never been manhandled in her whole life, never been slapped, spanked, no one had ever raised his voice to her, and here was this huge, temperamental guy, a two-hundred-and-twenty-pound Malaysian with a military brush cut and a flamboyant Hawaiian shirt he wore like a muumuu over his massive belly, squeezing her wrist, offering up a perfect opportunity for gallant intervention. Hampton had come quickly to their table and uttered the two-word question that became somehow the touchstone of their intimacy: What's happening? a question he has asked a hundred times since, each time conjuring a memory of Blueberry Hill and the beginnings of love.

"Nothing," Iris says.

Nothing is *never* the answer.

"Is the electricity out?" Hampton asks.

"Yes. We just lost it, twenty minutes ago."

Just lost it, twenty minutes ago? There's a bit of disarray in that sentence and Hampton senses it, the way you can enter your house and know something is wrong, some small thing has been slightly moved. "That's really pitiful. You'd think the infrastructure could cope with a little rain."

"It's snowing, that's what's doing it, the snow, it's been pouring snow for hours."

"Snowing?"

"And the leaves are still on the trees so they can't take the weight of it. It's so awful. Those poor trees. They tear the power lines down as they fall. There's sirens going all over the place. It's total chaos out there, it's like a war, except there's no enemy, just the snow. It's really strange to realize how easy it is to scramble everything. When you get here you'll see. Everything is broken, everything."

She is making no effort to keep the alarm out of her voice, in fact, she seems to be hyping it, letting him know that things are bad, maybe even out of control. Iris's way has usually been to keep him cool, to prevent him from overreacting, but now she is deliberately creating a sense of impending emergency, and Hampton wonders why.

"But the phone is working fine," he says.

"The phone lines are buried. But there's no lights, no heat."

"Then why not . . ." The words caught in his throat. "Why not go to a hotel?" Iris is particularly extravagant in hotels, and watching her raid the minibar is an advanced exercise in forbearance.

"You don't understand. We're snowed in. The roads are closed. It's dangerous out there. We couldn't go anywhere if we wanted to."

If we wanted to, that is an odd thing to say. Why wouldn't she want to leave a house that has no heat, no water, no lights?

"I'm worried about you," he says.

"We're safe in here. It's just a little claustrophobic, knowing you can't go out. And it might not be better tomorrow and I'm supposed to be at Marlowe for a thesis conference with Professor Shafer."

"Professor Shafer?" Her thesis advisor *was* an old Berkeley radical named Steven Pearlstein. That she is scheduled to meet someone else means she has once again abandoned her topic for a new one.

"He's great. He's new."

I'll bet he is. "Who's there with you?"

"Here? In the house? Daniel and Ruby. They came over after Wooden Shoe shut down." She pauses, lets it hang there, like a dancer stopping all movement, standing stock still while the beat goes on. "The whole town's shut down."

"What are they going to do?"

"I don't know. Stay here, I guess."

He hears a sound, a man's voice, distant and indistinct.

"What was that?"

"That was Daniel. He says hi."

"When's he going home?"

Iris turns away, says to Daniel, "Hampton says hello."

"Is he going to spend the night?"

"I don't really know."

The possibility of Iris spending a night in that house alone with Daniel Emerson renders Hampton, for the moment, mute.

"Don't do this, Iris," he finally says.

"What?"

Can she not hear him? Without quite meaning to, Hampton jabs his thumb onto the off button, breaking the connection. He had been standing during the conversation, but now he feels weak and must sit. He sits there clutching the phone. He thinks about racing up to Penn Station, getting on a train, and making it to Leyden before anything happens. How long would it take? It's half past six now. He has committed the train schedule to memory—his memory, which is like a shark looking for new things to eat, has long ago devoured it. The next train is at twenty past seven. The trip to Leyden is one hour and fifty minutes. That would make it ten past nine when he'd arrive. Ten minutes for a cab to come, ten more minutes to reach his house. Nine-thirty. Nelson doesn't go to bed until nine. That would give Iris and Daniel just a half hour before Hampton arrived. They would probably not have gone beyond longing looks, perhaps a kiss or two.

Yet as soon as he mentally goes through the paces of throwing a few belongings in a bag, flagging down a taxi in the rain, sitting on the Amtrak all the way up to Windsor County, making the trek to his house, and then having to do it all in reverse first thing in the morning in order to be back at work, his will to defend his wife against her own vulnerability to her desires, or from her weakness, all of a sudden is subsumed by a vast entropy.

This is not the first time he has sat in these rooms wondering if Iris is betraying him. He recognizes his own jealous nature, knows he could not trust the truest Desdemona, can recall with a measure of good-natured self-mocking that he was suspicious of Iris even when she was pregnant—he thought she had a crush on her obstetrician, a silver-haired Pakistani whom she would telephone for advice at the slightest physical provocation. Before going to his office for her regular appointments, Iris would spend two hours in the bathroom, showering, sprinkling herself with baby powder, polishing her nails, oiling her hair—and she'd wear something dark and vertically striped for the slimming effect, as if she wanted to camouflage her pregnancy. He saw how unlikely it was. Yet marriage to

Iris made his impulse toward jealousy practically hair-trigger, his heart is like a bank that has been outfitted with an alarm system that is far too sensitive, one that can be tripped by a little footstep.

Though Hampton looks back at some of his former suspicions and realizes they were silly and unjust, he must nevertheless continue to live with the degrading agonies of jealousy, and during these last months in New York part of his strategy for survival has been to commit small acts of unfaithfulness himself. He's not sure how he came upon this plan, but the fact is he can tolerate the idea of Iris's being touched by another man only if he can prove and re-prove to himself that mere physical intimacy is a matter of relatively small importance—he must, in fact, degrade the very thing he wishes to exalt. The adultery Hampton commits is highly controlled: he spends two or three hours a month with one of two prostitutes who, for $150 an hour, come to his apartment, spread lotion over his body, massage him, and masturbate him to a quick milky climax, the vehemence of which pleasantly surprises him every time. He has settled on these two particular women, after responding to several advertisements in the free weekly newspapers that carry in their back pages listings for escort services and unlicensed masseuses. He has seen ten different prostitutes in all and has had actual intercourse with none of them—though intercourse is available for an extra charge. He has come close to intercourse a couple of times—particularly with Mia, the Chinese girl, whose feathery touch up and down his buttocks, combined with the blank, stoned-out expression on her unhappy face, has proved particularly arousing—but he has, to this point, hung on to his resolve to not risk picking up a disease, and when Mia says "You wanna put it in me now?" he can, his mouth parched with desire, shake his head no.

The other woman he hires to arouse and release him is an African-American calling herself Anyuh—she has given him an engraved business card with her name and cell phone number, which he daringly keeps in his wallet. Anyuh—buxom, large-hipped, with a little girlie laugh, big smutty eyes, and long peach fingernails—also costs $150 for a massage and a hand job and twice that for real sex. At those prices, most of her clients are white. What this means is that she treats Hampton with an excess of familiarity that he finds off-putting; he does not want to be her one black client, her brotherly confidant, with whom she prattles on about her financial woes. Anyuh makes no attempt at coquetry, eschewing seduction for yawns and cabbagey little burps; while she works over his body, she places her cell phone right next to his pillow, where it continually chirps right into his ear as other clients pursue her far into the night.

He knows Mia's number by heart and he dials it quickly. Her voice on the phone sounds sad, a bit bronchial, but he chooses to ignore that and feels somehow that things are suddenly going his way when she says she can be over in twenty minutes.

Mia is never early for their appointments and the rainstorm will probably make her even later than usual. Nevertheless, Hampton hurries to prepare himself for her. He goes into his bedroom and as he strips off his dark-gray suit, his white shirt and striped tie, he also removes the framed photographs of Iris and Nelson from his bedside table, puts them in the closet, along with his clothes. Naked, he sits on the side of the modest double bed—the bed that he and Iris first made love in. A vision of Iris in this very bed—on her hands and knees, looking back at him over her shoulder. Oh, the pain of that.

From where he sits he can see himself in the wall mirror. He sits up straighter, sucks in what little gut he has, regards himself with some entirely personal mixture of admiration and disgust. He lifts his arm, smells himself. The workday leaves him acrid. He walks quickly into the bathroom, turns on the shower, makes it as hot as he can bear. When Mia arrives, he wants her to smell only the peppermint-scented antibacterial soap, the honey and almond shampoo. He opens his mouth, lets the steaming water rush in. It occurs to him for a moment that he is drowning himself; he turns his back to the shower, bends slightly, purifying his anus. The thought that Mia might pick up a whiff of something offensive while she works him over is intolerable.

———

Kate sits in Ruby's room, listening to her red radio. It amazes her that there are stations playing music, it seems unforgivable, like Nero's fiddling. With increasing impatience, she races through the dial, searching for news. She wants to be sure there are people out there who know that disaster has struck, who are putting it into some sort of context. How many people are trapped? How many houses are without electricity? How many roads are closed? She wants numbers. At last, she finds a news reader, a woman with a stainless-steel voice. Kate crouches forward in Ruby's dark little room, touches the radio as if it were a friend.

The newscaster is reporting new developments in the O. J. Simpson murder trial, now in its tenth month. Today's story is not so much about the case as it is about the reporting of the case—a reporter from one of the weekly magazines was heard calling Simpson a nigger (news radio said the reporter used "a racial epithet" but everyone knew what that meant) and now the reporter's employers have weighed in on the subject, releasing a statement to the effect that the writer's contract with the magazine has been terminated "by mutual consent."

After a couple more stories and a few noisy advertising spots, the national news switches to the local reports. Now a man, presumably close by, is reading the news. An estimated seventy thousand homes are without electricity. All major roadways are closed. County officials have no idea when things will be back to normal. The U.S. Weather Service says there may be as much as another foot of snow falling in the next eight hours. There have been eleven fatalities so far. "And in Leyden, there's a report that the power outage has disabled the security system at a local lockup for wayward boys, Star of Bethlehem. According to Star of Bethlehem officials, six of the youths have left the facility and are somewhere in the area." He pauses and then adds, "Wow."

Kate picks up Ruby's radio and walks out with it, into the candlelit hall. These candles were Daniel's purchase, scented ones, and Kate is repelled by their smell. She walks through the living room, where one candle burns, and into the kitchen, where she has lit a dozen votive candles. They send their plaintive light through beaded glass holders.

She turns the radio off, preserving the batteries, and sets it on the kitchen table. The temperature in the house is dropping, degree by degree, and in the place of homely warmth comes dampness and a growing sense of disorder. She wants something to drink, something to warm her. Something nonalcoholic. Tea. The stove is gas, so it doesn't matter if there's no electricity. She brings the kettle to the faucet, but the water pump runs on electricity and when she turns on the cold water, the pipes bang and only a faint unwholesome drool comes out.

Suddenly, she sees a flicker of motion from the corner of her eye. She turns quickly toward the window. At first all she can see is her own reflection. But then she sees it again: something wishing not to be seen.

She reaches for the flashlight, shines it through the window, but it throws its own shining face back at her. Kate then opens the window, letting precious heat escape, letting in a whoosh of snow that sweeps in like the tail of a comet. Now she shines the flashlight into the blizzard. Nothing. Nothing. But then she sees them. Footprints. Cratered into the snow, several pairs, stopping thirty feet from her house.

She feels a fear beyond any she has ever experienced, and she makes it worse by asking herself, *What if they come into the house?* The problem with the question is the answer—*They will rape me.*

Her heart pounding, and her stomach, too, like a second, sour heart, Kate pulls the window closed, locks it. She locks the back door, too, and as she does, she reaches for the phone. She pushes the on button—but there is no dial tone. It's a cordless phone, it works off electricity. She needs the phone upstairs in her study, the only old-style phone in the house. She is not certain whom she is about to call. Surely the police have too much on their hands to respond to some woman seven miles outside of town who is pretty sure she saw some footprints in the snow. Even if she were to tell them she has seen the escaped Star of Bethlehem kids— what would the police do? What *can* they do? They can't drive out in their cars, and even if they had helicopters, they couldn't fly them in this weather. So? Will they all jump onto their crime-buster snowmobiles?

She sweeps the flashlight back and forth as she walks through the house, an oar of light that rows through the sea of darkness. She realizes the only person she can call, the only person she wants to call is Daniel. Iris will probably answer the phone, and then hand it over to him. As Kate makes her way up the steps, there is a nerve-shattering death of a maple tree not fifty feet from the house, a noble old tree that seems actually to scream as it falls, as if its pulp were flesh. Kate hollers in fear— not that high, blood-curdling scream of the horror show damsel in distress, but the wavering, angry, monotone cry of real fear. She drops her flashlight, it rolls down the staircase, turning the house end over end until the flashlight hits the bottom and goes dark.

Kate is still making noise—a soft, stunned "oh-oh-oh." And then she gathers herself and shouts out, "Daniel!" She grips the banister, turns around. She wants to retrieve the flashlight. But no. Why walk back into that darkness? There are candles burning upstairs and the phone is there, too. She turns around again, stops. She remembers she still has not locked the front door, and so once again she turns around. She is turning around and around. And in the midst of all that turning she realizes that she is wet and clammy and there is a smell of urine in the air. Fucking tree. Fucking snow. Fucking gang bangers out there staring at her windows. Fucking Daniel, so far out there, so far away from her.

She clutches at her stomach, presses her hand against the wall to stop herself from tumbling down the stairs. She sits, feels along the side of her pants. Just a little dampness, not so bad. Her underwear, however, is soaked. Okay, that settles it. Upstairs, for a change of clothes. She starts to rise, but then sits again; there's still the matter of that unlocked front door. She cannot get up because she cannot decide if it would be better to continue upstairs or hurry downstairs, and the more she thinks, the more unlikely it seems that she will ever be able to make up her mind. She closes her eyes. The darkness within makes the darkness of the house seem like an ice cream parlor. She reaches up, grips the banister, pulls herself up. She sways, and with every bit of her will she forces a decision. She turns around and heads upstairs, where there are clean clothes and a working phone.

By the time she reaches the top of the stairs she hears the urgent knocking at her door. She knows it's them, the boys, the boys with nothing to lose. All she can think to do is pretend she does not hear it.

The bedroom has always been the coldest room in the house. She opens her dresser drawer, her undergarments feel cold and slippery in her hand. Then she finds a pair of jeans in the closet. She sits on the edge of the bed, undressing, dressing again, and through the noise of the storm she hears the pounding of the boys' fists against the front door. All she can think of by way of strategy is that if she ignores them they will eventually go away.

Dressed, dry, but still cold, she waits for the boys to give up. She places a votive candle on the bedspread and then holds her hands above it, warming her palms over the tiny flame. She holds her breath so that the sound of her respiration won't interfere with her trying to hear if the boys are still trying to get in. She hears nothing but the wind and the tortured groaning of trees, their canopies filled with ice and snow, any one of them liable to snap in two. Yet beneath the sounds of the storm, she can make out the urgent knocking of the boys' fists against her heavy front door. *Gun gun gun.* And then, suddenly, the knocking stops.

Kate pulls the phone off her bedside table and sits with it on her lap, her hand on the receiver. If she hears footsteps in the house, she will call the police. But she doesn't hear footsteps, she doesn't hear anything—all she has is a *sense* that those boys have found their way into her house.

She cannot sit there wondering. She goes down the stairs to see, and when she is halfway between the first and second floor landings she stops. Fresh snow is swirling in the foyer and still more is blowing in.

As quietly as she can, Kate backs up the stairs, and when she is at the top of the landing she turns and walks quickly to her bedroom. There is no lock on the door; she swats a pile of folded laundry off an upholstered chair, drags the chair across the room, and jams it beneath the porcelain door handle. Then she blows out the votive candle and the freestanding candle on the marble-topped dresser and the room slips into darkness.

She sits on the end of the bed, folds her hands onto her lap, and breathes as quietly as she can. She feels absolutely and without question that her life hangs now in the balance, that one stupid move, haste, panic, impatience, curiosity, anything but the most profound and disciplined stillness will lead to her death. Her fear—no longer relevant, no longer useful—seems to have been superseded by an exquisite clarity.

The fear remains in abeyance, even as she feels someone coming up the stairs. It is part of the house's idiosyncrasy that a footstep on the fifth stair vibrates along the master-bedroom floor. At night, she could always hear Daniel's gloomy trudge upstairs, and by day she could hear Ruby coming up to rouse her. That creaky step, and its harmonic convergence with the house's inner bone structure, is her distant early warning system; normally, it cues her to feign sleep, to pull the covers up over her chin, maybe place a pillow over her head. But tonight, all she can do is hold her breath.

The footsteps are in the hall, heading in her direction.

She cannot think of what to ask God. Asking for protection is like asking for a pair of skates. If he doesn't want you to die, then you're not going to die. If he does, you're certainly not going to talk him out of it at the last second. You don't pray for your safety, you don't pray for a home run, you don't pray that your next book is a Book of the Month Club selection. The only plausible prayer is for serenity of mind, for faith and acceptance, and Kate finds she has these things right now.

The footsteps stop before they reach the bedroom door. She hears another door close. Where did he go? The bathroom?

Silence. She counts it out to herself to keep from losing her mind, the numbers create a kind of pathway, bread crumbs in the forest. When she gets to thirty, she hears a voice shouting from the downstairs. It's the voice of a young man, someone she'd describe as obviously black. There is a foghorn quality to his voice, something to be heard over constant noise.

"Come on, Kenny, let's go."

"Lemme alone," a voice answers from the bathroom. Kenny. His voice is sharp, high, full of complaint.

"What are you doin' up there?"

"Taking a shit."

"Come on. Someone's gonna come in and find us here."

"I'm not shitting outside."

Kate leans back and gropes for the telephone in the darkness. She is not just going to sit here like some poor animal in a trap. She picks the receiver up, pressing her thumb onto the earpiece so that the hum of the dial tone won't carry.

She dials 911 and waits for one of the emergency police operators to pick up, one ring, two rings, three . . .

"Hey, Cyril," another voice is saying downstairs, "there's a bathroom by the kitchen." This kid pronounces it "baff-room," just the way Kate's father did when he did his imitation of his one black patient who always said, "I still wishin' I could go to the baff-room mo'." That he might use the bathroom in Dr. Ellis's office was a subject of joke-camouflaged anxiety—"lock da baff-room," and "git some bleach fo' da baff-room" were typical of the remarks Kate's father made.

Her call to 911 has yet to be answered. How many rings has it been? Fifteen? Twenty? Fucking hell, what is wrong with those people?

The husky-voiced boy calls up again. "This place is fucked. It's darker in here than outside. We're leaving!"

And not a moment after he says this, the maple tree that stands in front of the house, the proud, gnarled, forty-foot tree that as much as any other thing made Kate want to buy this house, suddenly cracks in two from the weight of the snow. The crown of the tree hits the roof, immediately tearing down the gutters; branches, half frozen, covered in snow, thrust themselves like monstrous arms through the windows on the east side of the house. One long branch smashes through the bedroom window; the branches at the end are cold and thin and they brush roughly against Kate's face. Wind and snow rush in.

Kate falls off the bed, onto her side, and rolls over on her stomach, covering her face. She uses her elbows and knees to push herself beneath the bed. And while she is there—hiding—she hears the boys leaving her house, screaming crazily, half in terror, half in excitement.

———

Daniel stands next to Iris in the guest bedroom, holding a flashlight for her while she makes up the sofa bed.

"You don't have to do this," he finally says. "I'm perfectly capable of making a bed." He nervously continues. "In fact, I used to make beds for a living. In college, or in the summers, actually, two years running I worked in a hotel in Delaware. I was a chambermaid."

"You were?"

"Or a chamberman, or maybe a chamber pot. I made beds, that's all I know."

"You can make the bed when I'm snowed in at your house," she says. She speaks softly, as if calming an excited animal.

And then, because he cannot let anything stand with her, nothing is enough, he says, "We're not really snowed in, we're *treed* in."

But she doesn't volley back, she ends the exchange with a smile, brief, insubstantial, that could be weighed but wouldn't register on any scale. She finishes her work. She has strong, useful hands; she smoothes her palm over the sheet and every wrinkle disappears.

"I don't even know what time it is," Daniel says. He tilts the flashlight beam toward his watch; a circle of bright golden light appears on his wrist.

"It's too cold to stay awake," she says. "Anyhow, when Nelson goes to sleep, as far as I'm concerned the night's over."

As best as he can make out, the sheets she has placed on his bed are dark blue. Surely, as in most households, these sheets have traveled from bed to bed, surely, then, Iris and Hampton have lain upon them in their own bedroom down the hall. He imagines Iris and Hampton on those sheets, their beautiful dark skin on the deep evening blue.

Iris steps back from the sofa bed and lays two fingers on Daniel's wrist. The tenderness of this gesture overwhelms him, it is as if she has kissed him. But all she is doing is redirecting the beam of the flashlight. She points it at the closet, where she finds extra blankets. "You're going to be nice and cozy," she says, dropping the blankets at the foot of the bed, and the proclamation, delivered in a throaty, good-natured voice, devastates him. He takes her to mean: Stay in your own bed. Don't come creeping into my room. You are here, these are your blankets and stay beneath them, be a good boy, nice doggie, stay.

"Do you have enough blankets in your room?" Daniel asks, bleating it, as if asking for mercy.

"Yes, I'm fine."

There are so many possibilities for speech or action; he could take her wrist, he could pull her toward him, he could say, "No, I want to sleep with you," he could sigh, he could say, "I think we both know what's going on here," he could play it cool and just say good night, he could place his hand over his heart, he could—somehow this, too, seems possible—burst into tears, yes, yes, he could try to boo-hoo her into bed. It's been done, what hasn't happened in the history of seduction? But finally Daniel can do nothing. He watches her as she moves toward the door. Then, a miracle. The bingo parlor of his mind comes up with a clear thought.

"I'll light your way," he says.

"Okay," she says. "You can be like a watchman, those guys who carried a lantern and saw people home."

"Useful work," Daniel says, with a kind of manic encouragement in his voice, one that borders on hysteria, and then to himself: *Shut the fuck up.*

He points the beam up and the light bounces off the ceiling and casts a pale gray glow. He walks behind her; her silhouette has put him into a kind of fugue state.

They have arrived at their destination: the master bedroom. He waits at the threshold, shining the light into the bedroom while Iris goes to the night table, opens a drawer, finds a book of matches, and lights a bedside candle.

He can no longer wait there for the impossible to occur. She is not going to ask him to lie with her in that bed. In fact, the quality of her silence now is pushing him away. She seems to have regained her balance. The drug of the storm is wearing off, she is coming to.

"Why don't I leave this flashlight with you," he says.

"It's okay. I've got one in here."

He forces himself to smile, not certain she can see his face. "Sleep well, Iris."

Here he is, standing practically in her bedroom, saying good night to her. *It's enough,* he tells himself. He's said *Sleep well, Iris,* he's always wanted to say that.

But lying in that sofa bed, pinioned by the cold and the darkness, he finds that the miracle of saying good night to Iris is *not* enough. Desire blooms in the darkness, he is choking on its scent. He is tormented by her nearness—how can he be letting this chance go by? He tries to force himself to sleep, but sleep gets further from him the more desperately he pursues it. Sleep has never eluded him as maddeningly since the months directly preceding his fall down the stairs, an assault that left him with a whole new vocabulary of pain—searing, metallic, throbbing, dizzying, freezing, burning, electric—and an enduring dependence on painkillers. Percocet and Lortab didn't really kill the pain, or significantly lessen it, but seemed to create a little chemical pavilion within his consciousness, a semipleasant place to which he could retreat and let the pain go on without him. It had not taken him long to increase his consumption from four pills a day to sixteen, and the number could have increased from there had he not, in a burst of self-preservation, stopped taking them altogether, leaving his body not only without its customary supply of synthetic endorphins but unable to recall how to make its own, as if the supply of opiates had lulled his body into a state of metabolic amnesia. At first, parts of his body that were not even injured began to throb and ache; he felt as if he had been dragged out of some weightless chamber and condemned to suffer the agonies of gravity. Then the wrist, the jaw, the ankles, the back—which never really got better—and throughout it all he was unable to sleep.

Which brought him to a couple of months of nightly sleeping pills and which bring him right now to remembering that Iris has sleeping pills, though of the over-the-counter variety. Daniel slips out of bed, steps through the darkness of the guest bedroom, and his foot lands on something furry and alive. He jumps back, frightened. He hears a low groan, and he turns on the flashlight. Scarecrow. She has been curled next to him all this time. She rubs against his legs, and when he bends to pat her she wiggles her hindquarters.

He finds his way to the bathroom. It's small. Cold. White-walled, tiled, strictly utilitarian. Tub, toilet, sink. He is as careful and quiet as possible. To the right of the sink is one of those novelty gift mirrors meant to look like the cover of *Time* magazine, with the words HAMPTON WELLES MAN OF THE YEAR embossed on the glass. To the left of the sink, a toothbrush holder affixed to the wall, with two brushes in it. A large and a small. He pulls out the one that is clearly Iris's. It has a zebra-striped handle, pigeon-pink rubber gum massager at the end, unusually full head of bristles. He touches it against his lips.

Daniel props the flashlight onto the side of the sink and opens the medicine chest. Hampton's shaving gear, four different kinds of children's cough medicine, liquid aspirin. Sominex. He pries off the cap, only to find the foil safety seal still intact. He peels it back without really considering the audacity of what he is doing. He shakes two tablets out and then realizes he must take them without water. Fine, whatever.

Just then, the ring of a telephone. He switches off the flashlight, holds his breath, as if he were not an overnight guest making a trip to the john but a thief about to be discovered. A second ring. And then he hears Iris's voice.

"Hello?"

Daniel grips the edge of the sink for stability.

"I was asleep," Iris says.

In the darkness and stillness of the house, her voice is everywhere, it is close, it is right next to him. "You know more about it than I do and I'm right here," Iris says. And then, a little later, she says, "Okay, if the power's still not on, we'll get to the train station and come and stay with you down there." And then, finally, "Me too, bye."

Daniel knows what "me too" means.

Iris hangs the phone up and a moment later Daniel sees the glow from her flashlight as she comes out of her bedroom and down the hall. Her footsteps are silent; the only way he can gauge her approach is by the brightening of the light. Should he pretend he was having a pee, quickly stand over the toilet? But what about the door—how can he be doing that with the door wide open? He could be washing his hands—but what sort of lunatic would be washing his hands in the middle of the night? Not to mention there is no electricity, no pump, no water.

Iris walks into the bathroom and captures him in the beam of her flashlight. She is wearing sweatpants and a turtleneck sweater, slipper socks, and a brightly colored Egyptian cap. "Are you all right?" she says. She reaches down to ruffle her fingers through the fur on top of Scarecrow's upturned head.

"Yes. I'm fine," Daniel says.

"I heard you in here," she says.

"I'm okay."

"I was going to check on the kids," she says. A little exhaust comes out of her mouth as she speaks.

He steps into the corridor and they walk to Nelson's room. Daniel turns off his flashlight, relying on hers. He is right behind her, with the dog at his side. The dog loves him, he feels this working in his favor.

Iris stops short, forcing contact. They collide softly, his toes on her heel, his chest against her shoulder blades.

She doesn't so much step back as shift her weight slightly toward him, increasing the contact. Contact displaces the still water between them, and in the splash of it intimacy rises in the wake.

Daniel lowers his forehead so it touches the back of her head. They are still. He breathes her in. She notches backward. His lips find her nape. She lifts her chin, exhales. He wraps his arms around her.

They have crossed a line, but it seems to him they have not ventured too far, not yet, they can still go back, no one will be the wiser.

Iris takes a step forward and Daniel releases her. They go to Nelson's room. Nelson is in the upper bunk; he has flung off the covers, his legs stick out over the side of the mattress. Ruby is on the bottom, a slowly dimming flashlight poking from the bedclothes and casting upon her sleeping face a cold white light, like the shine of a dying moon.

"I want to tell you something," Iris says, barely whispering. It's as if she is willing to wake the children.

"Let's go," Daniel says, pulling softly on her. "We don't want to wake them."

In the hallway, she pulls the door to Nelson's room three-quarters closed. "They're really sleeping deeply," she says. "They're so cold, the poor babies."

"Ruby always sleeps soundly."

"I can't sleep at all," she says. "I never can. I doze, I go in and out. I think sleep is too much of a commitment for me." She laughs.

"Maybe you have too much on your mind," he says. *Is that it?* She is suddenly exotic to him, opaque and unknown. No, that's not it. He just doesn't *get* her, he lacks that little snap of instant understanding. He must concentrate, she is something he must *work* at.

Daniel remains silent. It is like sitting quietly in the woods, things come to you, the life of the forest forgets about you and resumes. After a few moments, his silence draws her out, she comes softly to the edge of it like a deer.

"I'm going to tell you the truth right now," she says.

She sees alarm in his eyes and she places a comforting hand on the side of his face.

"I'm not going to say anything *bad*."

"Okay."

She is puzzled, she tilts her head, regards this strange creature.

"When I first saw you," Iris says, "I liked you so much. I mean right away. It was a very strange experience. You seemed perfect."

"That's me, all right."

"I'm serious. It was sort of frightening. First of all, you were taken and so was I."

She's talking about it in the past tense, thinks Daniel. *As if now we were free.*

"And second, I mean the thing that was even more frightening was sensing that if we were to get together and something happened, if you turned out not to even like me, or if you took advantage of me, I would never recover from it. I just knew from the start it would be fatal."

"I would never hurt *you,*" he says. He hears his voice in the strange dead air of that house.

"You wouldn't mean to," she says. She moves her hand away from him, but he catches her, presses his lips against her palm. The kiss goes to the pit of her stomach.

Ruby awakens. Their voices have found her in her sleep, carried her toward them. She calls for Daniel, her voice dry, cracked, and low.

Daniel goes back into the children's bedroom, sits on the edge of her bed. He feels something poking at him, at his ear, the side of his head. He realizes it's Nelson's foot, waving back and forth, though Nelson is still asleep.

"Are you all right?" Daniel whispers to Ruby.

"Yes," she says. "I have to go to the bathroom." She raises her arms, as if it's a matter of course that he will lift her, carry her.

When Ruby is finished, Daniel carries her back to Nelson's bedroom. Daniel carefully places Ruby onto the bed, she is practically asleep, but somehow the touch of the cold pillow awakens her. Her eyes are suddenly large, curious.

"We're staying here all night. Right?"

"That's right, Monkey," he says.

She is silent. A minute passes; he imagines her asleep. But then her cold fingers come to rest on the top of his hand. "I love you the most of everyone," she says.

———

Daniel lies next to her, and Iris cannot sleep. Her thoughts skip like stones over water. Nelson, the storm, a Japanese maple her father planted in their front yard, which she was always convinced irritated the white neighbors with its unseasonable purple leaves . . . Iris has never been able to fall asleep next to someone with whom she was in bed for the first time; choosing someone always meant giving up a night's sleep. Making love as a teenager was easier—she had to end up in her own bed, alone, and she could sink into sleep as if it were a kind of innocence. Even in college—and why why why did she allow her parents to talk her into attending Spelman, more than ninety percent black, a hundred percent female, a vast poaching ground for the men of Morehouse, brother-sister schools conceived, it seemed, for conception—even at college she developed a small reputation as the girl who always had to end up in her own safe little bed, the girl who says she has to get home because her teddy bear misses her.

It's been years since she has slept with anyone but Hampton. She has a moment of intense pining for him as if he were oceans away, irretrievable, dead. She misses the ease and comfort of being with a man who has seen her body week after week, year after year, and who is, as far as she can tell, blind to its small deteriorations. It has all happened gradually, and he has failed to notice. Hampton's criticisms of her are intellectual, spiritual, practical; he is more distressed by her forgetfulness than by her having grown older. He would rather her finish her doctorate—or junk it—than get a boob job. Even when it seems to her that Hampton holds her in contempt, his voraciousness for her body seldom varies. *I love your body,* he has said over and over, so many times and with such suddenness and disregard for her mood of the moment or what has been passing between them that she has come to find it an affront. It's all he seems to praise, his entire celebration of her is confined to that simple statement. He does not say *I need your advice* and he doesn't say *You fascinate me,* he surely doesn't ask her what is on her mind. He has little interest in her thoughts and sometimes she can barely blame him. But if her life is a little dull, then she sees no reason why that must be held against her, this life and her role in it is, after all, something they both made, it's a joint project. And when she has the emotional energy to refuse to be silenced, to speak up no matter what, she can see him *pretending* to pay attention, while it is heart-freezingly, face-slappingly clear that his thoughts are elsewhere. And after so disrespecting her, for him to look up and say how beautiful she is, how fucking hot she makes him: he may as well be saying, *Too bad you're not operating on my level. Too bad you're an idiot.*

Daniel seems to want to know everything about her. It's his nature, there is nothing he can do about it. He will want to know if she has ever been unfaithful to Hampton before, and if she tells him she has, then it's her guess that he will eventually want to know with whom, when, where, the reasons, and the results, and even if she says no, he will ask why not. He will ask her what she dreams, how the day was spent, what she had for lunch, where she buys her clothes, the names of her relatives, the route she takes from her house to school. He will devour her with love bites, he will lick the surface of her as if she were a scoop of ice cream until she gets smaller and smaller, until she disappears.

Iris reaches over Daniel's sprawled body, with its deep sonorous buzz and smell of sleep, and she gropes for the flashlight on the night table. But it's been knocked over in the commotion, it has tumbled onto the carpet, rolled onto the bare floor. She finally finds it, halfway under the bed. She hurries back to the nest of quilts and blankets, willing to awaken Daniel with the bounce of the mattress, but he sleeps through it all.

She switches on the flashlight. She puts her hand over its broad face to cut down on the silvery glare, and she points the beam of light at Daniel to inspect what she can see of his naked body.

The most puzzling thing is that he is naked at all. She wonders at the thermodynamics of this, how such white skin, which she imagines to be porous, diaphanous, and through which would pass all heat and light, how such pigmentless tissue could conceivably hold enough heat to allow him to sleep.

She moves the beam closer to him. A circle of light illuminates his chest. A sleek dark wave of hair rushes between his pectoral muscles. That ivory-white skin and that dark body hair. She stares at it, struck at how barbaric it looks. It makes her think of the stooped figures in schoolbooks, emigrating across ancient tundra two steps ahead of the glaciers. *How strange that whites ever compared black folk with apes, when it's the whites who are covered in hair.* Once, in college, Iris had entertained the idea of becoming a doctor; the notion—like so many of her inspired plans—had a short life span: by April she was bored with it, and by the end of the semester she could barely pass her finals. Still, she remembers: the dermis, the epidermis, subcutaneous tissue, dermal papilla, adipose tissue, the subpapillary network, and good old Meissner's corpuscle, the name of which she could never forget and the function of which she could never learn. Back then, she thought of all the components of human skin that are absolutely identical for Africans, Japanese, Europeans, and how we are all so similar beneath those topmost layers. But now, in bed with a Caucasian for the first time in her life, what strikes her is the difference, stranger and more unsettling than she would have expected. She rubs her fingertip across an inch or two of Daniel's skin, along the shoulder where the skin is bare, and cool to the touch, with little bumps, a kind of cottony grit. Without entirely meaning to, she slips a finger under his arm, feels the long silky hair, startling in its angora softness. A film of perspiration is on her fingertip now, she rubs it against her thumb, brings it to her nose, finds Daniel's smell within the bitterness of failed deodorant like the meat of a pecan surrounded by its broken shell.

She places her hand over the face of the flashlight more tightly so only a faint light escapes as she points it toward his face. His bushy brows, his long, somehow unsturdy-looking nose, his thin lips, the dark growth of whiskers on his chin, as if someone had rubbed iron filings onto his jaw. His hair rises in clumps in different directions. He looks slightly mad, pleasantly ruined.

She had been thinking about him in this way for months. How had it begun? What first drew her? She cannot remember. The quality of his attention as he listened to her? The gentle seriousness, the way an angel would hear you, not necessarily able to grant your wishes but able to know exactly why you've made them. Talking to him was like running a handful of riverbed stones through one of those tumblers, the kind that turn pebbles into shining things, almost jewels.

Her first time in bed with a white man. How the sweat poured off him, how he whimpered, how the breath broke in his throat like something frozen that's been stepped on, the copious, almost surreal amounts of semen that came out of him, the tireless frenzy of his fucks, his eyes staring at her, memorizing her, conquering her and surrendering at the same time.

Iris lifts the blanket and shines the flashlight further down Daniel's body. *Am I really going to do this?* But she doesn't stop herself, lets the light settle on his penis. Who was it who referred to every white man's penis as Pete Rose? Was that her father? No, impossible that something so naughty would come out of his pursed, prim mouth, a man who said sugarplums instead of shit. Her brothers? But they were so courtly around her—more dedicated than her parents to the exhausting, irritating project of keeping her the baby of the family. Yet someone had said it, and whenever she sees a picture of Pete Rose, with his schoolboy haircut and the Who Me? expression on his face, she invariably thinks: dick. Yet here, at last, is an actual white man's penis and she stares at it, flaccid and pink, looking so unprotected, vulnerable, raw, and unsheathed, like something that belongs inside the body, its own body, that is, something you are not meant to see. Like the real Pete Rose, this particular member does not seem as if he's going to make it into the Hall of Fame.

Yet he has pleased her, Pete Rose or not Pete Rose. He slipped in, and somehow the gentleness of the entrance, the unassuming, gracious, perfect guest aspect of his sexual presence caused in her an explosion of pleasure.

Suddenly, she remembers who calls the white penis Pete Rose. Hampton. The thought of him creates a guilty nausea in her: he must never know.

But what was Hampton doing talking about Caucasian sex organs? She can't remember. Surely some rant, some long riff of disparagement. Hampton, materially so well-off, so light complexioned, so privileged, seethes against the white world as if he were particularly oppressed, as if the indignities visited upon him had some greater resonance because they were happening to a man of his high quality. Even the gross misdeeds committed against less fortunate folk—the jailings, the beatings—were assaults against him, who perceived them so starkly and felt them so keenly. And so he feeds this disdain for whites into the furnace of himself, as if without it he would cease to be fully alive. His sense of white people is full of the feelings of injustice—how easy life is for them, how their power contradicts Darwin, for surely they are not the fittest—but without any great passion for justice: Hampton admires white hegemony, envies it, and he wishes it were the other way around, he wishes that the privileges were all his, and that to be born into a black family, a special black family, that is, one like his, would bestow on you the kind of birthright that the spoiled white brats took for granted. Inasmuch as possible, Hampton has chosen to live in that sort of world. The people he likes to be around, the people he does business with, drinks with, jogs around the Central Park reservoir with, are African-American strivers like himself, who feel all the proper respect for Hampton's pedigree—a lineage of accomplishment and gentility that no white person would even recognize, with fortunes based on such peculiarly Negro enterprises, such as cosmetics for dark-skinned women, Cadillac dealerships, weekly newspapers servicing the folks in Newark and the South Side of Chicago, radio stations at the back end of the dial. Wherever Hampton travels, from D.C. to Boston to Detroit to San Francisco, there are people like him, more than willing to pay their respects not only to Hampton but to his lineage, because to celebrate what it means to be a Welles, they also affirm the importance of their own family names, the majesty of their schools and clubs and summer resorts. They bow to one another as a way of genuflecting to themselves; they kiss each other like smooching with a mirror.

Daniel murmurs something in his sleep, and Iris clicks off the flashlight. She lies back in bed, rearranges her pillows, and recalls with a kind of

thrilled grief the sounds he made while they were making love, the pigeon
warble of mounting excitement, the sweet undefended cry of surrender.

———

The night has ended, the snow has finally stopped. Vast mountain ranges of
vapor have been heaved up by the storm, but between the clouds and the
horizon colors appear—pale blue, slate gray, and yellow. Inside the house
it is light enough to read, light enough to lift yourself up on your elbows
and look around the room and see the scatter of clothing on the floor.

Their noses are cold, their foreheads, their feet, the tips of their fingers. The furnace is still dead, the digital clocks are black.

"Good morning," Daniel says. "Did you even sleep for one second?"

"I'm not much of a sleeper anyhow," she says.

"I don't think I slept, it was more like passing out."

"It seemed," she says.

"Did I snore?"

She shakes her head no.

"So, let me ask you," he says. He presses himself against her. "Has the
myth of Caucasian sexual prowess been put into clearer perspective?"

"Yes," she says. "It has."

Daniel's smile slowly fades. He looks, in fact, unnerved. A little crack
of cold air opens up between them as he shrinks back from her.

"You were wonderful," Iris says. "You *are* wonderful. I can't tell you
how impressed I am. Seriously. Did your parents send you to sex camp?"

"Sex camp?"

"Don't white folks have all these different camps for their kids—
baseball camp, weight loss camp, computer camp."

He rolls next to her, gathering her closer. He is powerless not to. He
has waited too long to lie next to her, he has yet to get his fill.

"I'm sore," she says, removing his hand.

"You are?" he says, smiling.

"Aren't you?"

It dawns on him. He reaches behind him, feels the small of his back.

"My back doesn't hurt, which is a sort of Class B miracle. As for Mr. Johnson, he's been waiting for this his whole life."

She laughs, though she doesn't find it all that funny—what amuses her is his intention to amuse her.

She places her hands on Daniel's shoulder, as if to give him a little shove. But the feel of his flesh fascinates her, derails her impulse to rough him up a little. She squeezes his arm and then kisses his shoulder, touches her tongue against his skin—he tastes like a wooden countertop upon which someone has not quite cleaned up a spill of molasses.

He wants to make declarations. He wants to tell her how long he has dreamed of lying next to her, and he wants to tell her how the reality of actually being with her has exceeded his most fervid imaginings—but he has already said these things. He has discovered little imperfections in her body—brackish breath as she grew tired, a kind of abdominal fullness that suggests one day she will have a belly—but, of course, in the state he is in, these things have only made her more desirable: they have made her real, they have made her *his*. He wants to tell her she is beautiful, but how many times can you say that in twelve hours without it becoming suspect? Yet, he must declare something. Is he, for instance, meant to go home now and pretend none of this has happened?

She seems to have gotten there before him. She looks at him with great seriousness and says, "Say something to me. Tell me what I want to hear."

His first instinct is to declare his love, but something tells him not to.

"I'll tell you this," he says. "I'm not going to crowd you. I know your life is complicated."

"It is," she says softly.

"More than mine. If I lost everything, it wouldn't be that much. I'm not married. I don't have a kid."

"You have Ruby."

"She's not really mine."

"Yes she is, the way you love her. And if anything happened, you might never see her again. That would be so terrible."

"It's not like you. You have a good life. You have your son, school, your life, everything. I don't want to be a problem."

"So what do you think of me? What do you think of a woman who'd fuck some guy in her husband's bed?"

"I don't know. Maybe she should be taken out and stoned to death in front of a vast crowd."

He smiles to let her know he's kidding, but she doesn't find it funny, and the timing irritates her.

"Well, nobody needs to know, do they," she says.

"What are we supposed to do?" he asks.

"You think I'm going to change my whole life because you slept in this bed last night?" she says. Her voice is a little sharp, which she regrets. But, really.

"Yes, I think I do," he says. "I'm sorry. I'm going to figure out a better way to feel. And in the meanwhile, I promise to behave."

She makes a silencing gesture. She thinks she hears something, a noise from down the hall.

"Nobody's awake yet," Daniel says.

She listens again. He's right; the house is silent. She hears the distant whine of a snowmobile, powering through the white enameled stillness of the world like a dentist's drill. She kisses him.

"You'd better go back to the guest room," Iris says. "Nelson could walk in here any second."

"All right." He leans out of the bed, as if out of a life raft, reaching down for what is left of the night's wreckage—his shirt, his underwear, his pants.

She feels a sudden gust of desperation at the sight of him beginning to leave. What if this never can happen again? He looks at her over his shoulder as he gets out of bed. His reddish, slightly wrinkled little behind. She dives across the bed, grabs his hips, he makes it easy for her to pull him back into bed. When they have stopped rolling around, he has ended up below her, his head between her legs, his mouth kissing her opening as if they were the lips on her face. At this point, it is barely exciting, it's comforting, it feels warm and kind and devoted.

Footsteps. Have they been getting closer all the while? In a panic, Iris lifts herself up and twists away from Daniel. Her pubic bone bangs against his teeth. He looks bewildered, but she doesn't have to tell him to get up, he knows what's happening. There is a *pat pat pat* of footsteps getting closer. He rolls out of bed, grabs the clothes he gathered minutes before, makes a vain attempt to cover himself. Iris pulls the covers up to her chin.

It's Scarecrow. The old dog waddles in, head cocked, her long lilac tongue out, a good-natured glint in her blue eyes.

"Thank you, Jesus!" Daniel says.

They are so relieved, they share the hysterical laughter of the near miss. Iris does something she hasn't done since she was a little girl: she covers her mouth while she laughs her gummy laugh. And Daniel pretends to have a heart attack, grabbing his chest, staggering, falling back into the bed. Iris strokes his long, soft hair. She leans over, kisses the taste of herself off his mouth.

Nelson's footsteps are softer than the dog's. He is right next to the bed before they notice him.

"I'm cold," he says, staring intently at Daniel.

8

Hampton was still pinching black powder out of his back pocket, rubbing it between his thumb and forefinger. His fingers were long, poetic; you could imagine him playing piano, stroking a sleeping cat, caressing a woman. He tossed the powder into the darkness, as if scattering ashes after a cremation. Then he raked a handful of dead leaves off of a wild cherry tree, one that was still standing, and used them to wipe his hands. "I used to make Iris laugh all the time."

"I used to make Kate laugh, too," said Daniel. He said it because he had to say something. He couldn't simply let Hampton go on about Iris and not say anything in reply. It would be too strange, and it would be suspicious, too. However, what he said was true, meant. "First couple of years, I had her in hysterics."

He noticed that Hampton's shaved head had suffered a scrape. There was a little red worm of blood on the smooth scalp.

"Kate doesn't think you're funny anymore?"

"No, she doesn't," Daniel said.

"Iris thinks you're funny. Maybe you're funnier around her."

"Maybe she's just very kind."

"Or very lonely."

Daniel must move quickly now that Nelson has crawled under the covers to be next to Iris; he slips out of her bedroom and into the hall, where he dresses frantically and with more clumsiness than he thought himself capable of, before going into Nelson's room and waking Ruby. He shakes her awake. *Time to go, sweetie.* She nods, accepting the wisdom of his edict. She never argues with anything he says. She assumes he knows what is best for her and what is correct. If he serves her peas and corn, she eats peas and corn. If he tucks her in bed, she closes her eyes. If he tells her there are no such things as ghosts, she believes him, she doesn't even ask him to look in the closet. Daniel dresses her hurriedly, and then carries her down the stairs and through the door to the stunned, frosted, broken world outside.

His car has been spared. No trees have fallen on it during the night, though there are twigs and branches stuck in the snow on the roof and windshield. Next door, not thirty feet away, a dogwood has snapped in two; its crown rests on the roof of the house, right next to the chimney. Ruby stares at it with no small measure of awe, her eyes open so wide that the whites show above and below her pupils. Daniel gathers her closer, though he, too, stares at the tree, feeling creepy but spared.

No one has yet come out to shovel a sidewalk or clear a driveway, though the snow has finally stopped and the sky is a ridiculously cheerful blue. The blanket of untouched snow stretches as far as he can see—untouched, that is, except where trees or branches have plunged through the surface. At the far end of the block, a long coil of power line lies curled into itself like a snake in a basket, every now and then spitting out a warning venom of bright-orange sparks.

"We're going home, honey," Daniel says. His hands caress her cheeks, smooth as glass.

Though there is no road to drive on, Daniel goes through the motions of leaving anyhow. Feeling at once drunk and ill with the flu, he brushes the snow off the front-door handle, yanks the door open, breaking the brittle spun-sugar sheet of ice, slides into the car, and gets the engine started. Ruby climbs into the back and puts herself into the child seat, slipping the straps over her shoulders. While the engine warms, Daniel clears the windshield and the back window, and then brushes snow and debris off the roof. He gets back into the car and looks at Ruby. Her eyes are swollen with exhaustion, and she is shivering. "You all set?" he asks, and she nods. He puts the transmission into reverse and guns the motor, hoping to shoot over the hump of snow at the end of Iris's driveway. It doesn't quite occur to him that if the road crew hasn't cleared Iris's street right in the center of town, then there is no possibility of any of the roads being cleared, least of all the dirt road where he and Kate live, well out of town.

His car's back wheels spin uselessly. He puts the transmission into reverse, goes back a foot or two, and then puts it in drive, hoping to free himself by creating a rocking motion, back and forth. Soon, however, the spinning tires are melting the snow beneath their treads, and soon after that there rises the sharp odor of burning rubber.

"You know what?" Daniel says to Ruby, turning to look at her, smiling, trying to be as casual as possible. "Even if we get this stupid car out of the driveway, we still might not be able to drive all the way home. There's so much snow, honey."

"What about Mom?" Ruby asks.

"Well, she's the lucky one, isn't she? She's already home."

"Can't we go home, too?"

"Don't worry. We will." He looks back at Iris's house and tries to gather the courage to go back in. She is likely tending Nelson's abused sensibilities, but he has a little girl out in the snow.

Just then, he hears the urgent whine of a small engine revved to its upper limits, and a moment later an oversized, gaily painted snowmobile careens into view. It's Ferguson Richmond—airborne for a moment, as he comes over a rise, and then bouncing off the snowy street, raising up fans of pure powder. He takes a long, looping turn, and a moment later he pulls into Iris's driveway.

Daniel looks up at the second story, expecting that curiosity about this noise will have brought Iris to the window, but all he can see is a blaze of reflected sunlight in the glass.

"Enjoying Armageddon?" Ferguson asks. "Beats the hell out of locusts, doesn't it?" His voice rings out like a blacksmith's hammer. He wears neither a hat nor a helmet. His thinning hair is soaked, his bushy eyebrows hold little balls of ice. "What are you doing here?"

"Trying to get home," Daniel says. "What about you?"

"I *am* home," Ferguson says, with an excited, expansive wave. "And I wanted to see if this thing would work." He pats the snowmobile as if it were a horse. His hands are so red it looks as if the skin has been peeled off them. "And this Mexican kid who's doing some tile work for us was going crazy, so I took him over to the trailer park to be with his wife and kids. Since then I've just been cruising, surveying the damage. It's fantastic. Worse than I expected." He smiles broadly. "Want a lift?"

"Can you manage both of us?"

"We'll soon find out!"

They set off with Ruby sandwiched between them. Block after block of utter stillness and silence. Ferguson makes educated guesses where the turns would be, trying to adhere to what be believes is the road, and then he slows down as they drive through the center of town. No store is open and no one is on the street, except in front of the old brick firehouse, where a dozen volunteers are trying to clear the way, using chain saws and snowblowers.

At the far end of town, Ferguson cuts through a thirty-acre cornfield, taking a shortcut. The snowmobile hits an unexpected bump in the field. A splash of wet snow. The curved tip of the skis thrust black against the scrubbed blue sky. Daniel grabs hold of Ruby's jacket. Up. Up. And then down with a thud.

"Are you okay?" he cries out to her.

She nods nervously, her shoulders hunched, breathing shallowly through her mouth.

I'm putting her in danger, he thinks. *Is anything worth putting her in harm's way? Or even hurting her feelings? What was I thinking? And poor Nelson. What must it have been like for him to see his mother in bed with a stranger? Poor Iris.*

And now he is going back to Kate, whose intelligence he suddenly fears like a loaded gun. They are speeding through a landscape of ruined trees and blinding snow. They come to Chase Farms, where a dozen

Holsteins stand in a foot of snow, staring at one another, and then at the ground, and then at each other again. They seem puzzled by the sudden disappearance of their pasture. Above them, the blue dome of sky is starting to crack away like cheap paint, showing the cement underneath.

"Stop here!" Daniel calls out. Without asking why, Ferguson slows to a stop, and Daniel slides off the seat, gives Ruby a little squeeze, and then runs into the wrecked and tangled woods opposite Chase Farms. He is sure Ferguson assumes that he is going into the woods to take a pee. As soon as Daniel's out of sight, he pulls off his gloves, then scoops up a large handful of snow and presses it to his face, scrubbing back and forth. He must. Most adulterers have the luxury of modern plumbing with which to wash the scent of sex off before they return to their official life. But Daniel feels he bears the scent of every kiss, every secretion, on his hands, his face, his hair. It's a painful business, washing himself with snow, but his anxiety acts as a partial anesthetic, and when he finishes with his face he grabs still more snow and squeezes it between his hands.

———

As it happens, Kate is not in a position or a mood to detect the scent of infidelity on Daniel; she is frightened and a little drunk, and when Daniel and Ruby enter the house they find her in a frenzy of activity, trying to maintain some sense of domesticity in a house without lights, heat, or water. The only household appliance that works is the kitchen stove, which runs on gas that comes from two silver cylinders near the back door, and Kate hovers continually over this stove, cooking everything that would otherwise spoil, grilling the salmon, scrambling the eggs, broiling the chicken, and steaming the vegetables—without tap water, she uses club soda that she allows to go flat in the bottom of the pot before turning on the flame. At one point, Kate has something simmering on all six burners of their Garland range (inherited from the house's previous owners) and is swigging on a bottle of vermouth as well as a bottle of gin, as if to mix a martini in her mouth.

When she is not discussing in hair-raising detail last night's invasion by the Star of Bethlehem boys, Kate's spirits are darkly manic, her jocularity seems to scan the horizon for likely targets. To Daniel, she says, "This is some romantic, ain't it?" and pulls his hair, not quite hard enough to be thoroughly aggressive. "I hope you're hungry," she announces to the house, singing it out, like some nutty kid imitating an opera singer. "And I hope you like really really shitty cooking." Though it is cold in the house, she is flushed, little drops of sweat collect in her facial down. "Come on, Ruby, I'll play hide-and-seek with you." And when Ruby declines the in-vitation—the last thing the child wants to do is slip into a closet or slide under a bed in a house filled with darkness and cold, a house that is in-creasingly unnerving to her—Kate doesn't only look disappointed, she seems offended, as if she herself were a little girl, a lonely little girl, suf-fering the rejection of a playmate.

Without electricity, home life is less private than ever. They are cast back to some preindustrial reliance on each other. When the home technolo-gies are up and running, each member of the family can be a self-sustaining unit, in a private room with its own source of heat and light, listening to music on his own set, watching a movie, purchasing dried apricots from Haifa via the Internet. With only the fireplace for heat, the hearth becomes the locus of their lives. If Kate takes a candle to light her way to the bathroom, Daniel and Ruby are left in darkness.

Ruby has to be next to at least one of them, and the constancy of her presence, along with her nervousness and her boredom, begins to wear on Kate. Finally, however, Kate is able to coax Ruby to go upstairs, giv-ing her a candle and convincing her that the little red radio in her room will afford her some entertainment. When Ruby is finally out of earshot, Kate makes a martini for Daniel and hands it to him with a certain force-fulness that tells him he had better accept it, though, in fact, he would like to remain coldly sober, so as to defend himself if Kate should turn her intelligence against him, and also to continue trying to figure a way he could leave the house, make it back into town, and see Iris.

"You know when I told you about those men coming into the house last night . . ."

"I thought you said they were boys," Daniel says.

"They were men," Kate says. "Maybe some asshole lawyer could argue they were juveniles, but they were thudding around here like a herd of elephants."

He wants to say *By "asshole lawyer" I assume you mean me,* but why borrow trouble?

"And if they had found me," Kate is saying, "then I promise you it wouldn't have been some boyish prank."

"Well, thank God they didn't," Daniel says. He takes another sip of his martini and realizes that he has practically drained the glass.

When Kate veers closer he eases away from her. He is sure that he still reeks of last night, and then it strikes him that he ought to do some labor, something that might work up an exculpatory sweat. "I'm going to bring in some wood for the fireplace," he says. She looks at him a little strangely.

The sky is a deep blue, almost purple, with a crescent moon bobbing up and down in a stream of passing night clouds. The temperature is mild; with a fire in the fireplace, they'll be warm enough inside. Daniel stands for a few moments on the porch, where oak and ash logs are stacked against the gray clapboard of the exterior wall. The stillness and clarity of the evening are almost unbelievable—how could such tranquility follow such chaos? Daniel takes a deep breath, spreads his arms out: *Iris.* Two of the three old locust trees in the front yard are down, one has been split in two, the other has been completely torn out of the ground, its taproot unearthed. A few scattered stars pulsate, diamond chips in the velvet. He wonders if she is okay. She cannot bear the cold. She might have low blood pressure, she should have it checked. Maybe the road crews have already cleared out the center of town, maybe she's already up and around. Maybe the power has been restored on Juniper Street. He hopes so. She shouldn't be sitting alone in a dark house. He wonders if Hampton, learning the extent of the storm, has returned to his family.

He brings in several armloads of firewood, and places them all carefully in the large iron ring near the fireplace. The air is dank in the house. The smell from the fireplace is pleasant, however, and the three of them sit on the floor in front of it, enjoying its warmth and the comforting light. Kate continues to drink, though Daniel doesn't know exactly what's in her glass, and he doesn't feel able to ask her. But watching her drink makes him want to get drunk—despite the risk—and he makes his way into the kitchen, holding a candle that drips wax onto his knuckles with each step. He comes back with half a glass of bourbon and sits down on the hooked rug in front of the hearth, where he and Kate have been playing Uno with Ruby. Normally, playing with Ruby like this is one of the things that make Daniel feel life is worth living, and the same could be said for sitting in front of a successful fire, getting a little loaded, even going to bed with Kate after she'd been drinking. But tonight, everything seems fraught and dreary. How can he be here, stuck, trapped, put into a position in which every word out of his mouth is a lie? How can he be going through the motions in this sad and threadbare life, a life that now is— he hates to think it, but he must—little more than a terrible obstacle between him and simple human happiness?

Later that night, Daniel waits downstairs before going to bed, poking at the logs in the fireplace and hoping that Kate will have fallen asleep before he arrives in their bedroom. He extinguishes his candle when he is halfway up the stairs; all he can see in the darkness is the beady red lights of the battery-powered smoke detectors. He feels his way along the wall, down the hallway, and as quietly as possible into the bedroom. He takes his shoes off and gets into bed in his clothes—a pair of corduroy pants, beneath which he wears long underwear, two shirts, and a sweater, all of which he must wear for warmth, but which he also hopes will quarantine whatever evidence his body wants to give of last night's frenzies. He is operating on three hours of sleep, which he doesn't fully realize until he quietly slides into bed and an overpowering sense of exhaustion comes over him in slow, relentless waves.

And Kate is not asleep. She rolls next to him and drapes her leg over his.

"What were you doing down there?" she asks.

"Hitting a log with the fireplace poker."

"Oh, you man, you."

"That's me in a nutshell," he says. She presses herself against his hip, and he feels panic rising in him. Because it would seem strange and possibly even brutal not to, he puts his arm around her, though the very act makes him feel compromised, and even jealous—if he is capable of committing these little endearments, then Iris could surely be doing likewise. At this very moment.

"Do you really think I shouldn't call the police about those runaways being here last night?" Kate says.

"I don't know. There's not much they can do about it right now." He really doesn't want to talk, and he also senses that somewhere within this particular line of inquiry there lies trouble.

"You're a tiny bit on their side, aren't you?" Kate says softly, as if it were possible to lure him into believing she is not furious at the idea.

"Of course not. I hate that that happened. It was obviously terrifying. It terrifies me to even hear about it."

"Then what are you saying? That I should stop talking about it?"

"Kate. Of course not."

"But it is. That's what you're saying, that I should stop talking about it."

"Well, it's not what I meant to say."

"But it's what you said."

"Kate, I don't know what to tell you here. You're doing the subtext?"

"Yes, I'm doing the fucking subtext."

"Ah, the *fucking* subtext." *Shut up shut up,* he tells himself. But exhaustion, the bourbon, and acute sexual claustrophobia are having their way with him. He forces his eyes open. For a second he feels he might fall asleep—right in the middle of an argument.

"What?"

He tries to scramble back into the conversation, desperately. "If you want to call the police, call them," he says. "Or I will. I'll call Derek Pabst."

"Derek Pabst is an idiot."

"Then I'll call someone else. I'll call the attorney general."

"It's a big joke to you."

"No. It's not. I don't know what you want."

"I want you to care about what happened to me."

He wants to say that nothing really happened to her, but he manages to control himself. She continues with such vehemence, he may as well have said it.

"It's because they're black, isn't it?" she says. "You feel protective toward them. Like they're the victims, and the people who try to keep them under control are the bad guys."

"That's not what I think." He digs his elbows into the mattress to raise himself, but he doesn't have the strength.

"You're going to turn into one of those ridiculous white guys who secretly think they're black," Kate says. "Where's this coming from anyhow? You want to tell me?"

"I don't know what you're talking about. I don't think I'm black."

"But you wish you were."

"What I wish I was is asleep."

"It's like the Simpson case. When did you start believing that fucking O. J. is innocent?"

"I don't think that."

"Really? Do you think he's guilty?"

"I don't know! How could I know? I don't have all the facts. And the trial's still ongoing."

"The trial's still ongoing? The man butchered his wife, a poor girl who told her friends, 'If anything happens to me, O. J. did it.' Every reasonable person in America knows he's guilty, including his own lawyers, and all you can say is 'the trial's still ongoing.' " These last words are delivered in that mocking rendition of the male voice that women do— the voice of someone who's just had a cinder block dropped on his head.

Is that what I sound like to you? Daniel wants to say, in his eagerness to feel like the injured party. But even in the throes of passion, with all its attendant greed and narcissism, and with the self-centeredness and sociopathology of a man on the great emotional crusade of his life, Daniel cannot quite manage the moral contortion that would place himself squarely on his own side. His awareness that he is betraying Kate is too corrosively present. He is not only in love with someone else but he is keeping it a secret, and though there are surely worse things in the world that a man can do, there is nothing worse within a marriage, which is, he must finally admit, basically what he and Kate have. He would like to tell her that their time together is finished. They may have made a pledge to each other to be Swiss bankers of the heart, but banks fail. Still, he knows he cannot, must not tell her—telling the truth right now would likely put Iris in jeopardy.

"You know when you started thinking that O. J. is innocent?" Kate is saying.

"I never said he's . . ."

"Right around the time you started talking about Iris Davenport."

"Oh, come on, this is insane. *And:* you're drunk." He immediately regrets the aggression of this, but Kate seems not to have noticed.

"Does Iris think he's innocent, too?" she asks.

"I have no idea."

"Really? No idea? The whole county is obsessed with the case and you two have never mentioned it? That's interesting. What do you talk about, then?"

"I don't know. Nothing."

"Nothing? You talk about nothing? You were at her house for a day and a night talking about *nothing?*"

"Don't interrogate me, Kate."

"You can't invoke your Fifth Amendment rights in bed, buddy boy. All constitutional rights are waived between the sheets."

"Then maybe I should get up. I don't like being without my constitutional rights."

"If you leave this bed . . ."

"Kate, this is insane. Can we please just sleep? O. J.'s asleep, the jury's sleeping, the DA, everyone is." He waits for an answer, counts to three, and then closes his eyes, and when he opens them again it's morning, and he's alone.

———

Daniel and Kate collect buckets of snow, using some of it to flush their toilets, and melting a portion to use as drinking water. Kate, who is usually glad to allow Daniel to look after Ruby, is today somewhat possessive of the little girl; it leads Daniel to believe that she is trying to give him a sense of what his future will be like without the love of Ruby as a constant in his life. But other than this, her demeanor shows little of last night's suspiciousness and anger. When they are collecting the snow, she is playful, throwing little handfuls of it at Daniel. She makes him coffee. She is full of praise for the new morning fire in the hearth. Nevertheless, by eleven that morning Daniel is feeling so confined and isolated in their house, and so wild with desire to see Iris, that he feels his level of frustration is starting to become hazardous not only from a psychological standpoint but even from a medical one.

He must get out of here. Living in these conditions, with these new dictates of communality and wall-to-wall togetherness, makes it impossible to even call Iris. He casts desperately about in his mind, trying to think of a way to absent himself and somehow make it into town, and then, at last, at around noon, he goes upstairs to their sad and chilly bedroom, where there is a working telephone, and he calls Ferguson Richmond.

"Ferguson," he says, "Daniel Emerson here. I wonder if I could ask you a huge favor? If you're going to be out and around on your snowmobile, I wonder if you could come get me at my house and bring me into town."

"No problem," Ferguson says without hesitating. "When do you need to go? Now?"

Daniel is overcome by Ferguson's generosity and lack of inquisitiveness. "Yes," he says, sitting on the edge of the bed, "now would be fine. Anytime. Thank you so much."

He goes back downstairs, where Kate and Ruby are in the kitchen. Ruby is on the floor, playing with plastic horses, and Kate is melting some snow in a large cast-iron pot. She plans to fill the sink so that everyone can wash their hands and face.

"Who were you calling?" she asks casually enough.

"Ferguson Richmond," Daniel says.

"*Sir* Ferguson Richmond," Kate says. She likes to make fun of the local gentry, but her own southern background, with its emphasis on family and gentility, gives her an enduring interest in such things, and Daniel has always suspected that she admires the Windsor County aristocrats more than she lets on. "So what is he? Your new best friend?"

"He's actually going to do me a tremendous favor. He's coming out here on his snowmobile and he's taking me into town."

"You're kidding me."

"It's very nice of him."

"Yes. It's amazing. How far away is he? Eight miles, ten?"

"I don't know. I guess ten. It's what people always say about him. He's this total reactionary and a snob, but if you actually put something right in front of him, a problem, a person in need, there's nothing he wouldn't do for you. He's got bad ideas, but good feelings. He's got this deep, almost heroic generosity."

Ruby looks up from her horses. Her eyes are blurred and her skin is mottled; she looks like an abandoned child. "Where are you going?" she asks Daniel. She furrows her brow, purses her lips, to let him know she is worried.

"I need to go to work, sweetie," he says. "I have to go to my office."

"I want to go, too," she says.

"Do you want to?" Kate asks the child. "Take a ride with Daniel and see what's going on out there? Maybe some stores are open and Daniel can get you some Jolly Ranchers."

Ruby begins to pick up her toys, in preparation for leaving.

Daniel is appalled that Kate would use Ruby in such a cynical, manipulative fashion.

"I'm just going to my office," he says to Ruby.

"It's okay," she says.

He smiles, relieved.

"Your office is fun," Ruby says.

"What are you doing?" he asks Kate, lifting his hands in exasperation.

"What am *I* doing? What are *you* doing?"

"I am buried in paperwork. I have a dozen crises brewing, and a dozen more on the horizon, and I have no choice, I have to get to my office."

"Of course you do. But Ruby's not going to stop you from doing your paperwork. And that way she'll be a little less stir crazy."

"I want to go, too," Ruby says.

"And I'll be able to get a little writing done," Kate continues. "Or at least try."

"You're going to put her on the back of a snowmobile for ten miles?"

"It was fun," says Ruby.

"You put her on the back of the very same snowmobile," Kate says, "driven by the very same Samaritan who's coming to rescue you."

"That was an emergency. I was trying to get her home. I was trying to do the right thing. Jesus."

"Please," says Ruby. "It was so fun."

"I'm sorry, sweetie. It's just not going to work."

"I don't see why not," says Kate.

"Kate, you're being ridiculous. Really. Enough."

"It's so boring here," says Ruby.

"No!" Daniel says, his voice rising with temper and desperation. In the stillness of the house, it sounds as if he has shouted at the top of his voice.

Kate smiles a terrible, wounded, superior smile and shakes her head. "One question," she says. "How are you going to get back home after your . . . um, paperwork?"

"I'll get back." He is about to say *Trust me,* but he stops himself.

Daniel occupies himself while waiting for Ferguson by building up the fire and bringing in more wood. Nearly an hour passes, during which he almost loses hope of Ferguson arriving, but then he hears the manic whine of the snowmobile, and he races out to meet Ferguson, shouting his good-byes over his shoulder.

On the way into town, Ferguson fills Daniel in on the recovery effort. Though no snow has fallen since yesterday, trees continue to topple. Highway crews and repair crews from the power company have made virtually no progress in clearing the roads. The trouble has not been the amount of snow—not much more than a foot has fallen—but that the thousands of trees on the ground have made every emergency vehicle virtually useless. Squads of men with chain-saws are all over the county—they've come in from every county in the state, as well as Connecticut, Massachusetts, Pennsylvania, New Jersey, Vermont, and New Hampshire—and they are cutting up and removing the slaughtered trees one by one. Estimates are that the middle of town should be electrified either by tonight or tomorrow morning; beyond that, some areas aren't expected to have power for another three or four days, though Ferguson guesses it'll be longer than that.

Ferguson is wearing a dark leather jacket, weathered and cracked, thick wool pants, and a pair of boots that look as if they'd once belonged to a soldier in the First World War. The smell of gasoline and oil is all over him. He wears amber-tinted ski goggles that are so smudged and scratched it's a wonder he can see anything through them. His ears are as bright as freshly boiled shrimps and his graying hair whips back and forth in the wind as he speeds across a pasture, dodging trees, and then onto what Daniel guesses is Route 100, though all that indicates that it is a road at all are the occasional mailboxes standing iced and empty on their cedar stalks.

"An awful lot of people have been hurt," Ferguson is saying, in his firm, penetrating voice. "And we've had fatalities. Traffic, fire, and heart failure."

"Oh no, it's so terrible," Daniel says.

"It'll be a field day for the lawyers," Ferguson says. He looks over his shoulder and grins at Daniel.

Two black-and-yellow trucks from the power company are parked near an extinguished traffic light further down on Route 100. Two of the workers are standing around, drinking coffee and smoking, while the others cut an immense fallen oak into sections. A half mile later, there is a second crew, engaged in a similar task, and a quarter mile after that there is a third. Further off the road, the Schultz brothers, three long-haired, gray-bearded bachelors, who live in a hardscrabble compound in which they each own a trailer, and who drive fierce-looking pickup trucks with giant tires and furious bumper stickers directed against President Clinton, are hard at work chain-sawing fallen trees into three-foot lengths and heaving them into the backs of their trucks. Ferguson waves at them, and the brothers stare back expressionlessly, holding their saws like rifles, pointed down at the ground.

"They're making the best of it. They'll sell enough firewood to keep them in beer for the winter," Ferguson says. "Fellows like the Schultzes, they're the heart and soul of this county. They're our muzhiks, our own God-fearing serfs, and if all the city people coming out here drive up land prices—those crazy brothers are going to be swept right out of here."

Before reaching the center of Leyden, Ferguson makes a couple of stops, both of them to run-down, ranch-style houses, one occupied by an extended family of recently arrived Poles, the other lived in by an even more extended family of Mexicans. He keeps the snowmobile idling as he makes his quick visits, and then, assured that everyone is sur-viving the storm and its aftermath, he takes Daniel the rest of the way into town.

At the center of town, the sidewalks have been cleared and some of the larger trees have been cut and hauled away. Except for one of the gas stations, every business is still shut. Ferguson pulls to a stop in front of the Koffee Kup; though it's closed, a couple of the waitresses are inside, mopping the floor. Daniel slides off the snowmobile and staggers back a little—his legs feel distorted and anesthetized.

"Thanks so much, Ferguson. I really do appreciate it."

"Are you sure this is where you want me to drop you?" Ferguson says.

He takes off his goggles, rubs his left eye with a kind of startling vigor. "I could take you to Hampton Welles's place, it's only a couple blocks. Your car's still there, isn't it?"

"No, this is fine."

"Hey, look, if you need a lift back later on, give me a call."

"It's really awfully nice of you."

"Is it? Susan says I act as if I were the great *padrone* and it's my job to look out after all my little people. I just like driving this thing around. And I don't exactly despise being out of the house, if you know what I mean."

Daniel fusses with his car in Iris's driveway, hoping to create the impression that he has only returned for his vehicle, but soon she comes out, puts her arm around his shoulders, and steers him indoors. He is cold and wet; she makes him a cup of coffee, pours a little bit of brandy in it, and then takes hold of Daniel's chin and kisses him with fervor, openness, and engulfing warmth. They listen to hear if Nelson is busy in the playroom, and deciding that he is they begin to take chances. Thus begins the four days they will come to call the Rapture. He takes hold of her hips and presses her closer to him, hoping the pressure of her will relieve some of the agony of desire, and she lets out a soft moan of pleasure directly into his mouth. They sit at the kitchen table and keep an ear out for Nelson; they move their chairs closer so that they can touch each other, kiss, his hand is up her dress, she yanks her woolen tights down, opens herself to him, she is so concentrated on her own pleasure, she squints, and then suddenly it's upon her and her mouth opens and her breath comes in little puffs, it's like someone doing Lamaze, and when she comes it's convulsive. It seems to Daniel that his relief will have to wait, and he is fine with that, just watching her come is enough, but she quickly turns her attention to him, and he is fine with that, too. What does matter is that the next day is Friday and Hampton arrives in Leyden. By now, the roads are cleared, and the power is sporadically restored; Red Schoolhouse Road is still dark, but Daniel has driven his car back home the day before through a multitude of detours and now he can drive himself to his office, where he and Iris meet, with the blinds drawn, and the heat cranked up, and the door double-locked in case Sheila Alvarez should decide to put in an appearance, which she does not. Saturday afternoon. Daniel brings Kate and Ruby to the train station because Kate has decided to stay in New York until power is restored in Leyden, and twenty hours later Iris calls: Hampton has gone back to the city. Daniel is at her house in minutes. They bathe each other, nervous that Nelson might awaken, but unable to exercise any more caution than locking the door. "I never realized white people could get so dirty," she whispers to him, rubbing the soapy sponge onto his shoulders, smoothing the lather down his silky chest. "I look like a burn victim," he says, holding his arm next to hers, comparing the colors. They make love in the guest room, out of some shared tact, and sometime during it Iris says, "I feel really safe with you, it's such a pleasant way to feel," and though she says it in a purely conversational tone, as soon as the words are out she bursts into tears, and he holds her, afraid to ask why she is crying. He leaves her house as dawn breaks gray and pink in the high innocent sky, home of God and all the angels; never has he known such happiness. He drives past the twenty-four-hour road crews, waving idiotically at them, *bless you bless you all*. Iris is home from her seminar at two that afternoon, they have two and a half hours before it's time to collect Nelson. Conversation, confession, and sex. "You're killing me," she says happily. Soon all the roads will be cleared, even the houses miles out of town will have power restored, Kate will be back, life will return to normal. He no longer looks kindly at the road crews, their around-the-clock busyness seems like some terrible meddling. One last night with Iris, a few more hours, and the ferocious sexual project reveals itself: they are tearing each other apart, devouring the flesh until nothing separates them.

9

As far as Daniel was concerned, this was torture. It might be better just to come out with it, tell Hampton: I love Iris, and she seems to love me. We belong together. We do feel bad. Oh shut up about feeling bad. Do you think he cares? He'd like you to have brain cancer, that would be the sort of suffering he'd like for you. Why are you offering up your stricken conscience—to make him feel you've been punished sufficiently? Are you so afraid of him? And with that question, Daniel at last connected to the core of what had been plaguing him from the moment he and Hampton set off together in search of Marie. It was not really about conscience, after all. He'd been wrestling with his conscience for months now, they were old sparring partners, sometimes he pinned it to the mat, sometimes it slammed him, it didn't really amount to much, it was a show, like the wrestling on TV. And besides: the worst sort of remorse was preferable to what had preceded it, the infinitely greater agony of longing for Iris. Remorse was the payment due for the fulfillment of his great desire. And it was, finally, a payment he was willing to make. No, it was not his conscience that churned at the center of him, making him cringe inwardly when Hampton stepped too close to him. It was fear, physical fear.

Like many men who find love when they are no longer in the full bloom of vigor and health, Daniel has made a promise to himself to get back in shape. For a couple of nights, he tried doing calisthenics at home, but it seemed disrespectful to Kate to be grunting out sit-ups in the same room they conduct their wounded, slowly expiring relationship. Those exercises were a kind of celebratory dance of health, and his workout wear of baggy cotton shorts and a baggier old gray T-shirt was in fact the uniform of his new devotion: they may as well have borne Iris's name on the back. He is in training to be her lover. One day soon Kate will understand that the sexual Mount Everest Daniel is in training to scale has nothing to do with her, and when this grim domestic knowledge is complete Daniel does not want her to conjure a vision of him doing abdominal crunches on their bedroom floor.

As a less ostentatious form of body toning, Daniel decides to forego lunch and to spend the time vigorously walking through the village of Leyden, which now, nine days after the October snow, is just getting back to normal, with businesses long closed for lack of electrical power finally reopening, and employees finally able to show up for work. The mood of the town is festive, as if at the victorious end of a war. No one can get enough of talking about what befell them during the storm and the blackout, what they learned, what they lost, how they coped. Daniel's great story of the October storm, however, cannot be told, and its necessary suppression has dampened his normally gregarious nature. He is content to replay memories of his days and nights with Iris without any interruption as he walks the circumference of the town's commercial center. The problem really is that walking doesn't feel like exercise, and as soon as he makes it once around the village, he realizes that he looks half mad speed-walking in his suit and street shoes, and also that he is too young for walking, speed or otherwise, to make much of an impact on him. On his second time through the village, he hears someone call his name, and though he has promised himself that he will ignore all distractions, he stops immediately and turns to face Bruce Mc-Fadden, an old friend from Daniel's childhood days in Leyden.

"Hey, bro, what it is," McFadden says in some vaguely self-mocking approximation of black street slang, putting his palm out for a little skin.

McFadden, a tall, flimsily knit-together man, with long, lustrous brown hair, bright-green eyes, and a pale face with hectic bursts of color at the cheekbones, is about as black as a Highland fling, and normally he does not speak in anything approaching hip-hop patois. But a love of black culture is the original cornerstone of his friendship with Daniel, and Bruce still likes to black it up. And because, right now, Bruce doesn't happen to know any black people personally, saying "bro" and talking about Satchel Paige and Miles Davis, Chester Himes, Howling Wolf, Antonio Vargas, Peaches and Herb, Sonny Rollins, Sonny Liston, Sonny Boy Williamson, and all the other black Sonnys, is something he saves for his occasional meetings with Daniel.

Except for a few years in Albany, where he went to medical school, Bruce has never lived outside of Leyden. He is a part of a thriving medical group, but his personal life is conducted at the very pinnacle of circumspection—no one has any idea what he does when the sun goes down, if he drinks, or sits alone watching television, or whether or not he has a lover, and what the gender of that lover might be. Even Daniel, who loves Bruce, cannot say what the mysterious doctor has devised for getting through the nights.

"Why are you walking around like that?" Bruce asks Daniel, standing in front of the luncheonette, with a half-eaten tuna sandwich in one hand and a paper napkin in the other.

"Exercising," says Daniel.

"You can't get exercise walking around like that, man. You want exercise? I'll teach you the greatest of the white man's sports."

With that in mind, Bruce convinces Daniel to meet after work at Marlowe College, where Bruce is going to teach Daniel how to play squash. It's Friday; Hampton is coming back to town, and Daniel is grateful for the diversion, the company. Rather than go home and get his Nikes, shorts, and a T-shirt, Daniel buys all these things new and arrives at the gym a few minutes before his five o'clock date with Bruce. He immediately goes to the glass wall overlooking the college's swimming pool, an

immense turquoise parallelogram surrounded by red and white tiles—
Iris is a swimmer and Daniel is hoping that luck is on his side.

But the pool is empty. An elderly man, probably a professor, with an
enormous bald head, ears as large as fists, a barrel chest from which fur
rises up in fifty separate geysers, sits in a wheelchair at the edge of the
pool, grimacing at a young man with light olive skin and shoulder-length
hair, probably his physical therapist. The sight of the old man fills Daniel's
heart with urgency: time passes, bodies decay, every day spent without
love is lost forever, the time cannot be recaptured or made up for. The
professor's legs are as thin as a child's. He wraps his trembling, chim-
panzee arms around the young man's neck and allows himself to be
hoisted out of the chair and lowered into the deep end of the pool, just
to the left of the double-decker diving boards. As soon as the old man is
in the water, he disappears, and Daniel for a moment thinks he is the witness to a tragedy. But then the old man emerges; he has swum to the center of the pool, and he continues to propel himself with breast strokes,
expelling water from his mouth in a long arcing spew.

Bruce arrives, and Daniel follows him into the locker room. In the
large, windowless room, with its industrial gray carpeting and the smell
of sweat and chlorine in the air, a dozen or so college students are in various states of undress. Their movements are nervous, they dress hurriedly, with elaborate bashfulness about their young, fit bodies, slipping
into their shorts while they keep a towel wrapped around their midsec-
tions, showering in their bathing suits. The older men, the guys in their
fifties and sixties, display without shame their deteriorated bodies,
their flaccid bellies, hunched backs, saggy asses, and flamboyantly uneven
testicular sacs.

"Did you hear the news about those kids who broke out of Star of
Bethlehem?" Bruce asks.

"What happened?" Daniel cannot hear any mention of them without
a feeling of anxiety and remorse.

"Fucking crime spree, baby. All up and down the river." Bruce smiles,
shakes his head, it's hard to say if he means to be rueful or admiring.

"I guess they'll catch them sooner or later," Daniel says.

"I wouldn't bet on it. Cops up here are not used to anyone giving them any resistance."

Daniel and Bruce begin to undress and Bruce asks the inevitable question: "Where were you during the storm?"

"Actually, I was trapped in someone else's house for the first day of it."

"Oh my God, I would hate that," Bruce says. He tosses his loafers into the locker.

Daniel glances around the locker room to see if anyone is within earshot. Several lockers to the right, a skinny, gloomy-looking man in his late fifties, breathing heavily, bathed in sweat, unfastens a complicated knee brace.

"I was at Iris Davenport's house. I ended up spending the night there." Daniel has promised himself never to mention this, but now he can't quite recall why it's so important to keep the secrecy intact.

"Iris Davenport? What a fox. She looks a little like Whitney Houston, don't you think?"

"Not really."

"She's been to my office. Confidentially? I tested her for glaucoma. It runs in her family."

"When?"

"Months ago. She's a pretty girl," Bruce says in a distant voice, as if he were piecing together his memory of her as he speaks. "Her eyes are fine, by the way."

"Yes," says Daniel. "I could walk into her eyes and never come back."

Bruce glances away, clears his throat. "Whatever," he says. Then he adds, "What's she like, anyhow? I found her sort of hard to get a read on."

"She's honest, she's steady, she's always present. She's pure without being a puritan. She's liberated without being a libertine."

"All right. Now you're starting to frighten me."

Daniel blushes; in the company of another man, the pitch of his own ardor seems suddenly absurd. "I'm being undone by this whole thing," he murmurs. "I'm totally in love with her, Bruce." The relief of finally being able to say this to another person has upset his balance, the way you would lose strength in your legs and stumble forward after finally being relieved of a load of firewood.

"Oh dear," Bruce says. His sneakers are laced; he stands up and puts his hand on Daniel's shoulder and gives it a comradely pat. "It'll pass," he says, as if to comfort Daniel. "Let's not even talk about it."

The squash courts are on the second floor of the gym, a row of five white rooms with hardwood floors, the back wall of each made of shatterproof glass so that the games may be observed. All of the courts are empty when Daniel and Bruce arrive; they take court number one and Bruce teaches Daniel the rudiments of the game, beginning, as is the masculine custom, with the rules. Bruce seems fixated on the rules, rattling them off in a stern fashion, as if suspecting that Daniel might be trying to figure a way around them. When they finally begin to hit the ball, Daniel is confused by how little it bounces, how its hollowness and softness render it practically inert, and he wonders how this game will ever provide him with exercise. But the ball becomes livelier as it heats up, and after twenty minutes on the court Daniel is breathing heavily and feels the first trickle of sweat going down his spine.

They hear the thump of a ball being hit on an adjoining court; another game is in progress.

"You're a good beginner," Bruce says. "Want to get a drink of water?"

They open the glass door and walk out into the broad corridor, at the end of which is a water cooler. The first thing Daniel sees is Iris sitting on one of the brightly colored red-and-black benches in the hall. His heart flaps like a toucan in a cage. Iris sits there, with Nelson draped languidly on her lap. She wears a copper-colored down vest, a Baltimore Orioles cap, jeans, and rubber boots. She glances at Daniel, and then looks away. Surely she has known all along that he is here, they all must have seen him through the glass on their way to court two. Is this really her strategy? That they should ignore each other? It doesn't seem wise. And he is, of course, incapable of carrying it out.

"Iris!" he calls out, as if seeing her here were one of life's funny little surprises. He grasps Bruce by the elbow and steers him over toward Iris. "I believe you two know each other," Daniel says. He feels hot breath on his leg and looks down. It's Scarecrow, hitched to a dark-blue leash, wagging her tailless hindquarters and panting excitedly. Daniel is unreasonably happy to see her, as if the old dog had risen from the dead. "Scarecrow! Are you a member of the gym?"

"Hello, Iris," Bruce says. Noticing the confusion in her face, he adds, "It's Dr. McFadden."

"Oh yes, I'm sorry. I . . ."

"I'm out of context." He gestures toward his long legs. "You never saw me in shorts."

Daniel chooses to take this remark as somehow scaling the pinnacle of wit. In the midst of his laughter, he notices that Nelson is scowling openly at him, an exaggerated grimace, completely unencumbered by any sense of social grace. He is like a bad actor miming displeasure in a silent movie. Quickly, Daniel diverts his own attention to the squash game taking place in court two.

Hampton is playing against his younger brother, James. James Welles has his brother's—and, indeed, his entire family's—light copper complexion, but his appearance is far from Hampton's carefully groomed, businesslike image. While Hampton wears tennis whites, James is dressed as if to go fishing with a bamboo pole: in cutoff jeans, a faded rust T-shirt torn at the shoulder, black sneakers splattered with paint, and no socks at all. He has the merry and defiant eyes of a boy who always knew he was his mother's favorite, no matter what sort of trouble he caused. He has recently grown a little scraggly beard—hardly a beard, really, just three sprouts of whisker, a kind of Fu Manchu fountain springing from the center of his chin. His long hair is a complex nest of braids, culminating in a thick, glistening ponytail.

Daniel stands behind the glass wall and watches transfixed. James moves around the court as if scarcely subject to the laws of gravity, bounding and whirling, airborne, his braids flapping, his shoelaces flapping as well, letting out little yelps of pure animal joy, his youthful, handsome face alight with the bliss of his own physicality. The ball hits against the back wall, and James runs after it with the antic, spendthrift energy of a pup, in fact he overruns it, but no matter—he returns the ball by hitting it through his wide-open skinny legs, punctuating the circus shot with a whoop and a raised fist.

Hampton's reply to his younger brother's showboating is to return the ball in the most rudimentary, formal, and correct way possible. In fact, all of Hampton's moves on the court could be used in an instructional video, the way he cocks the racquet over his head before each stroke, the way he bends his knees, his short, punchy follow-through, his return to the center of the court after every stroke. His movements are dogged, mechanized, and tireless. The only emotion he shows is a slight reddening around the ears and throat when James makes a particularly unorthodox shot, since these are met with squeals and cheers from Nelson.

"Don't cheer against Daddy," Iris whispers to her boy.

"Uncle James is funny," Nelson says.

Bruce catches Daniel's eyes. *Let's go,* he mouths. Daniel shakes his head and Bruce sighs impatiently.

Daniel forces himself to turn away from the game, though by now it feels as if the fate of his love affair with Iris *requires* that Hampton be vanquished. "How are you doing?" he asks Iris.

"I'm all right. Nelson's Uncle James is visiting us."

"I see that," Daniel says. Daniel has always been moved by the quality of Iris's mothering; her kindness and her aptness around Nelson have appealed to Daniel so deeply that it is practically an erotic experience to see her with her boy, but just now Daniel wishes that she would speak only to *him.*

Still, he goes along with it. "Are you pretty excited to see your Uncle James?" he asks, directing his question to Nelson, who at first seems not to have heard him, and who then leers at him, first pursing his lips and then showing his little milky teeth. *Of course, now he hates me. He doesn't quite understand what he saw, but he'll never forgive finding me in his mother's bed.* "And how about you, Scarecrow?" Daniel says, squatting down to the dog's level. "Everything copasetic?" By way of an answer, the dog launches herself toward Daniel, ramming his eye with her wet nose.

"What's the score?" Nelson screams at his father and uncle. He squirms out of Iris's lap and hits his hard little hands against the glass wall. "Who's winning?"

"I am," James says, flipping his racquet up and then catching it by the handle. "I'm on fire, I'm unconscious, I can't be stopped."

Nelson doesn't shout in triumph, but he squeezes his hands into fists, goes rigid, and whispers to himself: "Yes." Nelson's expressions are exaggerated, feverishly intense; it's difficult to say whether these grimaces and gestures come from some molten, unmediated part of him, or if they are deliberately theatrical and insincere. Whatever their source, there is something troubling about them.

Hampton, in the meanwhile, has hit the ball in a slow, lazy arc over James's head, who then bats it wildly, with an equally wild accompanying whoop. The ball sails across the court, barely reaching the front wall, which it grazes, before dropping dead and unplayable, another point for the younger brother, who celebrates by spinning around on one foot with his arms outstretched.

James, having won the point, serves, and Hampton makes his usual methodical return—it's art versus science. James returns the shot with a dazzling and picturesque behind-the-back stroke, but from that moment on Hampton proceeds to dismantle him, wearing him down with his own refusal to lose. Hampton rallies to win the game 9-7.

Nelson has retreated to Iris's lap, and he sits awkwardly on her, his legs dangling, his arms folded over his chest, outraged over some shady business. Bruce, uncomfortable with standing there in light of what Daniel has told him, and also anxious to use his workout time, has gone back to court one, where he hits the ball to himself. Daniel, however, is powerless to move. He must see the match out to its bitter end. He has been crouched a few feet from Iris, as if he were a squash scout studying the game, looking for new prospects. He doesn't dare say anything to Iris, though he continually looks at her reflection in the squash court's glass wall. She glances at him and it seems as if her eyes are asking, *What are you doing?* but he cannot move.

At last, Hampton and James emerge. All of the levity and grace and joyousness and even youthfulness seems to have been beaten out of James, while Hampton, in victory, seems not noticeably different than he was in the beginning of the game, when he was losing. His long slender legs are bright with perspiration, his shirt has dark circles at the armpits, a long ragged icicle-shaped sweat stain down the middle, and his scalp glistens in the overhead light.

"You lost!" Nelson cries accusingly, jabbing his finger at the air between him and his uncle, as if to create a shock wave that would knock James to the ground.

"Sorry, O Great Leader," James says. His voice is weak, exhausted. "Your daddy's too much for me."

Pleased to hear this, Hampton smiles at James.

James slumps onto the bench next to Iris. "I feel sorry for *you,*" he says to her. "The man is tireless."

Daniel is offended by James's little joke. It is unbearable to think about Hampton's untiring ardor, the sexual machinery going on and on.

"He rinses his cottage cheese to take out the last one percent of milk fat," Iris says. "What do you expect?"

"Hello, Daniel," Hampton says. He opens his gym bag and pulls out a small white terry cloth towel with which he carefully dries, first his forehead, then the wings of his nose, then his chin.

"I was watching you play," Daniel says. "I'm just learning." He is acutely aware that everything he says could very well be subject to multiple interpretations, and that one day if—no, *when*—Hampton learns the truth, then it will all be remembered, ransacked for meaning.

Nelson has scrambled off Iris's lap. He takes the racquet from his uncle's hands and grabs the ball and hits it. It bounces and then rolls down the long hall, and then over the ledge, where it falls to the ground floor. Hampton snaps his fingers and points in Nelson's face.

"Get it," Hampton says. "Now."

Nelson doesn't say anything, but the skin on his face is suddenly drawn, mottled, he looks like someone who has been in the freezing cold.

"Take it easy, Hampton," Iris says. "That doesn't work with him." She turns to the boy. "Go on, Nellie, do as your father says."

"No!!" Nelson screams. "You get it."

The vehemence startles Iris and she lets go of the leash. Scarecrow goes straight for Daniel. After bounding up on Daniel and uncoiling her long tongue in the direction of his face, she suddenly lies down before him, resting her chin on her forepaws. Then, with a couple sharp barks, she rolls onto her back, exposing the bare pink-and-black skin of her belly, her eyes glazed with adoration.

"Scarecrow!!" Iris calls out, her voice sharp, nervous. "What are you doing?"

Hampton has folded his long arms over his hard, flat chest. "Seems like you've gone and won my doggie's heart," Hampton fairly drawls.

Meanwhile, on court number one, Bruce is hitting the ball to himself, harder and harder, until it sounds like gunshots.

———

"Do you mind if I sit next to you for a minute or two?"

Kate is sitting in the back pew of Saint Christopher's Church, which is eight miles outside of Leyden, on a curving dirt road, surrounded by open fields, where the dried remains of the harvested corn stalks rise and fall with the undulations of the land, in neat rows like markers in a cemetery. Startled by the soft, questioning voice, she turns to see the young priest next to her, tall, narrow, with an ascetic face and prematurely gray hair. He is the sort of man people say looks like a priest, even if he happens to be selling dress shirts in a department store, or walking in his baggy plaid bathing trunks on the beach.

"I didn't hear you sit down," Kate says.

"I'm sorry. Did I startle you? Were you praying?"

"I was really just closing my eyes. I'm collecting my thoughts."

"I see you come in here from time to time," the priest says. "I thought it was time we met."

"My name's Katherine Ellis. I'm not Catholic." She extends her hand.

"I'm Father Joseph Sidlowski. And I *am* Catholic." He takes her hand, shakes it. His touch is spectral, she could be dreaming him.

"I go to a lot of churches," Kate says. "But this one is just so lovely, it's one of the nicest in the area, I think."

Father Sidlowski looks up at the planked ceiling, the simple blue-and-yellow stained glass windows. "It really is," he says, as if the beauty of the place had never occurred to him before. "Do you know its history?"

"No."

"The farm right behind us and all the land around us, about four hundred acres, used to be owned by the Bailey family. Does that name mean anything to you?"

"I know Bailey Road."

"We're on Bailey Road, and there's the Bailey Building right in the village. The patriarch of the Bailey family was named Peter Bailey. He outlived three wives and ten of his thirteen children. In his seventies—this was in about 1880—he converted to Catholicism and built this church for himself and his family. There were no other Catholic churches nearby. It has something of the barn about it, don't you think? Anyway, he died in his nineties and he left an endowment to the archdiocese to keep Saint Christopher's open for one hundred years. The churchyard is filled with the remains of Baileys, as well as the graves of the priests who have worked here. Part of my own pastoral duties is to make certain those graves are well kept. The Bailey family is scattered now, and most of the priests who are buried here have no family to speak of. I think sometime in the next few years we'll see the doors to this chapel closed for the last time. We have a modest congregation and I suspect that when the hundred years are up and there is no income to support Saint Christopher's, they'll turn this place into an antiques shop."

"Just what the world needs."

Sidlowski shows his teeth in a slow approximation of a smile. "May I ask what brings you to Saint Christopher's?" His voice is low, confidential, though there is no one else in the church.

"It's very peaceful here," Kate says. She looks around the small church—the dark, heavily varnished painting of the dying Jesus recumbent in his stricken mother's lap, a few votive candles twinkling in their red glass holders, the simple wooden cross, unusually austere. "I've been thinking a lot about . . . things, and it's easier for me to have my thoughts in a church than it is at home."

"May I show you something?" Father Sidlowski asks Kate. "It'll only take a moment."

Kate follows the priest through the church. Their footsteps echo in the stillness and she wonders how he could have sat next to her without her hearing his approach. He leads her through a small doorway off the nave of the church and into his office. It's a small, windowless room, with books and magazines piled in every corner. A banged-up metal desk and a swivel chair are the only furniture. The fax machine on the edge of the desk is receiving a transmission as they walk in; Kate sneaks a peek at what's coming in—it seems to be from a travel agency, she sees a drawing of an airplane and the words "Christmas Travel Bargains." The walls are bare, except for one old painting in an ornate gilt frame. The image on the canvas is of a dark-haired woman in a modest brown robe, on her knees before a child's crib. Her hands are clasped prayerfully and blood drips from them. The crib is suffused with golden light.

"That's Saint Mary Frances," Sidlowski says, his voice suddenly intimate, suffused with gentleness, as if this were upsetting news he must break to her. "She died at the end of the eighteenth century and was canonized about sixty years after her death."

"I never heard of her," Kate says. "I don't really know very much about saints. As I said, I'm not—"

"Catholic," Sidlowski cuts in. "I realize that. But she's a lovely saint, one of my favorites. Not very well known here, but greatly loved in Naples. But do you see why I wanted you to see this painting?"

Kate redirects her attention to the image. The canvas is old, the paint is muddy, and the surface veneer is cracked into a thousand little jigsaw sections.

"She looks so much like you," Sidlowski says. "Don't you see the resemblance?"

Kate shakes her head. She sees nothing of herself in the face of Mary Frances. All there is in common is the dark-brown hair, brown eyes; everything else about Mary Frances seems merely average, even generic: average height, average weight. Oh, maybe a little something in the mouth, after all, that thin, broad upper lip, and maybe, also, a certain boyishness of chin. And the shoulders.

"I still think of myself as having blonde hair," Kate says. "Though I haven't since I was ten years old. But it was such a part of my identity, and such a part of my parents' celebration of me. The picture of myself that I carry within me will always be of some pink little girl with white-blonde hair. Oh my God, how my parents suffered when my hair went dark."

"It's not just the coloring," says Sidlowski. Whatever tact he had when first pointing the saint out to Kate is falling away now. His voice is eager, insistent. "It's the face, the shape of the head, and something else, something ineffable."

"I don't really see it," Kate says apologetically. "But thank you, I guess. I don't relate to saints, Father. I don't really believe in them."

"But it's a matter of historical record. And this is her birthday month. She was born October 6. October 6 was the day of the storm," Sidlowski says. "It made me think of her."

"Why is that?" Kate is uneasy with any mention of that unexpected, chaos-inducing snow. The storm has come to mean two things to her: her narrow escape from the roaming Star of Bethlehem boys, and Daniel spending the night with Iris, a night that, the more she thinks about it, almost certainly became the occasion for Daniel's long desire to finally find consummation. Kate cannot see a broken tree—and there are still thousands in Windsor County—without pain in her chest.

"Are you all right?" Father Sidlowski asks.

"Tell me about her," Kate says, gesturing toward the painting. "What's wrong with her hands? Why is she bleeding?"

"She was called Mary Frances of the Five Wounds." He waits to see if Kate understands those wounds refer to the five stabs of the Roman spears in Jesus' crucified body. "She had a very difficult life. Even after she joined an order, her father, who detested her, and, if you ask me, harbored and perhaps even acted upon incestuous feelings toward her, insisted she continue to live in his house as a servant. When Mary Frances's father was done with her, he passed her along to a local priest, a fanatic in the Jansenist tradition, who continued Mary's ill treatment. She remained the priest's personal servant for the rest of her life, thirty-eight more years. Yet even in the midst of her degradation, Mary insisted on caring for others. She practiced regular personal mortifications, many of them quite painful, asking God to place in her own soul the suffering of all those trapped in Purgatory, and asking, as well, to share the pain of her sick neighbors, most of whom treated her with contempt."

He looks at Kate, sees her pained expression, and lowers his voice, almost to a murmur.

"You said you were going from church to church. Would you mind my asking why?"

"I'm being treated with contempt, too, Father," Kate says. She steps toward him. The floor is soft, it seems as if her feet are sinking in through the wood. A sudden dizziness, the world spins, once, twice. *What's happening to me?* She grabs Sidlowski's arm to keep her balance.

———

Daniel is wracked with jealousy now that it is the weekend and Hampton is home. He suspects that there is no one in the world who would sympathize with his agony, not even Iris. And what puts him even further from sympathy's comforting embrace is that he is harming other people. He is lying to Kate, though he tells himself that he would tell her the truth and take the necessary steps to separate their lives if only he hadn't promised Iris not to make any precipitous moves. The fact is that Iris's swearing him to silence fits in with his own reluctance to say the terrible thing to Kate. He is betraying Hampton, who is not really a friend or a man toward whom Daniel has ever had warm feelings, but who is, at least, a fellow human being, and worthy of respect and decent treatment. And he is betraying Iris—he has slept with Kate as a way of keeping a modicum of domestic peace, simply a matter of slapping up some wallpaper to cover the cracks in the plaster.

His only comfort is the Windsor Bistro, which he discovered a couple of weeks ago quite by accident. Before the storm, the Windsor Bistro seemed well on its way to being a losing proposition, a small, pleasant place, with a little gas fireplace and a Colonial chandelier, but there were never more than six or eight people eating at the same time. The owner and cook, Doris Snyder, a shy, frugal woman with a starburst birthmark on her forehead, stocked as little fresh food as possible, afraid, as she was, that most of it would end up in the garbage. By the time of the October snow, the Windsor Bistro was beginning to have that doomed air of a fighter looking for a place to fall. But then the storm hit, and the Bistro was the first place in Leyden to reopen, and anyone who was brave or restless enough to leave home gathered there for companionship. Doris's confidence grew each time the door opened, and soon she was greeting everyone personally, serving free drinks and complimentary desserts. After a couple of nights, she convinced her boyfriend, a mentally unstable but handsome man named Curtis, who had not left their house in six months, to bring his guitar in and sing his repertoire of Neil Young, Jim Croce, and Jackson Browne songs.

Daniel has become a regular. The place is crowded tonight and it is only his position as one of the original, favored customers that allows him to occupy a table all to himself. The owner's boyfriend has not come in; his place on the stool to the side of the bar is taken by an old grade-school friend of Daniel's, a bushy-browed man named Chris Kiley, who accompanies himself on a little Yamaha keyboard while he sings sultry rhythm and blues songs about marital chaos, such as "Me and Mrs. Jones" and "Who's Making Love to Your Old Lady (While You're Out Making Love)." These songs feel like anthems in the confines of the Bistro, which, aside from being the only place in Leyden open past midnight, seems to have become a refuge for people whose deepest impulses have brought them into conflict with what society expects of them. There at the bar sits the principal of the high school with the new second-grade teacher fresh from college in Colorado. There at the table next to Daniel's sits Clive Mason, whose wife is dying of breast cancer, with his arm around Mary Gallagher, whose husband is a state patrolman serving three years in prison for grand larceny. And now they are joined by Ethan Cohen, who owns a women's clothing shop next to the George Washington Inn, and Shane Chilowitcz, who teaches performance art over at the college, where he lives with his Polish wife, who is at home minding their six children.

> Got no one to turn to
> Tired of being alone
> Feel like breaking up
> Somebody's home.

Ah, truer words were never sung, Daniel thinks. He looks up from his book, habitually scanning the place for Iris. Though in the week he has been coming here every night, he has yet to see her, he continually expects her to walk in at any moment. It's maddening to be constantly on the lookout for her, but it gives him a gambler's fervid hope that something transforming is just about to happen.

The singer sways behind his keyboard, surrounded by customers, who are also swaying to the music—a few are singing along. It has become even more crowded around the bar. There are people standing three deep, talking, laughing with piercing animation, signaling the newly hired bartender for drinks.

Standing near the bar is Mercy, Ruby's baby-sitter. She is dressed to look older than her age—plenty of makeup, a tailored brown jacket over a black scoop-necked blouse, ironed jeans, heels. She looks like one of the young women at the bank—sobriety and trustworthiness mixed with a kind of singles-bar brassiness. She has been trying to get Daniel's attention, and now that he has finally seen her she smiles and walks over to his table.

"Hello, Mr. Emerson," she says. She has put so much color on her lashes it seems a struggle to keep her eyes open. She holds a glass of beer with a thin slice of lime floating in its amber.

"Hello, Mercy," he says. He almost asks, *What are you doing here?* But, the custom of the Bistro prevents such snoopiness.

She takes his smile as an invitation to sit. She arranges herself carefully in the bentwood chair, as if she were taking her place on a jury. The rim of her glass is faintly red from her lipstick. "I've been thinking about that stuff you told me," she says. Her voice drops to a whisper. "About becoming an emancipated minor?"

"It's a big step, Mercy. It's basically a desperation move."

"I really have to get out of there," she replies, and as she says it the man with whom she arrived at the Bistro strides from the bar to Daniel's table. He is more than twice her age. His name is Sam Holland, he is one of the area's writers, not the most celebrated but possibly the richest, and he is someone Daniel knows. A couple of years ago, just when Daniel, Kate, and Ruby were moving back to Leyden, Holland's teenage son had gotten himself into a lot of trouble, and Sam had talked to Daniel about handling the kid's defense.

Whatever chagrin Sam might feel about being away from his wife, or from being seen with a girl two years younger than his son, is nowhere in evidence as he thrusts his hand out and grasps Daniel with a manly grip.

"Hello, Danny," Sam says. He is wearing a blazer, a white shirt, and blue jeans; his thick, suddenly pewter hair is swept straight back. "How'd your house make it through the storm?"

Daniel thinks about this for a moment. "We took a couple of hits," he says.

"We were decimated," Sam says, with a wide, radiant smile. He has dragged a chair over and sits close to Mercy. Daniel imagines their knees are touching. "Were you home for it?" Sam asks.

"Not in the beginning."

"At least I was home," Sam says. "That made it semimanageable. Where were you?" he asks Mercy.

"At my girlfriend's. They let us out of school early and like ten of us walked over to her house."

"Party time," says Sam.

"Kind of, if you call not being able to watch TV or wash your hands a party."

"That's exactly what I call a party," he says. "That's the trouble with your generation, you don't know a goddamned party when you see one." He turns back toward Daniel. "So where were you when the storm hit?"

"I was at Hampton Welles and Iris Davenport's house," Daniel says.

"My girlfriend baby-sits their kid," Mercy says. "He hit her on the head with like a toy truck. She had to get twenty stitches on her scalp, but you can't see them because the hair's grown back."

"That's a lot to endure for three-fifty an hour," Sam says.

"Try eight," Mercy says.

"Well, for eight dollars an hour I might take getting hit by a truck— you did say it was a *toy* truck, didn't you?" He looks at Daniel, as if he, at least, would understand the joke: the ways we disfigure ourselves in order to put bread on the table.

"No one wants to baby-sit that kid," Mercy says. "He's like really really mean."

"He's not even five years old," Daniel says. "Maybe your friends are reacting to something else."

Mercy, having no wish to antagonize Daniel, and, in fact, wanting only to keep him on her side, lowers her eyes.

"I have to go to the ladies' room," she says.

As soon as she is safely away, Sam leans closer to Daniel.

"I'm helping her with her homework," he says, deadpan.

"Take her home, Sam," Daniel says. "You really have to stop seeing her. Her father's crazy and a cop, it's going to end very badly."

"I know," Sam says.

"Don't you worry about her, Sam? Do you know what happens to those girls? They end up dancing in a cage with spangles on their nipples. You know what I mean?"

"Look, it's not that simple. I could end up dancing in a cage somewhere, too."

"You could end up in jail, is where you could end up. She's a kid."

"I love her. I'm drawn to her, and I don't have a list of reasons why. It just happened. You think I wanted this? My whole life is in the process of going down the drain."

"Then do something about it."

"I tried. Do you have any idea how foolish I feel, being here with . . . with someone so inappropriate," he says. "But the thing is, I can't help it, I literally cannot help it. Everyone thinks being with a young girl is like finding the fountain of youth. The truth is, it's just the opposite. First of all, I can barely concentrate on sex because I'm so busy sucking in my stomach. And then, when I get out of bed and I make these little groans, you know, the way a man does, the knee hurts, the back, a little sore shoulder, whatever. You groan, after forty-five you get out of bed and you make a little noise, I don't care if you're Peter Pan. So I get up, straighten myself out, and Mercy's all breathless, panicked. 'What's wrong, what's wrong?' she's asking. 'Nothing,' I tell her, 'absolutely nothing.' And she says, 'But you were making these noises.' And I have to tell her, 'Honey, that's what you do when you wake up in the morning. You groan.' And she nods, trying to be a good sport about it, but I swear to God, Daniel, I have never felt so fucking old in my entire life. These guys who think they're going to get a second at bat in the youth league by hanging out with some young girl, they've got it exactly wrong. You want to feel young, find yourself some old broad and run circles around her."

Tonight's singer is finishing up; the applause sounds like rain on a tin roof. Daniel's eyes habitually scan the room; he cannot let go of the dream of Iris suddenly appearing. He imagines her sashaying through this convivial throng, her sitting next to him, a tilted, slightly apprehensive look of arrival and surrender on her face, her bony knee knocking against him, her night voice an octave lower, cracked with fatigue, the whites of her eyes creamy, like French vanilla.

Through the pack of people comes Ferguson Richmond, grinning maniacally, wearing a pair of catastrophic brown pants, his hair slicked back. On his arm is the blind girl, Marie Thorne, who, though her eyes are secreted behind dark glasses, looks festive and in high spirits.

Ferguson greets him like an old friend, and Marie, too, is effusive. It makes Daniel think that the two of them have been talking about him, speculating about his having spent the night at Iris's, and that now, seeing him here, at the nocturnal headquarters for the town's transgressors, their hypothesis is proved. Without waiting to be asked, Ferguson drags two more chairs over to Daniel's table. He sits Marie next to Daniel and then squeezes himself between Sam and Mercy. As he sits, he seems to notice for the first time how young Mercy is—in fact, he does an almost comic double take.

And then, with no apparent provocation, Ferguson reaches across the table and takes Marie's hand and brings it to his lips, and he kisses her with loud, smacking sounds, almost in a burlesque of affection. The gesture is shocking and everyone at the table laughs, including Daniel, though the sight of Ferguson's fantastically uncivilized behavior makes Daniel's longing for Iris all the more excruciating.

Ferguson sees the dismay in Daniel's face. "Seen much of the lovely Iris Davenport lately?" he asks.

"No," Daniel says, in a voice not quite able to bear the weight of even a one-word answer.

"Old Daniel found himself at her house the first night of the storm," Ferguson explains to the rest of them, curling his fingers into quotation marks when he says "found himself."

"So he tells us," says Sam.

———

At home that night, Kate sips her way through a bottle of zinfandel and talks on the phone to Lorraine Del Vecchio, whom she thinks of as her best friend, though now that Kate has moved out of New York City, they rarely see each other, and their phone calls, which even a year ago were daily, now take place only two or three times a month, though what they have come to lack in frequency they have made up for in duration. Except for her undergraduate years spent across the country at Reed College, where she studied Plato and abused amphetamines, Lorraine has never lived anywhere but Manhattan. When Kate first met her, Lorraine was an editor at *Cosmopolitan;* Lorraine had read Kate's novel, *Peaches and Cream,* and had fought to have it excerpted in *Cosmo,* only to be overruled at the eleventh hour by the editor-in-chief.

By the time the deal had fallen through, Lorraine and Kate had already established a telephone rapport. Lorraine loved Kate's acerbic style, her pitilessness that didn't stop with the skewering of subsidiary characters but also included the novel's narrator, who was, Lorraine assumed, a stand-in for the author herself. But what Lorraine particularly loved about the novel was its depiction of the beauty business as a world of harpies from which intelligent girls must rescue themselves—in fact, it was precisely the novel's send-up of dermatology, and its underlying fury at a world that attached such value to appearance, that prevented Lorraine from buying it for her magazine, where half the articles and nearly all the advertising were meant to encourage young women to be ceaselessly fretful about their appearance. When running a portion of *Peaches and Cream* was torpedoed at the last minute, Lorraine called Kate personally to break the bad news, and she sounded so distressed that Kate agreed to meet her for lunch at the end of the week.

Daniel had warned Kate about Lorraine. He didn't know Lorraine, but he was getting a sense of the women who became Kate's most passionate readers, and he had duly noted the expressions on their faces when they finally met Kate and realized that she, unlike her heroine or themselves, was quite beautiful. Like the heroine, Kate had been entered into Beautiful Baby contests when she was an infant, and her parents *did* openly grieve when her hair turned from blonde to brown, and they did give her Clairol rinses when she was nine years old and send her to bed with her hair wrapped in a scarf soaked in lemon juice, and when, at thirteen, a birdshot spray of pimples appeared on her forehead, her father, a doctor himself, sent her to a dermatologist in Washington, D.C.—but not, as it occurred in the novel, all the way to Zurich. The other indignities visited upon the novel's teenage narrator—how she wakes up one day with virtually a full mustache, the involvement with a Santeria cult, her entire body being encased in defoliating wax, the liposuction performed at midnight like a backstreet abortion—were entirely fictional, as was the section in which the mother's bridge club accidentally drops the narrator's diet pills into their coffee, having gotten them confused with saccharin tablets, and the subsequent freak-out, during which the ladies go after each other like wildcats and one of them ends up dying of a heart attack.

"You've struck a chord with all women with unfortunate looks," Daniel said. "And when they see you they feel ripped off, like you've tricked them into believing you're one of them."

To Kate's immense relief, the woman she found waiting for her at the Russian Tea Room was completely presentable, in fact, great-looking—with short black hair, bright-green dramatic eyes, the serene, commanding face and ample bust of a figurehead carved into the prow of a whaling ship. "Oh, look at you," Lorraine exclaimed upon first seeing Kate. "You're gorgeous, you bum." She clutched her heart. "How could you do this to me?"

The accusation was made humorously and it might have been meant to flatter Kate. Yet she felt she had just been slapped in the face, and despite the fact that their rapport soon moved beyond what Kate considered the hallucinogenic stage—a kind of jokey alternative reality in which Lorraine pretended Kate was ravishing and she herself was homely and doomed—and onto a truer rapport, that first remark created a shadow presence in their friendship. This shadow presence insisted that Kate was the fortunate one and Lorraine, despite her well-paying job, numerous sexual adventures, supportive family, and brownstone apartment with a fireplace and two skylights, was the hard-luck case. It meant that Kate was somehow beholden to equalize things between them, by deferring to Lorraine.

Tonight, Lorraine has a cold, and she uses the first part of their phone time complaining about it. Lately, Lorraine has become a little screwy about her health. As she approaches thirty-eight, the age her own mother died of cervical cancer, Lorraine is more and more putting herself in the care of not only doctors but also an acupuncturist, a masseuse, an aromatherapist, two nutritionists, and even a psychic whose specialty is disease.

"I spent the day in bed," she says.

"For a cold?" Kate asks, hoping her disapproval isn't apparent.

"Yes, for a cold. And I was in a major O. J. mood. I really wanted to watch the trial in the privacy of my own home. Watching it at the office sucks, so many interruptions."

"So? Did anything happen?" Kate could not watch today's proceedings because, oddly enough, she was too busy finishing an article about the trial—an article that Lorraine herself had commissioned.

"I just had this wild premonition that he was going to crack, and stand up in the middle of the court and confess."

"That's not going to happen."

"I realize that. How's the article going?"

"I should be done in a couple more days." Kate feels the subtle change, she is suddenly in her writer-fending-off-an-editor mode. "Three at the most."

"It's not going to do us any good if the trial's over."

"The trial has got months to go."

"Not if he confesses. What about Daniel? What's his take on this whole thing? I mean, doesn't he see it as a kind of indictment of the legal profession, this guy who has so obviously assassinated his poor wife and now he's just dragging out the proceedings, thanks to the efforts of a team of high-priced lawyers, all of whom have probably entered into pacts with Satan."

Kate is silent for a moment. "Daniel's starting to make noises as if he believes O. J. is innocent."

"You're kidding."

"He thinks racist cops might have tampered with the evidence. The Fuhrman thing. He thinks all sorts of things."

"He actually thinks O. J. is innocent?"

"I don't know." Here is the hard part. "Let me take a sip of wine and tell you what I really think."

"Sip away."

Kate finishes the entire glass, dabs her palm against her chin, where a single red drop clings, and then refills her glass.

"He has a wicked crush on this black woman and I think he's tailoring his O. J. opinions to suit her fashion."

"Oh, Kate, are you sure?" Lorraine's voice sounds warm, motherly. Lorraine's compassion always comes as a sort of pleasant surprise, though she never fails to show it.

"No, not really. But . . . I'm pretty sure."

"Who's the woman?"

"Oh, just some local mom, a perpetual grad student, with an absentee husband."

"I'm not getting a clear picture."

"Her name's Iris. I really feel like killing her with my bare hands, I feel like O. J.-ing her. She's reasonably attractive, in a freckly sort of way. She has Adored Daughter Syndrome, she just sort of sits there and expects all this attention. She has some demented kid who Ruby likes, so there's all these occasions to get together, Daniel and Iris. You should see them together. Daniel's entire body becomes one big boner."

"And you?" Lorraine asks.

"What do you mean? What about me?"

"Are you going to let this temptress take your boyfriend away?"

Lorraine is being far too lighthearted about this, and as a way of telling her so Kate lets that last remark hang in the air for a few extra moments.

"I don't know what I'm going to do, Lorraine. When I first started noticing how fixated on this woman he was getting, I thought to myself: Oh well, who cares, live and let live, screw and let screw, whatever."

"And now?"

"It's getting to me. It's having a perverse effect."

"Oh yes, I know how that works. You're starting to fall in love with him again, right?"

"Something like that. I don't require a lot of care and feeding, you know. I don't need to be adored, or ravished, I don't need little poems slipped under my pillow, or a rose on my breakfast tray. But, I really do *not* want him to leave me. That really doesn't work for me."

"We're such idiots."

"It's not as if I fell *out* of love with Daniel."

"I know."

"I'm used to him, with all the good and bad that implies. Anyhow, we had sort of an arrangement. We're both moderates, you know what I mean? We hate excess, neither of us even likes *Romeo and Juliet*. I feel betrayed in that way, too. Suddenly, I sense this willingness in him to be crucified on passion's cross. Ugh. He's becoming a different person."

"And then there's the small matter of Ruby," says Lorraine. "I thought he was so devoted to her."

"I'm not even thinking about that. He's not going to *leave* me. He would never do anything to upset Ruby. He worships her."

"What's the café-au-lait absentee husband like?"

"His name is Hampton."

"Oh God, they have the best names. Hampton what?"

"Welles. He's Ivy League, Wall Street, so bourgeois he makes Martha Stewart seem like Karen Finley."

"And does he think O. J. is innocent, too? It would be interesting to find out."

"I don't know. O. J. may be a little dark for Hampton's taste."

Just then, Kate hears wracking coughs coming from Ruby's bedroom. She has been in and out of respiratory sickness ever since the storm—the ride home on the snowmobile did her in.

"Can you hold on for a minute?" Kate asks.

"Did you get another call? Don't take it."

"No, Ruby's coughing her brains out. I better look in on her."

"Where's Danny boy?"

"Out. I'm not actually sure where." As soon as Kate says this, two things occur: Ruby's coughing stops, and a heavy, soggy sense of emotional panic settles over Kate. "Oh good," she says, "false alarm," while in fact she is just now feeling her first intimations of real alarm.

"He's out and you have no idea where?" Lorraine says. "That's not like him."

"Well, lately it has been."

"There's nothing to do up there, nowhere to go. Where does he go?"

"There's this place in town, a bar. Lately he's been going there."

"A bar?" Lorraine's voice is full of the kind of scorn that tries to masquerade as incredulity.

"It's not that extraordinary, is it?" Kate tries to sound bemused, but her blood has begun to race. She has an impulse to simply slam the phone down and get in the car, surprise the little fucker right in his new nighttime haunt. Yet just as she is about to hang up, she realizes the reason she has called Lorraine in the first place. "We had this monster snowstorm," she says.

"I know, I saw it on Fox. Weird."

"We didn't have electricity for four days, no heat, no water, nothing. And we were trapped here, no cars were moving, every road was closed."

"You should really move back to New York."

"Last year a water main exploded under your street and your entire apartment was filled with mud."

"True, but at least I had heat. I had lights, I could read. And I could leave, I could go to my health club, I could have a watercress-and-goat-cheese salad at Cafe Luxembourg."

"It was sort of fun, getting back to basics, the three of us camping out. And when the snow stopped the sun came out and it was sort of mild."

"I don't ever want to be in a position where I'm glad the sun came out."

"But for the first day I was here alone, and *that* was a little weird."

"Where were Daniel and Ruby?"

"At Iris's."

"You're fucking kidding."

"And while I was here alone, some boys broke into the house."

"What are you talking about?"

"There's a home for delinquent boys, mostly black kids from the city. Some escaped during the power outage and they ended up here."

"Oh my God. Are you all right?"

"Yes, I'm fine. They never even saw me. They came in to use the facilities."

"They shit in your house?"

"In the toilet."

"Well, that was civilized."

Kate is about to say something and realizes her voice is suddenly not available to her, it seems submerged.

"Were you hiding?" Lorraine asks. "Where were you?"

Kate takes a deep breath. *Okay,* she thinks. *Steady.* "I was pretty scared," she says. "These were not nice boys."

"They could have raped you, killed you."

"I suppose. A tree hit the house and they ran like hell."

"A tree." Lorraine snorts contemptuously. "And Daniel was at Iris's house."

"That could not be helped. He couldn't get home."

"The poor lamb. Listen to me, Kate. Okay?"

"No, please. Don't be smarter than me about this, don't open my eyes to the obvious, I don't want to be pummeled with your insight."

"I'm just—"

"I know. I'm just not ready. Anyhow, I'm getting out of here."

"Where are you going?"

"To that bar Daniel's been hanging out at. Windsor Bistro."

"Good. And if he's there with her—"

"He's not."

"Just remember, if O. J. can get away with it, so can you."

After hanging the phone up, Kate sits in her chair and finishes her glass of wine, waiting for her pulse to stop pounding. She goes to the window at the front of the house—the repairman who replaced the panes did a sloppy job and there are smears of putty on the mullions—and looks out at the night. The sky is a steep dome of bright stars. The moon is pale and wafer-thin; it casts its light down on the split and toppled trees around the house; a little patch of brightness reflects on the chrome of her car's back bumper.

She remembers: Ruby, with a kind of start, the way you do when you drive away from the house and suddenly remember you've left the stove on. How can she go to the Windsor Bistro and leave Ruby all alone? How far away is it? Ten minutes, okay that's twenty minutes round-trip. Let's call it twenty-five, allowing for petty delays. And all she would need is fifteen minutes at the Bistro. That's forty minutes altogether, and possibly a lot less.

She walks into Ruby's bedroom. The room is softly visible through the glow of a fairy princess night-light. Kate stands over her daughter's—her captor's—bed and gazes down at her. She sleeps on her back, with the satin border of the blanket drawn up to her chin. Her skin is creamy, her brows dark and sensuous. Deep childish breaths, with a little bronchial burr at the end of each one. Ruby is a deep sleeper, she plunges down through the barely lit terrain of her own inner life, one hundred fathoms deep, dreaming of gigantic doors and talking animals. She almost never wakes during the night—even those wracking coughs left her sleep undisturbed. *Forty-five minutes,* thinks Kate. *She'll never know the difference.* Yet a moment later anxiety takes its customary spot in Kate's consciousness, sits with the authority of an old fortune-teller and turns the cards over one by one: here is the child waking, she is calling your name, here is the furnace leaking noxious fumes, here is an invisible frayed wire festering in the wall, here is a thief, here is a kidnapper, and this card is five black boys coming back for who knows what. What are you thinking? What could possibly be in your mind? You are staying in this house. And he knows it.

10

The problem was there was no space to walk in; the woods had imploded. They were walking in circles, continually tripping over vines, stumbling over fallen trees, getting scraped by branches, stomping into sudden pools of still water, sometimes walking right into a standing tree. It was strangely insulting, like being toyed with. Isolated in their despair, they walked for half an hour without speaking.

Then, suddenly, a stretch where last month's storm seemed to have done little damage. They walked for three minutes without having to change course. And though they didn't know what direction they were going in, the mere fact of keeping a constant course gave them a bit of encouragement. They were not, after all, in the middle of some vast uncharted wilderness. They were only a hundred miles north of the city. How far could you go without ending up on some stretch of asphalt or in someone's backyard? But then they reached a devastated grove of locusts, the saplings with bark spiked with thorns, like giant, petrified roses. There were so many of them down on the ground, or leaning against each other in a swoon, that it would have been impossible to get through them or past them even in daylight.

Nightlife. Daniel comes down the stairs. In flannel pajamas, a House of Blues T-shirt. Here comes the approximate orphan, here comes the almost father, here comes the world's worst ersatz husband. But he feels none of these things. Night is the time of desire and love seizes him, shakes him silly. Outside: a gay dancing little flurry of snow blows past the porch light. His heart sings like a cello inside his chest.

Being alive is a ceaseless project of self-forgiveness, and Daniel forgives himself. He knows he is acting badly. He knows he ought to be feverish with shame. But he's not, he has resisted it, like those doctors who tend a ward full of infected patients but who themselves don't fall ill. Daniel has resisted his own feelings of guilt, he has become immune to himself.

The beauty of the world is, finally, overwhelming, it's too fragile, too perfect, he must turn away. He faces a wall and glances at the aerial photograph of his house hanging there. Last year two men appeared at the door, a squared-off pilot with a rough face and a failed mustache, a lanky photographer in Trotsky glasses and a Planet Hollywood satin windbreaker. For three hundred dollars they offered to fly over the house and take a picture of it from above. "We can see ourselves as God sees us," Kate had said, strangely enthusiastic about the idea. The finished product was delivered six months later when the barnstormers were back in Windsor County, and it hangs now in the living room, behind the green sofa.

Daniel, whose lover's heart has sprouted wings, now is airborne himself, and he enters the photograph in full flight, hovering above his own house and its snow-dappled ten acres. The smoke from his chimney, a slightly darker gray than the cold, sunless air, rises up, stings his eyes. His arms are extended, he swims away from it, wondering if at any moment he will come crashing down to earth but somehow knowing he is safe. He points his hands upward, hears the whoosh of the air as he zooms toward the dawn moon, which remains fully risen, stuck in the sky like a coin frozen beneath a thin sheet of ice. He tucks his chin in, peers down at the little town—the cold air crashes like cymbals against his eyes. There is the river, a blue-gray serpent upon whose chilly scales the waning moon reflects. The mountains to the west are humped in mist and darkness; the lights of a few houses and headlights flicker like the sparkle of dew on the coat of a sleeping bear.

He flies in through the window of his parents' bedroom, where Carl and Julia sleep side by side on their backs, as still as carvings on a sarcophagus. The electronic numbers on their digital clock, burnt-orange, pulsate in the darkness of the room. On Julia's side of the bed, the night table is stacked with books, but all Carl's table holds is a lamp and a wristwatch, as if he already knows everything he cares to know. Upon the old Crouch and Fitzgerald trunk at the end of the bed, where extra blankets and fragile quilts are packed in mothballs, they have lain their matching plaid robes. The tidiness and modesty of the room makes Daniel ache with love and a mysterious sort of pity, a pity that is also the deepest kind of respect. The room smells of liniment, eucalyptus, detergent, and slow human decay. Daniel hovers above them, wanting to touch them but hesitating, for either he is incorporeal or they are. He rests his ear near his father's chest, listens to the ruminative thump of the old man's heart. It is time to start spreading all that forgiveness he has been giving to himself. *Thank you for feeding me, thank you for sending me to school, thank you for staying the course.* He kisses Julia's cool forehead, a smooth stone in a rushing stream. *Thank you thank you.*

He backs out through the window, the branches of a tall hemlock scrape against him as he gains altitude. He sees a police car, the beams of its headlights are going from side to side. He flies alongside it. His old friend Derek Pabst is at the wheel, sipping from a Styrofoam coffee cup, his uniform cap on the seat beside him. He has xeroxed pictures of the boys who escaped from Star of Bethlehem taped to the dashboard of his car. He is driving fast, his lips are gray and pursed, they are like a wall through which no words can penetrate. Derek pulls off the county road and speeds across a short, singing bridge onto an unpaved road. His tires churn up long choking curls of dust.

Daniel is above the river now, sailing past the mansions. He enters Eight Chimneys. Squirrels are in the entrance hall, wildly chasing each other around. The air is cold in the old dank house, colder than outside. He hears a sound and finds Ferguson in the huge, cluttered, far from clean kitchen in his pajama bottoms, standing in front of the refrigerator, scratching idly at his pale bare chest. He suddenly grabs the heel of a roast beef and a carton of orange juice, and he heads back upstairs with it, with Daniel following. On the second story of the house, Ferguson turns right, walking past a dozen closed doors, until he comes to the staircase to the third floor, where once the servants lived. Marie is waiting for him at the top of the stairs, naked. Her little tangle of pubic hair looks particularly black against her colorless skin. The skin around her nipples is wrinkled with cold. She stands on her toes, writhing with happiness and anticipation. "Hurry," she whispers. "I'm so thirsty." As soon as Ferguson is on the landing, Marie takes the carton of orange juice from him, sniffs it, and then drinks it down. She finishes with a loud, comical *Ahhhh,* shakes the carton to make sure it's empty, and then lets it drop and puts her arms around her disheveled, confused lover. He lifts her up as they kiss, she wraps her legs around him.

Daniel flies to Iris's house with one beat of his winged heart, blessing every house beneath him as he sails toward his beloved. She is in bed, awake and alone, propped up with the pillows behind her, and her portable computer resting on the hammock of blanket between her knees. He lights next to her, puts his arm around her, nuzzles her neck, kisses her cheekbone, the corner of her eye, and looks at the screen. *Dear Daniel,* she has written, but that is all. Her fingers rest on the keys. When Kate writes, her expression is avid, she is being fed and enjoying every bite, but Iris has a kind of shyness even within the privacy of her own thoughts, as if she is observing one part of herself while the other is half hidden behind a pillar.

Thank you, he says to her. Surely there is some way she can hear this. *Thank you for being so beautiful, thank you for not being too beautiful for me, thank you for your life, thank you for your breasts, let me touch them, can you feel that? That's my hand, this is my mouth, thank you for being so open and wet, thank you for putting me in your mouth, thank you for grabbing at the sheets when I kissed you between the legs, thank you for digging your fingers into my back, thank you for letting me sit at your table, thank you for letting me play with your dog, thank you for looking at me with your deep clear eyes . . .*

Iris lets out a long sigh and shuts her computer off. She reaches right through him as she places the little Compaq on her night table. She puts the pillows back in their normal places and lies flat, pulls the covers up to her chin.

And it is then that it strikes him: this will not end well. He has exceeded his capacities, he has somehow gotten more than he deserves, he has the sudden terrible knowledge that happiness of this magnitude can only lead to sorrow. Joy lifts you up and joy casts you down.

Now she is turning off the lamp on the night table. Her touch is too emphatic, the lamp totters, but she catches it before it falls, sets it right. *Good girl*. He lies next to her in the darkness, no living ghost has ever loved more fervently. He brings his nose almost into the crook of her neck and breathes her in, the smell of laundered cotton, and some ineffable spice.

Airborne again, flying close to the treetops, heading home. He slips into his own bed, Kate is sleeping deeply. A scent of alcohol comes off her skin. He props himself up on one elbow, disentangles a few of her hairs that have gotten stuck into the moist corner of her mouth. "I'm sorry," he whispers into her ear.

She opens her eyes. She looks damaged, badly used. "What did you say?" she asks.

11

They continued to walk, hoping to find a clearing, a way out. Once, most of this
land was pasture, grazed by cattle, but it hadn't seen a plow in over a hundred
years and left to its own had become a wild place. They climbed yet another hill—
this might have been steeper because they both had to hold on to trees to pull them-
selves up, or else they were getting tired.

And once they had scaled it, all they could see was more trees—except on one
side, where there was a sharp drop-off, leading to what looked like a large pond
filled with black water.

"We came from that direction," Hampton said uncertainly. He was pointing
down the hill upon which they stood, and off to the left. The night was gathering
quickly, the darkness was rushing in like water through the hull of a ship, cover-
ing everything.

Kate has prevailed upon Daniel to take a day and a night away from
home, together, and he cannot decently refuse her. They leave Ruby
with Carl and Julia, and then head out of town on County Road 100A, a
curving blacktop that winds its way past Leyden's two surviving commercial dairy farms—sagging wire fences, Delft-blue silos, black-and-
white Holstein cows—until it runs into a T-junction, at which they turn
onto the road to Massachusetts, where Kate has booked them a room—

their old room, their first room—at a huge ramshackle hotel in Stockbridge called the Sleeping Giant Inn.

On the drive, Kate reads to Daniel from the article she has just written about the O. J. Simpson case. As Kate reads, Daniel is silent, his jaw set, his eyes hooded—she has never seen him pay such fanatical attention to highway conditions, even the shadows of the wind-rocked hemlocks make him brake, he is continually readjusting his side and rearview mirrors, changing the tilt of the steering wheel, checking the gas and temperature gauges, anything to escape her two thousand words on O. J. Kate realizes that bringing up the case is not the best way to begin their Saturday getaway, but, perversely, she is unable to refrain. She isn't about to pretend that she has the slightest sympathy for a man who so wantonly committed murder and who is now trying to buy his way out of it. And she cannot help but feel that if she can only find the right fact, the right tone, the right line of logic, then Daniel himself will snap out of his ridiculous spell and see, as everyone else she knows and respects sees, that O. J. is as guilty as the Boston Strangler, or Richard Speck, or any of the other monsters.

"What do you think?" she asks. They are just turning off the Taconic, onto the road to Stockbridge, where there is an old roadside diner, with a neon sign showing a vast, noble Indian.

"Inadmissible," he says.

"Probably," Kate answers. "It's for a magazine. You know? For people sitting under hair dryers." Yet she cannot let his legal point stand unquestioned. "But why couldn't such information be used in court? It *is* relevant that he's been violent in the past, it helps establish a pattern of solving domestic issues in a completely brutal manner." No, this is not what she wants them to be talking about, but she can't give up the search for the right words, the verbal alchemy that would bring him around. Even as she drills through layer after layer of murk, she keeps her hopes up for the ultimate strike, that surging thrilling gusher of epiphanous recognition.

"I think if I were accused of some terrible crime," Daniel says slowly, seemingly as reluctant as Kate to discuss this case, "a lawyer or a writer could probably find some old girlfriend who'd be willing to trash me."

"Well, I certainly never would. No matter what anybody said, I would always think you were a good man."

He glances at her and colors. It looks for a moment as if he might even cry, and Kate thinks to herself: *Good. One for my side.*

———

The early afternoon train from Leyden pulls into Penn Station, and Iris, who has slept most of the ride and who nevertheless can barely keep her eyes open, stands up unsteadily and pulls her black nylon travel bag down from the overhead rack. She has packed one change of clothes, a night-gown, a plastic zippered bag full of toiletries (including her diaphragm), and a couple of thick, heavy books—what Hampton calls, in his Johnny Carson voice, "weighty tomes"—she has been meaning to read for thesis research purposes, and which take up more room than everything else she has brought with her to New York. She has settled into a kind of fugue-state of emotional neutrality, allowing the two hours' silence and the rhythmic rocking of the train to lull her into a strange, sad peacefulness. She realizes this time in the city alone with Hampton may well require of her a degree of watchfulness, a certain deftness of emotional ma-neuvering.

The arrangement is that she will taxi down to the apartment, and Hampton—who is meant to play squash at the Downtown Athletic Club with a Jamaican rum bottler—will meet her there no more than half an hour later. But as soon as Iris steps off the train, she sees Hampton wait-ing for her on the platform, craning his long neck and trying to pick her out of the stream of arriving passengers. She knows this is meant to pleasantly surprise her, but the sight of him makes her spirits plummet. He looks like a teacher striding down the rows of desks, passing out the questions to a surprise quiz.

He sees her. He raises his hand to signal her and she sees that—hor-rors—he is holding a long-stemmed rose. He has undoubtedly bought it from one of the vendors right here in Penn Station, but nevertheless he waves the flower at her, to signal her that this Saturday in Manhattan is meant to be one of high romance.

"What happened to your squash game?" Iris says, as Hampton kisses her cheek, takes her bag off her shoulder and hefts it onto his.

"I wanted to meet you," he says.

This leaves the question about his squash game unanswered. It isn't like Hampton to put personal life over business—actually, Iris has always *liked* this aspect of him—and she suspects he is here on the warm, smoky, stinking-of-diesel-fuel platform because his game has been cancelled.

She lags behind him as they make their way out. There's an escalator, but Hampton always chooses the stairs, for the sake of fitness. She admires his body as she walks behind him. He is wearing his Saturday attire: khaki pants, a white polo shirt under a dark-green cashmere sweater, brown loafers. Even his casual clothes are carefully chosen, crisply ironed, but of course there are no casual occasions for Hampton, not at the dinner table, not in bed, and certainly not out in public.

"Everything okay up in the country?" he asks. "How's Nellie?"

She doesn't bother to answer. He doesn't really expect an answer, he's just recording the fact that he's asked. Yet when they reach the main hall of the station, Hampton surprises her and repeats the question.

"Everything cool with Nellie?"

The simple, truthful answer would be: No. Nelson has been agitated, clingy, explosive, nagging, and oppositional. He has been putting Band-Aids on his hands and knees without any physical reason for doing so. He has been cruel to Scarecrow to the point where the usually patient and forgiving old dog will leave the room when she hears Nelson's footsteps. Every night since the storm—except when Hampton has been home—Nelson has come into her bed between midnight and two and slept there until he woke both himself and his mother by peeing his pajamas. And when she has whispered to him, "Nelson, get up, let's change your pj's," he has screamed at her like some crazed motorist on the freeway after a fender-bender. This morning, when she was backing her car out of the driveway, he was straining to break free of Iris's sister, who had driven her sporty little green Mazda up from Baltimore two days earlier to spend a little time with Iris before the weekend, and to give Nelson time to get used to her. Whatever level of trust and comfort he had reached seemed to be obliterated by the sight of Iris actually leaving: he was not only kicking and howling but he was also trying to sink his teeth into his aunt's restraining hand.

"He's okay," Iris says. "He was nervous about my leaving, but he loves Carol, so that made it a little easier."

"He'll be fine," Hampton says. He dislikes Carol, thinks of her as promiscuous, brassy, silly, unread; he cannot bear her prattling on about her real estate business. She is unmarried, her days are full of office tasks and her nights are full of boyfriends. Yet he cannot say anything critical of Carol, not now. It was, after all, his idea that he and Iris spend the weekend alone in the city together, and it was, he supposed, up to her to choose who would mind Nelson.

He knows that the energy is down between them right now and he has a pretty clear idea what the trouble is: she feels neglected, the romance of their life together has been subsumed by dailiness, it's an old story, even the men he sees in business, with whom he almost never has a personal conversation, hint that their own clever wives grumble about the lack of attention being paid to them, even if the wives themselves are in business, making deals, returning calls through the night. And Iris feels isolated, maybe even abandoned up there in Leyden—it cannot help but add to the mix of Iris's difficulties that she is swimming in a white sea.

And so, without exactly planning it that way, Hampton escorts her on a black tour of Manhattan: lunch at a black-owned, mostly black-frequented restaurant in the theater district, a place of large comfortable booths and Art Deco mirrors, where gorgeous black women in black pants and black silk shirts serve them crab cakes and collard greens, and after lunch a cab ride up near Harlem, where Hampton shows Iris a block of derelict brownstones a developer is in the process of snapping up. The developer is looking for investors and he has come to Hampton to help him put together an offering statement, but what Hampton wants to know is if Iris thinks it might make sense for they themselves to put in one hundred thousand dollars, that way they could make a little money and do a little good, it's always nice when the two can be combined. From Amsterdam Avenue, they go to a newly opened Black Culture Museum, which was inaugurated with some fanfare on Adam Clayton Powell Boulevard a month ago, and which turns out to be not much more than a storefront but has a nice exhibition of nineteenth-century photographs. The place is filled with people whom one does not normally see in a museum—church ladies dressed like birds of paradise in their vermilion, chartreuse, and salmon dresses, and wrinkled old men in baggy suits.

After, Iris and Hampton take a taxi all the way down to Jane Street, through crawling, seething, honking Saturday traffic. Hampton, to keep himself from staring at the taxi's meter, and to make the most of his time with Iris, does something that is not exactly his style: he begins to kiss her, right there in the cab, with the Chinese driver undoubtedly spying on them. Iris has always been the one pushing them to be a little cozier with each other in public, the one sort of thing that struck Hampton as exhibitionist, distasteful, and, frankly, unsafe—you never knew who would be triggered by the sight of two African-Americans kissing. And now, when he is not exactly in the mood for public display but nevertheless feeling that a little conjugal vulgarity might be just what the doctor ordered, he discovers that he has, alas, been successful in training Iris away from kissing in cabs: her lips barely respond to his, and when he presses them more forcefully against her, she gently shoves him away and looks at him as if he were a naughty little boy, or a fool. "I feel a little sick from that lunch," she says apologetically. "I think the crab might have been a little off." And then, as if she were systematically obliterating the day, like someone knocking the heads off flowers with a walking stick, she says, "I don't think we should be investing in those apartment houses, Hampton, I really don't. I think they're depressing, and all those developers are going to do is make them suitable for some gullible buppies and I don't want to be a part of that."

Back at the apartment, Iris looks at the eastern sky; a few clouds are tinged with the reflected red glow of the setting sun. The windows of the Sheridan Square buildings and, further east, Fifth Avenue, blaze iridescent orange. Below, the cars are suddenly turning on their headlights, the light streaming from them as cool as the moon. Hampton is in the bathroom and has been for several minutes. He has never gone into a bathroom without taking an inordinate amount of time. She has never asked him what takes him so long, she doesn't know and has never wanted to know. Maybe he has some disorder he is keeping secret from her. Maybe he just needs to be by himself for fifteen minutes a few times a day. Right now, she is glad for the privacy; she cannot shake that sense of being unprepared for an examination, or perhaps a cross-examination.

She sees Hampton's reflection in the window, coming at her, superimposed over the skyline, floating like a ghost. He has taken off his sweater and his T-shirt and, unless she is mistaken, he seems to be shimmying toward her, in a kind of Calypso rhythm. Iris understands that Hampton, when he needs her, feels vulnerable and somehow trapped beneath the ice of his dignity. Often, he will cover his own desire with a protective irony. She has in the past found it endearing, but now his little dance seems ludicrous, and a little demeaning. He visits the pleasures of her body like a tourist who behaves on vacation in a way he never would dream of at home. And like the tourist who raves about the island hospitality, there is, in Hampton's adoration of her, a bit of colonial condescension. She is his refuge from the hard realities of life. He has decided that she is more natural than he, more in tune with the primordial—motherhood, cooking, listening, fellatio, that sort of thing.

She goes to bed with him; to refuse him this afternoon would be unwise, unthinkable. She feels he is trying to impress her, to renew his claim on her, and, even as it breaks her heart and makes her feel she is the most unfaithful, unworthy woman who ever drew breath, all of Hampton's exertions cannot dislodge her mind from its secret orbit around her memories of Daniel. Each of Hampton's kisses is not only what it is but what it is not.

She puts one hand on Hampton's chest, grabs his hip with the other. She shrinks back from him until he is dislodged and then she turns over, presses her forehead to the mattress, puts her arms out over her head, raises up on her knees. He is covered in perspiration. He is behind her, she is beginning to pick up his personal scent making its way through the layers of Irish soap and Italian cologne. He is saying her name, low, guttural. Then there is a moment's silence as he aligns himself with her and then she feels him going back into her. She squeezes herself away from him, grabs his cock, and then, rocking back, presses the head of it against her anus. She is relatively dry, but he is slick, oily. His breath catches when he realizes what she is proposing.

"Are you sure?" he whispers.

"Yes. Do it. Just do it."

He sprawls across her, his weight is crushing. He opens the drawer of his night table and takes out a jar of some sort of coconut-scented cream. Her eyes are closed now, she doesn't want to get involved in the practicalities. She hears the plastic whisper of the lid being unscrewed, and then hears Hampton's suddenly belabored, overly excited breathing. He scoops some of the cream up and then throws the jar onto the floor. He slaps the cream onto her, gruff and impersonal. She can feel the warmth of his fingers behind the slimy chill of the cream. And then he is astride her again. Whenever they have done this she has imagined her mother walking in. He is finished in moments.

He falls to his side of the bed, covers his eyes with his forearm.

"Did I hurt you?" he whispers, not looking at her.

"No. A little. I'm fine." She is wondering what she will say when he asks her if she wants to come, too. But he is not his usual obliging self.

"I feel afraid of losing you, Iris."

She is silent. The room has gotten suddenly darker, colder. She scrambles to get under the covers. The weight of Hampton's body presses the sheet and blankets down on her.

"Should I be?" he asks. He raises himself up on his elbows, looks at her through the corners of his eyes. She feels his keen, predatory intelligence. He ought to have been a lawyer, he loves to come after you with questions. "Is there any reason I should feel as worried as I do?"

"What are you asking me, Hampton?" she manages to say. She has history on her side; he has been suspicious and jealous for the entirety of their marriage, and even before. "Is this why you asked me to come to the city? To ask me these *questions?*"

He is silent. She can feel him retreating, but it doesn't feel like he's going very far.

———

The Sleeping Giant is a huge white clapboard hotel, with shuttered windows and rickety iron fire escapes. The first time they arrived, just a few weeks into their relationship, it was on one of those dark-blue autumn evenings, when the last of the sunset outlines every hill. But today, the sky is cement, there will be no sunset, and their original room, which Kate has requested, is not as they remember it. Daniel and Kate stand there, looking at the four-poster bed, which looks noisy and uncomfortable, and which takes up more than half the room's space, and at the little secretary desk, and the grim little GE television set on a metal rolling table, and the beige wallpaper with its pattern of overly vivid, practically rapacious peonies. Daniel sees the disappointment on Kate's face. "I think there's something sort of nice about this room," he says.

"It's changed," says Kate.

"Well, we've all changed. The room's probably having a hard time recognizing *us.*"

She feels the generosity of what he is saying and for a moment it draws her to him, but quickly it crosses her mind: he can *afford* to be generous, he is that happy, that full of life.

Now, at the Sleeping Giant, they leave their room, first for the main desk, where Kate uses the fax machine to send her article in to Lorraine, and then on to the Dragon's Lair, one of the hotel's two bars. It's a dark room, with old scarred tables and poster-sized photos of the Three Stooges on the wall. The free happy-hour snacks have a contemporary flair—little chunks of sesame chicken and fried plantain simmer in the aluminum warming trays—and the music is supplied by a heavy, open-faced young man in a turtleneck sweater singing songs by U2 and REM and accompanying himself on the guitar.

"Sit, sit," Kate says, pointing Daniel toward an empty table. "I'll get us some drinks. What do you want? A Heineken?" She barely waits for an answer. As she hurries toward the bar, she calls to him over her shoulder, "Score us some apps." She cringes at the sound of her voice—she sounds to herself like some office flirt. Still, she is glad she is the one talking to the bartender; she doesn't want Daniel involved in how much she will be drinking.

The TV above the bar is tuned to a Saturday afternoon football game being played in Florida. The male cheerleaders are tossing the women high into the dark-blue air. The bartender is a man in his sixties, tall and stately, with delicate broken veins in his hollow cheeks and thick author-itative eyebrows. He looks like a New England Protestant patriarch, he should be a county judge, and Kate wonders what wrong turns have brought him to this place, standing behind a noisy bar wearing a red cut-away jacket and a black bow tie.

"I'd like a large Tanqueray martini, no olives, no ice, very dry, and a Heineken," Kate says.

The bartender narrows his vaporous blue eyes, while his trembling hands, dappled like the hide of a fawn, worry the silver tops of the mix-ers slotted into the inside of the bar. "I'm going to have to see some sort of ID," he says pleasantly.

"Are you serious?"

"A driver's license, preferably."

"You're making my day." She waits, but the bartender doesn't move. "What's the drinking age in Massachusetts?" she asks. "Forty?"

When Kate gets back to the table, she finds Daniel has struck up a conversation with a couple at an adjoining table. The man, who appears to be about fifty, wears a heavy blue fisherman's sweater; his short hair is the color of pewter, and his skin is richly, intensely black. The woman with him, who, as Kate approaches, has reared her head to let out peals of shrill laughter, is young and white. She wears a short, spangled skirt that Kate thinks would be risky even for a woman with long, slim legs. Kate simply cannot help thinking this, that the black man might very well be blinded by the woman's whiteness as well as her youth, and has not yet noticed her stockiness.

"Kate!" Daniel says, with an odd excess of enthusiasm, the way men do when they've been caught at something and are trying to pretend everything is just great.

Kate sits and Daniel makes the introductions. The man's name is Erick Ayinde; his accent is a mixture of British and something else far more exotic, which Kate guesses is African. The woman's name is Christine Kirk; she speaks softly, carefully, as if in vigilance against her real voice.

"Erick's a private detective," Daniel announces.

"Really," says Kate. "Imagine."

"Daniel tells us you're a writer," Erick says.

"I wish I had more time to read," Christine says. "I love books. Do you think you might have written something I've read?"

"I'm not sure," Kate says. "Tell me what you've read."

Daniel has heard this reply before and knows he must laugh to cover the aggression of it.

"And what about you, Christine?" Kate says. She takes a long drink of her martini. Too much vermouth, it tastes slimy. "Are you a detective, too?"

"Yes, I am, an investigator," Christine says, with a small, satisfied smile. She knows she has been underestimated. "Erick and I were in business together, but it got *way* too incestuous."

"What kind of detective work do you mostly do?" Kate asks. "Matrimonial?"

"Not so much of that," Christine says.

"Mostly business and industrial," Erick says.

"And missing persons," says Christine. "Which I prefer."

"Do you mind if I ask you something a little on the personal side," Daniel suddenly says.

"The personal side is our bread and butter," Erick says, smiling. He tilts back in his chair, drapes his arm around Christine.

"I take it you two are married?"

"Correct," says Erick.

"Do you get a lot of hassle, being an interracial couple?"

Kate cannot believe he has asked this question. It is not so much its considerable impertinence, but that it reveals what is really on Daniel's mind.

"Do you want to handle this?" Erick says to Christine.

"No, it's okay. You go ahead."

"Well, first of all, thank you for your question. Actually, Chrissy and I wonder why more people don't ask us about this. Even our friends fail to ask us what it feels like to be going through this experience."

Here, Christine interrupts. "Short answer? It's extremely trying. We're always being looked at."

"Or pointedly ignored," adds Erick. "We live in Beacon Hill, in an upscale neighborhood. So, in a way, we're sheltered from some of the more virulent forms of racism. We live in a cocoon. Where we shop, where we eat, it's not a problem."

"I see things Erick doesn't," Christine says. "I see it in their eyes."

"I can live with what's in their eyes," says Erick.

This is a fucking nightmare, Kate thinks. *Our evening is being hijacked by these people. And I have to sit here while Daniel fantasizes about Iris by proxy.*

"But how does it affect your relationship?" Daniel asks. He has always had this earnest wide-eyed aspect to his personality, but it has never seemed so infantile and jejune to Kate before. She feels like dragging him from the bar by his hair. "It seems to me that it would either tear you apart or cement you together."

"Oh, we circle the wagons, if that's what you mean," says Erick. "No question but that sharing the antipathy of small-minded people bonds us. But that's not our marriage's source of strength."

"Then what is?" asks Daniel.

His behavior reminds Kate of something her English publisher once said about Americans, how they can say more to a stranger on an airplane than an Englishman generally says to his closest friend.

"Well, what binds us is what people said would drive us apart—our differences," Erick says. "The terrible trap married people fall into is believing that their spouse is actually a version of themselves, and that they will act as they act, want what they want, believe what they believe. When the spouse fails to do this, when, let's say for argument's sake, the husband acts in some contrary way, the wife cannot help herself from believing he is doing so just to annoy her, or out of disrespect, whereas he may very well be acting in accordance with how he was raised, his own particular psychological dynamic, but she can't see this clearly because she feels that fundamentally they are the same, two sides of the same coin, as much brother and sister as husband and wife."

Kate looks in wonder at Daniel, who is rapt, as if this blowhard were some sort of fucking oracle. She casts wildly about in her mind, trying to come up with a gesture or phrase that could instantly extricate them, move them on to dinner or, better yet, back up to their room, their dear, old, immemorial room, where, Kate thinks, they can screw their way back into each other's good graces.

"But with Chrissy and me," Erick continues, "our differences are obvious and undeniable. I was born in Nairobi, educated in Wales and Montreal, and then Palo Alto, and she comes from Worcester, Massachusetts, her father was a policeman; and we bear this in mind, all of it, the whole curious burden of history. Our life together is a constant struggle to understand. We have no assumptions, and few expectations. It's a journey, do you see?"

"I do," says Daniel. "I see what you mean."

"How'd you two happen to meet?" Kate asks. "I'm curious."

"Erick was one of my professors at Boston College," Christine says. " 'Controversies in Twentieth-Century Criminology.' "

Kate smiles. "Really," she says, "I thought universities sort of frowned on things like that."

"Kate!" Daniel says, admonishing her, but in a somehow teasing way, as if she were merely being irascible and eccentric.

If Erick and Christine feel insulted by Kate's remark, they nevertheless remain serene. "How about you?" Erick asks. "How did you two happen to meet?"

Kate notices a familiar face on the TV above the bar—it's a flushed, balding, stocky man who looks like a sinister presence in a German Expressionist painting. His name is Otto Fisher and he is one of the networks' main correspondents at the Simpson trial. What's he doing on TV on a Saturday?

"Shhh," Kate says to Daniel, Erick, and Christine. They look at the TV and Christine lets out a little groan of displeasure. "Bartender?" Kate calls out. "Would you turn the volume up? Please."

Otto Fisher is standing in front of the courthouse in Los Angeles, looking hot and displaced in his dark suit with the bright-blue sky behind him. He has gotten word that one of the lawyers defending Simpson is threatening to quit the so-called Dream Team because he is objecting to the strategy of playing the so-called Race Card. The lawyer is quoted as saying, "As this trial has proceeded, it has become more and more about politics—especially the politics of *race*—and less and less about the letter of the law. I believe in Mr. Simpson's innocence, but I also believe in the law . . ."

"That motherfucker," Kate says, shaking her head. "He believes in the law like he believes in the tooth fairy." She picks up her martini, discovers it empty. "He spends months helping to drag prosecution witnesses through the slime, and then suddenly he's too delicate to stay on the case?"

"I've never seen such a fuss made over a trial in all my life," Erick says.

"That glorified ambulance chaser is leaving because he knows O. J.'s going to be found guilty," says Kate. "Mark my words. He's covering his own fat ass. And he hates the new DNA guy, there's total conflict between them."

"You seem to know a great deal about the personalities involved," Erick says.

"Oh, forget it. I'm totally addicted to this trial."

"I wonder why."

"You wonder why?" Kate says. "The man killed his wife."

"Probably, but who knows?"

"He killed his wife."

"Well, surely he's not the first man in history to commit such a crime. Why all the attention this time?" Erick says.

"Yes, I wonder," says Christine.

"That's ridiculous," says Kate. "He's rich, he's famous, he's great-looking, and he killed his wife. Why wouldn't the world pay attention?"

"You don't think it has anything to do with the fact that he's a man of color married to a white woman?" asks Erick.

"You know," Kate says, "if men of color murder their white wives, it's still against the law."

Erick is about to say something but stops himself and instead emits a breathy, contemptuous laugh.

"What about you, Daniel?" Christine asks. "Didn't you say you were a lawyer?"

"I'm glad I'm not on the jury," Daniel says. "I find myself thinking one thing one day and another the next. I was a huge fan of O. J.'s when he was playing ball."

"No, you weren't," says Kate. This is mutiny, out-and-out betrayal. Daniel seems to her to be actually making things up. "You don't give a shit about sports."

Erick places a twenty-dollar bill on his check and then stands up so abruptly he almost tips his table over. "I think it's time for dinner, Chrissy," he says in a tight, enraged voice. He makes a brisk Prussian nod in Daniel's direction and says, "Good evening, Daniel."

Daniel starts to stand up, but Erick gestures for him to remain seated. Christine gathers her purse and her angora shawl and in a few moments the two of them are gone.

"My God," Daniel says, shaking his head. He is visibly upset. "How did that happen?"

"I will quote Czeslaw Milosz," Kate says. " 'In a room where people unanimously maintain a conspiracy of silence, one word of truth sounds like a pistol shot.' "

"Is that what that was? The overwhelming sound of truth?"

His eyes look reptilian and blank as he says this, and Kate thinks, *I have my work cut out for me.*

They leave the bar with the vague thought of going on to dinner, not because either of them is hungry but because it is dark now and it just seems time. As they make their way toward the dining room, Kate takes Daniel's arm and says, in a kind of haunted-house scared voice, "What if *they're* having dinner now, too?" What she hopes for is that Daniel will shudder, too, and they'll be bonded by their wish to see no more of Erick and Christine, and that, further along, the story of the old black detective and his dumpy young white wife will become a part of their own lovers' folklore, taking its place in that shared history of mishaps and faux pas that constitute the fabric of all enduring relationships.

But Daniel is not amused. He stops short and then says, "You're right, we can't go in there. So? What do you propose?"

What she proposes is they go back to their room. "It's too early to eat," she says. "In the old days we never had dinner before nine o'clock, sometimes we'd eat at midnight."

"That was in New York. If we wait too long out here, we're going to end up with a bag of chips from some Seven-Eleven."

"Well, at least let's wait until nine, or even eight-thirty." She wants to get him into their room. It's time for her to be abject, it's time for her to worship him, to go through all the phallocentric rituals. She tugs at him, she hopes it feels playful to him but she wonders if perhaps she's pulling a little too hard. Everything's a notch or two off, he's really making her work for this, he's putting her through the mill, and once she wins him back he will have to be punished for this, not severely, not even so he will know he is being punished, but he will suffer nevertheless. *As God is my witness, I will never be humble again.*

Room 301. Now that they are back in their old room, it occurs to Kate that this four-poster bed with its dour Yankee spread and foam rubber pillows is hardly a monument to ecstasy. That first night together had been awkward, tense, a bit of a botch. *We accomplished it but we weren't very accomplished* is how she described it to a friend. There's a lot to be said for establishing a friendship before sex, there's a sweetness to it and even a possible synergy, but in their particular case all of those hours of conversation and chastity were not so much a prelude to sex as an alternative. She and Daniel had already established routines that had nothing to do with sex, they had learned to be relaxed with each other, they had developed a sense of safety, and as wonderful as those things were, they had very little to do with the fierceness and desire, the mindlessness and abandon of erotic joy. Their friendship cast a pall over their lovemaking. The friendship needed not only to be overcome but jeopardized, renounced.

"Remember our first night here?" Kate says, sitting on the edge of the bed, patting the mattress and inviting him to join her. "We were so shy."

"Yes," Daniel says. "I remember it well." His back is to her, he is standing at the window, looking out at the town's main street. A truck is going by, the sound of its grinding gears like the roar of a lion. Workmen have set up ladders and they are braiding Christmas lights around the poles of the streetlights and through the branches of the maple trees.

"Don't you want to sit next to me?" Kate says. She means for this to sound teasing, and that slightly pleading tone of voice is meant as a kind of send-up of the whole notion of a woman trying to get a man's attention, but the satire is leaden. It's too true to be amusing.

"You were really weird with the people down there," Daniel says.

"I know, it's fine. They're off somewhere circling the wagons."

"I don't know why you did that," Daniel says, shaking his head.

"Why were you so interested in them?" Kate asks. She can't help herself, the self-righteousness in his voice offends her. "Because they're an *interracial* couple?"

"My God, listen to you," Daniel says. The dull sheen seems to be lifting from his eyes, he is coming alive suddenly. "You really have a problem with it. You feeling a little racist in your old age?"

"My old age? How fucking dare you."

"You see? You're more worried about your age than you are about being called racist."

"Well, my dear, the fact is that I *am* getting older, so I'm sensitive to it. And the fact also is that I am *not* racist, so I'm not sensitive to that. Okay?"

"You're obsessed with the Simpson case, and the Star of Bethlehem kids—"

"Those black delinquents were in our house and it seems like you're on *their* side."

"I'm not on their side. But the fact is, half the kids in that place are locked up because they're black. You know it, I know it, everybody knows it."

"They were in our house," says Kate, her voice rising. "How did I know what they were going to do? They could have easily killed me, or raped me, or both. I was alone, I was completely alone." She is standing now. She walks toward Daniel, stops. They are facing each other, less than a foot apart. "While you were all cozy and warm at Iris Davenport's house."

"I know, I know," says Daniel softly. "It must have been frightening. I'm sorry."

"What was really going on at that house, Daniel?" Kate says. She reaches for him, but he moves away.

"Let's not do this, Kate."

"It's too late for that, Daniel. I want to know what was really going on in that house."

"We were snowed in, just like everybody else."

"I know you were snowed in. That's not what I'm asking."

Daniel shrugs, as if unable to imagine what more she could want.

"What I'm asking is did you sleep with her?" As soon as the words are out, she regrets them. And in the ensuing silence she casts frantically about for some way to turn this conversation around, or off. Is it possible to simply throw her arms around him and say, *Never mind, I don't want to know*? It seems she could go for decades not knowing, but if the knowledge is there it will pierce her, it will shoot its poison into her, and then she will have to save herself from it.

"Well?" she says. "You're very quiet."

He backs up a little, he seems to be shaking. He seems to have an appetite but no talent for treachery. "What do you want me to say, Kate? I don't know what to do here."

"What kind of question is that? You want my fucking guidance, for Christ's sake? Just tell me, get it over with. Did you sleep with her?"

"Yes. I'm sorry. I did."

For a moment, she doesn't believe him. He's just throwing it in her face, giving her a taste of what it would be like, trying to shock her into shutting up. And then the moment passes, and she still does not believe him, yet at the same time, she knew it all along.

"Did you really?" she says, sitting on the bed again.

"I'm sorry, Kate. It kills me to think of hurting you."

Kate laughs, but she can see by his expression that laughter, or any other sign of instability, will be playing right into his hand. He would like nothing more than to withdraw into the relative safety of deciding she's a little crazy right now.

"I think we should leave," he says.

"Really? Any place in particular? Do you have a hot date or something?"

"No," he says quietly.

"Do you mind if I ask you a question?" she asks. "Would that be all right?"

He shrugs. His eyes are suddenly bright red, as if the sight of her is like knives going into them.

"Are you in love with her?"

He is trying to say something, but his lips are trembling, he will not allow himself to cry, he will not try to elicit her sympathy. He nods his head.

"Is that a yes I see?" *The handle toward my hand. Come let me clutch thee.*

He covers his face. It seems suddenly important to Kate, a matter of life and death, that he not do that. She springs from the bed, grabs his hands, and pulls them down. His face is soaked with self-pity.

"Get out of here!" she screams. "Just get out of here!"

He backs away, gives her a wary look, somehow implying that the problem between them is her mental health. He seems to like the idea of just getting out of there. His hand is on the door, but he keeps his eyes on her, as if she might attack him. Is he going to take the car? Drive back to Leyden, go right to Iris's house? *I told her, she knows,* he'll say.

"Where are you going?"

"I don't know. You said . . ."

"No, don't go. We're going to work this out, okay?"

"Kate."

"Get another room, but you're not leaving me here. You can sleep in another room, you can dream of your little sweetheart in peace. But you're not taking the car and abandoning me. We're going to work this out in the morning, or whenever. But I'm not letting you do this, you understand me? You're not doing this to Ruby, or to yourself, or me."

"Kate, I think we just have to move on."

"Move on? What kind of talk is that? Move on. What are we? Cowboys? You get another room and we'll talk in the morning."

He stands there. He is silent. He closes his eyes. Is this an act of contrition, or is he weighing his options?

"All right," he says.

Her heart floods with relief. His agreeing to get another room gives her a sense of direction and triumph. She has come up with a plan and he has agreed to it. She stands there as he goes to their overnight bag and takes out what he needs.

And then he does something intolerable. He flips his toiletries kit up in the air—a light-brown leather bag that she gave him a couple of birthdays ago—and catches it. She feels the blood in her face. Her muscles tighten so swiftly it feels like she's growing taller.

"Call Ruby," she says, as he is about to let himself out. "Let her know what you think is important."

Their eyes meet, and she feels what she believes to be the miracle of her own strength, her own survival. Thoughts come to her like the drip of anesthetic. He has not destroyed her, and he has not destroyed *them*. The bomb has exploded but the hole is not big enough for him to crawl through. And just look at him, he knows it, too, he's not going anywhere. Let him have this night, let him weep and tear out his hair. Tomorrow in the cool morning she will appear freshly bathed and combed, she will be wearing faded jeans and a black cashmere sweater, a little bit of makeup, the Arts and Leisure and the Book Review sections of the Sunday paper tucked under her arm, the car keys in her hand, and a bag full of breakfast goodies for the road. Then, once they are rolling, she will say the words that will end this insanity: she will forgive him.

Carol Davenport has spent the past two hours reading to her nephew, who lay in his little bed, staring up at her with his dark obdurate eyes—even as he yawned, he refused to close them. After going through a dozen of Nelson's books, Carol was feeling frantic with boredom and exhaustion. If she had to keep reading to put the kid to sleep, she could not bear to read any more about headstrong bunnies and brave little toasters, so she read to him from the novel she herself was reading—a Barbara Kingsolver book chosen by her reading group back home in Baltimore—and that, in fact, did the trick. Now, she stands in the darkened second-story hall of her sister's house, listening anxiously for any signs of wakefulness from Nelson's room.

Hearing none, she goes downstairs, wondering if she is tired enough herself to go to bed. She has forgotten her book back in Nelson's room, but she doesn't dare risk waking him by going back to retrieve it. She sits on the sofa, picks the TV remote control up off the coffee table. Suddenly, the phone rings and she lunges for it, afraid that the high electronic twitter of it will awaken Nelson, who has been so stubborn and confrontational and whom she fears she will throttle if he says another word to her before morning.

"Hello?" she whispers into the phone.

"Oh, thank God it's you," a man's voice says on the other end. "I know you can't talk. Can you? Are you alone?"

Carol is so startled by the urgency—and the whiteness—of this voice that she is momentarily speechless. She feels exposed, out there in the middle of nowhere, with only white people, whites in cars, whites in their houses, whites in the police station and the hospital, she feels fantastically and perilously alone.

"I told Kate, she knows," the man says. "I just wanted you to know. And this too, this too. I love you. When can I see you?"

Carol summons her courage. She grips the phone tightly and brings it close to her mouth, so that this man can feel the heat of her scorn. "Who the fuck is this?" she says.

[12]

"I think we've already been here," Hampton said.

"Really? What makes you think so?"

It was too dark to see Hampton's face, but Daniel could tell from the quality of the silence that Hampton was glaring at him. Even friends would have begun to get irritated with each other by now. Being lost brought out the sort of fear that dovetails into rage.

"What makes me think so?" asked Hampton. His voice seemed completely unconnected to his feelings; even in anger, it was melodious. Or maybe there was a connection, but Daniel didn't know him well enough to make it.

"I think we're making progress," Daniel said.

"Well, we're not, we're going in circles."

"Hampton. I've been following you. All right?"

"We're going in circles."

"Well, you've been taking us there."

"Daniel?"

"What?"

"Can I make a suggestion?"

"Sure. What?"

"Go fuck yourself."

There was a rock nearby, embedded deeply into the forest floor, covered with moss and lichen. Hampton thought to scale it, hoping to see a break in the woods, *but the soles of his shoes were slippery, and as soon as he stood on the rock he slipped and fell hard onto his hands and knees, and just stayed there, with his head down, for several moments.*

Daniel went to his side, touched him softly on the shoulder.

Hampton glanced up at Daniel. "Damn," he said.

"Here," Daniel said. He put out his hand. Hampton's fingers were hard and cold; he grasped Daniel's hand like a statue come to life. Daniel stepped back and pulled Hampton to his feet. It was strange to be touching this man who had once had, and was now losing, everything.

Weeks pass. Anxiety. Cunning. Lies. Daniel and Iris meet whenever and wherever they can. The danger is, of course, an aphrodisiac—an Afro-disiac, Daniel thinks, but does not say it. Iris has made it clear that she is not going to be his Black Girlfriend. She has also made it clear that she is not ready to tell the truth to Hampton, which means Daniel must somehow make certain that Kate doesn't speak to Hampton herself. And so when Kate wants to make love he makes love with her, and when she insists that they begin to repair their relationship by seeing a therapist he must acquiesce to that, as well.

And now it is Tuesday, two days before Thanksgiving, three in the afternoon, and Daniel and Kate are in the waiting room of the Windsor Family Counseling Center. Daniel picks up an old, well-worn copy of *Redbook,* just for something to do with his hands and eyes, opens it up to a picture of a delirious golden retriever bounding up to its human family in an open field, an ad for canine arthritis medicine.

They are going to talk to a therapist on Kate's insistence, but they have come to this specific office on Daniel's recommendation. Daniel asked the shrink who worked down the hall from his law office for a name and was told that the best person for that sort of thing was Brian Fox. But getting the referral didn't complete Daniel's manly reparations, nothing could. "You call him, this mess is your doing, you make the appointment," she said, and rather than argue the matter, Daniel found it simpler to make the call. Now they are here, and Kate seems appalled by the informality of the place, already in some agony over what they have come to discuss, already feeling that her privacy is being invaded, her dignity compromised, her wounded pride put on display.

Daniel stretches his feet out before him, looks at the tips of his shoes, places his hands on his knees. He must gather himself, think of what he will say, what he will not say, when Dr. Fox brings them in for their two-fifteen. He closes his eyes.

A couple of days ago, after making love to Iris in her bedroom, they were both covered in perspiration, and Iris pulled from her closet a small tan-and-blue rotating fan. She plugged it in, placed it on top of her dresser, and then grabbed his hand to pull him out of bed and stood with him in front of the cooling, drying breeze. "This is better than a shower," she said. "I don't want you to just wash me off you."

He tries to rivet his attention on the magazine. He looks again at the ad for canine arthritis medicine and thinks about Scarecrow, poor Crow, slowing down week by week, day by day, tottering around Iris's house and yard exuding beneficence. Daniel has never known such a perfect dog in his life, though he realizes that his virtually worshipful attitude toward the dog is consistent with his virtually worshipful attitude toward everything in Iris's house, the orderliness of her spice rack, the scent of her hand soap, the clarity of the ice cubes, the amusing nature of her computer's screen-saver (kangaroos in sunglasses), the silk Turkish carpet her brother brought back from Istanbul, the black-and-white photographs of Nelson in their austere wooden frames, pictures Iris took and printed herself during the brief period she was interested in photography.

A door next to the receptionist's window opens and Dr. Fox emerges, wearing a dark-blue suit, a white shirt, a blue-and-white tie. With his close-cropped hair, wire-rimmed glasses, and elegant goatee, he looks like a diplomat from a small Marxist nation. "Katherine? Daniel?" he inquires softly, with a kindly smile.

Kate stares at Fox with palpable amazement and then, despite herself, she begins to laugh. Daniel, who himself was not expecting a black man, understands that Kate is feeling the irony of their having made an appointment with an African-American to discuss their domestic difficulties, but he nevertheless feels she is behaving badly.

If Dr. Fox senses some racial content in Kate's laughter, he gives no evidence of it, and he ushers them into his office, a small, dimly lit room filled with books, green glass lamps, a small collection of antique typewriters. His window looks out onto an old apple tree that was split in two by the October storm. When they are all seated—Kate and Daniel in khaki director's chairs, Fox in a tufted burgundy leather seat—the relationships counselor begins the session by asking them their names, their ages, what insurance they carry. His voice is steady, at once emotionless and insistent, it's like being pulled over by a highway patrolman.

"We're here because Daniel has been seeing another woman," Kate suddenly says, no longer patient enough to allow Fox to collect the standard data.

Daniel is surprised at how raw this sounds. Every scoundrel he knows complains about being quoted out of context, but having his behavior reduced to the simple act of infidelity strikes him now not only as inaccurate but unjust. What about all the pointlessly lonely nights that led up to it? What about never having known passion?

"How have you come to this knowledge?" Fox asks, with funereal tact.

"It was quite obvious," says Kate.

"I told her," Daniel adds softly.

"Well, then," Fox says, taking a deep breath. He pinches the skin around his Adam's apple, purses his lips. "So let me begin with you, Katherine—and Daniel, you'll have your chance to speak, too, but I want to begin with Katherine, if that's all right with both of you. Katherine, this situation you find yourself in, how would you like to see it resolved?"

Kate's face colors, and the sight of it stabs through Daniel. She is nervous to be here, humiliated, and she who is so deft with words seems tongue-tied.

"I want to save what amounts to my marriage," she says, her voice barely more than a whisper. She clears her throat. "We may not have any official documents, but this relationship means a great deal to me. Certainly more than my actual marriage, which was just . . . crap. More than anything, I guess. And I miss my old life, I miss the way things were before all this chaos. If we could go back to that, back to that nice life, I think I would be willing to forget everything that's happened since October."

Daniel feels he is being lured into what a man in his position must never do: looking into the heart of the person he is leaving. He thinks for a moment that maybe he ought to get out of his chair and leave. He cannot offer her hope, nor solace. If Kate is here to protect herself, or to heal her wounds, then he should not be here. He is the cause of her pain, he is the source, that churning in her stomach, he put it there, that sense of exclusion and exile—it comes from him. But what can he do? He cannot be for himself and for her, too. Their interests are in collision. There is no middle ground. What he wants is what is tearing Kate apart, and he cannot and will not stop wanting Iris, Iris is the most real thing.

Fox strokes his goatee, and his deep, almond-shaped eyes seem to soften, which Daniel notes, as if trying to assess a juror's sympathies. "Can you say more about that?" Fox asks.

Daniel sits back in his chair, waiting for the sharp sting of Kate's reply. He knows her well enough to imagine how irritating Fox's insipid invitation must be to her.

But Kate tries to do what Fox has asked. "I'm very angry, and very hurt," she says. "As Daniel knows. The atmosphere at home is obviously tense. Very tense. Practically unbearable. We're all walking on eggshells. We're waiting to see what Daniel will do. I think even Daniel is waiting to see what he'll do. He's a decent man and very kind and he's terrific with my daughter. I'm sure this whole situation is killing him."

Fox turns briefly toward Daniel, not to elicit a response or any further clarification of Kate's remarks but, it seems, just to see the expression on his face.

"And you say you were previously married," Fox says.

"Yes, to a man whom I wasn't in love with. And about whom I rarely think. He has no relationship with my daughter, he lives in Hawaii on a little bit of family money, and he is completely irresponsible."

"Which brings us to Daniel," says Fox.

"I've asked him to stop seeing this woman."

"I see," says Fox. "And has he stopped seeing her?"

They're talking about me as if I weren't actually here, thinks Daniel.

"I don't think so," she says.

In fact, he has seen her this morning, their parting is just three hours old, and he feels, as usual, half mad from either having just seen her or from being about to see her. Today, he accompanied her to an immense supermarket twenty miles south of Leyden and followed her up and down the aisles while she shopped for her family's Thanksgiving dinner. Despite everything, Iris was excited about the holiday, which was her favorite of all the holidays—a fact that confounded Daniel, who would have ranked it close to the bottom, rivaled only by Christmas in the categories of forced jollity, depressing cuisine, and awakened feelings of emptiness, isolation, and loneliness. Iris's parents were coming in, as well as her sister, Carol, and her brother, Andrew, with his wife and two children. Hampton's parents would be there, too, along with his aunt Margaret, his sister Victoria, with her family, and his brother James, and the prospect of housing them all, the improvisation of beds and bedrooms, the finessing of small privacies, the worries over laundry, water pressure, the orchestration of bathroom times, Aunt Margaret's sudden allergies to pecans and oysters, without which a proper Thanksgiving dinner was unimaginable to Iris, all these and a dozen more domestic preoccupations were absorbing Iris as she filled her cart with bags of cranberries, cartons of beer, gigantic bottles of seltzer and Coke, three pounds of butter, bags of marshmallows, a ten-pound bag of sugar, a twelve-pack of toilet paper. Listening to her as he tagged along made Daniel ache with envy of all those people who were to be the recipient of her care. Imagine! Pressed into this marathon of housewifery and to somehow keep her enthusiasm and her love of family intact. She was an emotional genius. If only he could somehow escape the frozen Butterball turkey sitting sullenly in his own refrigerator, somehow be spirited away from the embattled dinner that waits to be served at his table at home, if only all the laws of logic and propriety could be suspended and he could find himself at Iris's house for that meal, with Ruby at his side, and Hampton not only vanished but completely forgotten, gone like a puff of smoke.

"Daniel?" Fox is saying. "This is a heavy time for you, isn't it."

"Yes," says Daniel, though not quite certain to what he is agreeing.

"I hear you."

"Yes," says Daniel automatically. "Thank you."

"Is there something you'd like to say to Katherine right now? Let's imagine we are in a little circle of safety, and we can say whatever it was that was in our hearts and there will be no blame, no blame at all. What would you like to say in the circle of safety?"

"I'm sorry."

"That's good, Daniel, but you're looking at me."

He turns to face Kate. "I'm sorry."

"We're not really in a circle of safety, Dr. Fox," Kate says. "We're more like in a circle of hell."

Daniel's heart floods with fondness for Kate, a strangely nostalgic outpouring of remembered love, as if she were long departed. Wouldn't it be nice if Iris said biting and sophisticated things like that? But wit is not the source of Iris's allure. Hers is a different sort of grace, unadorned and total, the grace of the sea, the grace of angels, and sex.

And as for Kate: she is suffering, but how can he protect her from it, how can he even soothe her when he himself is misery's messenger? The unmentionable truth is that he has moved on. No. Worse. He has moved *up*. He has entered a higher plane of feeling, a higher plane of devotion, and a higher plane of pleasure. How can he make Kate understand this? He is not only leaving her, he is leaving himself, leaving everything familiar behind, he is slipping over the border with only the clothes on his back.

"I didn't think we'd have to talk about a certain aspect of this whole thing," Kate says, crossing her legs, "but since we're here and . . . you're here." She gestures elegantly toward Dr. Fox. "It seems worth mentioning. The woman Daniel was, or maybe we should say, *is* seeing is black."

"How is that relevant?" Daniel says, much more insistently than intended.

"Oh please, Daniel. It's completely relevant. You always wanted to be black, and now you've figured out a way to be black by proxy."

Daniel hazards a glance at Fox, whose brief, black eyebrows have raised up practically to his hairline. "Is this true?" Fox asks.

"About the woman being African-American? Yes. But, I'm sorry, I think there's something a little bit racist in what Kate's saying."

"Daniel," says Fox, "you're looking at me."

"I know."

"Do you want to say this to Kate?"

"She heard me."

"And she won't dignify it with a reply," Kate says.

"She's practically making a living out of writing articles about O. J. Simpson," Daniel says to Fox, as if appealing to him, forging some sort of bond, and instantly feeling the folly of it as the therapist shifts in his seat.

"Are you still seeing her or not?" Kate says, her voice level, composed. She cocks her head as she looks at Daniel, somehow creating the impression that whatever he answers will come as a relief to her.

But he's not convinced. It seems entirely likely to him that if he tells Kate he is still actively in love with Iris, and he sees her whenever possible, then Kate will not only suffer but she will retaliate.

He wishes that Iris would tell Hampton herself. *Soon,* she has said. *I can't,* she has also said. She fears him, fears the pain it will cause her, and is exhausted to contemplate the mess that will ensue. She worries about losing custody of Nelson—though surely Hampton could not delude himself into believing he was set up or temperamentally suitable to take care of the boy.

If it were up to Daniel, Hampton would already know. Then he would simply stay in New York, and those unbearable conjugal visits could cease. But Iris is more than reluctant to tell him, she seems terrified of the possibility, which makes him wonder if she fears Hampton will do some violence to her, that he will pummel her, that beneath that golden-brown exterior of affluence and elegance, family roots, princely entitlements, and fraternity-boy competitiveness lurks the narcissistic, sexually preening, and ultimately predatory black man who prowls, sulks, and rages through Kate's articles on O. J.

"Well, are you or not?" Kate asks, her voice a little wobblier this time, like a tightrope walker working without a net who's made the mistake of looking down.

If he tells her the truth, he will pay for it. She will try to put a wedge between him and Ruby. She will make his life hell.

"I've already answered this question," he says.

"Answer it again," says Kate.

He shakes his head no, thinking that in some malignantly petty way this silent No can be taken to mean that he isn't seeing Iris anymore, or it could also mean that he doesn't want to "answer it again." He knows he is losing his honor with these infantile games with the truth, but, then, if he's willing to lose his family why not jettison honor, as well?

"What do you think about that?" Dr. Fox asks Kate.

"About what? He hasn't answered me. He shook his head, that could mean anything."

"I'm not seeing her," Daniel blurts out. "I'm not seeing Iris. Okay?" Telling this lie isn't as sickening as he'd anticipated, he was so close to it anyhow, it wasn't difficult, he just let himself drift into it.

"What do you think about what Daniel has said?" Fox asks again.

Kate shakes her head. "I don't know. I'd like to believe him."

"You don't believe me?" asks Daniel, as if incredulous.

"No. I don't."

"Then have me followed. Hire a private detective."

"I have."

Daniel's first thought is of this morning, after he and Iris left the supermarket and drove north back toward Leyden—wasn't there a car following close behind, a nondescript sedan, just the sort to be driven by some professional snoop? A mile into the drive they pulled into Windsor Motors; Iris wanted to check out the new Volvos, and Daniel would have gone anywhere for a few extra minutes with her. Had the sedan followed them in? They walked around the lot, a light snow fell for a few moments and then stopped. A salesman descended upon them. Iris pointed to a car she liked and the next thing they knew the salesman had slapped a pair of dealer plates on it and he was waving so long to them as Iris steered the new car out of the lot for a test drive, with Daniel in the passenger seat. Her eyes were brimming with tears. *What's wrong,* he asked her. She shook her head, pulled out into traffic, started driving a little too fast. He saw a tear roll down her cheek, he stopped it with his fingertip—remembering Kate once saying that human tears were filled with bodily waste, more toxic than piss—and then licked his finger clean. *You're crying,* he whispered. *He just gave us the car,* Iris said. *He didn't ask for identification, a credit card, nothing.* "*Here's the keys, see you in a while, drive safely.*" She sniffed back what remained of her first response to this novel situation, and then looked at Daniel with something utterly wild, something practically feral in her expression, as if she had just entered a realm in which more was permissible than she had ever dreamed.

"Look at his face," Kate says to Dr. Fox. "You must be somewhat of an expert on the faces men make when they are totally fucking busted."

Fox's clock is digital so there isn't even a ticking, all that can be heard is the long *shhhhh* of the white-noise machine, like the sound of an enormous punctured balloon. And then, from another of the center's offices, the sound of a muffled male voice crying out, "Not at meal time, that's all I'm asking. Not at meal time!"

"What's that?" Kate asks.

"Somebody else's misery," Daniel answers.

"Not that. That."

"It's the white-noise machine," Fox says.

"Ah," says Kate, smiling. "Then shouldn't it be whining?" She starts to laugh.

"I can't believe you hired someone to follow me around," says Daniel.

"Well, I didn't. But I'm never going to forget the look on your face when you thought I had."

"All right," says Fox. "I'd like to try something here, if that's okay with you two."

"He still hasn't answered my question about whether he's seeing her or not."

"What I'd like to try . . . ," says Fox.

"Just a second, Dr. Fox. Please? There's no point going forward with this little session, if Daniel's not willing to answer my question."

"He did answer your question," Fox says, his voice rising with alarm, which Daniel notes with relief for himself and a feeling of some pity for Kate—poor Kate, fifteen minutes into therapy and she's alienating the doctor.

"Let me tell you something about Daniel, Dr. Fox. He's not terribly straightforward. He'd rather lie than hurt someone. He's a negotiator. No, here's what he is." She uncrosses her legs and then recrosses them in the opposite direction. "He's like an orphan. He's always covering his ass, making sure he doesn't get sent back to the home. He doesn't feel as if he belongs anywhere. He moves back to his hometown—and moves me back with him, by the way. He has no idea why. His parents cut him out of their stupid little will? He barely reacts. He wants something big to happen to him, something to tell him who he is, or make him something. There must be a name for that, he must be a type, or something. He can tell you anything. He may end up saying that he's black. I wouldn't be surprised. People like him can never tell the truth, because they don't know the truth. He's a sweet guy, and a good man, and despite his behavior he's really pretty ethical. But Daniel's been spinning his own feelings for so long they're a mystery even to him."

Fox nods, somewhat sagely, but when he strokes his goatee, his fingers are trembling. He clears his throat and murmurs something about "trust issues," and something further about that most unfortunate "circle of safety."

Abruptly, Kate reaches over and squeezes Daniel's knee as hard as she can. She speaks to him through curled lips and clenched teeth. "Say something."

"Do you love me, Kate?" he asks, his voice soft, almost sleepy. The pressure she exerts on the muscles right above his knee is vaguely painful, but relaxing, too. The physical punishment seems to siphon off some of the other, more persistent agonies.

"That's really not the issue here," Kate says. "Anyway, of course I do."

"I'll take that as a no," he says.

"You see? I can't win."

"All right, then let me ask you this . . ."

"It's better to just express your own feelings," Fox says. "And not ask questions."

"I agree," says Daniel. "But let me get these questions out of the way first."

"He said no questions, Daniel," Kate says.

"You've had your chance to cross-examine me. Now it's time for the defense."

"The whole idea of couples counseling," Fox says, "is to keep you *out* of court."

"Have you ever felt the kind of love for me," Daniel says to Kate, "that you'd rather die than live without me?"

"What do you want me to do? Audition?"

"I'll make it easier for you. I don't think you ever have, at least not toward me. And I think it's a sad life, and a waste of heart. We are capable of it. If I am, then you are . . ." He points to Dr. Fox, who seems to be staring at him with alarm. "And you are, too. We all are. It's in our wiring, in our DNA, it's the poetry that we all are capable of writing, if we can find the goddamned courage."

"I think you have lost your mind," Kate says, slowly taking her hand away from him. "Who are you? The fucking Johnny Appleseed of Love? How can you say these things to me?" She looks for a moment as if she is going to be furious, as if she is going to scream at him, smack him, rake him with her fingernails, but then her face crumples and she begins to cry. She takes a handkerchief out of her handbag and covers her eyes.

If she thinks what he says is awful, she should hear what he does not say. He is here trying to mollify Kate, when what he might really be interested in is shaking her until she sees how he has changed, that he is no longer the emotionally anemic man she somehow chose. He wants to ask her: *Have you ever made love for six hours barely stopping? Have you ever had nine orgasms in a night? Have you ever seen me weep from the sight of your beauty? When was the last time we slept in each other's arms? Have you ever seen my savage side? Have you ever known me to be absolutely helpless with passion? Has anyone ever stuck their tongue up your ass? Have you risked disgrace for me? Have you made a double life and been willing to hurt another person for the love of me? Have you ever been willing to give up everything for another person? You wouldn't even do that for Ruby.*

Fox finally releases them, and they hurry out of his office, angry and ashamed, with their eyes down, their faces closed. They have made an appointment for next Wednesday, but they both know they will not keep it. Neither of them ever wants to be in this place again. The medicine here cannot cure them.

The November sky is the color of a cellar sink; a cold wind blows through the parking lot as Daniel follows at a safe distance behind Kate on the way to her car. She lets herself in and he waits there for a moment, giving her a chance to pull away without him, if that's what she wants to do. His car is at his office, a ten-minute walk, which he would prefer to being in cramped space with Kate. Yet he cannot bolt out of the parking lot and make a run for it; despite the danger, he feels the logic of life, the rules of decorum insist that he get into the passenger seat, close the door behind him, strap on his safety belt. The car's engine turns over. The radio comes on, a blur of excited talk that Kate instantly switches off.

"Ready?" she says. And then, without waiting for his answer—he was about to say sure, fire away—she throws her car into reverse and backs it quickly and without hesitation across the center's small parking lot, straight into the front end of a blood-red Toyota. Daniel is hardly dislodged from his seated position, but Kate, lighter, has pitched forward and banged her forehead against the steering wheel. She barely reacts to this, not so much as touching the oozing welt with her fingers. She throws the car into drive, her car extricates itself from the Toyota, and she drives it headlong into a gray Honda parked on the other side of the lot. By the time the center empties out—no one inside has failed to hear the twisting metal and shattering glass—Kate's car is immobile and she and Daniel are screaming at each other.

———

The next morning, desperate to see Iris and to tell her what has happened at the counseling center, Daniel brings Ruby to My Little Wooden Shoe at the normal time, but to his ravishing disappointment Nelson is already there. As he helps Ruby out of her jacket, Daniel's eyes search the suddenly grim and airless little day care center in case he has somehow overlooked her presence, in case she is talking to a teacher, or maybe helping out in the kitchen. Stiff with unhappiness, his fingers fumble with the buttons, and Ruby looks up at him with dismay.

Nelson, seeing Ruby, comes to her side and tugs at the sleeve of her shirt. "Come on," he commands her. Generally, Ruby is compliant around Nelson, but today she resists. She raises her little square hands toward Daniel and puckers for a good-bye kiss, while Nelson glowers at them both.

"Okay, you guys, have a great day," Daniel says.

"I don't even like you," Nelson replies, raising his eyebrows, extending his lower lip, shrugging.

Ruby is appalled by what Nelson says. Her cheeks blaze as if slapped. "Yes you do!" she fairly cries. "He's my dad."

"No he's not," says Nelson. He smiles as if Ruby has walked into his trap. To complete his mastery of her, he takes Ruby's arm and pulls her away.

Daniel drives away from My Little Wooden Shoe, with no destination in mind, only vaguely aware of traffic and the fact that he is in charge of a heavy moving machine. His mind is not so much processing information as pinned beneath it, pierced on one end by the absence of Iris and on the other by the fact that Nelson is harboring a great malevolence for him. At the end of the winding, residential road that the day care center shares with a scatter of one-story houses, where Daniel would normally turn right to head toward the village and his office, he instead turns left, which brings him to Chaucer Street, which in turn empties out onto the state highway leading six miles north to Marlowe College. He presses the power button on his cell phone to tell Sheila Alvarez he'll be in an hour or so late, but the battery has worn down and the phone remains dark. *I'll call my office when I get there,* he thinks.

But get where? All he knows is that there's a good chance that Iris is at the college, and a good chance that if he drives over to Marlowe there is hope of finding her.

Life, it seems, can be really very simple: you feel where you want to go, and you go there. You let your legs take you. At least the body, dog that it is, tells the truth.

Seventy years ago, Marlowe College was a sleepy, mediocre Episcopalian school with an enrollment of five hundred young men. Now, it is nondenominational, with four thousand students, twenty-four hundred of them women. The original old buildings still exist—ivy-covered, gray stone buildings, with leaded windows and burgundy slate roofs—but they are now overwhelmed by the modernist additions, the glass-and-steel fitness center, the broken geometry of the art center, the Bauhausian dorms. The campus has grown, but it is still only thirty acres, with one north-south road winding through it, and another going east to west, and now Daniel is navigating his car, driving slowly as students stroll across the road without so much as a cautious glance. The air, cold and humid, is like a soaking sheet. A couple of very large crows land on a power line and swivel their heads toward each other as the wire sinks beneath their weight.

Daniel finds Iris's car in the parking lot between the gym and the student center, and he decides she's more likely in the center and tries there first, where he immediately spots her, in the cafeteria, seated at a small wooden table in the company of a prematurely gray, olive-complexioned man in his late thirties. He wears a silk shirt and a long, luxurious scarf, and he holds a pen as if it were a cigarette as he leans toward Iris. Iris is dressed in a smart black skirt and a dark-green chenille sweater, with a silver bracelet and matching earrings. Daniel, struck by the sight of her, and then further struck by seeing her in conversation with the handsome man at her table, freezes in his tracks. A steady stream of young students flows past, parting ways to walk around him. Daniel is fixed to his spot, suddenly gravely dubious about having come here, and feeling a sick stirring of jealousy at the sight of Iris seated with another man. Within moments, however, Iris happens to look in his direction and gestures for him to come and sit with her. She doesn't ask what he is doing here, and, of course, gives no indication that they are anything but two people whose children go to the same preschool. She introduces him to John Ardizzone, who, it turns out, is her newly appointed thesis advisor in the American Studies Department. Daniel, though unasked to account for his sudden appearance, says that he has come to use the college's library to check up on some local history as a part of his research about Eight Chimneys, but as soon as he is embarked on this unnecessary fiction he regrets it and simply lets it trail off. Ardizzone quickly excuses himself, saying he has a departmental meeting. He taps his pen a couple of times, as if dislodging an ash from its tip, and, before hurrying off, he tells Iris that he likes her new ideas for her thesis and he hopes she can have a draft of it before the end of the spring semester.

"You have a new thesis?" Daniel asks, as soon as Ardizzone is safely away.

"Yes. So, what are you doing here?"

"I don't know. I think I'm stalking you. I'm sorry."

"It's strange seeing you here." Her voice drops to a whisper. "It's strange seeing you with your clothes on."

"Don't excite me," he says.

"You missed a spot shaving," Iris says, touching his upper lip. Her short hair glistens and her fingers smell of the oil she has rubbed into her scalp. "Are you having trouble facing yourself in the mirror?"

"No."

"I am."

"I've given myself over to a higher power," Daniel says, smiling. "And you're it."

"Sounds convenient."

"It's a lot of things, but if convenient is on the list, I haven't noticed."

"It's okay," Iris says. "I'm not trying to hassle you. But I'm finding this very difficult."

"I'm sorry, Iris. I don't know what to do."

"You want to know the truth? I'm miserable, frightened, guilty, sleepless, I feel like a criminal, and I think I'm getting a flu or something, and I'm happy, happier than I've ever been." She looks over her shoulder. "Oh shit, here she comes, perfect timing."

"Who?"

"Kalilah Childs. This girl, this kid, I keep running into her in the library. She keeps trying to get me to join the Black Student Alliance."

"Maybe if we start necking she'll go away."

"Too late," Iris says.

Moments later, Kalilah Childs is at their table, a dark, fleshy nineteen-year-old girl in faded denim overalls and work boots, wide-eyed, cornrowed, wearing a multitude of rings, bracelets, and necklaces. The jewelry is, for the most part, African, though she also wears a pearl necklace given to her by her parents when she graduated first in her class from her Quaker high school in Philadelphia. A scent of sandalwood is on her clothing. Rarely serene—she is acknowledged as a genius at Marlowe, and the pressure is immense—Kalilah now is particularly agitated. She looms over Iris and looks as if she might pounce upon her.

"Have you heard what happened to Alysha?" Kalilah says. She doesn't acknowledge Daniel's presence. "Three guys jumped her at that pizza place out on Route One Hundred, and one of them kicked her in the ear."

"Oh no," Daniel says, though as soon as his expression of shock is uttered, he realizes that in this particular situation he is meant to be quiet.

"Is she all right?" Iris asks.

"She had to go to the hospital. Now she's in her dorm. Her mother's coming up from Brooklyn to take her home."

Iris nods, taking it in. "Actually," she says, "I don't think I know Alysha?" She says the name uncertainly.

"You would if you ever came to a meeting," Kalilah says. The finger she shakes at Iris has three rings on it.

Iris presents Kalilah with a slow, composed smile, one that would have stopped Kalilah in her tracks if she were two years older or ten percent more perceptive.

"When am I supposed to go to a meeting, Kalilah?" Iris says. "I'm trying to get my work done and raise a family. And going to school when you're older is really difficult. You can't understand. You've got a supple young brain, and all this fire and certainty and sense of purpose. I'm struggling just to get through, and don't have anything left to go to any damn meeting."

"You're not old!" Kalilah says, her voice rising—it's hard to say if it's out of conviction or discomfort. "And we need every one of us. Look at what happened to Alysha."

"I'm sorry for what happened to her." Iris puts particular emphasis on the final pronoun.

"Well it could have been you, or me, or any one of us," Kalilah says. "That's why we need the Black Student Alliance, and that's why you need it, too." As Kalilah says this, she turns slowly and lets her eyes fall to rest on Daniel.

"You know what, Kalilah?" Iris says. "I don't join clubs, or groups, or any of that stuff. Okay? Oh, sorry. Kalilah Childs? This is Daniel Emerson."

"Nice to meet you," Daniel says, half rising from his chair.

"Hello," Kalilah says, her face pleasant, a little placid.

Daniel thinks this would be as good a time as any to leave. Iris senses his thought and places her hand on his wrist.

"What if my friend Daniel wanted to join your club?" Iris says. "Would that be all right?"

"No, and anyhow I bet he's not even a student here."

"Well, let's say he was. Then could he join?"

"Come on. It's for African-Americans only, students and faculty."

"Well, I would never join that kind of thing. I don't think I could be friends with Daniel if I joined a club that excluded him. How do you think I'd feel if Daniel belonged to an organization that didn't allow African-Americans? Do you think that would be all right with me? You think that wouldn't be grounds for ending the friendship?"

"Well, he does belong to a group that excludes you," Kalilah says. "It's called the white race. I presume you've heard of it. Try joining it."

"Daniel didn't join it," Iris says.

"Well, he's in it."

"Actually, I resigned," Daniel says, at last able to speak. "But it's like the Mafia, you know, they keep pulling me back in."

"That's pretty funny," Kalilah says.

Iris looks at her watch. "I've got class," she says. She picks up her briefcase, zippers it shut. A tremble goes through her hands and Daniel realizes just how angry she is. "You know, Kalilah," she says. "You've got a great future ahead of you in politics, if that's what you choose."

"That sounds like a put-down, coming from you," Kalilah says.

"You just don't take no for an answer, and maybe that's good. But it doesn't work with me. You think you're the first person who's ever told me I need to be doing this or that for my people? You think I haven't heard it from both sides of my family? And both sides of my husband's family, too? I'll tell you the same thing I say to them. You believe in freedom? Great. Then let me be free. Is that so hard? I've got one little life to live, that's all, that's the whole thing. Don't I have the right to live it the way I choose? Why do I have to do what you want me to do? Why do I have to join your group, and say you're like me and I'm like you and we're all together? It's really shit. You know that, Kalilah? It's total shit. And if you want to talk about racism, let's think about this—you look at me and all you see is brown skin. You don't know what I'm going through in my life. You don't know what kind of responsibilities I'm dealing with, or what the pressures are, or anything else. You don't know what I eat, or where I live, or what I want, you don't know if I sleep on my back, or if I'm wanted for murder in Tennessee. All you're registering is the pigmentation. So how are you different from some white racist?"

"You don't give us a chance to know you," Kalilah says.

By now, Iris is standing. "That's what I'm doing now," she says. She kisses her fingertips and touches them against Daniel's cheek. Then, before another word can be said, she turns and walks quickly away.

Daniel and Kalilah watch her cross the cafeteria, and then are left with each other and the silence between them.

———

Thanksgiving arrives. Daniel and Kate are fleetingly bound together as they collaborate on a story to explain the bandage on Kate's forehead, as well as her black eye, as they sit at the dutifully laden table with Ruby, and with Carl and Julia Emerson.

The Emersons are amazed but not inquisitive as they listen to the story of Kate's car's jammed accelerator, and Daniel, to lend some verisimilitude to the tale, hints darkly that a very serious lawsuit may be in the offing and that Kate may be living on easy street by next year. "And I'm going to get my beak wet on this one, as well," he says, uncorking the wine, walking nervously around the table and filling glasses.

Carl and Julia look as if they have recently graduated at the head of their class in the Prussian Posture Academy. With their shoulders squared, their backbones straight as pool cues, they surreptitiously warm their hands, rubbing and squeezing them under the cover of the starched linen tablecloth. When the turkey is brought steaming and fragrant to the table, they follow it carefully with their eyes but make no comment, no *oooh* of pleasure, no *ahhh* of anticipation. Their faces show no gaiety; in fact, they came close to not showing up at Kate and Daniel's house at all. After more than seventy Thanksgivings, the thought of missing one struck them as being something less than tragic, and, further, they both suspected that somewhere during the long, gluttonous, tryptophane-infused afternoon there was a very real chance that their son would finally vent his rage over being eased out of their will.

Daniel, for his part, has no such plan. He is glad his parents are here, glad he and Kate and Ruby do not have to face this holiday feast on their own.

Kate, too, is glad for the Emersons' presence. Though she does not find them altogether agreeable company, and, more important, she is quite sure they don't care for her—her southernness makes her seem alien to them, her life as a writer seems vain, her single-motherhood was bad planning, and they also suspect she is a lush—they are, nevertheless, family, and right now the idea of family seems important to Kate.

As for Ruby: everyone's voice seems too loud. The food smells like medicine. Her patent leather shoes, unworn for months, feel full of sand. She feels continually as if she has to go to the toilet, but when she does nothing comes out. Her stomach has hurt her all day, and the day before that, and the day before that, too. She cannot stop wondering what everybody would do if she pounded her fists on the table and screamed.

Three hours later, Carl and Julia, exhausted by the meal, by the concertina-wire tension in the house, Ruby and her constantly imploring them to get down on the floor with her and watch her play with her Legos, or to read to her, leave. They leave what is left of the fifteen-pound turkey, leave bowls of stuffing, quivering masses of cranberry sauce, a casserole of yams and Brussels sprouts, two pies, pumpkin and pecan, they leave a spatter of candle wax on the heirloom white of the table-cloth, bowls of nuts, wine glasses blurred by greasy fingerprints. In the end, not very much food has been consumed, and even less of it has been enjoyed, but the meal is registered in the Great Book of Holidays, and Daniel's parents, much to his surprise, give him a last-minute embrace as they are making their way out the door—a little eruption of affection that he believes to be expressive of their boundless relief to be finally getting out of there. "Stay in touch!" Carl shouts over his shoulder, as they scamper toward their car. The sky is a flat chalky black, the murkiness of water in which a paintbrush has been swirled.

Daniel closes the door, turns to survey the conditions of his house arrest. He cannot see the dining room, but he can hear the angry clatter of dishes being cleared; nor can he see the little den in which they keep their TV, but that, too, he can hear. Ruby is watching *Little House on the Prairie,* her favorite show. It seems to be a Thanksgiving special, she wants to watch make-believe people enjoy the holiday. Daniel will wait a few moments before going in to join Kate on cleanup—right now, he is sure she is slugging back the wine people have left in their glasses, and he doesn't want to walk in on it, doesn't want to have to react. He checks his watch. It is only a few minutes past eight o'clock and he stands at the edge of what remains of the night, feeling hopeless and beset, as if peering across a river too broad to cross. He imagines the dinner over on Juniper, probably in all the confusion and conviviality of a large family gathering they are just sitting down to eat. He imagines the laughter, the little side comments, the well-worn repartee of brothers and sisters.

Daniel forces himself into the dining room. Sure enough, the wine glasses are all empty. They are all four on their side and placed around the turkey carcass on the great white platter, which Kate has just lifted off the table. Daniel collects the two bottles of Chilean cabernet and, as he suspected, they are both empty, not even a little tannic slosh at their base. He hates to calculate, but the math of this is inevitable. Two bottles equals twelve nice glasses of wine. He himself has had two, his father one, his mother her usual festive zero, leaving nine for Kate. Nine glasses of red wine do not a lost weekend make, but nevertheless: it's still nine glasses. But wait! There'd been *cocktails* before the first bottle had been uncorked. A dish of olives and a little platter of smoked salmon, both of which Daniel had picked up himself that morning at one of Leyden's new gourmet shops, obligingly open Thanksgiving morning. The little appe-

tizers had been laid out and Kate had asked, "Who wants a drink?" Nobody really did, but Daniel, thinking he was somehow covering for her,
said he'd have one, too, and she brought out a quart of one of the Nordic
vodkas and poured a neat one for Daniel and one for herself, and now
that he thinks of it she drank it down with nary a shudder, so the chances
are it was not her first little taste of the day.

Daniel is unable to help himself from making a bit of a show of putting the empties in the recycling sack. "Poor old soldiers," he mutters
over their socially responsible grave, and when Kate fails to react to that
he pushes the matter. "That was pretty decent wine, wasn't it?" Kate is at
the sink, with her back to him. The scalding water rushes out of the
tap—he's got to remember to turn down the temperature on the hot-
water heater, while he is still on hand—and a cloud of steam rises from
the basin. She is motionless; the plates and glasses remain on the counter
next to the sink, and Daniel figures that she is waiting for him to do some
real work here, something a little more useful than checking the empty
wine bottles. He joins her at the sink—he will rinse and she can put
things into the dishwasher, the pots and pans can soak until morning. But
as soon as he is next to her, or, really, a few seconds after that, because it
takes a few beats to come up with the courage to glance at her, he sees
that her face is a deep sorrowful pink, her eyes are shut, and her hollow,
downy cheeks are slick with tears. He places a hand on her shoulder.

"Get your fucking hand off of me," she says in a whisper.

He lifts his hand slowly, lets it hover in midair for a moment, and then
brings it to his side.

"What do you want me to do, Kate?"

"I want you to die."

He sighs, shakes his head, and says, "Short of that." He can scarcely
believe he's said something so glib, he tries to cover it quickly. "Why
don't I clean up here? You did most of the cooking."

She picks up the five dinner plates and drops them into the sink. They
land with a crash, yet somehow none of them break. Then she goes for the
platter upon which the turkey still stands, but Daniel stops her before she

drops that, too. He slowly wrests the platter from her. At first she resists, but then she seems to lose interest in creating any further havoc. She puts her hands up, steps back, like a criminal who has just been disarmed.

"You want to do the dishes? Do the fucking dishes," she says.

He is so imprisoned by the grisly emotional logic of a love affair at its end point that he almost shouts, No, goddamnit, he will *not* be doing the dishes. True, Kate cooked the turkey but he, always the more domestic one in their sinking domestic partnership, was responsible for the cranberry sauce, the vegetables, the salad. And what is there to cooking a turkey? You put it in the oven, deck it out in some sort of Reynolds Wrap biohazard suit, peek in on it every hour or so, and in the meanwhile you can be sneaking little pulls on the old Absolut. But then, sanity and self-interest, not always boon companions, do a little synchronized swimming across his brainpan and he realizes that his relieving Kate of all household duties would be the very best thing he could do right now.

"Fine," he says, "I'll be glad to. You should get some rest."

She looks him up and down, wanting to quarrel but too exhausted and too full of wine to bother speaking. She is wearing flowing black trousers, a white satin blouse, she has braided her hair up in a little deft twist, but all her beauty has fallen into a heap. She drags her feet as she trudges across the kitchen, the little squared heels of her black pumps scrape and bang against the floor; they are the noisy, tottering footsteps of a little girl wearing her mother's shoes. Daniel doesn't say anything more, he is afraid to look at her. He doesn't want to do anything to impede the progress of her retreat. All he wants her to do is go upstairs, lie down, and then pass out, dressed, undressed, makes no difference.

He rinses the dishes, the glasses, the silverware, sticks everything that fits into the dishwasher, and then, thinking that if Kate is really going to pass out she will have done so by now, he creeps up the steps and looks into their bedroom, where, sure enough, she is not only in bed but under the covers, with the lights out. A little exhausted sigh of light from the hallways casts its pale dull depressive patina into the bedroom; Daniel can make out what seems to be Kate's white blouse and the tips of her shoes on the floor. So: she has undressed. Meaning: she is not napping, she is turning in for the night; this is not a pit stop, this is a crash. Kate rarely mentions her brief husband, but more than once she has told Daniel that Ross loved to fuck her when she was passed out loaded. Alcohol was like cement blocks tethered to her sleeping brain, sinking it twenty fathoms deep, rendering her impervious to human voices, barking dogs, sanitation trucks, phones, alarm clocks, light, cold, heat, shaken shoulders, kissed lips, fingers up her vagina, and, from time to time, full copulation. Every so often, however, she would be briefly aroused from her stupor and come streaming up to the surface of consciousness like a scuba diver swimming up through a thick red velvet ocean of wine, and catch Ross at it. She would either tell him to stop it, or she would not—both responses had their dark satisfactions.

The result of one of those sneaky copulations was Ruby, and now Daniel slips out of the bedroom and goes downstairs to check on the little girl, who has dozed off in front of the TV. Some nitwit in charge of programming has decided to show *Platoon* on Thanksgiving night. The Samuel Barber Adagio for Strings is on the soundtrack, its piercing melody accompanying the men as they kill and die in the lush jungle. Daniel digs beneath the sofa cushions and finds the remote, mutes the sound, hoping to protect Ruby, but the sudden absence of sound awakens her.

"Hey, Monkey," Daniel whispers, hoping she will remain drowsy.

"What's this?" she says, looking at the screen.

"Nothing," he says, hitting the off button. "It's time for bed."

"What was that?"

"A movie."

"Can I watch it?"

"You won't like it, honey. It's not for kids." He sits next to her. "Are you feeling okay?"

She hates to admit it—mainly because she doesn't want him to use it as an argument against her watching the TV. Nevertheless, she would like some sympathy, the occasional magic of an adult's commiserating voice. "My stomach hurts."

"Still?" he asks.

She nods. She detects alarm in his voice and it brings tears to her eyes—the strange kind, the kind she knows will not be shed.

"Where does it hurt?"

"My stomach."

"But where?"

She moves her hand in an indistinct circle around her abdomen, as if waxing a tabletop.

"Does it feel more throw-uppy, or more poopy?"

She shrugs, looks away, suddenly delicate. He has the feeling of having misspoken on a date.

"How long have you had it?" he asks. "Since dinner?"

"Every day," she says. She reaches for the remote control; Daniel pulls it away from her, but she persists, and he gives it to her. She presses the on button and the set comes on just as one of the soldiers in *Platoon* catches a bullet in the back. Her face is so impassive, Daniel can't tell if she has registered the image. She begins to scroll through the channels, one after the next, looking for a station showing cartoons.

"Where's Cartoon Network?" she asks.

They have had a satellite receiver on their roof for months now, but with hundreds of channels to choose from, Daniel is still the only one who knows where the various networks and cable stations are on the scroll. Even Kate, a hard-core aficionado of CNN, often asks Daniel for her show's three-digit address. He is the one who brings the groceries home, who lugs them from the car, he is the one who mows the lawn, rakes the leaves, shovels the snow, salts the icy sidewalk, carries the firewood in from the shed and stacks it next to the hearth, he is the one who opens the flue in November and yanks it shut again in May, he is the one who pushes the reset button on the boiler when it inexplicably shuts down, who sets the Havahart traps for the squirrels in the kitchen, who traps the milk snakes in the dirt-floor cellar, who opens the windows so that the occasional bat can escape, he is the one who changes the batteries in the smoke detectors—what in the world will they do without him?

"It's too late for cartoons," he says to Ruby.

"What time is it?" A note of desperation in her voice—she knows what's coming.

"Almost ten," he answers, yawning.

"Where's Mom?" she asks.

"She's sleeping, too. Come on." Daniel stands. He grips her by her armpits, the heat comes straight through the fabric of her cotton turtleneck. He lifts her, she grips his ribs with her knees. What if this is the last time he ever lifts her into his arms? Of course it's not, he tells himself. But he also knows that day will come. In the end, she may come to love him again, but first there will be hurdles to jump in a long steeplechase of hate.

The usual bedtime ritual for Ruby—the washing, the brushing, the stories, the back scratching—usually runs close to an hour, but tonight she allows herself to be put to sleep in twenty minutes, after which Daniel checks in on Kate again, and after that he goes downstairs, puts on his overcoat, and leaves. The night air is cold and tastes of wood smoke. The stars pulsate like wounds. He slides into his car, starts the engine, and backs away from the house without putting on his headlights. When he is safely away from the house he switches on his lights and surprises two deer who have been standing on the side of the road. He wonders if he is making a terrible mistake—the kind you can never live down, the kind that defines your life, that creates a before and an after—by leaving Ruby alone in the house with her mother. But he comforts himself: Isn't that how the world goes? Aren't there at this very moment millions of kids in their little beds, with their drunken parents right down the hall?

When he has put that proverbial country mile between himself and his house, Daniel realizes that once again he has no destination. The Bistro is closed for the holiday—though surely half its clientele could use a place to repair to—and he neither wishes nor dares to drive by Iris's house. He finds his cell phone in the glove compartment and dials her number. One of Daniel's clients, a postmarital stalker, from whom

Daniel has unconsciously learned certain desperate techniques of information gathering and track covering, has told Daniel that if you want to make a phone call and don't want your number to show up on caller-identification hardware, or to have your number retrievable by the recipient's pressing *69, then you can block your number from coming up by dialing *67 before making the call, which Daniel does now before dialing Iris's number. His plan: If Iris answers, ask her to meet him at his office; if anyone else picks up, simply terminate the call.

The call is answered on the second ring. A man's voice. Hampton. *Fucking hell*. Daniel hits the off button on his phone, tosses it aside, and steps on the accelerator, plunging the car deeper into the night.

Guided only by the logic and habits of driving, he speeds through the village and turns onto a little two-block stretch of frame houses, given the grandiose name Vanderbilt Drive; from there, he takes a left onto Hammersmith, to his office. Irma Thomas is playing on his tape deck: *It's raining so hard I can scarcely catch my breath* . . . He pulls into the driveway that leads to the parking area behind the building, which is just an unlighted patch of blacktop, with amateurishly drawn yellow lines indicating the parking space for each of the building's clients, and he doesn't notice Iris's car until he is turning into his own slot and the outer edge of his headlights sweeps against the side doors of her blue Volvo.

He bangs his fist against the steering wheel, rocks back in his seat.

Iris has gotten out of her car, she is walking toward him. He opens the door. He hurries toward her, takes her in his arms.

"It's you," he says, talking and kissing her at the same time.

"I was just going to leave," she says.

"Do you have time?"

She shakes her head no. "Do you?"

"Kate's asleep. Passed out, actually." It strikes him as a terrible thing to say, but even as he realizes that he proceeds to make it worse. "I actually feel nervous leaving Ruby alone with her."

"You should go back. We both should."

"How did you know I'd be here?" Daniel asks.

"I didn't. I just had to get out of the house and I decided to come here. Hampton's brothers Jordan and James—"

"I met James," Daniel interjects.

"And his sister Victoria are completely obsessed with this fucking video game James brought over. All that brotherly competition, it's really exhausting. And they've got Nelson all gooned up over it. It's the worst kind of violent fantasy game for a kid like Nelson, but try telling that to Hampton. He just laughs, like there's something cute and naïve about my concerns."

"Leave him then, live with me."

Without any particular change of expression, the look of frustration and anger on her face changes to melancholy, it's like moving a radio dial the breadth of one cricket leg and hearing completely different music. "Don't," she says. "It's not funny."

"Am I laughing? Am I even smiling?"

"Where were you all my life?" she says. "Why weren't you there when it was time to get married? Where were you? What were you doing?"

"I don't remember," he says, pulling her close. "Let's go upstairs," he murmurs into her ear.

They have already been at each other a few times in his office; they have made love on the floor, with Iris on Daniel's lap and Daniel in his chair, with Iris naked and bent over the desk, propped up on her elbows, her hands clasped as if in prayer, or with her arms outstretched and her hands grasping onto the edge of the desk for traction while Daniel empties himself into her from behind. As they walk in tonight, and Daniel turns on a floor lamp and then steps behind Iris to help her off with her coat, they both realize that more than any other single room, this utilitarian space, with its sense of grievance and redress in the glassed-in bookshelves, with its evidence of time wasted and time standing still in the standard-issue magazines on the low table in the waiting room, and the tax-deductible elegance in the blue-and-gold weave of the Turkish rug Daniel bought at an auction at a Holiday Inn across the river, this two-room suite, this place of business, this professional outpost of a man who willfully jettisoned his main chance to make any kind of name for himself in his field, this is as close as anything they have to call their own. Where in the world can they go? They have used her house, going from room to room, trying to find a bed in which they don't feel criminal, they have parked like teenagers along various dirt roads and woodland paths, and they have been together at the Catskill Motel, the Bittersweet, the Stuyvesant Motor Lodge, a Sheraton, a Motel 6, the Flying Dutchman, and in Cabin 3 of a squalid scatter of tiny tourist cabins calling itself the Morpheus Arms, always checking in under assumed names and paying in cash, sometimes only able to stay for a half hour, and never returning anywhere a second time.

"Where does everyone think you are?" he asks her, hanging her coat on the coatrack, and then putting his own over hers.

"Hampton's mother wants some Pepto and I said I'd find someplace open and get it for her." She glances at her watch, shrugs. "We actually have some in the house—Pepto-Bismol is to the Welles family what chicken soup is to Jews—but I just hid it in my purse so I could have an excuse to get out of there." She takes an unopened bottle of the lurid pink liquid out of her pocketbook and shows it to Daniel.

He is thrilled by her cunning. Its dishonest, calculating nature doesn't disturb him at all.

"Kind of low, isn't it?" she says, dropping the medicine back into her bag.

"I think when people love each other, they'll do anything to be together," Daniel says. "Everything that is in the way has to get either shoved to one side or beaten into dust. You do whatever is necessary."

"Great. Let's go on a killing spree."

Daniel gestures toward the oak file cabinets. "Most of my cases, there's not much passion behind them, but now and then I have to represent someone who's driven by some desire—for another person, for money, whatever—and I never understood how someone could risk wrecking their life, or ruining the lives of people around them, or actually hurting someone, just to get what they want. But I think that's because I never really wanted anything myself, I mean really wanted it, the way I wanted you."

"You mean you don't anymore?"

"Now more than ever. It's the only real thing."

"There's no place in the world for us, Daniel. Nothing will ever come of this. Just memories, fantastically painful memories."

"That doesn't have to be true."

"Too much is against us," Iris says. "Do you see how people look at us when we're in public?"

"Fuck them."

"Well, one day we're going to be tired of being in a freak show."

"That's because we're here in Tiny Town. We could go to a city."

"Where could we go?"

"Anywhere. New York."

"New York? That belongs to Hampton. I could never. Where could we go? We couldn't stay here. Or Washington, Atlanta, San Francisco, Chicago. He's got family in so many places. Where could we live?"

"Anywhere. London. Hong Kong. Amsterdam. Oslo. What difference does it make? I would go anywhere. And I'd do anything. I'd crawl through broken glass if I could just be sure that at the end of the day I'd be getting into bed next to you."

"You're too focused on what you want, Daniel."

"I can't help it. I think I was hardwired to be with you. I'm telling you, Iris, nothing else matters. To me." He has grabbed her elbows and is pulling her closer to him, but she turns her face away.

"I love being with you," she says. "I love what you see in me, and I like who I am around you." She looks at him, with such sudden seriousness it almost makes him laugh. "It's the greatest freedom I've ever known," she says. He is about to say something but she stops him. "But what are we going to do?" she says. "If I ever tried to leave Hampton, it would be like a war."

"Fifty percent of marriages end in divorce," Daniel says.

"Not fifty percent of Hampton's marriages, or anyone else in his family. With them, every wedding is a royal wedding, part of some grand alliance. They're all demonstrating some idea they have of perfect family life, and I can guarantee you one thing, he would make my life hell. He'd be merciless. In terms of finances . . ."

"Who cares about that?"

"I do, Daniel. Come on, be realistic here. This is my life we're talking about. And Nelson's, too. He'd go for custody, Hampton would, he would try to hurt me in any way he could."

"He could try for custody. That doesn't mean he's going to get it. He won't. The courts are used to these guys who suddenly are Father of the Year. Hampton's not set up to raise a kid. And he's not that great with Nelson. He bullies him."

"You know, these family court judges," Iris says.

"Idiots," says Daniel.

"Yes, well, a lot of them are African-American. African-American women. I think they'd give Hampton whatever he asked for. They would, wouldn't they? Tell me I'm wrong. Please. I wish you would. But you can't! I'm not going to lose my son!"

"Iris . . ."

"And I'll tell you another thing," Iris says. "If Hampton thought I was leaving him for a white guy, that would make it all the worse."

"I'm not all that white."

"I'm being serious, Daniel."

"Sorry. But he's not all that black, that's for sure."

"What are you talking about? He's not all that black? You don't really know what you're talking about. Hampton is a black man, he feels it, his world is based on it, his social life, his business, his identity, he may be light-skinned and think like a banker, but I can promise you if he ever found out I was fucking some white guy, he'd be Louis Farrakhan before the day was out. It would be the ultimate betrayal."

"Is this what you came here to talk about?" Daniel says. He lets go of her, and, just as he feared, his touch was all that was keeping her close.

She drifts away from him, stands at the window. Drops of moisture—rain? snow?—are forming on the black glass.

"No. I wanted to come someplace where you might be, or at least somewhere that belongs to you. I'm just so crazy about you, it's ridiculous."

The phone on his desk rings with a sound as sudden as a rock through a window. Daniel thinks, *This is either a wrong number or trouble.* The answering machine picks up, Sheila Alvarez's soothing voice. After the tone, Kate's voice: "I just called you on your cell phone but you're not answering, so I'll leave this happy holiday message for you at your office, Asshole. I woke up from the little nap you so considerately convinced me to take, and guess what I found? An unattended child and a sink full of dirty dishes. So, Asshole, are you having fun?"

Daniel finally rouses himself and turns the volume off on the machine, so the only evidence of Kate's continuing diatribe is the light—as red as a pinprick of blood—blinking off and on.

[13]

There was a break in the black sky and the platinum moonlight poured down on them. The whites of Hampton's eyes glittered. His shirt was dirty, his khaki trousers were covered in burrs and black with mud at the knees. Daniel looked down at his own hands. There was a scrape on the heel of his hand. And then the crack in the sky healed, and the moonlight disappeared.

Two Sundays later, there is an afternoon party at Eight Chimneys, to inaugurate the Eight Chimneys Foundation, which Marie Thorne has set up as a first step in turning the old house into an official New York State Historical Site. Despite Susan Richmond's antagonism to the project—she can't bear the thought of ticket-holding strangers traipsing around her property, and she also knows that the entire scheme has created a little dome of privacy, a secret spot in which Ferguson and Marie can carry on their repulsive flirtation—leaving the planning of the party itself to Ferguson and Marie is beyond her powers of forbearance. Ferguson is as domestic as Buffalo Bill, and Marie's ideas for the party are pathetic, culled from some grotesque guide to "elegant living"—caterers cooking and serving hot appetizers, expensive booze, chamber musicians from Marlowe College, vases filled with Casablanca lilies. Marie, despite having been born and raised on the property, seems to have no idea that such froufrou touches have no place at Eight Chimneys, where one entertains simply and cheaply. Susan feels that ostentation is the province of the middle class, who always seem to be saying "Look what we have!" whereas at Eight Chimneys one likes to behave in such a way that implies "We've all had enough chamber music and porcini tarts, and the long, tiresome trek through the gardens of plenty has led us to believe it's a hell of a lot more fun to fill up a few bowls with potato chips, get store-brand sodas at the Price Chopper, jeroboams of cheap wine, and not make such a big deal out of everything." Susan cannot resist a chance to express her own artistic talents, and on each of the ninety invitations sent out she creates a tiny watercolor, usually just a few wavy blue lines to symbolize the river, but sometimes a finely wrought chimney, or a cow.

The invitation in Kate's hand has been personalized with the wavy blue lines. Beneath the times of the party, from 2:00 to 4:00 P.M., there is a line that reads DONATION: TWENTY-FIVE DOLLARS PER PERSON. On Daniel and Kate's invitation, Susan has drawn a circle around the amount, with a line running off the circle that leads to the message NO EXCEPTIONS! Kate has been going on about the boorishness of this reminder since its arrival on Tuesday, and now, sitting at her dressing table, putting on her lipstick, with the invitation propped up against the mirror, she suddenly sees Daniel in the glass and begins again.

"Does Susan Richmond really think we're going to try and sneak in without paying?" she asks. She doesn't turn to face him but watches his reflection in the mirror. His hair is still wet from the shower; his eyes are dark and startled in the middle of his scrubbed face. He has lately become meticulous about his grooming, as he has with every other detail of domestic life, from getting up with Ruby every morning and making breakfast for the family, to the dutiful little good-night kisses he places on Kate's cheek at night. He is like a British officer in captivity, keeping up his own morale with close shaves and crisp salutes.

"I'm sure it's a joke," he says. He checks the time. "You look very nice." Which is his way of saying, "Hurry up, it's time to leave."

"I've started a new novel," she suddenly announces.

"That's good. It's great. I'm really glad."

"You are?"

"Of course I am."

"Yes, well, we'll see. But it does seem that connubial bliss was interfering with my creativity. Ever since . . . you know, the big confession, I've really felt inspired. And this book—well, I don't even want to talk about it. I don't want to jinx it. It could all disappear. I could spend the rest of my life just writing articles."

"I'm really glad," Daniel says. "Are you almost ready?"

"Ruby?" she asks, still gazing at him in the mirror.

"I think she's all set. I'll go check."

Except for not loving Kate, Daniel has been a model partner since his confession in the hotel room two weeks ago. No socks on the floor, impeccable table manners, he has even purchased over the Internet some spray he squirts on the back of his throat at night, which has virtually eliminated his snoring. The respect he shows for her sleep is boundless. Not only has the snoring stopped, but he no longer tugs at the blanket, and when he rolls over nothing of him so much as grazes her, she cannot even feel his breathing, he has less presence than the dead, and in the mornings he is quieter than the rising sun when he slips out of bed to mind Ruby and get her off to school. Yet he is not entirely cold, not like someone who is furious, or who wishes to punish you. If she rolls next to him in bed, he is accepting. If she presses herself against him he gathers her in. If she kisses him, he kisses her back. If she wants to fuck, he fucks. He is entirely at her disposal. Her every wish, it seems, is . . . no, not his command, but his opportunity to commit some further act of penance. "Got me one of dem penitent boyfriends," Kate said to Lorraine over the telephone the other day. "Dem's the best kind," answered Lorraine.

Daniel finds Ruby in her room, brushing the bright-yellow hair of a chubby-faced doll with a pug nose, a prissy mouth, and blue, unforgiving eyes. Neither Daniel nor Kate would have bought such a toy for Ruby—they would rather supply her with little cars, plastic horses, building blocks, books—but she'd fallen under the doll's spell at day care and the teachers let her take it home. "Are you about ready, Monkey?" Daniel asks. He feels so guilty around Ruby that he has made his voice overly cheerful.

"I want to play with Ginkie," Ruby says. She turns the doll around on her lap, gazes into its bright blue eyes.

"You can bring Ginkie with you, if you want."

"No. She can't go out." Ruby has long contended that the doll is afraid to leave the house—it seems part of a strategy to make certain that it never gets returned to the day care center.

"It's going to be fun," says Daniel. "And besides, there's not going to be any grown-ups home, so you have to come along."

"What about Mercy?"

"She's busy."

"Is she going to be at the party?"

"You never know."

"Can I really take Ginkie?"

Daniel picks Ruby up, notches her onto his hip. The weight of her balances him, somehow damps down the anxiety.

The three of them drive to the party, through a mild November afternoon. The sun is high and hazy in the pale-blue sky, it looks like a little stain on a shirt. The wreckage of last month's storm is still everywhere in evidence—collapsed old barns, fallen trees, heartbreaking wreaths on the side of the road where people lost their lives.

He drives slowly, not wanting to telegraph how anxious he is to arrive at the party. Kate, who since beginning her novel has taken up smoking again, lights a cigarette and cracks the window to let out the smoke.

"Don't smoke!" Ruby cries out, the way they all do in unison at her day care center, during Awareness Training, when the kids are introduced to all God's dangers: *Don't smoke! Don't drink! Don't touch me!*

Kate rolls her eyes, inviting Daniel to share her exasperation, but at the same time she reaches behind her and gives Ruby's knee a humorous little squeeze.

"Are there going to be other kids at the party?" Ruby asks.

After a brief silence, Daniel answers. "I don't really know for sure. I imagine so."

"I want Nelson to be there," Ruby says. "Was he invited?"

"I don't know who was invited," Daniel says. He feels Kate's eyes on him, and his voice wavers.

"Oh, I certainly hope Nelson is there," Kate says, taking one last drag of her cigarette and then tossing it out the window. "With his lovely parents. That would make everything special."

"He's nice," Ruby says, stretching her arms and legs. The child seat seems suddenly a size too small for her.

"Oh, he's fantastic," Kate says. "The whole family."

She glances at Daniel, notes his discomfort, and wraps her hand around the crook of his right arm, momentarily throwing his steering off. They are riding through the village now, past the church in which the four of them heard the *Messiah* a few weeks ago. It seems like months, years. She remembers Daniel and Iris, the little looks they traded. Was he already fucking her? He claims not, but it's probably ridiculous to assume scrupulous honesty from him. Maybe he was. Maybe Kate was already being played for a fool. When she was young the thought of somehow being the butt of a joke was at the absolute zenith of her jealousy, nothing was worse than thinking someone might be reveling in putting something over on her. But now, to her surprise, the possibility that Daniel and Iris might have taken some grotesque pride in fooling her barely registers in Kate. It seems the most trivial part of the story. This is a story about sadness and loss, about getting a shocking wake-up call to put her house back in order, this is a story about what she had to learn in order to make things right again. She wonders if she is deluding herself, but that thought is simply too painful. Instead she thinks: *I should thank them,* trying that one on for size. But no, it doesn't fit, either. Too big. Or too small. Something.

They drive on the curving, bucolic blacktop that goes past Leyden's riverside mansions. The estate next to Eight Chimneys, which for two hundred years had been known as Eliade, has finally been sold off by the dissolute progeny of its original owners and is now called Leyden Farms.

A wooden roadside stand has been built across the road from the entrance gate where bushels of golden delicious and Macintosh apples are sold—a puzzling bit of frugality on the new owner's part. He is a middle-aged television producer, specializing in hospital dramas, and he paid close to eight million dollars for the estate. It's difficult to see how the two or three hundred dollars made annually from selling apples could make much difference to him. Perhaps they're a tax dodge.

A mile later, they come to the crumbling stone gates of Eight Chimneys. The estate's gatehouse sits at the edge of the road—a small stone house that is an architectural miniature of the mansion, and in even worse repair.

"These people are so crazy," Kate says. "Everything is falling apart, it's just chaos everywhere."

"I'd think you'd like this sort of thing," says Daniel. "It's sort of southern. It's Faulknerian."

"If I wanted to be in the South, I would have stayed in the South. I think people ought to take care of what they have. I hate things going to wrack and ruin. And Daniel? This isn't Faulknerian. Everything creepy and southern isn't Faulknerian, just like everything annoying isn't Kafkaesque."

The long driveway between the road and the main house has somehow gotten worse since the last time he drove it. The potholes have doubled in depth, and now Daniel must dodge the crowns of fallen trees—once he drives directly into one of the craters. When they reach the main house, there are only five cars in front, and one of them has no tires and has obviously been there for quite a while.

"You said it was going to be a big party," Ruby says.

"It will be," Daniel says. "We're just a little early."

"When's Nelson coming?" Ruby asks. She hugs her doll close to her.

"I don't know if he's coming at all, Monkey," Daniel says. "But there will be other kids, I promise."

"You promise?" asks Kate, amazed.

"Yes," Daniel says. And Kate shakes her head, clearly implying that Daniel, if he had the proper humility, would never make another promise for as long as he lived.

They are met at the door by Susan, wearing a rust-colored corduroy jumper, such as you would see on a schoolgirl. Her graying hair is twisted into a long braid. Her face looks moist and dense, like the inside of an apple.

"Hello, Kate," Susan says, extending her hand. Her voice is frosty, edged with contempt. She is punishing him for his participation in Ferguson's and Marie's scheme. "It's nice to see you. We're putting coats in here." Then, turning toward Daniel, "If any of the politicians show up, I'll leave them to you. I can't stand politicians."

She leads them into what had once been the conservatory, a large room with floor-to-ceiling casement windows. The room is empty, except for an antique telescope standing gawkily in a corner, and a long oak table upon which the guests can deposit their coats. "Isn't this the room where Professor Plum did it, using a . . . candlestick?" Kate murmurs to Daniel. Susan is walking a few feet in front of them, with her hand resting on Ruby's shoulder.

"We haven't met," Susan says to Ruby. "I'm Susan Ferguson."

Ruby has never been addressed in quite this tone. There is no inflection in Susan's voice that would suggest she is speaking to a child. Confused, and a little thrilled, as well, Ruby looks up at the strange woman. "Is this your house?" she asks. She holds her doll behind her back to hide it from Susan.

"Oh please, don't remind me. Look." She gestures toward the wallpaper, faded blue and dirty white, showing a repeated pattern of a little girl in a pinafore holding a hoop through which jumps her dingy little dog. "Not to mention . . ." She points to the warped floorboards, then the copper-colored stains on the ceiling. Susan sighs, takes Ruby's coat from her. "You know, at a certain point, you just give up." She looks down at Ruby, gives her a curious little frown, as she wonders why this child seems so unresponsive. "Are you in school?" she asks.

The party is centered in what the Richmonds still call the ballroom, and, in fact, it is a room where dancing sometimes occurs—though now it is either raucous, sweating rock and roll, or the sacred, ceremonial steps of Apache rain dancers or Sufi dervishes, performers brought in by

Susan. People are beginning to arrive, but Daniel is too nervous by now to do more than nod a distant hello to each of them. It is striking him with some force that coming to this party is a grave mistake. If Iris doesn't show up, it will break his heart, his indelible disappointment will show like blood on a sheet. If she does appear—then what? How will he be able to keep away from her?

He stands, with Kate, near the fireplace where four-foot white birch logs are smoldering. The brick wall of the hearth is coated with creosote, black and sticky. Kate speaks to him through the side of her mouth. "Thank God we hurried getting here. I think it's important to be among the very first to arrive. Don't you?"

"There's no kids here," Ruby says.

"There will be, I'm sure of it," Daniel answers.

"I want Nelson," says Ruby.

Daniel stares at the fire. He knows Kate is looking directly at him, but he pretends to be absorbed by the progress of the flame as it slowly burns through the logs. His face is scalding; the fire burns his thoughts away, and he stands there as if hypnotized. When he finally steps away he sees a few more people have arrived, and that Ruby has found the food on the other side of the room and is grabbing handfuls of potato chips. Susan has taken it upon herself to point out a mural on the ballroom's ceiling to Kate, who has a plastic cup of wine in her hand.

"Ferguson's great-grandfather Payson Richmond commissioned a Portuguese artist to make this mural. Payson wanted a picture of heaven, he wanted stars, which you see, and a moon, over there, and he wanted to see God. More than anything he wanted God up there, looking down on all the wonderful people. But the artist, whose name was Barbieri, was a devout atheist. You see, no saints, and certainly no God. Payson insisted that Barbieri get back on the scaffolding and find a place for God and Barbieri of course refused, and before anyone could intervene the two of them were fighting like kids, slapping each other in the face, pushing, and Payson ended up slipping on the floor and hitting the side of his head, which caused him to lose the hearing in his right ear."

Kate seems amused as she listens to this. She has a taste for the sort of ceaselessly self-referential anecdotes families like the Richmonds like to tell. She herself uses phrases like "old family" and "good family." She believes in genealogy, she believes in birthrights, she feels that the deeds and misdeeds of our ancestors are a large part of who we are. Daniel prefers not to believe in such things, the idea that who we are is determined by our ancestors has never appealed to him, and now, of course, it is repellent. Yet he is relieved to see Kate staring up at the mural with Susan. Kate's neck is long and still firm. She is wearing a black skirt, flattering and tight, a bolero jacket, clip-on pearl earrings. Her hands are on her hips. She looks lithe, high-spirited, if he didn't know her he would want to. How strange it feels not to love her. That love had once felt so stable, dependable, its very lack of drama made it feel eternal, and now, to feel so little, to feel almost nothing outside of respect, and a desire not to hurt her too badly, is like waking up one morning and finding that you no longer can enjoy the taste of bread.

Ferguson, meanwhile, is on the third floor, in the room into which Marie has moved. There's a little hooked rug on the floor; the walls are bare except for an old brass bell that used to be connected to a system of pulleys controlled from a panel in the butler's pantry and could be rung to summon whatever maid might be using that room. Ferguson sits on the edge of Marie's bed, dressed in work pants, a frayed white shirt, while she dips a comb into a glass of water and grooms him. "Hey, take it easy," he says, as she rakes the comb through his hair, but she is determined to bring his unruly mop under control. She combs his hair straight back and when she finally finishes, Ferguson stands up and walks stiff-leggedly to the window, where he sees his faint reflection swimming in the old wavy glass. "Great," he says. "Now I look like a Mexican."

"I doubt it," says Marie. She kisses his forehead. "If I help you save Eight Chimneys . . ."

"I'll be forever in your debt," Ferguson says.

"That's sort of what I'm counting on. It'll put us on the same level. I won't be poor little Marie, I'll be the girl who saved you."

When the party is in full swing, Marie plans to make a little speech. She wants to thank everyone for coming and to give a brief overview of the Eight Chimneys Project, which is what she is now calling the plan to turn the house into a historical site. Ferguson has come to her room, however, not only to kiss her, and to walk with her down to the old ballroom, but to talk her out of making her speech. Susan must not be overshadowed in that way, it will be humiliating to her, and that would be unkind and even a little dangerous. But now that he is with Marie he finds that he doesn't have the heart to tell her not to address the guests. She deserves the credit and she deserves the recognition. And the personal significance that this afternoon must hold for Marie has suddenly become touchingly clear to him. What a triumph, what a turn of events, what a change of fortune. Here, after all, is a girl who was raised by one of the estate's old servants, a girl whom destiny seemed to have marked for a life of utter insignificance. How could anyone with a heart interfere with her moment of glory? *I'll stand next to Susan while Marie makes her speech,* he thinks. *Maybe I'll put my arm around her.*

"Are you ready?" he asks Marie.

She touches her throat, and then the pearl necklace that Susan and Ferguson gave her on her sixteenth birthday. She is dressed in an oatmeal-colored woolen suit. It seems like something women wear to the office. Ferguson has no idea how she chooses her clothes; he's meant to ask her but it keeps slipping his mind.

"Do I look all right?" she asks.

"You're beautiful. You make me very, very happy."

She seems truly surprised by his tenderness. He rarely says sweet things to her if they aren't in bed—in fact, the best part of sleeping with him is getting to hear that gentle voice.

"I wish Dad were here," she says.

"I do, too, honey," says Ferguson. "I really do. Now let's go down there and shock the hell out of everybody."

Marie stops in her tracks. "What do you mean?"

"I don't know. Nothing. I have no idea why I said that. Fumes from the lead paint on these old walls." He links his arm through hers and steers her through the doorway.

Ferguson and Marie come down just as State Senator Phil Russell joins the party. Russell is a stocky, ravenous man, dressed in a brown suit. Thirty years ago, he was a football star at Sacred Heart, a Windsor County Catholic high school, and his chin, nose, and forehead still show the scars of his three years on the offensive line. He surveys the room with wary eyes—this bastion of the faded aristocracy is not on his regular beat. Russell runs on the Republican and the Right to Life tickets; he has been warned by his staff that while the Richmonds' Republican roots are deep, Ferguson and Susan are at the end of the line and their house is a gathering place for eccentrics and flakes.

As Ferguson and Marie make their way toward Russell, Susan swoops him up and escorts him over to meet Daniel. By now, forty or fifty people have shown up, but not Iris, and Daniel is trying to keep his composure.

"Daniel, I'm sure you know Phil Russell," Susan says. "Mr. Russell, Daniel Emerson has agreed to act as our attorney in this whole business. Isn't that nice of him?"

For a moment, Daniel wonders if Susan is somehow under the impression that he's not going to bill them, but then he realizes this is merely her manner.

"Nice to see you," Russell says, squeezing Daniel's hand, his shoulder. "What a wonderful party."

"It certainly is," Daniel says. He has found a place to stand near the center of the room where he can feel the cool draft whenever the front door opens, so he knows when new people have arrived. He feels the flutter of the breeze on his pant legs, but when he looks past Russell he sees Upton Douglas, a portly, white-haired real estate broker, swinging his way in on a pair of yellow crutches. Douglas was knocked to the ground by a falling branch during the October storm and he broke his leg in four places. They've known each other casually for years, and when Douglas sees Daniel staring at him he smiles.

Daniel suddenly notices that Phil Russell is looking oddly at him, and

Daniel quickly says, "It'll be great to see this old place brought back to its former glory."

"It's really something," Russell says. He has been taking in his surroundings and his eyes are registering some alarm. Eight Chimneys' derelict state unnerves him, it seems to suggest a kind of madness. "What do you think the square footage is in this place?"

"I don't think houses like this *have* square footage."

"Yeah, I know what you mean." He smooths his shirt over his cinderblock stomach. "It's going to take a lot more than state historic money to put this puppy back on its hindquarters again. We're going to have to think about the Fed, and private donations." He smiles his high school hero smile. "But that's okay, we're going to make it happen because it's the right thing to do."

Daniel sees Kate across the room, talking with noticeable animation to a man in his fifties, a writer from the city named Barry Braithwaite. Braithwaite, a small, sickly man with bloodshot eyes and yellowed fingers, has written several articles about O. J. Simpson, mostly concentrating on the sociopathology of the coddled athlete. Kate has her hand on his shoulder and whispers something in Braithwaite's ear. Braithwaite tucks his chin in and looks at her with considerable amazement, as if she has just made the most transgressive remark he has ever heard, and then he laughs.

Just then, Derek Pabst comes in, dressed in a dark-brown suit, a yellow shirt, and brown tie. He looks uneasy as he sways in the entrance to the ballroom, squeezing his large hands together, rolling his broad shoulders, and casting his eyes around for a familiar face. It is not that Derek is a stranger to the people here, but most of them are too wealthy and too grand to be a part of his social life. He has issued them speeding tickets, brought them sad news about missing dogs and cats, shot rabid raccoons on their porches, been in their homes after break-ins, and even responded to a couple of domestic abuse calls, but drinking wine and chatting with this collection of doctors, lawyers, academics, writers, and the idle well-to-do on a Sunday afternoon in a mansion by the river is outside his usual experience. When he sees Daniel across the room, his face lights up with relief.

"Hello, good buddy," he says, grabbing Daniel's elbow.

"Hello, Derek," Daniel says. He is about to ask, *What are you doing here?* but he stops himself.

Derek looks around, taking in his surroundings. "You hear all these rumors about what this place is like on the inside, but it's not so bad, not like I thought."

"Derek Pabst," Daniel says. "This is Phil Russell."

Russell puts his hand out and Derek shakes it, but he is clearly distracted.

"Is Kate here?" he asks.

"She's over there. What about Stephanie?"

"She's home with Chelsea." Derek peers around the room. "Where's Kate. I actually need to talk to her." He senses the confusion in Daniel's eyes. "I've got a little more information about those runaway kids from Star of Bethlehem, I know she's concerned." He suddenly sees her. "There she is." He smooths his tie against his shirt. "I'll be right back."

As soon as Derek is gone, Russell looks at his watch. "Point Mary Thorne out for me, will you?" he asks Daniel. "She's the one who sent us the invitation."

"Marie. She's right over there, come on, I'll introduce you."

Russell repeats the name softly to himself, committing it to memory.

As they make their way to the other side of the ballroom, Daniel looks for Ruby, who is suddenly not in sight. By now, most of the guests have arrived. The talk is loud and excited; people are still telling their storm stories. Ferguson is in front of the fireplace, heaving a four-foot birch log in, and Susan is at his side, with her finger hooked through his empty belt loop, and looks to be speaking to him with extreme displeasure. Marie, holding a plastic cup of white wine, is talking with Ethan Greenblatt, Marlowe College's young president. Marie's attention is rapt, though she seems not to realize how unusually tall Greenblatt is and her eyes are fixed not on his face but his chest. If Greenblatt finds this unnerving, he is nevertheless undeterred from going on at some length about oddities in the history of Eight

Chimneys—though born in Montreal and raised in Palo Alto, Greenblatt knows as much as any of the river aristocracy about the town's grand past.

"Do you know," he says, in a voice that is at once declamatory and ironic, "Mark Twain, Charles Dickens, Edith Wharton, and Ernest Hemingway all have spent the night in this house, and there is no other structure on record in which all four of these luminaries have stayed." When Greenblatt sees Daniel and Russell approaching, he rests his hand on Marie's shoulder, as if to prevent them from stealing her away. "And its political past is actually more extensive and, well, paradoxical than its cultural past. Dorothy Day, Frederick Douglass, Winston Churchill, Octavio Paz, all the Roosevelts, of course, Woodrow Wilson——"

"Sorry to interrupt," Daniel says.

"I'm just finishing, Daniel," Greenblatt says. "I'm making a plea." He raises both hands as if to hold Daniel off, and then petitions for Marie's attentions again by touching her lightly. "I would like Marlowe College to be somehow involved in the Eight Chimneys Project, in either curating or administrating the museum, if it so happens that it comes to pass. Obviously, we can't help in terms of finances, but we could bring a lot of expertise and legitimacy to the project, and it would be a real boon to our history department, which, by the way, already rivals the best history departments in the country."

"We're okay on legitimacy, Ethan," Marie says. "What we're looking for is money."

Just then, Daniel hears Ruby's voice rising high above the wall-to-wall murmur of the party. At first, the sound alarms him, but then he hears it for what it is: a long trill of joy, and he knows there is only one person who can make Ruby quite that happy. Nelson's here.

Daniel hurries to the entrance hall. Ruby holds Nelson's hand and jumps up and down, trying to incite him to her level of frenzied joy, but Nelson is having none of it. He is glancing over his shoulder at his parents, who are taking their coats off and looking around, trying to figure out where to put them.

"Ruby, Ruby, calm down," Daniel says, making his presence known. He would like to think he is smiling casually, though he can't be sure.

"You were right!" Ruby says. "They're here!" She pushes her doll onto Daniel. "Hold this," she says, and then turns to Nelson. "You want chips?"

"Hey, you two," Daniel says to Iris and Hampton. In his desire to sound chipper, his voice comes out far too strongly. "Coats are in there, in the conservatory." A rush of dizziness. It seems he has forgotten how to distribute his weight when standing. He tries to look only at Hampton but is unable to keep his gaze off Iris. She is wearing a black sweater and jeans; she has a little Band-Aid on her right thumb and he resists the impulse to ask her how she hurt herself, and further resists the more absurd but equally powerful impulse to take her hand and kiss it. Iris has Hampton's coat and she carries it off with her own, leaving the two men alone for a moment. A wild stab of disappointment goes through Daniel—if Iris had given the coats to Hampton, she and Daniel could have had ten seconds of privacy.

"Nelson, come back here," Hampton commands. Nelson stops as if on the end of a leash and turns around to look at his father. Hampton crooks his finger and Nelson dutifully walks back to his side. Like Daniel—just like Daniel, in fact—he wears khaki trousers and a blue blazer, though his are more expensively tailored. The ceiling fixtures cast a brilliant light on his hairless dome.

"Where are we?" Hampton asks Nelson.

"Sorry," Nelson says.

"Question repeated. Where *are* we?"

Iris emerges from the coatroom. She is pushing up the sleeves of her sweater. Her face is expressionless.

"In a house," Nelson says.

"Correct. So? Can we please have *inside* behavior? Which means no running, no loud voices. All right?"

How would it play if I slugged him? Daniel wonders.

Nelson nods yes, and backs out of the entrance hall without taking his eyes off Hampton, as if to never turn his back on the king.

Then Daniel and Hampton, and Iris between them, walk into the ballroom, without looking at each other and without saying a word. Ferguson is standing on an old harp-backed chair in front of the fireplace, with his hands cupped over his mouth. "Attention, everybody," he calls out. His voice is authoritative, but with something good-natured in it, too, something that recognizes the absurdity of shouting at a roomful of people in Windsor County on a warm Sunday afternoon in November. "We're going to take you all on a grand tour of this house, this wonderful house, which I speak of not with the pride of ownership but the humility of stewardship." There is a smattering of applause; someone even says *hear hear*.

"What's this about?" Hampton asks.

"We're here to support the house," Iris says. "So they want to show it to us. Why is that a problem?"

Hampton shakes his head. He is clearly here against his wishes. He sees Nelson and gestures for him to come, which the boy does, immediately, with Ruby following.

Ferguson jumps off the chair and tosses wine from his plastic cup into the fireplace, igniting a sudden whoosh of flame. "Everybody line up along the west wall, and we'll exit the ballroom through the double doors, and go straight to the portrait gallery."

The guests are good-natured and compliant, and a line immediately forms. "I'm going to find Kate," Daniel announces, forcing himself away from Iris and Hampton.

He cranes his neck, trying to find her in the crowd.

"Ruby can come with us," Iris says.

The suggestion seems intimate and kind. Daniel cannot even look at her for fear of giving everything away. There is still no sign of Kate, and Daniel is the last out of the ballroom as the tour begins. Then he sees her, coming out of a bathroom near the main stairway. She seems startled to see all the guests in a line, making their way up the stairs. The tip of her nose is red; it looks as if she might have been crying.

"Tour," Daniel says.

"Let's get out of here." She looks at the doll in Daniel's hand, furrows her brow.

"We just got here. Come on. They'll show us around. You've never really seen this place."

They can hear Ferguson's voice from the landing of the second floor. "On the way to the portrait gallery, you'll notice quite a few first-rate paintings in the hallway. And you'll also notice a few blank spots, where paintings have been taken down and brought to Sotheby's."

"Did you know she was going to be here?"

"Who?"

"Please, don't insult me."

He hadn't meant to, it was just the first word out of his mouth. "No," he says. "How could I?"

"Don't answer my question with a question. I'd actually rather be lied to than subjected to that. It's how my father spoke to me, that demeaning, patriarchal bullshit."

"I didn't know she was going to be here." He feels he could make things a little easier if he could only touch Kate right now, just put a hand on her shoulder, but he is somehow unable to manage the gesture. It is as if that hand, the hand that could bring comfort to Kate, has been amputated, he has cut it off like Van Gogh's ear.

Kate exhales as if she has been holding her breath for a long while. "We should have brought two cars," she says.

The tour passes directly over them, thunderously, shaking the ceiling. Marie says in her high, ringing voice, "The rooms to your left will not be public space, but over here, to the right . . ."

"They're being given a tour by a blind woman," Kate says.

They are interrupted by the sound of footsteps coming down the stairs. It's Susan Richmond, moving in a daze, holding on to the banister for support. She stops midway and peers down at Daniel and Kate, and then shakes her head and continues her descent, holding her chin up now, to affect a certain grandeur. "Intolerable," she says, and then when she has reached the bottom of the stairs she walks up to Daniel and Kate, as if they were exactly the people she had hoped to find. "That little weasel is leading a tour of my house. If I stayed up there for one more second I was going to go insane." She steps in front of the mirror hanging in the entrance hall, the glass wavy, the backing showing through, framed in plain wood and shaped like a large slice of bread. She peers at her reflection, frowns. "Hmm. Maybe I've already gone insane." And then, turning toward Kate, she says, "I never told you how much I enjoyed *Peaches and Cream.* I just roared, that poor, ugly girl, and all the troubles she had. I gave it to Ferguson to read, but he never reads anything. Oh well, at least he doesn't pretend to, he'll actually come right out and say he hates reading. Either he disagrees with the author, in which case it annoys him, or he agrees, in which case it's a waste of time."

"I don't see how he could agree or disagree with my book," says Kate. "It's a novel, it would be like disagreeing with someone's dream."

"Yes, I see what you mean. That's marvelous." She turns to Daniel. "We're going to have to pull the plug on this, Daniel," she says. "I don't care what Fergie and his little friend say. This is intolerable. If we're having money problems we'll just have to find another way to solve them, even if it means that we go into the village every day and work at the hardware store. Anything would be better than this."

As Susan announces this, the tour, with Marie at the head of it, begins down the stairs. The force of the collective footsteps is so great that a faint cloud of plaster fills the sunlight that pours into the entrance hall.

"Next," Marie is saying, "we'll go down to the house's original cellar, which was part of the famous Underground Railroad, in the years preceding and during the American Civil War." The strain and the excitement of conducting this tour seem to be exacting their price. Marie's voice has become a little shrill, and she gestures wildly, as if waving away a swarm of gnats. "We envision this as one of the highlights of the tour. Right now, you'll have to use your imagination, but when we have everything set up it will be a sort of diorama of the period, with lifelike figures of slaves." She turns to face the guests and suddenly loses her footing. Ethan Greenblatt, who is directly behind her, manages to catch her by the jacket—if it weren't for him Marie would be in a heap at the bottom of the stairs.

"She's not above a lawsuit," Susan says to Kate. Then, to Daniel: "Don't mention anything to Marie about our stopping this ridiculous project of hers. I'll tell her myself, it seems only fair."

Marie is rattled by her near fall, but she continues with the tour, bringing the guests down to the ground floor, turning left in the entrance hall and leading them all through the conservatory, the dining room, the main kitchen, and then the summer kitchen, where the door to the cellar can be found.

Iris and Hampton walk through the entrance hall, followed by Ruby and Nelson. When Ruby sees Kate and Daniel, she calls out to them with her customary exuberance. "You're missing it, you guys. Come on, we're going down to see where the slaves hid." She holds her hand out.

"Let's take a look," Daniel says to Kate, taking Ruby's hand.

Ferguson has seen to it that the cellar is well lit for today's party—there are standing and clip-on lamps every few feet—but he has not been able to dispel the dank gloominess of the place. With its packed dirt floor and thick, fabriclike cobwebs, it seems more like a cave than a part of someone's house. It smells of rain and mold. Strips of pink fiberglass insulation hang from the ceiling. Generations of broken wooden chairs line the walls, awaiting repair. In fact, the entire place is a terminal ward for stricken furniture, some of it too valuable to dispose of, some saved for no apparent reason. Old leather chairs ooze cotton, dozens of old oak chairs stand along the wall with their cane seats torn, unraveled, or missing altogether. There is a small Queen Anne sofa upon which someone seems to have poured white paint. There's a rolltop desk missing all of its drawers, and with one of its legs replaced by an unpainted two-by-four. There are skis, tennis racquets, a croquet set, sleeping bags, a punching bag covered in dust hanging from a beam. There seem to be literally hundreds of paint cans, some without their tops appear to be empty, others seem brand-new. There are at least twenty large cartons of china, a dozen rolled-up rugs secured with twine and stood up on their ends, drooping and leaning into each other like a family of drunks. In a corner, someone has abandoned an old, elaborate model train set, its tracks ravaged, its cars toppled, its miniature landscape of trees, cows, and water towers scattered—it looks like the transportation system of a country that has lost a long, ruinous war.

At the north end of the old cellar is a cast-iron coal-burning furnace, unused for decades. Some twenty feet to the side of the furnace, the dirt and stone wall is paneled over with wide wooden planks, newly painted white. Marie stumbles for a moment on her way to the wall, and then when she reaches it she rests her hand on it. "Is everybody watching?" she calls out.

She spreads her small hand out as far as her fingers will reach, and then, applying pressure, slides a false panel in the wall over a few inches. Then she grabs hold of the edge of the opened panel and drags it further to the side, revealing a vast, dark emptiness.

"This is where the runaway slaves were kept," she calls out. "Sometimes there'd be just one or two of them, sometimes as many as ten. Then, when the coast was clear, they'd get herded out and sent on their way—to Canada, mostly. Where they'd be free. The great thing about this space is that the temperature is always sixty degrees, winter and summer, as is true with many of the rooms in Eight Chimneys."

Marie goes on for a while longer, telling everyone about Wendell Richmond, who was the master of the house from 1820 to 1882, and about the escaped slave who gave birth to a child in this cellar, and about the artifacts of that time that have recently been recovered—the little tin earrings, the diary filled with sketches of trees, fields, and other fleeing slaves, the unexplained human teeth. Then, finally, she steps into the old cloister and feels in the air for the lamp that has been set up—she has never looked more like a blind girl than at this moment, groping for the switch with almost spastic waves, like a kid pretending to have lost her sight.

The light comes on, revealing two mannequins that Ferguson got from the Fashion Bug at the Windsor Mall. One of them is dressed in overalls and a straw hat, the other in an old gingham dress, and both of them have been freshly painted brown. Ten by ten, the guests walk into the secreted room, have a look, and presumably imagine themselves hiding and hungry in such a place. It smells of mud that has been there forever, and the paint that only yesterday was sprayed on the mannequins' faces. When Daniel crowds in to look around for himself, Kate, refusing to be a part of the tour's grand finale, has already left, and when he feels the tip of a finger against his backbone, Daniel's heart quickens: he knows it is Iris's touch. He takes a deep breath and feels it again. It is just one finger, a circumspect gesture, a child's, a prisoner's, but the force of her fingertip stirs his blood. Then it is time for them all to turn around and let the next wave of guests come in to look at what is, after all, just a storage room in the cellar of an old house. When Daniel faces the other direction, he is behind Iris and Hampton, Nelson and Ruby. He could return the secret little touch, but he doesn't dare. He doesn't trust his hand; it is not inconceivable that once he touches her he will not be able to stop.

Upstairs in the ballroom, the party has become more animated. The guests, released now from the dutiful march through the house and its claustrophobic conclusion in the cellar's secret room, and further released from the slightly hectoring quality of Marie's voice, are gossiping and joking with each other in increasingly excited voices. Daniel is looking to see where Kate is now and finally sees her across the room, standing with Derek, whose face is very close to hers and who is speaking to her with what appears to be great seriousness. Daniel sees Iris, too; she's talking with Ethan Greenblatt. Then he sees Susan with Marie. Susan is holding Marie by the upper arm and seems to be scolding her. Marie tries to yank her arm away but Susan's grip is too strong. She continues to speak to Marie, with a rather cruel, powerful smile on her face, and suddenly Marie breaks free.

Marie leaves the ballroom and heads straight out of the house, without so much as a jacket or a sweater. Seeing this gives Daniel a small jolt of concern, but before he can give it much more thought, Daniel is set upon by Upton Douglas, who swings his way over on his crutches, accompanied by a willowy middle-aged woman with an elegantly unhappy face, a widow from Buffalo, to whom Douglas has been showing houses in the area. Upton wants Daniel to talk to her about how grand it is to live in Leyden, its beauty, and convenience, its friendly atmosphere and myriad cultural events, and Daniel is trapped in this seemingly endless conversation.

Finally, he feels a tug at his back pocket. It's Ruby.

"Can I have Ginkie?" she asks.

It takes him a moment to understand she wants her doll, and another moment to realize he no longer has it in hand. And then he remembers: when he felt Iris's finger on his spine, his hands instinctively opened and the doll slipped from his grasp.

"Oh, you know what, Ruby?" he says, scooping her up. "I think I accidentally left her downstairs."

"Where?"

"Just wait here. Find Mommy, and I'll find Ginkie."

He sets Ruby down and waits there for a moment while she hurries off to find Kate. When she has disappeared into the crowd, Daniel walks out of the ballroom and makes his way through the dining room, the kitchen, and the summer kitchen, where he finds Ferguson and Derek huddled together in intense conversation. Ferguson's shoes are covered with fresh, wet dirt; there is a muddy patch on his right knee.

"Daniel," Ferguson says, "Marie's gone missing."

"Have you seen her?" Derek asks.

"I saw her leave," Daniel says. "Maybe half an hour ago." He has his hand on the door leading down to the cellar. He can barely even form this thought in his own mind, but the fact is that he hasn't seen Iris for a while and he cannot help but wonder if she is still somehow in the cellar.

"Well, you know what *I* think," Derek says to Ferguson. "She's blind. I don't care how well she knows the property, things are torn up out there and where there used to be paths there's nothing but fallen trees. And those boys from the juvey home are still at large and for all we know they could be out there right now."

"My God," says Daniel. "You and Kate are really focused on those kids."

"You would be, too, if it happened to you," Derek says sharply.

"What do you think I should do?" Ferguson asks.

"You want me to call it in?"

Ferguson sighs, looks away, and Derek presses him.

"I appreciate your wanting to be discreet . . ."

Ferguson sighs. "Call it in," he says.

"I'll be right back," Daniel says, opening the cellar door.

"Where are you going?" Ferguson asks.

"My kid left her doll down there," Daniel says. He waits for a moment and then quickly heads down the stairs, holding on to the banister, his legs trembling.

A few lights have been left burning and he easily makes his way past the Richmond family's cast-off possessions. The sliding door to the secret room is still half open, and by the time he pulls it all the way to the side his heart is pounding violently.

"Hello," Iris says. She has been sitting on a small, rough-hewn bench and she rises as Daniel walks in. She is holding Ruby's doll. She and Daniel stand there facing each other for a moment, and then she hands the doll to him. "Here."

"Thank you," he says. The two painted mannequins seem to be staring at him. He looks at Ruby's doll for a moment and then lets it drop from his hands. He puts his arms around Iris.

"I was waiting for you," she whispers.

[14]

Daniel and Iris rearrange their clothes. They are reeling. Their legs are weak. Desire summoned but unresolved leaves them nervous yet vague, like people awakened while dreaming.

"Wait here," Iris whispers, her lips an inch from his mouth. She turns to leave but he catches her, stops her, just to show that he can. She slips away from him and hurries out of the cellar, he hears the heels of her shoes clacking against the wooden stairs, *bang bang,* it's like being buried alive and listening to the hammer driving the nails into the coffin.

He waits, and when he finally comes back upstairs, he is still trembling, but no one pays attention to his arrival, no one asks where he's been, or what the matter is. They are gathered in front of Ferguson, who is addressing them all.

"All right, then," he's saying, "here's what we're going to do. First, I want to thank you all for your help. My family appreciates it and I appreciate it, and I think if we go out there, and just do this in an orderly way, we'll find Marie before she hurts herself. The police have been informed, but there's not a hell of a lot they can do right now. I don't know what we're paying our taxes for, but it's not for helicopters. So it'll be up to us."

Nine men and five women volunteer to form a search party to find poor Marie. Everything capable and charismatic in Ferguson is on display as he addresses the volunteers. His voice is powerful, confident; he has even produced a topographical map of his holdings, and he stands before it now and taps at it with his blunt, oil-stained forefinger.

"This is where we are right now. The house is right in the center of the property, plus or minus three degrees. We can radiate out from the house, and since we'll have seven teams, each team can cover roughly a forty-five-degree slice of the pie."

Susan has come up close beside him. Her expression is at once proprietary and serene, like a cat about to stretch out next to something it has killed. She is holding a large wicker basket with both hands; it is filled with what appear to be thick, red cigars, with pictures of medieval lions printed on them.

Gathered in the entrance hall, beneath the stained and sagging grandeur of the painted ceiling, the volunteers choose their partners. Daniel doesn't care whom he is paired with, as long as it's not Hampton, but luck would have it otherwise. Hampton may not like Daniel but at least he knows him, however uneasily, and without actually saying anything he stands next to Daniel, as if their searching for Marie together is a foregone conclusion.

"We need a way of signaling when we find her," Susan is saying. "I've got Roman candles and everyone should take one. If you find her, light the fuse, and the rest of the search party will know."

"Where did you get those?" asks Ferguson.

"Remember when we had that Burmese purification ceremony two Septembers ago?" Susan says, dropping the basket onto the floor. She cannot help reflecting upon how Ferguson had mocked the ritual, as he mocked all rituals, or anything new—except the ritual of infidelity and the novelty of a new young body. "Help yourselves," she says. She figures that everyone here knows that Ferguson is screwing Marie, and probably they assume that Marie has fled the house because Susan finally told that little whore what she thinks of her—and they are essentially correct in that assumption, though "finally" might not be the right word, since Marie has known of Susan's enmity all along, and why she picked today of all days to overreact is anybody's guess. Of one thing, however, Susan is certain: Marie will try to find a way of turning this irritating little drama to her own advantage.

"Be careful," Susan announces, as the guests take the Roman candles out of the basket. "They pack quite a wallop."

The search party files out of the foyer, onto the porch. Daniel and Hampton head south-southwest, across a ruined expanse of wild grass that soon leads to a dense wood of pine, locust, maple, and oak.

Once they are in the woods, the remains of the afternoon light seem to shrink away. The shadows of the trees—a shocking number of which have fallen to the ground from the weight of October's sudden snowstorm—seem to pile on top of each other, one shadow over the next, building a wall of darkness. There had always been paths through the woods, made by the herds of deer that traversed these acres, or left over from the old days when there had been enough money to maintain and even manicure the Richmond holdings. But the October storm had dropped thousands of trees, and the paths are somewhere beneath them, invisible now. Daniel and Hampton can't take two steps without having to scramble over the canopy of a fallen tree, or climb over a trunk, or a crisscross of trunks, slippery with rot. And where there aren't fallen trees there are thorny blackberry vines that furl out across the forest floor like a sharp, punishing fog.

Here and there are little white throw rugs of snow.

"These vines are like razor wire," says Daniel. Everything he says seems potentially disastrous, every word packed with black powder and a short fuse.

"Damn!" said Hampton. A snarl of vines has caught his cuffs, and as he yanks his leg free, the thorn tears his skin right through his sock.

"Are you all right?" Daniel says. They are halfway up a gentle slope—it seems to Daniel that if they could get to the top of the hill, they might be able to see over the trees and gain some sense of where they are.

"Yeah, I'm fine." Hampton touches his ankle and then looks at his fingertip: red. "I just wish Ferguson took care of his own mess."

"You mean Marie?"

"He's sleeping with her in his house, with his wife there. Insanity. What does the man expect?" Even now, he speaks formally, his voice deep and honeyed, every syllable distinct.

"Not this, probably." Daniel stands ten feet from Hampton. He feels moisture from the forest floor seeping through the thin soles of his Sunday shoes. "Anyhow, are we really sure Fergie's sleeping with Marie?"

"That's what Iris tells me," Hampton says. "Ferguson's known Marie since she was a little girl. And since he and Susan don't have children, it's like a sublimated incest."

"Is that what Iris says?"

"Hasn't she said it to you?" Hampton asks, raising his eyebrows.

Oh Jesus, he's closing in, thinks Daniel.

They walk. The crunch of their footsteps. The cries of invisible birds. Daniel cups his hands around his mouth and calls Marie's name, silencing the birds. The noise of their footsteps on the brittle layer of dried leaves that covers the forest floor is like a saw going tirelessly back and forth. They have no idea where they are going.

They zigzag around fallen trees and swirls of bramble. Daniel walks in front. He looks over his shoulder. Hampton is having a hard time keeping his balance.

"I'm ruining these shoes," Hampton says. He leans against a partially fallen cherry tree and looks at the sole of his English cordovan. The leather is shiny, rosy, and moist, like a human tongue.

"Are you all right?" asks Daniel.

Hampton nods curtly. "I hate the woods," he says. "I don't even like trees. I prefer landscape that's flat and open, where you can see what's out there."

"Well, you're a long-range planner," says Daniel. "So that figures."

Hampton frowns. He seems to be questioning Daniel's right to be making glib generalizations about him.

"My wife tells me she sees a lot of you during the week," he says.

"Well, you know, the kids," Daniel says. "Kate's daughter worships your son. It's Nelson this and Nelson that. Constantly."

Hampton tries to remember the little girl's name. He recalls it was the name of one of his aunts—but his mother has four sisters by blood and three stepsisters, and then all those sisters-in-law. Hampton was raised in a swirling, scolding vortex of large, vivid women.

"It's like seeing what it'll be like when Ruby falls in love," says Daniel.

Ah, right: Ruby. Actually, none of his aunts had that name, no one came any closer to that than his aunt Scarlet, a well-powdered librarian, whose upper arms were like thighs, and who, nevertheless, was usually in a sleeveless dress, which displayed not only her fleshy arms but her vaccination, a raised opacity of skin and scar the size of a pocket watch. And Scarlet wasn't even her name—it was Charlotte, but one of the other nephews mispronounced it and Scarlet stuck.

Hampton presses a button on the side of his watch, the dial lights up like a firefly for a moment.

"It's almost five o'clock."

"It'll be dark soon," says Daniel. "I wonder if anyone's found her."

"This is so messed up."

"Marie!" Daniel shouts, but his voice drops like an anvil ten feet in front of him.

"I have to be on the nine o'clock train tonight. That Monday morning train's no good for me."

Daniel keeps quiet about that, though he is by now, of course, fully aware of Hampton's hours of departure and arrival. Infidelity is an ugly business, but it makes you a stickler for detail. You're an air traffic controller and the sky is stacked up with lies, all of them circling and circling, the tips of their wings sometimes coming within inches of each other.

They reach the top of the small hill, but the sight lines are no better than below. The only sky they can see is directly above them, gray, going black.

"What do you think?" says Daniel.

"I think we're lost," Hampton says, shaking his head.

"Next they'll be sending a search party after us," Daniel says. He notices something on the ground and peers more closely at it. A dead coyote like a flat gray shadow. Sometimes at night, he and Kate could hear coyotes in the distance, a pack whipping themselves up into a frenzy of howls and yips, but this desiccated pelt, eyeless, tongueless, is the closest he has come to actually seeing one.

"What do you have there?" Hampton asks.

"The animal formerly known as coyote," Daniel says.

Breaking off a low, bare branch from a dead hemlock, Daniel pokes the coyote's remains. Curious, Hampton stands next to him. A puff of colorless dust rises up. The world seems so deeply inhospitable—but, of course, it isn't: they are just in the part of it that isn't made for them. Here, it is for deer, foxes, raccoons, birds and mice and hard-shelled insects, fish, toads, sloths, maggots. Hampton steps back and covers his mouth and nose with his hand, as if breathing in the little puff that has arisen from the coyote will imperil him. Iris has often bemoaned her husband's fastidiousness, his loathing of mess, his fear of germs. He has turned the controls of their water heater up and now the water comes out scalding, hot enough to kill most household bacteria. There are pump-and-squirt bottles of antibacterial soap next to every sink in the house; if Iris has a cold, Hampton sleeps in the guest room, and if Nelson has so much as a sniffle, Hampton will eschew kissing the little boy good night, he will shake hands with him instead and then, within minutes, he'll be squirting that bright emerald-green soap into his palm.

An immense oak tree lies on the ground; Hampton rests his foot on it and then shouts Marie's name. The veins on his neck swell; Daniel has a sense of what it would be like to deal with Hampton's temper, about which he has heard a great deal from Iris. No wonder Iris hasn't told Hampton a thing. She is afraid. *How could I have not seen it before?* Daniel wonders. *She has not told him, she will never tell him, and if she does Hampton will kill her. Or me.*

Discouraged, exhausted, Hampton sits on the fallen tree—and immediately springs up again. He has sat upon the Roman candle in his back pocket and it split in two. He quickly pulls it out, with frantic gestures, as if it might explode, and tosses the top half of the candy-striped cardboard tubing as far from him as he can.

Now his back pocket is filled with the Roman candle's black powder, a mixture of saltpeter, sulfur, arsenic, and strontium. *If I kick him in the ass, he might explode,* thinks Daniel. He has a vision of Hampton blasting off, sailing high above the tree line, smoke pouring out of his behind.

Suddenly, in the distance is a pop, and then a plume of iridescent smoke rises above the trees, a vivid tear in the dark silken sky.

"Someone's got her," Daniel says. "I just saw a flare."

Hampton looks up. Only a small circle of sky is visible through the encirclement of trees. "What's a damn blind girl doing out here? Even with eyes you can't make your way."

"She was raised here," Daniel says. "Her father was the caretaker. She came back to look after him when he got sick. Smiley."

"Smiley? What do you mean?"

"That's what everyone called him. I used to see him in town when *I* was a kid."

Hampton shakes his head. "These people, they're living in another century. They got their old family retainers, their fox-hunting clubs, their ice boats, they play tennis with these tiny little wooden racquets, and New Year's Eve they put on the rusty tuxedos their grandfathers used to wear."

"They can be pretty absurd," Daniel says. "They're half mad, but it's okay, if you have a sense of humor about it."

"That was the first thing Iris ever said about you, how you have this terrific sense of humor."

"Class clown," says Daniel. "In my case, middle class."

Hampton is still pinching black powder out of his back pocket, rubbing it between his thumb and forefinger. He tosses the powder into the darkness, as if scattering ashes after a cremation. He rakes a handful of dead leaves off of a wild cherry tree, one that is still standing, and uses them to wipe his hands. "I used to make Iris laugh all the time."

"I used to make Kate laugh, too," says Daniel. He says it because he has to say something. He cannot simply let Hampton go on about Iris and not say anything in reply. It would be too strange, and it would be suspicious, too. "First couple of years, I had her in hysterics."

He notices that Hampton's shaved head has suffered a scrape. There's a little red worm of blood on the smooth scalp.

"Kate doesn't think you're funny anymore?"

"No, she doesn't," Daniel says.

"Iris thinks you're funny. Maybe you're funnier around her."

"Maybe she's just very kind."

"Or very lonely."

As far as Daniel is concerned, this is torture. It might be better just to come out with it, tell Hampton: *I love Iris, and it seems she loves me. We belong together. We do feel bad* . . . Oh, shut up about feeling bad. Do you think he cares? He'd like you to have brain cancer, that would be the sort of suffering he'd like for you. Why are you offering up your stricken conscience—to make him feel you've been punished sufficiently? Are you so afraid of him? And with that question, Daniel at last connects to the core of what had been plaguing him from the moment he and Hampton set off together in search of Marie. It is not really about conscience, after all. He's been wrestling with conscience for months now, they are old sparring partners, sometimes he pins it to the mat, sometimes it slams him, it doesn't really amount to much, it's a show, like wrestling on TV. And besides: the worst sort of remorse is preferable to what preceded it, which was the infinitely greater agony of longing for Iris. Remorse is the payment due for the fulfillment of his great desire. And it is, finally, a payment he was willing to make. No, it is not his conscience that churns sickly at the center of him, making him cringe inwardly when Hampton steps too close to him. It is fear, physical fear.

They continue to walk, hoping to find a clearing, a way out. Once, most of this land was pasture, grazed by cattle, but it hadn't seen a plow in over a hundred years and left to its own had become a wild place. They climb yet another hill. This one might have been steeper—because they both have to hold on to trees to pull themselves up—or else they are getting tired.

And once they have scaled it, all they can see is more trees—except on one side, where there is a sharp drop-off, leading to what looks like a large pond filled with black water.

"We came from that direction," Hampton says uncertainly. He points down the hill upon which they stand, and off to the left. The night is gathering quickly, the darkness rushes in like water through the hull of a ship, covering everything.

It seems to Daniel that they have walked *down* the hill, as well as walking up it. In fact, they may have traipsed up and down it three or four times. But he chooses to not argue the matter.

"All right," he says. "I have no idea." He touches the Roman candle in his back pocket. Maybe set it off right now, before it got any darker. But how much darker could it get? Better to save the flare for later, if needed.

"Do you know how to get out of here?" Hampton asks.

"No."

"Then let's go."

"Fine, lead the way."

They half walk and half slide down the hill, with their arms in front of their faces to protect themselves from the saplings.

The problem is there is no space to walk in; the woods have imploded. They seem to be walking in circles, corkscrewing themselves into oblivion, continually tripping over vines, stumbling over fallen trees, getting scraped by branches, stomping into sudden pools of still water, sometimes walking right into a standing tree. It is as if they are being toyed with. Isolated in their despair, they walk for half an hour without speaking.

Then, suddenly, a little stretch where last month's storm seemed to have done little damage. They walk for three minutes without having to change course. And though they don't know which direction they are going in, the mere fact of keeping a constant course gives them a bit of encouragement. They are not, after all, in the middle of some vast uncharted wilderness. They are only a hundred miles north of the city. How far can they go without ending up on some stretch of asphalt or in someone's backyard? But then they reach a devastated grove of locusts, the saplings with bark spiked with thorns, like giant, petrified roses. There are so many of them down on the ground, or leaning against each other in a swoon, that it would have been impossible to get through them or past them even in daylight.

"I think we've already been here," Hampton says.

"Really? What makes you think so?"

In the blindness of the night, Daniel can sense from the quality of the silence that Hampton is glaring at him.

"What makes me think so?" asks Hampton. His voice seems completely unconnected to his feelings; even in anger, it is melodious.

"I think we're making progress," Daniel says.

"Well, we're not, we're going in circles."

"Hampton. I've been following you. All right?"

"We're going in circles."

"Well, you've been taking us there."

"Daniel?"

"What?"

"Can I make a suggestion?"

"Sure. What?"

"Go fuck yourself."

There is a rock nearby, embedded deeply into the forest floor and covered with moss and lichen. Hampton tries to scale it, hoping to see a break in the woods, but the soles of his shoes are slick, and as soon as he stands on the rock he slips and falls hard onto his hands and knees, and just stays there, with his head down, for several moments.

Daniel goes to his side, touches him softly on the shoulder. "Here," he says. He puts out his hand. Hampton's fingers are hard and cold; he grasps Daniel's hand like a statue come to life. Daniel steps back and pulls Hampton to his feet. It is strange to be touching this man who once had, and is now losing, everything.

"You know," Hampton says, "even in the dark I can still sort of see you. Your white skin picks up every little bit of light there is."

"Yeah?"

"I guess you can't see me at all, can you?"

Daniel doesn't want to say no; he just shakes his head. He wonders if Iris's scent is on him—surely Hampton would recognize it. He moves a little farther away. This great secret life suddenly feels like groceries coming out of a wet paper sack.

"What's it like being lost out here with a big old African-American man who you basically do not know."

"What are you talking about, Hampton?"

"Just that. I'm curious. I see white people all the time, but I rarely have the opportunity to ask them certain things. Do you know many black people, Daniel?"

"A few. I used to know more. Out here, it's more difficult, obviously."

"But here's where you are, it's what you chose, you *moved* here."

"Not to get away from black people."

"Are you sure about that?"

"If you want to know the truth, I think my prejudice goes the other way. Black people have something I've always wanted."

"Rhythm?"

"That's ridiculous." He backs still farther away, stumbles, rights himself.

"All right. Sorry. What is it we black people have that you've always wanted?"

"Family. Community."

Hampton laughs—a sudden, rude bark of amusement.

"I know how it sounds," says Daniel. He searches his mind for something to substitute, some innocuous generalization, something admiring of black people that won't seem too utterly stupid and condescending.

Hampton is silent. He takes a deep breath, a man controlling his temper.

"Is that what you see in Iris?" he finally asks. "Someone in touch with her feelings who can put you in touch with yours?"

So here it is, thinks Daniel. A kind of exhaustion of strategy begins to overcome him, a growing incapacity to dodge and maneuver. The lies he has told weigh him down, it is as if they were stones with which he has filled his pockets. His psychological step is increasingly heavy and un-sure. One day, Daniel thinks, Hampton will replay this conversation in his mind and every lie he has told will be vivid and repulsive to him. But, for now, Daniel must stay the course.

"I see everything in Iris," Daniel says quietly.

"Don't be deceived by her skin and her hair. She's as white as the bankers I see down in the city."

"Let's not do this here, okay, Hampton? You want to talk about this, I'll talk about it. But let's get out of these woods, go someplace where we can sit down."

"So you're making the rules?"

"I'm asking."

Another silence. Daniel hears Hampton exhale.

"Fine. Wait here for a second, all right? I have to urinate." Even this announcement is made in Hampton's public speaker's voice.

There's a break in the black sky and the platinum moonlight pours down on them. The whites of Hampton's eyes glitter. His shirt is dirty, his trousers are covered in burrs and black with mud at the knees.

"I'll wait here," Daniel says.

Hampton's footsteps crunch over the dried leaves, fainter and fainter. Where is he going? Uphill? It's hard for Daniel to tell which way Hampton is walking, and then, ten seconds later, fifteen at the most, he can't hear him at all.

Daniel walks a couple of careful, shuffling steps until he feels the hard presence of yet another fallen tree. He crouches down, runs his hands along the bark. No branches, no large knots. He sits carefully on the tree trunk and waits. He cannot continue with these lies—he remembers thinking this, the nearness of this confession is what will come to haunt him. He will remember thinking that the ordering of events, the careful timing of when the truth can be released, all of it is being taken out of his hand.

Hampton's piss seems to be taking an extraordinarily long time. The cold wind rustles the treetops. A presence of spirits? Who knew? From someplace quite near comes the sound of a pack of coyotes, a frenzy of yips and yowls.

Daniel loses patience, stands. "Hampton? You all right?" There is no answer. Even the coyotes are silent, for a moment. Daniel wonders if Hampton has simply decided to ditch him, to abandon him in these ruined woods. A rush of malevolence streaks through him, like a comet with its rock- and ice-strewn brilliance, its searing, filthy light. For a moment, he despises Hampton as much as he had during the very worst nights of longing for Iris, when sleep was impossible and there was no end to the hatred he had for the man who had everything Daniel wanted.

"Hampton?" Daniel says, much louder this time. He hears the slight hysteria in his voice, feels it in his throat. "Hampton? Hampton! Are you there?"

He makes some vague, stumbling effort to find him. Seeing almost nothing, Daniel makes his way up the steep hill. He must grab on to the trees along the way to power himself up. Hadn't they been on this steep hill before? Isn't this the one with the sharp drop-off into a pool of black water fifty feet below? Or is this another one just like it?

Daniel scrambles to the top of the hill. His face stings and when he touches it he realizes that he must have gotten hit by a branch. His fingertips are wet. He is bleeding.

"Hampton?" Silence. He feels a wind at his back and turns quickly. He is right on the edge of that fifty-foot drop-off.

A jolt of fear goes through him. He has a vision of Hampton springing up and hitting him on the shoulders with his open hands, and sending him falling off the hill and into the water.

And as soon as that thought occurs, he realizes that is exactly where Hampton is, in that black water below. He has fallen. Those shoes, those pricey, prissy fucking shoes. He is down there, probably facedown in the water.

Daniel stands there, not knowing what to do. Should he skid down and see if he can find Hampton? It seems insane. He might have gone in another direction, he might right now be back at the spot at which they'd parted, wondering where Daniel has gone.

The cold wind parts the clouds and moonlight shines down again. Daniel looks down, sees that he is only a foot from the edge of the hill. Again he steps back. His heart is leaping up and down inside of him, like a creature trapped in a well. He is suddenly exhausted. He has an over-powering desire to sit down, close his eyes, but forces himself to care-fully inch closer to the drop-off. The ground is an impasto of pebble, pine needle, and slippery cold mud.

He gets down on his hands and knees. The clouds are already making their way back to the moon, he has only a few moments of light. He peers down at the pond—and there it is: the unthinkable. Hampton. Facedown in the water. Arms stretched out before him, jacket balloon-ing, making him look like a hunchback.

Daniel claps his hand over his own eyes, turns away, sits there, draws up his knees, shudders.

Do something.

It seems as if he were paralyzed.

Do something. Now!

If only he had raced down, if only Daniel had taken that steep, plung-ing run toward the water with total abandon. He was screaming, *Oh my God, oh my God,* but he was not selfless. He kept his face covered. He slowed down when he lost traction and began to skid. And when his foot caught on an exposed root and he fell to the ground, he stayed there for an extra heartbeat or two, trying to gather his strength. He would re-member the clumsy caution of his descent.

When he is nearly down the slope, he loses his footing again. He does not fall but he has to run in an awkward, stiff-legged way to keep his balance. His momentum takes him into the water, right up to his knees. The cold is like being hit in the shins with a tire iron. Hampton's form has drifted to-ward the center of the pond. Daniel calls his name. This time his shout is not stillborn, it blooms in echoes. But there is no reply, no movement.

Daniel takes another step and the bottom of the pond falls away. Instinctively, he rears back, stops himself from going forward, from going under. Panic is upon him, merciless and annihilating. The water rushes into his clothes, it is like the paralyzing sting of an insect, something to render him helpless so he can be consumed. He has never been a strong swimmer, in fact, he can barely swim. There is no chance of his rescuing Hampton, if there was any Hampton left to rescue. Daniel backs up a step, and then another, he reaches into his pocket and pulls out the Roman candle.

He crouches at the edge of the pond, jams the base of the Roman candle into the ground. The fuse is plastered to the side of the cardboard cylinder and Daniel has to tease it up with his fingernails, makes it stand straight out so that he can light it. He digs in his front pocket for matches. Quarters fall out, as well as his keys. He finds the matches. They are damp, and the first one doesn't light. But the second one does. His hands are shaking but he finally gets the flame to the fuse. It sparks up with a sudden, nervous hiss. Someone will see it, someone will come. In the meanwhile, he will try to force himself back into the water, if it is at all possible. The wind is parting the clouds again, the moonlight is starting to come through, a long platinum spoke of it. The fuse burns slowly for the first couple inches, but then accelerates.

He realizes that the candle is pointing right at him, that it is going to fire into his face, and he jerks his head away and quickly pushes the candle forward.

He scrambles up. Then, in the darkness, against all probability: he hears a voice. "Hey, what are you doing?" He looks up at the sound and sees Hampton standing at the top of the hill.

There is an instant when Daniel is almost wild with relief. It is as if he loves Hampton as much as he loves Iris.

The Roman candle ignites, and the first fireball from it rises and flies, making a sound like air being sucked out of a pipe. It launches at a forty-five-degree angle and never reaches the sky. It strikes Hampton and buries itself deep into the softest part of his throat. Hampton just stands in place. There is enough moonlight now to see his expression. He is stunned, hurt. His mouth opens. His hand clasps the object in his throat, but he doesn't appear to be trying to pull it out. It's almost as if he's holding it in place. His legs buckle and then they are useless. He sits down, heavily, his head falls forward and then his body tilts to the side. He topples over and starts to roll.

Daniel runs up the hill, shouting. But even now his progress is impeded; he looks over his shoulder, back down at the pond. He is still in the grip of the notion that Hampton, another Hampton, the real Hampton, is in the water, he can't quite shake it. Though now the clouds are moving quickly and the moonlight is streaming down, and Daniel can see what he could not see before—in the water is a partially submerged log, the top half of a tree that has been snapped in two by the storm, its ganglia of dead branches surrounded by leaves.

Six months pass. The spring is winding down, reverting to the insolent, unpredictable nature with which it began, cold one day, warm the next. Though the schools have weeks before closing for summer, the Leyden teenagers are behaving as if their vacations have already begun, prowling the streets beginning in the late afternoon and staying in their packs through the evening. Now it's about four in the afternoon, a bright, mild day, the sky like a child's drawing, and Derek Pabst drives his patrol car through Leyden's small commercial neighborhood, past the Koffee Kup, which seems to serve everyone in town who drives an American car, and then past the Taste of SoHo, where most of the customers drive imports, and then past Windsor Hardware, which has begun stocking more Italian crockery and ornate English fireplace utensils. For the most part, the stores on Leyden's little Broadway are the same ones that were there when Derek was a boy—the Smoke Shop, Mountain Stream Realty, Buddy's Card Shop, Candyland, Donna's Uniforms, the Windsor Pharmacy, Sew and Vac, Kirk's Variety Store, Fin and Feather, Tack and Tackle, and the Stoller and Hoffman Insurance Agency.

Derek cruises through town without expecting to see anything he will have to react to. Except for traffic violations, he has never seen a crime in progress in his twelve-year career. He has been, for the most part, after the fact—showing up after a house has been burgled, after a wall has been covered with graffiti, after a wife has been smacked around by her drunken husband. Finding Marie Thorne in the Richmond woods last November had been the most dynamic moment of Derek's career, and the satisfaction of that feat was all but cancelled by, first of all, her not wanting to be found, and, secondly, by the hideous accident that took place in those same woods a half hour later. Nevertheless, Derek remains alert as he makes his customary rounds. You make your presence known, you show the flag. It reminds people they are living under the rule of law, it makes everyone feel safer, it brings out the best in them. He stops at the town's central traffic light, where Broadway intersects with Route 100, the county's main road that goes south to New York City and north to Albany. The wind swings the hanging traffic light back and forth like a censer. A processional of high school kids crosses the street in front of him, fifteen- and sixteen-year-olds in cargo pants and tank tops, a mixed group of boys and girls, horsing around, shoves, laughter, their skin glistening, all of them in hormonal overdrive.

As is Derek himself. Spring always awakens his longing. He thaws like a river, his blood rushes, he can hear it as he lies in his bed and waits to fall asleep. The constellations wheeling in the spring skies seem to exert undue influence on him. It is not only that he is seasonally overcome with lust, but that the lust itself has such a melancholy weight to it. He watches the teenagers as they make their way through the white lines of the crosswalk and come percolating up onto the sidewalk. Is that Buddy Guyette's daughter in those pale, distressed jeans? My God, the ass on her. He feels a little twist of sensual agony. Then he sees Mercy Crane, whose father is also a Leyden cop. She is alone, walking with her eyes cast down, wearing baggy clothes to hide her shape. She looks dejected, her hair hangs lank and dirty over her eyes, she slings her backpack over her shoulder and holds on to the strap with one hand.

Mercy looks up, sees Derek through the sun-struck windshield, with its reflections of rooftops and upside-down trees. She raises a practically lifeless hand in greeting, ekes out a tiny smile.

Derek drives another quarter mile and turns into the driveway leading to the Richmond Library, originally funded by Ferguson Richmond's family a hundred years ago. Now it's a public library, funded half by the state and half by the town. It's a pleasant old brick building, with something of the Russian dacha about it, flanked by locust trees. Derek likes to come here to smoke in private, sitting on the hood of his car, savoring the taste of tobacco, letting the nicotine simultaneously jack him up and cool him down, and think about his life. A few years ago, the town built a basketball court behind the library, and though the cement has cracked and the baskets aren't regulation height, there's often a decent pickup game going on for Derek to watch while he smokes.

He steers his car with the heel of his left hand, using the right to pluck a cigarette out of his breast pocket. As he swings around the library and approaches the court, he can hear the excited young male voices, the pounding of the ball on the cement, and then he sees something that galvanizes him, sends a rush of adrenaline through him.

Two African-American males, fifteen to eighteen years old, one tall, the other taller, one thin, the other thinner, one black, the other blacker, and both of them fitting the description of two of the escaped Star of Bethlehem boys who are still at large. Unsnapping his holster strap as he gets out of the car, Derek walks quickly toward the basketball court. It's a two-on-two full-court game, shirts versus skins, both the black kids have their shirts off. Derek approaches from the north and the action is under the south basket, so no one sees him right away. But then someone makes a basket, the ball is taken out of bounds, and the flow of the game reverses. Derek is still fifteen or twenty yards from the fence surrounding the court. As soon as he knows he's been spotted he breaks into a run, shouting, "Hey, you, stay where you are. Don't move."

The white boys do as they're told, but the blacks know better. They practically fly through the gate on the south end of the court and into the cornfield that's on the Richmond Library's eastern edge. In the past, the corn would not have been knee-high this time of year, but the farmer who normally harvests these thirty acres moved to Arizona, and last year's crop, ten feet tall and dark brown, is still standing. The boys are invisible.

Derek doesn't bother to chase them in. As a boy, he ran from friends, rivals, and even the police through this very same field of corn, and he knows exactly where the boys will emerge—they will take the natural path that empties out onto the open land right behind the VFW post. He walks quickly back to his car, but before he gets in he shouts at the white boys: "You be here when I get back."

It takes barely a minute to drive to the VFW. It's a squat little asphalt-shingled lodge, with squinty little windows and white pebbles in the parking area. Two flags snap smartly in the breeze—the red, white, and blue and the black POW-MIA. Derek parks his car in front and makes his way to the rear of the building. A long sloping lawn heads right down to the cornfield. He walks a few feet into the dried brown rows of last year's crop, just deep enough in to conceal himself, about ten feet to the right of the deer path that boys have been using for probably a hundred years. His heart is pounding with anticipation. He will listen for their footsteps, and when they are almost out of the field he will step into their path with his gun drawn. For a moment, he considers unlocking the safety, but he thinks better of it. He is not without self-knowledge and he senses within himself a desire to do some harm.

Derek waits in the field. The drone of an airplane passing overhead, the drone of traffic, the drone of a million flies who have come to feast on the corn's rot, the drone of a motorcycle just picking up some speed. He feels a cold trickle of sweat going down his spine. He disengages the safety on his gun.

After ten minutes, it's obvious that those black boys must have found some other way out. Nevertheless, Derek continues to wait, while the sweat accumulates at his belt line and the humming of his mind winds tighter and tighter, higher and higher. At last, he forces himself to concede his plan has not worked. He walks back to his car, returns to the basketball court.

The white boys have waited for him, as instructed. He's watched these two grow up. They used to blush, literally wring their small hands with pleasure when he spoke to them, but now they are at the age of secrets and not one of them can look directly into his eyes. They claim not to know the name of either of the black kids they were playing ball with not fifteen minutes ago.

"Ever see either of them before?" Derek asks, pretending to believe them, keeping up the fiction that they are all on the same side in this matter.

This isn't even dignified with an answer, not a grunt, not even a slight shifting of weight.

"What about it, Todd?" Derek says, figuring he'll have better luck singling one of them out. He chooses Todd because Todd's a good kid, with a brother in the Marines and a schoolteacher mother, on the one hand, and a father who took off for Hawaii to live in a nudist commune, on the other hand, so Todd's got to know right from wrong.

"We don't know them, Officer Pabst," Todd says. Christ, what a piece of work this kid's become, the insincerity wrapping around his voice like red stripes on a candy cane. "We were just playing a little B-ball with them."

"A little B-ball," Derek says.

"Are you charging us with something?" asks Avery Hoffman, an aging cherub with a messy mustache. Avery's father is a lawyer with the public defender's office who has argued so many losing cases that he's become one of those crackpot small-town cynics who sense a deal, a fix, or a conspiracy in every transaction. Derek thrusts his eyes upon Avery with the force of a nightstick, but the kid doesn't fold. "Cause if you're not," he continues, "we'd sort of like to get back to our game."

Derek laughs invitingly, but the boys remain silent, removed. "I'll tell you, this was a real nice town to grow up in." The boys exchange glances, which Derek quickly tries to evaluate. Are they treating him like an old-timer? Bad enough. Or are they acknowledging some little secret held among them? Worse. He lowers his voice, moves it to one side, like folding back the lapel of your jacket to reveal a shoulder holster. "And I want to keep this a nice town, you understand? Those individuals you were playing basketball with? They don't belong around here, not running around."

"Why is that, Officer Pabst?" asks Todd, laying it on pretty thick now.

"Because they escaped from a juvey home," Derek says, letting Todd think he's being taken at face value. "And since then they've been breaking a whole lot of laws. They've been going up and down the river, breaking in, bothering people, taking shit, making their own rules. They almost raped a woman right here in our town."

"If you know so much about them," Avery says, "then how come you're like 'What's their names' and everything?"

"Come here," Derek says, softly beckoning Avery forward.

"No," Avery says.

"I said come here." Derek grabs Avery's shirt and pulls him forward until their noses are touching. "Be nice," Derek whispers into the boy's suddenly gray face.

"We really don't know those guys," Todd says, his voice rising. "We were just playing and they came over. We don't know them."

Derek listens to Todd but keeps his eyes on Avery. "Is that right?" Derek says, barely whispering, and he holds on until Avery finally caves in, nods. Derek pushes him away.

Back in his patrol car, Derek has ample time for reconsideration and regret. He has forgotten little of his own youth, recalling not only the scrapes with the law, the lies, the reckless adventures, but also remembering with a painful clarity how it all *felt*—that sacramental sense of loyalty toward your friends, how it swelled in your heart, that mad belief in each other, how you'd do anything for them and they'd do as much for you and with all of you pulling for one another no one could bring you down. As far as those boys are concerned, he's the enemy, not only old but a cop.

Without admitting to himself where he has been driving, Derek pulls into Kate's driveway, just as a yellow-and-black van from Centurion Security Systems is backing away from the house, its wheels spinning, throwing up pebbles. Kate is still in the doorway, holding the signed copy of her maintenance agreement with Centurion, and when she sees Derek she waves the sheet of paper over her head, because he has been after her for months to get the house wired up.

As has become their custom, she invites him in for a cup of coffee. She gets her coffee delivered by UPS from a warehouse in Louisiana, bright-yellow cans of dark roast with chicory, and Derek tells her with each cup that it is the best coffee he has ever tasted. "And as a cop, let me tell you, I know my coffee." She knows he is flirting with her when he says this, but she is willing to let that happen. When she and Daniel first moved to Leyden, she dreaded somehow being involved with Daniel's former life in the town, and Derek was emblematic of all the old friends of whom she wished to steer clear. Derek was worshipful and beseeching around Daniel, and his wife, the perfume-soaked and the socially ambitious Stephanie, with her bleached hair, and coarse skin, was anathema to Kate, and provided yet another reason to avoid Derek. But now, Kate looks forward to Derek's visits and his interest in her offers moments of relief from the loneliness of her days as a single woman. He is surely not what she would have chosen for herself, but she enjoys him the way she enjoys TV, as a slightly enervating diversion. He has a pleasant voice, deep and manly, beautiful hands, with long, tapered fingers, and the hair on his arms is like a boy's, the color of honey.

"I don't know why I waited so long to have a security system put in," Kate says, nursing a cold half inch of coffee while watching Derek enjoy his fresh cup. They are seated in the living room, on the black corduroy sofa in front of the fireplace, which is now filled with dried goldenrod and purple loose strife.

"I feel better that you got it done," says Derek. "Especially . . ."

"What?"

"Well, I wasn't going to tell you this, but I think I saw two Star of Bethlehem kids on the loose today, two from the gang who broke into your house."

"Where?"

"In town. I tried to talk to them, but they saw me coming and they took off. Any doubts I had about them being the two . . ."

"It's so strange. They just won't go away, will they. Why don't they go back to the city, or wherever it is they came from? They want to live in the country, near the river, and enjoy our various cultural and natural resources. Is that it?"

Kate laughs, but her voice is soft, far from her usual tone of sly provocation. When Derek first started coming around, Kate adopted a more feminine and compliant voice in a kind of compensatory spirit, the way very tall people will stoop a little around others so as not to tower over them. She didn't want to intimidate Derek—whom she calls "poor Derek" when she mentions him to people like Lorraine—and she slipped into a somewhat frail persona with him, seeking his advice, deferring to him on matters of worldly practicality, and keeping in check such verbal habits as sarcasm, arcane cultural references, and wordplay. Derek, for his part, has also constructed a kind of alternative self for his meetings with Kate. Rather than sitting at her table as a man who has lived his whole life within the confines of one small community, a man who has married his high school sweetheart, he has changed himself into a kind of exiled big-city cop who has ended up in Leyden because of some secret catastrophe back in the big city. That both Kate and Derek are in disguise makes their time together unreal yet relaxing; it's like being at a masquerade ball, but one in which the disguises are not so elaborate, and you always know with whom you're dancing.

Kate and Derek continue to talk about her new alarm system. Kate says that one of the reasons she agreed to move out of the city was that she liked the idea of living in a place where she wouldn't have to worry about crime. Derek tells her that crime in Windsor County has gone up nearly ten percent in the past four years, though it's been mainly in the larger towns in the south of the county. Then they talk awhile about the O. J. case, though here Kate has to be careful because Derek knows next to nothing about it, he keeps falling back on the simplest statements, like, "Man, that guy had everything, and now look at him." They are doing their best to avoid the inevitable conversational juncture when they will begin talking about Daniel, whose behavior, motives, and present-day life have ended up at the center of their every conversation.

This time, it's Derek who brings it up. "Any word from our wandering boy?" he asks. The way he talks about Daniel is different from how he discusses crime and safety. His voice when he mentions Daniel is tolerant, bemused, and morally superior.

"As a matter of fact, I talked to him today."

"Really?" Derek says, his voice rising a little.

"He wanted to pick Ruby up at day care."

"You're kidding me."

"Well, it was just as well for me. I knew I was having the alarm system put in, but they wouldn't give me an exact time."

"So? Is she going to spend the night there?"

"Yes," she says. "I could use a night off."

"Well, I guess it's good for her to have a male role model or something."

And now the subject is properly launched, it wafts above them like a big lazy balloon.

"This place where he's living," Kate says. "I finally got the courage to go over and take a look at it."

"He's over on Salter Turnpike."

"A little suburban-style house, with a carport and fake shutters." She stops herself, realizes that sort of architecture wouldn't disturb Derek, that in fact his own house could be described like that. "And inside, really dreary. I asked him, 'Who decorated this place? Lee Harvey Oswald?' "

"Three years ago, I was called out on a domestic abuse on Salter Turnpike and the guy turned out to be my tenth-grade English teacher, Mr. Machias. Man, I loved busting that guy, and he's like trying to strike a bargain with me while I'm leading him out to the car, he's saying, 'Mr. Pabst, we're both men of the world.' Men of the world. His poor old wife's in there with a broken nose and a chipped front tooth and he's trying to bond with me."

"So what are you saying, Derek? That it's a bad neighborhood?"

"Here's what I think. There are no bad neighborhoods, there's just bad people."

Oh, thank you for your hard-won wisdom of the streets. "Daniel looked really uncomfortable, having me in his house," she says. "He was swaying back and forth, talking a mile a minute, and he had his hand sort of tucked behind him, massaging his kidney like he does when he's very, very nervous."

"He was nervous? He should be *ashamed*. He should be on his knees begging you to forgive him."

Kate shrugs, but Derek is saying exactly what she wants to hear. She finds that she has a practically limitless need to hear her side of things affirmed when it comes to the breakup of her household. Once, she would have guessed that she would want to preserve her pride, that she would put up a brave front and mount the traditional romantic defense of nonchalance, or philosophical acceptance. But that hasn't been the case. Kate wants there to be no mistake in anyone's mind about whose idea it was to separate. She is the wronged party, any spin on that is immoral. And whenever she thinks she has had her fill of pity, she finds that she has a craving for just one more helping.

"He looks terrible," Kate says. "He must have lost at least twenty pounds, and he's got these crepe paper dark patches under his eyes. His health is shot."

"He shouldn't even be talking to you about his health," Derek says. "He's lost that right."

"It's not like cops and robbers, Derek, this is real life. Whatever he's done, he's still important to me. And if he's developed some kind of heart condition . . ."

"He had a heart attack?"

"I don't know what he had. But I do know he's wasting away. And for what?"

"Hampton Welles," Derek says softly.

"But that wasn't Daniel's fault!"

Derek nods. It is, in fact, what he, too, believes, but he doesn't like to hear Kate say it.

"And I do think," Kate continues, "that in terms of him and Iris, it's been devastating to them. I think it's hard for them to even see each other."

Derek is entirely sure that Daniel and Iris are seeing a lot more of each other than Kate cares to realize—he has seen them coming out of the Windsor Bistro, seen her car in front of Daniel's house—but he thinks better of making the point. Sometimes you can lose by winning.

"You're a very brave lady, Kate," he says. "I mean it. You're really taking it well."

"Can I offer you another cup of coffee?"

"No, I better not. I'm having trouble sleeping anyhow. And this stuff is a whole lot stronger than anything I get at home."

"Meow," says Kate, making Derek laugh with such a burst of manic nervous energy that his face goes crimson. Kate looks at him with a mild gaze, but soon she is laughing, too, and they continue to laugh, as if her joke were a kiss and they wanted to prolong it.

And then the laughter subsides and they are left with each other and the silence, which Derek, finally, cannot endure.

"You ask yourself," he says, shaking his head.

"What?"

"What you'd do in her particular individual situation."

"Iris? With Daniel, you mean?"

"Whatever anyone says about it being an accident, Daniel lit the fuse. What would you do with someone who did something like that to your husband?"

"Well, first I'd like to actually have a husband." She realizes as soon as the words are out that it's not a good or even acceptable joke. She knows Derek is attracted to her, that he has been coming around with the hope of one day taking her to bed, and she doesn't want to encourage him, any more than she would want to absolutely discourage him. And, sure enough, the wisecrack has made him uncomfortable. He shifts in his seat, recrosses his legs.

"You know Hampton, don't you?" Derek asks.

"A little."

"What's he like?"

"Extremely dignified, what people used to call a Credit to His Race."

"Man," Derek says, with a sad shake of the head, as he so often does when Hampton's fate is discussed. He touches the hollow of his own throat, also a practically ritualized gesture between them.

"Poor Daniel," she says. "I can't help thinking Iris is sort of holding him hostage."

"Hostage?"

"Psychologically."

Derek glances away, as if this were a bit rarefied for his tastes.

"Daniel feels responsible . . . And Iris is no fool. She's perfectly capable of manipulating the hell out of Daniel, without even half trying. He's doing her shopping, he's mowing the lawn, he's like her servant."

"I can't believe you," Derek says. "You're sitting here feeling sorry for him. The whole town's talking about what a rat he is, and the person he hurt the most is feeling sorry for him. You're a very understanding person."

"I'm not understanding. I'm hurt. I feel incredibly hurt. It's just . . . well, it's *Daniel*. He's a sweet man. But he's rootless, that might be the problem. I should have put it together when he came up with the plan to move back to this place. He wanted to be near his parents, strange as it sounds. All that unfinished business, it's true what they say. Some of those unloved kids have the hardest time leaving home. They think it's always just about to happen, the things they've been waiting their whole life for. And then they get fixated on the idea of passion, some big bang theory. You know what I mean? An explosion that will create, or re-create, the world. Maybe that's why he got so attached to this woman, this woman who is really basically a stranger to him. He wants to be rescued from his own emptiness. And I think he sees her as the perfect mother, too—even though she was willing to throw her marriage out the window. But she's very touchy-feely with her kid. Daniel loves that, because he understands it, and it's what he missed. Then you take all that, and you mix in all of Daniel's goddamned pro bono idealism, and his whole fixation on the *black* thing, and how they're supposed to be more feeling than us, more emotionally present. All that nonsense."

"Nonsense? You call what he did nonsense?"

"Daniel doesn't want to hurt anybody."

"But he has," says Derek. "He's lucky he's not facing charges."

"It was an accident, I think that much was obvious to everybody. It was just the worst horrible freak luck. That thing, that rocket goes off and severs poor Hampton's carotid artery. God. It would have been better if he'd died right then and there."

"He pretty much did."

"That's not true. He's getting around, he's walking, feeding himself. He's probably fucking that wife of his." She puts her hands up as if to shield herself. "Sorry. I don't know where that came from."

A silence descends upon them. From outside the house, they can hear the blue jays raucously quarreling around the bird feeder; they seem perfectly willing to slaughter each other over a beakful of thistle. Sometimes it seems so obvious: the world is a place of relentless brutality, the only reason anything is alive is that it can kill something else.

Derek has left the window down in his car and the squawk of his radio drifts toward the silence of the early evening.

"Your radio," Kate says.

"I can hear it."

"What's it saying? What's going on?"

"Not a damn thing." And then, in a moment of inspiration, he decides to risk it all in one sentence. Suddenly it's easier than holding back, easier than pretending he has not been dreaming of Kate, has not fallen in love with her. All that has happened has happened for a reason, starting with Daniel getting kicked down the stairs and moving back to Leyden, and then the freak early snow, and those black kids terrorizing Kate, the whole karmic chain of events, including Marie Thorne getting lost in the woods. It all had to click together just so.

Kate is frowning at the open window, through which the noise of the police radio drifts.

"Should you be paying attention to that?" she asks.

He takes her hand. "Everything I really want to pay attention to is right here," he says.

[16]

Despite his being in a constant state of tension from recalling and reliving the moment he lit the fuse of that Roman candle, despite his flulike feelings of remorse over breaking up his family, despite his constant worry over Ruby's well-being, her psychological health, her physical health, and even her moods, despite his having taken down the photograph of the dear little girl because the sight of it on his beige bedroom wall makes him weep, despite the many times he has called her on the telephone when she seems indisposed, distracted, and does not want to talk, despite his taking her to feed the swans that live near the shore of a nearby monastery and turning around for a half minute and her disappearing for nearly ten minutes, despite having received numerous nighttime drink-and-dial telephone calls from Kate, despite his sometimes wondering how he could have thought for a moment that he could live without her, despite his having let down more than a few of his clients, despite the wreckage he has made of his practice, his career, and his reputation, despite his going from a respected and well-liked figure in his little town to a person about whom people gossip, of whom people do not approve, around whom people seem less than comfortable, despite the difficulties he and Iris have seeing each other since Hampton's injury, despite his having developed a searing, steely pain in the middle of his heel, as if it has been pierced by an arrow, especially in the morning, when he can barely get out of bed the pain is so severe, despite the fact that his assistant, Sheila Alvarez, has turned contemptuous toward him, and snapped her fingers in his face and said, "Hello?" when he failed to answer one of her rapid-fire inquiries, despite Iris's little boy's continuing in his dislike for Daniel, his squirming away from his touch, glaring at him from across the Burger King booth, despite bouts of feverish nostalgia for his old domesticity, its regularities and comforts, despite his more or less despising where he now lives, where he has yet to get a decent night's sleep, where he is obliged to buy cumbersome, backbreaking bottles of spring water because what comes out of the tap smells like leprous frogs, where the idiot landlord, who has never had a tenant before, continues to hover around, mowing the lawn on Saturday mornings, watering the scraggly, parsimoniously producing rosebushes, pruning the juniper bushes, which smell like cat urine, and who compulsively continues to chaperone Daniel's relationship to the house as if the depressing little bungalow were a young virgin and Daniel himself a notorious Lothario, despite his having lost ten pounds of muscle and not an ounce of fat, despite wiry curls of gray hair suddenly appearing on his sideburns, despite his having begun fifteen books without getting to the end of any of them, this is the happiest he has ever been.

Much of this happiness is purely physical. It is an animal joy, a stunning erotic completeness such as he has never experienced. Daniel had always secretly believed that people who went on about their sexual happiness were exaggerating, they were like those restaurant reviewers who compare a bowl of soup to a glimpse of heaven. They were sexual gourmets, they were like those wine critics who justify their expense-account indulgences with words that not only elevated their simple human pleasure into some bold adventure of the senses but also claimed to be extracting arcane nuances of pleasure that only they could discern.

Yet now that he is with Iris, Daniel has become *one of those people*. Since the night of the October snow, he is a connoisseur of sex, and if there were anyone in the world with whom he could share his newly found joy, he would have become a proselytizer for the holy church of physical love.

For one thing, he is finally able to make love while positioned on top, which he has not been able to do since getting kicked down the stairs back on Perry Street. The long fall left him with a strained lower back, a proclivity toward muscle spasms, and a sciatic nerve that was like the third rail in a subway tunnel, humming with pain. It also left him unable to do what the missionary position requires, and so, week by week, and then month by month, Kate mounted Daniel and, in her words, "did all the work." But now the pain is gone and its absence is fantastically rejuvenating to him. Daniel is restored to his youthful self, shot through with the vigor and flexibility of a man in his twenties, but a chastened, wised-up man in his twenties, one who will not waste his youth.

It is night and Daniel hovers a mere fifty feet above the town, sitting in the air just as comfortably as if it were a chair, his legs crossed, his hands folded in his lap, his thumbs tapping each other. The first couple of times he became airborne, he expended absurd amounts of effort moving around, or just staying aloft. He would thrust his arms in front of him because this is how Superman made himself aerodynamic in the movies. Then, after a while, in a moment of irritation and exhaustion, he thought to himself: *I don't really mind if I come crashing down,* and he gave up, he simply offered himself to the elements like a swimmer succumbing to the sea, and it was fine. His presence there is as easy and uncontested as his presence on earth. He has already flown over the entire town, beaming down his prayers of love and happiness to all who are sleeping, and to all whom sleep eludes.

Now, rocking back and forth on the currents of night air, able to move himself from here to there on the power of thought, he hovers protectively over Iris's house, feeling all the ferocious animal longing for her that he once felt when touching her was but a dream, feeling, in fact, more desire for the Iris who he has come to know than he had ever felt for the phantom Iris. The Iris he has come to know, the Iris who he has kissed, the Iris he has is not exactly the Iris for whom he once longed. That Iris was cast into the shadows when Hampton had his stroke. None of the changes that have come over her are really what he would have once hoped for. The Iris he once so deliriously craved was languid, while the Iris he knows now is exhausted, the Iris he courted wanted to be amused, and the Iris he has achieved wants to be comforted. And not necessarily by him.

And then, as he floats back and forth, just a few feet above her roof, but unable to enter her house even as a specter, Daniel first learns that he is not alone in the nightlife of the skies over Leyden. At first, he thinks he has seen an owl or some other nocturnal bird of prey, and his second thought is that some small object has fallen from space, a meteorite, a scrap of cosmic garbage. He turns and sees, of all people, Derek Pabst flying rapidly, wildly due west, dressed in a pair of dark-blue boxer shorts and a Boston Red Sox T-shirt. Derek seems not to have noticed Daniel, and though Daniel has no desire to speak to Derek, some instinct of camaraderie overtakes him and he calls out to his old friend. Derek, a look of great anxiety on his face, turns toward the sound of Daniel's voice, fails to see him, and then begins to tumble head over heel, zooming out toward the outskirts of the village like a ball of lightning.

When he turns to resume his watch over Iris's house, she is there, facing him. She is only inches away, her nightgown streaming behind her, a look of wonder and bewilderment on her face.

"Am I dreaming?" she asks. She starts to drift away and he catches her by the wrist, pulls her close to him.

"You're awake."

"I've had a terrible night, such a terrible, terrible night."

"Hampton?"

"When you spend all this time with someone who cannot speak, it forces you down into yourself, but in the worst way. We're not meant to be silent, but to him words have no meaning. So I sit there with him, and I think about you, and if there's no one else around . . ." She stops herself, looks down. She starts to lose altitude and Daniel catches her again. She presses her lips to his palm and then places it on her breast. Her breath comes in broken pieces, as if it must turn at right angles to escape her. "If there's no one around," she says, "I just say what I'm thinking. I say, 'Hampton, I'm in love. I'm in love with a man who thinks I'm smart and beautiful.'"

"Everyone thinks you're smart and beautiful, Iris."

"I stopped loving him, Daniel. Long ago. Being with someone so broken—even if you love them, it takes everything. How do you do it when you already stopped loving them? When you already felt trapped. When your heart is . . . elsewhere. He's grotesque now. He's frightened, he cries, and every day he gets physically stronger. But how can I leave him?" A sudden wind comes off the river and pushes her closer to Daniel.

"Everything in the world is telling us we don't belong together," he says miserably.

"Don't you love me anymore?"

"Of course I do. But it doesn't have anything to do with that, not now. How much can love do? It's buried."

"I don't feel buried. I used to, but not now. Look at me!" She spreads her arms and then raises them above her and begins to gain altitude, slowly at first, and then she soars.

"I want to see him!" Daniel shouts after her, but if she hears him she gives no sign of it, she continues to rise. Unnerved, Daniel returns to his own bed.

He switches on the light on his bedside table. The lamp is shaped like a calla lily; he bought it in town, thinking that it was an iris, and that Iris would be touched by it, or at least like it. But no matter how many times she has come to this room, she seems never to notice the lamp. Nor has she mentioned the expensive brass bed he's installed, or the five-hundred-dollar goose down comforter, or the black lacquered end tables, or the Navaho rug, or the Parisian jazz club poster, with a piano keyboard curling across it like a black-and-white woolen scarf. It all seems like a miscalculation, the fancy boudoir accoutrements. He props a pillow against the chilly brass bars of the bed's headboard, picks up the book he's been reading. He remains on his back, turns the page, and then switches to his side, propping up his head with one hand. The hand covers his right eye and the world instantly disappears. He sits bolt upright, his heart racing; as soon as he removes the heel of his hand from his right eye the world returns. He covers the eye again. Darkness. He is blind in one eye.

Daniel is learning how to live with one sighted eye, learning to cope with the peculiar flatness of the world, the odd augmentation of sound, the unnerving momentary losses of balance, the trepidation before stairways, the sense of plunging while merely stepping off a curb, and he is even learning to live with the pervasive feeling that there is something or someone just behind him, or just to the side of him, a threatening presence that is out of range of his reduced arc of vision, and that this peripheral, punishing phantom is about to pounce, grab, push, stab, or shoot him. What he is still having particular trouble with is keeping the secret of his sudden infirmity. He wants to talk about it, he wants help, he wants a little credit for how well he's coping; concealment is against his nature, and now he must add the arrival of this partial blindness to his stockpile of secrets.

Finally, however, Daniel submits to a series of tests, under the aegis of Bruce McFadden. First, Bruce conducts his own examinations, and then, finding nothing amiss, he sends Daniel to Windsor Imaging, for an MRI and then a CAT scan, and when all the results are in he sits with Daniel in his office to go over them. Among the other decorations in McFadden's office—and it's an eccentric old space, filled with angles and oddities— are framed black-and-white photographs of some of his favorite blind musicians: Ray Charles, Stevie Wonder, Roland Kirk, Al Hibler, Ivory Joe

Hunter, Blind Willie McTell, the Five Blind Boys of Mississippi *and* the Five Blind Boys of Alabama, together in the same photo, which makes it an artifact of unusual distinction, and the English jazz pianist George Shearing, the one white face in the lot.

"It's the old joke," Bruce says, tilted back in his Swedish orthopedic chair, with its childishly bright-blue upholstery and its brilliant chrome hardware, "the one that goes, 'I've got good news and bad news.'" His feet are on the desk, he has knit his fingers behind his neck. "But the good news is good enough, maybe you won't even care about the bad. There's nothing wrong with your eye, Daniel. The retina, the cornea, the optic nerve, everything's shipshape. In fact, you've got the ocular vigor of a teenager. You don't even need glasses."

"Except that I can't see," Daniel says.

"Yes, well, that's the bad news," Bruce says. "We're going to have to explore the possibility that the origin of your difficulty is not physical."

"Meaning?" Daniel asks, though an instant later the question answers itself.

"Your eye is fine. Your vision will most likely come back. After your life—"

"You think my *life* has made me blind?"

"I don't know what's made you blind, Daniel. All I can tell you is what the tests say. And they all say your eye is healthy."

Daniel falls silent. He hears a sound, turns toward it. The branch of a maple tree, its leaves large as hands, blows in the breeze, scraping against the outside of the window.

"Guilt's a bitch," Bruce says. He sits forward, folds his hands, he's coming to the end of the time allotted.

"I don't feel guilty. How could I? I've turned a blind eye to everything."

Bruce smiles, he looks relieved. "It may turn out to be as simple as that," he says.

"I'm *joking,* Bruce." Daniel's chin juts forward, he widens his eyes. "Jesus."

"I feel sorry for you, Daniel. I really do. You're under a lot of pressure."

Daniel tries to smile, but then, failing that, he tries to compose himself into a sort of manly grimace, but even that will not hold. He feels his lips quiver and he feels the surge of tears. He takes a deep breath, covers his eyes. There are certain things he has not been able to say, not even to Iris. She, into whose consciousness he has wanted to pour himself since first meeting her, she turns out to be perhaps the last person to whom he can reveal the remorse he feels over Hampton, over Ruby, over Kate. She already has a broken man in her life. Every step he has taken into the light of Iris's love seems to have ushered him along on an equal journey into, if not the heart of darkness, then, at least, the darkness of the heart. It is not what he had expected. What happened to the world opening wide, what happened to joy? How could the achievement of all that he has desired cast him into such withering isolation?

"I don't think this needs to be said, Daniel," Bruce says. "But nobody blames you. You realize that, don't you?"

Daniel reaches across the desk and clasps Bruce's hand. "Oh my God," he says. "I can see! I can see!"

For a moment, Bruce looks confused, as if he is about to believe some kind of miracle has occurred. But then, he regains his composure. "Very funny," he says. "Ha ha ha."

——

Even with the appalling evidence of Hampton's ruination an inch or two from her face, the reality of what has befallen him, her, all of them, remains elusive to Iris. The waking dream of everyday life obscures his injury, there is so much else to do, so many people, so much work—dishes to be washed, clothes to be folded, tunes hummed, a minute goes by, ten, and the space in her mind labeled "Hampton" will, without her governance, be silently, unconsciously occupied by the familiar man to whom she once swore allegiance and then betrayed, that infuriating, belittling presence.

And the parade of people who march in and out of her house. It's like Memorial Day. Here come the fire trucks, here comes the Little League, here come the Elks. Iris has kept a journal, meant at first to be a receptacle for her pain, for the remorse, the guilt she must share for what has happened to Hampton, and a place to map and describe the dark sea of sex and happiness in which she is sometimes swimming, sometimes sailing, and sometimes sinking—but little of that ever makes it into the diary. It is crowded out, eclipsed, and then obliterated by a constantly expanding cast of characters, the people who come in and out of the life of the house.

There are the doctors, the nurses, the medical technicians, all with names, all with stories, one has a limp, one is diabetic, one lost three fingers to frostbite in the peacetime Polish Army, one smokes clove cigarettes, one is a Sufi, one sang backup for Paula Abdul, each and every one of them stakes a separate claim on her attention.

And then: family. There are pages and pages in her journal about the comings and goings of her family, and Hampton's family. They have all risen to the occasion. Iris's sister Carol is a constant presence. Of the first ninety days of Hampton's convalescence—though that perhaps is the wrong word for it, convalescence implies a process, an end point, and Hampton's global aphasia is permanent—Carol was living with them more than half the time. But not counting Carol, the first to arrive was Hampton's mother, who descended into the hell of Juniper Street in her dark-blue suit and wavy silver hair, wearing orange lipstick and a large diamond ring, and seemed to think that if she taught Hampton to speak once she can do it again. Then came Hampton's brother James, who for all his hippy ways, his bewildering openness to spiritual marginalia, could do nothing useful; he sobbed and wailed, in a frenzy until finally it fell to Iris to comfort him. Then arrived Hampton's oldest brother, Jordan, a Congregationalist minister in Bethesda, gaunt, widowed, and remote, who, when Iris asked if he was going to pray over Hampton, looked at her as if she had asked if he handled snakes or rolled on the floor speaking in tongues. Next came her two favorite brothers, Louis and Raymond, in business together back home, getting rich selling BMWs (LouRay Motors) and speculating in real estate (Davenport Development, Inc.). Then her father arrived, a month after the accident, as if waiting for the smoke to clear so he could set matters straight, strolling into the ruination like Yojimbo, somehow carrying with him the medical authority of the entire Richmond Memorial Hospital, where he had been head of Food Services for thirty-eight years. Then Hampton's old friends, the Morrison-Rosemonts, up from Atlanta, and then more brothers, more sisters, his parents again, her parents again. She is running a bed-and-breakfast for the genuinely concerned, throwing in lunch and dinner, too. All of them have different ideas, different needs, different dietary requirements. Some are helpful, some are pains in the ass, and all of them, each and every one of them, wants, finally, to know the same thing: Who has done this thing to Hampton?

"Oh, the man I love, the man I will sneak out of here to see as soon as the coast is clear, as soon as I hear you snoring behind the guest room door," is what Iris does not say. "A friend of mine named Daniel, it was an accident," she also doesn't say. "If you need someone to blame, then blame me," is likewise on the list of unuttered things. But she can't remain silent, she can't refuse to answer their very reasonable question, she cannot drum her fingers on the side of her head and say "Da da da." And so she tells the story again and again, drawing it out so it can seem she is not stinting on the details, beginning with the party at Eight Chimneys, the trouble between the Richmonds, the disappearance of Marie Thorne, the storm-wrecked woods, the flares, and on and on, and no matter which way she spins it the end is always the same—her silence mixes with the silence of her listener, and the two silences combine in the air and create a kind of Holy Ghost of the Unspoken, and that spirit looks down upon them and whispers: *a white man did this to him.*

It's late at night, one day or another, Wednesday, Thursday, it doesn't really matter anymore. Daniel has fallen asleep in front of the TV set, with his hands folded in his lap and his feet up on the coffee table. It is a shabby threadbare sort of sleep, mixed in with the sounds of the movie he has been watching—*The Guns of Navarone*—as well as the still unfamiliar ruminations of his house. His dream life is thin and discontinuous, just images, moments, nothing quite memorable, it's like reading the spines of the books in a vast secondhand shop. Here he is decanting a bottle of red wine, trying to push a mower through wet grass, being driven to court by Anthony Quinn, and then Ruby appears, she looks overheated, as if she's been running, she opens her mouth and instead of words or any human sound there comes the chime of a doorbell, *dingdong dingdong* . . . Daniel awakens, his heart racing. He tries to get up but his legs are granite. He grabs his trousers, pulls one leg off the table and then the other, it feels as if he's been left for dead on the side of the road. The ringing of the doorbell is continuing. "Just a second!" he cries out.

He doesn't have the presence of mind or the sense of self-preservation to ask who it is, he simply drags himself through the living room, passes beneath the little oval archway to the foyer, and opens the door to find Iris on his porch, wearing a sweater that is much too large for her—Hampton's?—and dark glasses, though it is eleven at night. The air smells of night-blooming flowers.

"I need to see you," she says.

He reaches for her, pulls her to him, and as he embraces her he feels a sickening twist of intuition: Hampton has died. She nuzzles her face into the crook of his neck. He pulls away to get a better look at her.

"Are you all right?" he whispers.

"I just had to get out of there."

"What's going on? Has anything happened?"

"Hampton's mother is there, and his sister, with her daughter, Christine, this skinny ten-year-old nervous wreck, scared of her own shadow, constantly bursting into tears. They're all nervous wrecks, and between them and the nurse there's no room for me. I can't pee without someone knocking on the bathroom door."

"How's Hampton?"

"The same. Every day, the same. Except stronger. He takes walks, he eats, but the speech thing, you know. He can't leave the house because he cannot speak. He has one word. Da-da. Da-da, da-da. It means yes, it means no, it means I'm hungry, I'm cold, it means whatever he wants. And believe me, everyone is meant to understand that this da-da means

he wants a soft-boiled egg and that da-da means he wants a back rub."
Her voice is level, slightly hard, but her eyes show the injury, the pity,
and the fury of living with a man who has been ruined.

"It feels really strange," Daniel says. "You know. That I've never seen him."

"How can you? What would you do? Walk in? Pay him a visit?"

"I don't know. But it just seems strange. I feel I should. After all . . ."

"Well, it just can't happen." She is startled by the harshness in her
tone. "Maybe sometime," she adds. "Just not now."

"I need to take responsibility," Daniel says.

"I'm taking responsibility," Iris says. "Every day. And that's enough.
He doesn't even know exactly what happened to him. He certainly
doesn't think it had anything to do with you. I would have to draw him
a series of cartoons, and he still probably wouldn't understand. Come
on. Please. I don't want to talk about it. I need a break from all that."

Brusquely, even roughly—he forgives and even enjoys the bullying
haste of it—she leads him to the bedroom, pushes his shoulders. He falls
onto the bed and she swoops onto him in a fury of need. He tries to
speak against the sorrowful pressure of her kisses and their teeth click
against each other.

He feels that she isn't ready yet, but she wants him inside of her now.
Her sudden intake of breath whistles through her clenched teeth. Her
eyelids flutter and she presses her fingers into his back, urgently. She
whispers the details and the extent of her pleasure into his ear, and even
as he feels the joy of being with and within her, a thought presents itself:
Why, he wonders, *didn't she let me make her ready before I entered her? Why
didn't she let me touch her, why did she want me to push my way in?* It is a thought
of surpassing pettiness—how could the man who once had longed so fervently for the chance to kiss the instep of her foot now quibble over the
details of lubrication? But even as he continues to make love to her, even
as he feels the sweat pouring off of him, even as he times his movements
so as to bring her pleasure, to hear that stunned, despairing, and undefended little yell she makes, even as her grip tightens and he feels himself
drawn into the inevitable engulfing swoon of coming, even now he cannot

repress the memory of that sharp little intake of breath. The conclusion is inescapable: the forceful penetration is what she is used to, that is what she once had with Hampton, and this is what her body craves, this is what she hungers for, and—right now—this is what she requires.

Yet somehow, through force of will, and by doggedly obeying the commands of his own desire, he is able to stay with her, and now they lie next to each other, panting and relieved. In the dim light of his bedroom-in-exile (he cannot imagine making his life in this house; he occupies it like a fugitive), Iris dozes off, her legs pressed together, her arms at her side, like a child miming sleep. A gentle snore hovers above her lips. Daniel props himself up on his elbow and gazes down at her. Her breasts are nearly flat against her, the nipples elongated and with a slight droop from two years of nursing Nelson. Her belly gently swells with each breath. What if his child were growing in there?

Not wanting to disturb her sleep, and not trusting himself to keep from touching her, Daniel slips out of bed and walks as softly as he can into the front room. Naked, he sits on the sofa, finds the remote control under a cushion, and turns on the TV. *The Guns of Navarone* is no longer playing, and he flips through the channels looking for something that can hold his interest for ten or fifteen minutes, after which time he feels he ought to wake Iris. He settles on one of the all-news cable channels, where a black lawyer named Reginald McTeer is holding forth about the O. J. Simpson case. Daniel has often seen McTeer's endlessly smiling, media-friendly face on TV. The program must have sent a crew to McTeer's office because he is seated at a grand desk, with shelves of law books framing a view of midtown Manhattan behind him. RECORDED EARLIER TODAY flashes on the bottom of the screen. McTeer is a stocky man in a dark suit and his signature ten-gallon cowboy hat, bright white with a red satin band. A picture of his light-skinned wife and their three fair children is on his desk, as well as photographs of McTeer enjoying his expensive hobbies and vacations—on safari, in the cockpit of his Mooney, on horseback, and with various well-knowns from the worlds of politics and entertainment. He speaks like a man comfortable with the sound of his own voice, with the exhorting enthusiasm of a preacher, or a Cadillac salesman.

"You know, Jim, all the media's going crazy because Mr. O. J. Simpson got himself a team of first-rate lawyers. Everyone's going on about justice for sale. And I say: more power to him. This is America, baby. Everything's for sale. You think the poor get the same medical care as the rich? Everything is for sale, top to bottom. What you've got to understand is that's how the system works, that's just what the man's got to do. In America green trumps black *and* white."

McTeer smiles, and then suddenly the TV shows Jim Klein sitting in the cable station's studio, watching McTeer on a large monitor. Klein, a silver-haired man in a blue blazer, once a newscaster for one of the networks, and now nearing the end of his broadcast career, swivels in his chair and faces another large monitor.

It's Kate, in Leyden, sitting on the sofa in the living room. Daniel stares at her image for several seconds, not even entirely believing it is actually her. She looks relaxed. Her legs are crossed, her delicate, patrician hands are folded onto her lap. She wears a white blouse, a strand of pearls. As she speaks, her name appears in writing on the bottom of the screen: KATE ELLIS   AUTHOR AND SIMPSON EXPERT   NEW YORK.

"You know, Jim, it's very interesting," Kate is saying, "and not without significance, that, for all his talk about the law and justice, and about the green and the white and the black, Mr. McTeer fails to mention that he was himself part of the original team of lawyers put together for Simpson's defense." As soon as she says this, the broadcast goes to a split-screen format and McTeer can be seen shaking his head, and waving his hand dismissively at the camera, clearly indicating that Kate's comments are beneath contempt.

But Kate cannot see McTeer and she continues, undaunted, her cultured voice brimming with self-confidence. Daniel leans forward, his hands resting on his square, bare knees. She seems entirely herself, yet at the same time somehow perfect for television. It's been months since he has seen her looking so relaxed. "Mr. McTeer was asked to be a part of

O. J.'s Dream Team and he declined. Why? Well, a statement Mr. McTeer made to the press last year should put his actions in a clear light. He said . . ." Kate glances at a little notebook she has left next to her on the sofa. With a lurch, Daniel recognizes it—it's a little spiral notebook with a picture of a whale on the cover, which he bought for her two summers ago on a weekend trip to Nantucket. " 'Life is too short, and life is too precious, and there are still things on earth that money can't buy.' "

"With all due respect, Ms. Ellis, you can't believe everything you read in the press," McTeer says. "There are more writers out there than you can shake a stick at, and some of them are putting groceries on the table by writing a lot of damn foolishness about O. J. Simpson."

"Okay," Jim Klein says. "Let me ask you something, Kate Ellis. You've been perceived by some as O. J. Simpson's most potent enemy in the press, and there have been a few—and I'm sure you've heard this, so I'm not saying anything you haven't dealt with, and I'm certainly not trying to imply any agreement with this statement—but some have said that your articles about the case . . ." Klein picks up a thick, glossy magazine and holds it up to the camera: the cover is a portrait of O. J., his skin several shades darker than its actual color, posed on a dark street, grinning, holding a pair of leather gloves in one hand, with the other hand hidden behind his back. "Show a certain insensitivity to the racial implications of the case against Mr. Simpson."

"There are no racial implications, Jim. None that matter, anyhow."

"Mighty easy for you to say, Miss Ellis," McTeer says with a laugh.

"This is a murder case, Mr. McTeer," Kate says. "Not a debate about civil rights."

"Are you a lawyer in your spare time, Miss Ellis?" McTeer asks.

"No. But, if it matters, I happen to live with a lawyer, and a very fine lawyer . . ."

Instinctively, Daniel grabs the remote control, but then is unsure whether he wants to turn the volume up or down. He points it toward the set without pressing any buttons. Behind Kate, not quite in focus, is the fireplace, the mantel covered with framed snapshots of the three of them.

"I fell asleep."

Startled, abashed, as if caught with pornography, Daniel looks at Iris. She, too, is naked, with one hand massaging her eyes and the other fig-leafed over her middle.

"A woman has been brutally murdered," Kate is saying, "and there is at this point a good chance that the man who is clearly responsible for her death is going to go free. All the talk about racist cops . . ."

"What is this?" Iris asks, sitting next to Daniel, draping her leg over him.

"TV," says Daniel.

"Who is she talking about?"

"O. J. Simpson. Who else?"

"I don't know."

"That this man has become some sort of rebel-hero to the African-American community," Kate is saying, "is completely ludicrous, and of-fensive. That rappers and other prominent blacks are wearing 'Free O. J.' T-shirts is also ludicrous and offensive. We have to ask ourselves: Are we a nation of laws, or aren't we?"

"We are a nation of laws," McTeer says.

"Who's that freak?" Iris asks.

"Reginald McTeer, a lawyer."

"And the foundation of our legal system," McTeer continues, "is a man or a woman is presumed innocent until proven guilty. Without that presumption, there is no justice. And without justice there is no peace."

Kate rolls her eyes. "I don't know anyone who doesn't believe that O. J. Simpson murdered Nicole Brown and Ron Goldman."

"I know plenty of people who have grave doubts about that, Miss El-lis," McTeer says. "You should get out more. The whole world isn't in the editorial offices of some fancy magazine. Go into the kitchen in some of the lavish restaurants where you eat and ask the people who have been cooking your food, ask them what they think, or ask the woman who cleans your house."

"I'm the woman who cleans my house, Mr. McTeer, and I say he's guilty."

"She's in your house," Iris says.

"I know."

"Look at the windows. It's light out. When was this?"

Daniel puts up a hand to silence her. "Wait." He has surprised himself. A few months ago he would have gone to practically any lengths to hear the sound of Iris's voice and now he is shushing her. "I just want to hear this," he adds softly. Then, still nervous that he may have hurt her feelings, he further adds, "It was videotaped earlier today." He pats her knee reassuringly.

Iris grabs his hand, ferocious yet playful. She kisses the back of it, turns it over and kisses his palm, and then puts first one finger and then a second into her mouth, and sucks on them, and then, when he lets out a little involuntary whimper of pleasure, she slides off the sofa, positions herself between his legs, forces his knees apart—not that he resists her in any but the most perfunctory way—and buries her face in his lap, kissing his cock until it rises, at which time she moves her head back a little and accepts him into her mouth.

"We have witnessed a travesty of justice," Kate is saying.

Daniel, his eyes closed now, gropes for the remote control and turns off the set.

———

Iris leaves shortly after. Daniel returns to his bed, which is full of the warmth and aromas of sex. He tries to sink into it, but sleep seems to have turned its back on him, and he gets dressed and drives into the village for a drink or two (or three or four—who cares?) at the Windsor Bistro, though it is after midnight. As he nears the Bistro and sees that its dark-red neon sign is still lit, bleeding its deep, pleasantly lurid colors into the black air, he feels a little swoon of pure gratitude for the place and everyone who makes it run: how monstrous the night can be without a place to go.

It's crowded at the Bistro, more crowded than he's ever seen it. Is the entire town wracked with desire, unable to sleep? Daniel stands near the entrance, next to the coatroom, which, now that it's summer, is filled with elaborate arrangements of flowers. He looks in on tonight's crowd, he is not quite ready to venture further in. It's not as if the people here tonight are strangers to him—everyone in Leyden is familiar, to a certain extent—but they are not people he really knows, not people he can confidently call by name. They're a boisterous bunch, gathered together in groups of six, seven, or eight, with wild laughter being the order of the night. Tonight's customers are acting as if they were having their last manic round of grog on a sinking ship. The owner's normally saturnine boyfriend, rather than playing from his usual repertoire of folk-rock torch songs, is leading some of the customers in "Rainy Day Women." *And I would not feel so all alone / Everybody must get stoned.*

Daniel thinks of himself as one of the original customers of the Bistro, one of its founding fathers, but whatever favoritism Doris Snyder, the Bistro's owner, used to show him is not available tonight. She works feverishly behind the bar, mixing margaritas with one hand and filling bowls of pretzels with the other, and when Daniel makes a little imploring gesture in her direction her eyes are as expressive as thumbtacks.

He finds a small, empty table in a distant corner and sits down, resigned to a long wait before he is served. He scans the room, looking for Deirdre, Johnnie Day, Calliope, or any of the other college-aged girls who have not yet managed their way out of Leyden, and who supplement their lives of pottery, yoga classes, organic garden design, and whole foods catering with employment at the Bistro. However, the first person with whom he makes eye contact is Susan Richmond, who is holding a beer mug and swaying to the music, like a shy person all alone who wants to appear to be enjoying herself.

An hour ago, she was back at Eight Chimneys, lying in her own bed, unable to sleep, and her mind in that vulnerable state had been seized with a desire to see her husband—it was as if wakefulness had compromised her mind's autoimmune system, made it easy prey to resentment and longing. The jealousy was like rabies, it commanded her, the infection of it made her want to sink her teeth into something. She felt helpless against its power. She paced through the vast gloom of her sighing, creaking house, turning on lamps, going into rooms she hadn't visited in months, surprising the visiting Bulgarian folk dancers who were drinking gin and poring over old maps in the library, and then coming in on the busy chipmunks in the ballroom, the circling bats in the kitchen, and even braving a peek into Marie's little cell.

Susan has agreed to let Marie stay on at Eight Chimneys. It seems less humiliating that way. The girl can stay but whatever happens between Ferguson and his blind whore must remain private, not only from Susan herself but from the outside world—particularly that, particularly the outside world. Yet despite the agreement, Susan knows that sometimes Ferguson and Marie slip off the property, and the Bistro is one of the places they go. Susan has come here to find them, and has not, though she has remained here for over an hour, partly to prolong the charade that she is simply out for a bit of night air and a couple of drinks, and partly because those drinks have made her drunk.

Her face lights up at the sight of Daniel. She has never held any particular fondness for him—in fact, his association with Ferguson and Marie, and then his so catastrophically injuring Hampton on her land, with *her* Roman candle, has put him in her "bad news" category. But tonight she responds to the sight of his familiar face with a wave and a broad smile of relief, because for her entire time in the Bistro she has not seen anyone she knows.

"Hello, there," she says, seating herself heavily at his table. The scent of alcohol wafts off her skin. "What a crazy place!"

"Hello, Susan," Daniel says, giving her name particular emphasis. He likes to use her name frequently when they happen to meet, largely because he is sure she is having trouble remembering his. "I must admit, Susan, I'm a little surprised to see you here."

"Why do you keep saying my name? My God, it's annoying."

"I'm sorry. Annoying Susan Richmond is surely the last thing I want to do."

"Is it because you think I don't remember you? I know exactly who you are. You're Daniel Emerson and you ditched your perfectly lovely, smart-as-a-whip wife. You're one of the boys." She fixes her large, bleary eyes on him, and then raises her mug in mock salute.

Daniel wonders how to respond to this—should he just take it in stride, pretend it's nothing more than a little rough kidding—or should he strike back at her? A waitress comes to their table. Susan orders another beer, though her mug is far from empty, and Daniel asks for a cognac, and decides on the path of least resistance: he'll pretend she means no harm.

But before he can say anything, Susan breathes up a bitter snort of laughter and wags her finger in his face. "When do people around here start living up to their responsibilities? You'd think that almost killing a man would have brought you up short, but from what I hear you and Iris are still going at it hot and heavy."

"Hot and heavy?" Daniel is reduced to this, pointing out little excesses in diction.

"Yes. It's curious, isn't it? On the face of it, you and Ferguson couldn't be less alike. He comes from all this historical tradition, and you come from nowhere. He's all about contemplation and you're all about work. But beneath it all, you're both men, or aging boys, that's more like it, and you're carrying on in exactly the same revolting way. What my uncle Peter used to call 'Letting the little head think for the big head.' May I ask you a question?"

"Look, Susan, this isn't—"

"What gives you the right, that's what I can't understand. What gives you the right to cause so much damage, and to hurt people? To really, really hurt people. And it's the worst kind of pain, worse than slapping someone in the face, or stabbing them. Because what are you doing, when you get right down to it? You're making a fool of someone."

"Are you calling Kate a fool? That would be making a big mistake."

"What would you think if right now your wife was home and feeling so brokenhearted that she decided to drink poison? How would that make you feel?"

"Are you thinking of poisoning yourself, Susan?"

"Me? I should say not."

"Then what makes you think Kate is?"

"Some people do just that."

"Most don't."

"I just think that what you're doing is very dishonorable, that's all I'm saying. The whole thing is shabby."

The waitress returns with their drinks and places them on the table. "Doris sends these over with her compliments," she says.

Daniel realizes that Doris is making up for the empty stare she dealt him when he first walked in, and then, quite without meaning to, he wonders if she would be making these liquid reparations if he were sitting with Iris instead of this bulky, somewhat ridiculous woman, with her blotchy white skin and fierce, entitled eyes. Iris has already given him the tour of Leyden and pointed out the various shops in which she is routinely treated like a thief, either physically trailed by an employee or constantly scrutinized by whoever is working the cash register. All the once benign spots of his youth.

The tour came last Saturday, when he dared to accompany her on an errand to the Windsor Pharmacy, where, in fact, the clerk treated her with friendliness and respect—since Hampton's convalescence, she was a regular there and they'd come to know her. After she bought surgical gloves and a sheepskin mattress cover, they chanced a stroll down Broadway, with Daniel carrying her packages as if they were her books and he were walking her home from school. She would in all probability never have mentioned her run-ins with Leyden's commercial class if Daniel hadn't sighed and gestured to all the little shops and said, "Such a sweet little place, isn't it?"

"Depends who you are," she said softly, because it depressed her to have to talk about all of the instances of prejudice, the sheer rudeness that entered into practically every day of her life. Iris did not care to discuss the details of her life as part of the long and terrible story of Race in America—she thought she deserved both more and less than to be counted among the victims of racism. Yet there was something in

Daniel's voice when he called Leyden "sweet" that made her want to bring him up short. She wanted Daniel to know that *here* is where she was forced to sit for fifteen minutes before anyone came to take her order, and *here* is where she had to show three pieces of identification before they'd take her seventeen-dollar check, and *here* is where she would never buy a Danish backpack if her life depended upon it because the bitch who owned the store had rubbed the top of Nelson's head, and then whispered to a friend, *It's supposed to be good luck.*

Daniel has not been paying attention to what Susan is saying, and when he forces himself to focus on her, widening his eyes in an approximation of interest, his attention is seized by the sight of Kate winding her way through the Bistro on her way to his table. Her friend and editor Lorraine Del Vecchio follows behind her. Both women wear summery black dresses, with spaghetti straps, and both women carry snifters of cognac. Without any fanfare, Kate sits in the empty chair closest to Daniel, letting her breath out with a little sigh and allowing her shoulder to graze his for a moment. Lorraine, however, is left standing.

Nervously, his voice booming, Daniel introduces Lorraine and Susan, but Susan's energy is turned onto Kate. "I was just giving your stupid man here a piece of my mind," Susan says.

"Well, you have to be careful," Kate says. "Daniel's already of two minds about most things, and now if you've given him a piece of yours, that might be more mind than he can handle."

Daniel feels a nostalgic twinge of gratitude toward Kate, for coming to his defense without seeming to, and for being so quick off the dime: her playful caste of mind, which was sometimes, during their time together, numbing and de-eroticizing, turns out to be one of the things he misses most about her.

"I saw you on TV," Daniel says.

Kate makes a little yelp of dismay, covers her face, but spreads her fingers so she can peek out at him.

"Wasn't she *fabulous?*" Lorraine says, pronouncing it so as to leave little doubt that she isn't the sort of person who normally says "fabulous."

"You were great," Daniel says. "I loved the crack about cleaning your house."

"That show goes on so late, I was sort of hoping no one would see it."

"And she looked *fantastic*," Lorraine says, again with comic, distancing emphasis.

"You really thought I was okay?" Kate says to Daniel. "That means a lot, coming from you." She reaches for his hand, pats it as if comforting him. Her touch is as warm as breath. Her perfume is a mixture of musk and orange. The lines around her eyes have deepened. She is wearing a delicate little cross that has half disappeared into her cleavage. "I didn't even want to be home when they aired it. Lorraine's here to distract me."

Lorraine notices an empty chair at a nearby table, but as soon as she makes a move to retrieve it the doors to the Bistro fly open and three men, or boys, charge in, one of them holding a handgun and the other two carrying rifles. Their faces are covered by rubber Halloween masks: Frankenstein, Dracula, and Mickey Mouse. Frankenstein, who has the handgun, leaps onto the little stage behind the bar and holds a gun to the singer's head. Dracula and Mickey Mouse push their way into the room, waving their rifles back and forth, shouting, "On the floor, on the floor, get your sorry asses on the motherfucking floor." And even though the Bistro's customers are plunged into a collective terror, it takes several long moments for any of them to comply.

Daniel and his party lie upon the floor. He and Kate both lie face-down, chins resting on left forearms to keep mouth and nose off the boozy grime, and their right arms reaching toward each other, until their fingers touch.

"Don't worry," Daniel whispers.

Kate doesn't make a sound, but she mimes the word "fuck."

What was once a raucous crowd of nightlife revelers is now fifty-eight extremely quiet men and women, all of them on the sticky floor, except for Doris, who remains standing behind the bar. Her boyfriend is wide-eyed, his face drained of color, he is a corpse with a guitar. He remains in his folding chair, with a gun to his head, held by a robber disguised as

Frankenstein. Sometime during the transition of this being a room full of drinkers to this being a room full of people lying flat on the ground, someone has told Doris to open up the cash register and now she is handing its contents to Frankenstein, who looks weirdly attenuated and graceful, reaching toward her to receive his bounty while keeping his gun pressed against her boyfriend's temple. When he has the money, Dracula comes over and takes it from him, and drops it in a mesh laundry bag, at which point Frankenstein yanks the wires of the bar phone out of the wall. He grabs the singer by the back of the shirt, lifts him out of the chair.

Mickey and Dracula go from person to person, collecting cash, credit cards, cell phones, keys, watches, and jewelry. Mickey Mouse stands over them, crouching, to collect their worldly goods; Daniel, despite having told himself to do nothing to antagonize him, cannot resist the impulse to peer through the eyeholes in the masks, to somehow make contact with the human eyes within: shiny brown eyes, young, arrogant, glittering with energy. He drops his wallet and forty dollars in cash into the laundry bag, which tops it off. Mickey pulls the drawstring, ties it in a knot, and then slides the unshapely sack across the floor, toward the bar, where Frankenstein picks it up. Dracula has another laundry bag under his shirt, he pulls it out and holds it open in front of Kate. She is slow to empty her purse into it, and he prods her with the greasy barrel of his rifle—it stencils a little broken O on her skin, and she utters a sound of distress, more from surprise than anything else.

"All right," Daniel says, in a level, almost paternal voice. "We're all going to be real, real careful here. Okay?" He doesn't want to make a reassuring gesture with his hand, or any gesture, but he slightly widens his eyes, as if to say, *Listen to me, I know what you're going through.*

"Fuck you," Dracula replies, his voice muffled behind rubber. Eventually, with everything of value collected—even tie pins, cuff links, and cigarette lighters—the three masked men leave. No one has tried to be heroic. Even as those who have been told to lie down begin to get to their feet, the Bistro remains fearfully silent, except for the sounds of feet and furniture scraping on the floor. Kate has put her arm around Lorraine, who is sobbing softly, and Daniel, who now that the crisis has passed feels light-headed, almost giddy with relief, stands next to Kate, pats her shoulder reassuringly.

"It was those boys, wasn't it," Susan Ferguson says. "The ones who ran away during the storm. I heard they were still in the area, taking things, camping in the woods, or in empty houses. It was them."

Kate nods slowly, her lips pursed. "I think you're exactly right," she says.

"Oh, we don't know that," Daniel says. "We don't know anything." His voice is completely wrong, he sounds like he is trying to jolly them out of their thoughts.

Marcia Harnack, a lawyer who specializes in real estate, is standing nearby and has heard their conversation. "That's what I was thinking, all through it," she says. She is a woman with the body of a strong man and the voice of a shy little girl; she clasps her hands when she speaks, as if asking for forgiveness for being too large. "Star of Bethlehem. It's what I thought when they first came in."

"Why did you think that?" Daniel asks.

"They were definitely black," says George Schwab, short, hard, and hairless, a little seersucker bomb in his blue-and-white suit. He has been selling off five-acre parcels of his family's old orchards, and Marcia has been helping him structure the deals.

"And how'd you figure that?" asks Daniel.

"I saw their skin, that's how," says George. He rises up on the toes of his tasseled loafers and clenches his small fists, as if a lightning bolt of fury has just gone through him. "We were almost slaughtered like a bunch of cattle in here."

"You didn't see their skin, George," Daniel says. "No one did."

"Don't tell me what I saw and didn't see," George says, his voice getting higher, as if it, too, had toes to rise upon. "You've got your own agenda."

By this he clearly means Iris, and Daniel's attachment to her, but Daniel has no choice but to ignore it. By now, two of the customers whose cell phones have been overlooked are calling the police; others join in the speculation and argument.

"They're the ones who robbed the Goulianos house," Fortune Pryor says.

"They completely trashed that sweet little house where Esther Rothschild used to live," Libby Young says.

"This is really fucked up," Daniel says. He feels like standing on a chair and exhorting the lot of them. His neighbors have become a dangerous collective, drunk on its own bad ideas. "This is really really really fucked up," he says, louder now. He feels Kate's wifely, cautioning touch on his elbow. "They could have been Chinese," Daniel shouts out. "They could have been Mexican, Polish, they could have been kids right from here."

"Shut up, Emerson," someone bellows from the front of the bar. There is a scattering of applause, murmurs of agreement.

"No one saw their skin," Daniel says, as forcefully as he can.

"I did." This is shouted by George.

"I did, too."

"I did, too."

"I did, too."

The more opposition Daniel meets, the more righteous indignation he feels. His eyes burn in their sockets, fury courses through him, his legs tremble. "I'm ashamed of this town," Daniel cries.

Now Kate's gentle touch has become an urgent tug. She pulls him toward her and says into his ear, "Daniel. Please. We've all heard you."

"Can you believe this shit?"

"They just think you're going on like this because you're with Iris." She says it with extraordinary kindness. Her eyes are soft with sympathy, she shakes her head.

"Let's just get out of here?" Lorraine says. "Can we please?"

Derek Pabst and another Leyden cop are the first of the police to arrive, followed shortly by four members of the state police. It takes nearly two hours for statements to be taken and reports to be written up, and when the Bistro's customers are finally able to leave it is nearly three in the morning. No cars have been stolen, but since all the keys have been taken, the customers must either call for a ride home or walk. It is Daniel's habit, however, to leave his keys in his car and he leads Kate and Lorraine through the cool night rain to his car, two blocks away.

As he drives them back to what was once his house, Lorraine, in the backseat, exclaims, "I just don't get it. You left your keys *in* your car? I just don't understand why you'd do that."

"He always leaves them in the ignition," Kate says. They are already a mile out of the village, driving through the wet, luminous night.

"It doesn't make sense," Lorraine says.

It strikes Daniel that perhaps she means to suggest some foreknowledge on his part, or even a degree of collusion with the robbers. And though confronting Lorraine is as far from Daniel's temperament as reaching over the backseat and giving her a smack across the face, he cannot resist asking her, "What are you suggesting, Lorraine?"

"Everyone in the whole place seemed to know who those guys were," she says. "And you were jumping through hoops to make them think otherwise."

"And?"

"It's just weird, that's all." Lorraine is slumped down, the back of her hand is pressed against her forehead.

"Our nerves are shot," says Kate. "All of us. I've never been robbed before." She clutches her chest, trying to make light of it. "Oh my God. I'm a crime statistic."

"They didn't rob you the first time they came to your house?" Lorraine says.

"No, not really. I told you. They wanted to use the facilities."

"Gross." Lorraine shudders. "But you were right next to them. Were they the same ones who just held us up?"

"How can she know that?" Daniel says.

"It's important," Lorraine says. "They should catch those fucking kids and feed them to the wolves."

"I agree," says Daniel. "Or maybe a lynching."

"Our nerves are shot," Kate repeats. She pats Daniel's knee, and then leaves her hand resting on it.

"They took two hundred and thirty dollars off me," Lorraine says.

"And my wallet, my address book, my Filofax, all my credit cards. My *life* was in that bag."

"That could be the problem right there," Daniel says.

"Fuck yourself," Lorraine says.

They arrive at Kate's house. The windows blaze with light. A weather-worn old Ford is in the driveway. Kate sees Daniel react to the unfamiliar car and tells him, "That's the baby-sitter's." He nods, surprised by the little trickle of gratitude that goes through him. Lorraine climbs out of the back door, waits for Kate with her back to them both. Kate powers down her window and says to Lorraine, "I'll be right in. I just want to talk to Daniel. For a minute." Lorraine shrugs without turning around and trods off to the house.

Kate waits for Lorraine to let herself in, and then she turns to Daniel. "I miss you. What do you think about that? Do you miss me?"

"Derek was acting so strange toward you in there. Did you notice that? It was as if he was furious with you."

"It's fine. We had a communication problem, and it's all ironed out. Can you answer my question? Do you miss me?"

"Of course I do. And Ruby. How is she?"

"Fine, we're both fine, we'd like you to come home." The ping of that little hammer blow of confession breaks her voice.

"Kate . . ."

"You know what?" she says. "I never told you, I mean I never actually said the words 'I love you.' But I do. I love you." Her eyes glitter, the color rises in her face. She seems moved, even inspired by her own words. Having said what was for so long unutterable, she now feels capable of saying anything. "I love you. You're my guy, you're my sweet man. I just assumed you knew, but now I see that sometimes it needs to be said."

"This is so painful, Kate."

"You're involved in something with her that's simply never ever ever ever ever going to work out, and I want to give you the chance to get out of it, and come back. You deserve that chance, Daniel. You really do. People get stuck in their bad decisions and they think nothing can undo them. Can I be honest with you? You look like you're about to pass out. But I know what's going on in that house of hers. That man's not going to suddenly get better. She's going to be looking after him for a long, long time. And that's the best-case scenario. We don't even want to talk about worst-case. But the fact is, you did this to him. For whatever reason, it was you."

"Whatever reason? It was an accident!"

"Maybe you've been looking to even the score ever since those black guys kicked you down the stairs."

"That's the stupidest fucking thing I have ever heard."

"Blacks and whites don't get along," she says. "Too much has happened. It's ruined. If something doesn't begin well, how can it end well?"

Daniel is silent, trying to think of something to say, some way of ending the conversation without enraging her, a way of sending her into the house that won't be humiliating. But Kate interprets his silence as Daniel's somehow being swayed, or even *moved* by what she is saying, and she puts her hand on his chest in a familiar, nostalgic way, and then quickly leans in to him with a deep, possessive kiss.

[18]

Morning. Warm dusty light pours through the uncurtained windows. Daniel has kicked the covers off his bed, and though he has slept only four hours, he is awake. His penis is hard, in a slightly disconcerting and even irritating counterpoint to his otherwise grim state of mind. *Relax, you idiot.* He stares at the ceiling, with its chicken-skin paint job, and thinks about the money he lost last night. His mind is pierced by the picadors of sudden money anxieties. He has made the mistake of totaling up the money he would have made had he stayed in New York at his old firm. He is minus about three hundred grand from that lovely decision. Two years now, he has been living in the half-life of his former affluence, but some time ago, without his admitting it to himself, his savings were depleted, the clothes he had bought when he was flush had begun looking like old clothes, his hair has forgotten what it is like to be cut by a master, and he no longer has that cheerful, ironic, healthy animal sheen of a young man with more money than he needs. He has never computed how much money he had been saving by living with Kate. Even coming up with about half of the monthly mortgage payments—and lately he has come to suspect that the sum she requested was less than half, that she was floating him to an extent—he was exempt from phone, electric, and heating bills; and groceries, which he usually paid for in full, used to cost in a month less than he was now spending in restaurants in a week.

Courting Iris has cost a king's ransom. Before he secured this little $1,400 per month tract house—he knows he is being robbed—he was spending hundreds of dollars per week on hotels, motels, and inns. He has spent $3,800 he can't afford on a pair of diamond earrings Iris can't wear. (Sometimes, she puts them on when she comes to see him, but mostly she forgets them, and last time when he asked why she wasn't wearing them she said that diamonds make her think of apartheid, which struck him as unfair and aggressive.) He spends money on having her sidewalk shoveled and her lawn mowed when he is unable to take care of it himself. He brings bags of groceries into her house when the coast is clear, and leaves them on the porch when members of Hampton's or Iris's family are on hand, and he has never collected a penny in reimbursement. He has brought her car into the shop for a new transmission and simply paid the bill. He bought her a purple-and-black Amish quilt that was hanging in the window of an antique store in town because when they walked by it one day she slowed down and looked at it. He forces himself to stop thinking of the tabs he has picked up, the munificence that has been his second nature. He is not regretting it, not a gesture, not a penny. Receiving these things never failed to delight Iris, who, as it turns out, is becoming very careful with her money; Hampton's coffers are rather full and his disability insurance is not only coming up with biweekly checks that approach what he was making before the accident but is also paying out for those occasional medical expenses his health insurers manage to duck. Nevertheless, Iris's frugality seems to be growing. She patrols her house, turning off lamps. Daniel has watched with amazement as she scratched a single postage stamp off a letter because the post office failed to cancel it and she thought it could be used again. If anything is left over on her dinner plate, even at the humblest restaurant, she will ask the waiter to have it wrapped—a half of a baked potato, thirty peas, a chicken wing. One of the reasons Daniel often asks her to wear those diamond earrings is sometimes he suspects she has sold them.

Money money money.

Daniel's phone rings and he lunges for the receiver. It's only seven-thirty. He has not had time to settle on a plausible narrative why someone would call him this early, and there is a moment of pure fear before he hears Kate's voice, which for some reason settles his nerves.

"I'm not waking you, am I?" she says. This is a continuation of an old relationship myth—because he sleeps less than Kate, she acts like he needs no sleep at all.

"What's up?" he asks. He struggles to sit up in bed; as soon as he stirs, the shifting of his blood recalls the feel of her kiss five hours ago.

"Ruby is freaking out here. She's just desperate for you to take her to school."

"Really?"

"Can you manage it? It would mean the world to her."

He suspects there is something less than the absolute truth in what Kate is saying. Ruby may have said she would like Daniel to bring her to day care, but it was most likely a matter of Kate asking her, *Would you like Daniel to bring you to school today?* and Ruby saying okay. After all, months have passed since Daniel moved out of the house and not once in that time has Ruby requested his chauffeuring services. It seems more than coincidence that Ruby would suddenly ask for him on a morning when Kate is in particular need of a few hours more sleep, and after a night when she had kissed him. And Kate's willingness to turn Ruby over to him is also a little suspect—she has been consistently grudging in allowing him to spend time with the little girl who was practically his stepdaughter. When permission is granted it is always qualified with the warning that he better not be taking her to Iris's house, and that Iris and even Nelson not be included in whatever little plan might be in the offing. Nevertheless, Daniel is not about to turn down a chance to spend time with Ruby and he says he will be over to pick her up in twenty minutes.

He arrives, in fact, in less time than that. Although he comes here regularly to pick Ruby up for their sad little dates, and, in fact, was just here a few hours ago dropping off Kate and Lorraine, he is taken somewhat by surprise by the loveliness and tranquility of the house and its acres. The rosebushes, after two reluctant summers, seem to have found their confidence and now are in full red-and-white flower. The lawn is a particularly luxurious dark green. The shutters have been painted at last; concrete urns ablaze with geraniums sit on the porch. Has the place ever looked so relaxing? A nasty little stab of envy. He lives in a crummy rented house. Iris's house, though certainly adequate, is also rented. Of the three of them, Kate is the one with roots—and how strange, since it seems to him she is the one with the least reason to be in Windsor County. Kate has left the door open, which he takes to mean that the alarm system has been deactivated and he is to simply let himself in, but he knocks and waits for her nevertheless. She comes to the door and her eyes peer out skeptically beneath furrowed brows, she seems to be implying he is being deliberately difficult by not waltzing right in.

"Is she ready?" Daniel asks. Ruby hears his voice and races in from the kitchen, in practically maniacal high spirits. He hasn't seen her in a couple of weeks and the first thing he notices is she has gotten a little chubby. In fact, she has gone from stocky to rather fat. Noticing this makes him feel petty and ungenerous, and he picks her up and holds her tightly, as if to make it up to her. "My God," he says, without meaning to, "you're getting so big!"

"It's nice of you to do this," Kate says. She looks surprisingly fresh and composed, considering she usually requires nine or ten hours of sleep and is operating on four at the most.

"I'm so glad to have the chance. Is Lorraine still around?" He doesn't even know why he's asked, he's simply lofting the ball back to Kate's side of the net.

"She fled the countryside for the safety of the city. I looked out the window at six o'clock and there was a taxi in the driveway, and then I saw her running for it. I guess she was trying to make the six-twenty."

She rakes her fingers through Ruby's hair, untangling it, but keeps her eyes fixed on Daniel.

He gets Ruby out of there as quickly as decently possible—he cannot shake the idea that Kate has engineered this whole thing as a way of further implicating him in the life of his old family, and since he cannot fathom that there is the slightest possibility of his being drawn back into the old domesticities, it seems more humane to be brief and even a little remote. He makes only minimal eye contact with Kate as she hands him Ruby's insulated snack bag, made of bright scarlet fabric with a Velcro flap. Yet when he has Ruby strapped into the child seat in the back of his car—he has kept the clunky gray-and-beige thing there despite his changed circumstances—he feels an unexpected swoon of loneliness and nostalgia. Buckling the straps of the seat recalls those mornings that now seem a lifetime ago when he began every day with Ruby, and the pleasures of those drives to My Little Wooden Shoe, when her sweet physical presence filled the car, and her little piping voice was like birdsong, and for ten minutes he could see the world through her unjaded eyes, ten minutes when the trees were goblins, the crows were looking directly at her, the sky was a zoo, and the grammar school a shining city on the hill.

"How's everything going back there?" he asks. He reaches back to pat her but misjudges her position and touches nothing but air.

"Fine," she says. She catches his fingers and squeezes them affectionately.

Oh I wish, I wish, I wish, he thinks, though he could not say for certain what he wishes for. To be back with Kate? He does not believe that is the case. To have Ruby somehow belong to him? It's out of the question. Yet there is something he longs for, something he has lost, and then, in a little flare of self-knowledge he knows what it is. The privilege of his own comfort. He has lost his easy life. He has lost Kate's house, her conversation, her soft, beautiful hair—he can barely believe he is thinking this, but then: there it is. He has lost Ruby, he has lost sleep, he has lost his energy, he has lost his sense of humor, he has lost his sight in one eye, he has lost if not his mind then at the very least his untroubled mind. And he has given it all away for something that seems to be slipping through his fingers.

When they are close to My Little Wooden Shoe, the familiar feeling of anticipation comes back to him, a pure and wild animal eagerness. Iris could very well be pulling into the parking lot at this very moment. It's fifteen minutes past eight o'clock. He knows she has a nine o'clock seminar at the college. The nurse who helps look after Hampton on the morning shift sometimes brings Nelson to day care, but Iris tries to do it herself whenever possible, and now, beneath a low, soft, blue-and-gray early summer sky, Daniel speeds the last mile of the way.

Her car is there, its doors dappled with mud. Hurriedly, Daniel takes Ruby out of the car seat and carries her across the parking lot, the pebbles crunching eagerly beneath his feet.

Before he and Ruby reach the door, Iris comes out in what appears to be a great rush. She is wearing a maroon skirt and jacket, black high-heeled shoes. She looks hurried but hopeless. Nelson is beside her, trying to keep pace. Then Iris sees Daniel, with Ruby in his arms. Daniel's first thought is that Iris will somehow misconstrue this, will think that he has spent the night at Kate's house, or is in some aspect of reconciliation. But Iris, in fact, does not seem to be speculating about anything.

"Mrs. Davis just called the school," she says, moving right past Daniel. "She has to leave in fifteen minutes and there's no one home to look after Hampton."

"Oh no," Daniel says, following after her. "What happened to Mrs. Davis?"

"What difference does it make? I have to get home. He's sleeping, he won't be up until noon, at the earliest. But he can't be in an empty house."

Daniel places Ruby on the ground and she and Nelson begin talking, smiling, and gesturing, like old friends in their mid-forties.

"You're all dressed up," Daniel says. "Are you supposed to be somewhere?"

"Yes." She gestures helplessly, a mixture of temper and surrender.

"I've got a meeting with my advisor. I don't know what I'm going to do. Fucking Mrs. Davis!" She doesn't bother to lower her voice. "And now this one . . ." She waves in Nelson's direction. "He's insisting on coming home, too. May as well. No sense putting him in day care if I'm going to be stuck in the house no matter what." She reaches toward Nelson, pulls him close to her, caresses his face, his head. For a moment he luxuriates in his mother's love, but then, suddenly, he squirms away from her.

"I thought all those people were there," Daniel says.

"They're gone, they left early this morning. Who can stand it?"

"I can look after him. He's sleeping. He won't know. I'll just be there."

"You can't do that," Iris says.

"How long do you need?"

"An hour and a half, two at the most. No, I can't. It's too strange."

"It's okay. Don't forget." He smiles. "I have almost no career. All I have to do is make a couple of calls, I can do that from your house." He is about to say, *It's the least I can do,* but he stops himself. Iris is looking at him intently; it takes him a moment to realize why: she is trying to decide under what rules of conduct it would be permissible to have Daniel looking after Hampton, even if it's only ninety minutes, even if Hampton will never know, even if there are the emergency phone numbers Scotch-taped onto the wall next to every phone in the house, even if this will never ever happen again.

"You're not going to see him, you know," she says. "Not unless you go upstairs and watch him sleep. And, Daniel, I don't want you to do that. I forbid you, I really do, I forbid you to do that."

"I won't. I wouldn't. I'm trying to help you here, Iris."

"I'm sorry."

"Okay, then?" he says.

"Okay."

"Good, then that's it." He is wringing his hands, trying not to touch her.

"I really appreciate it. You don't have to do anything, all you have to do is be there."

"You better hurry."

"Thank you." She is surprised how formal this sounds. She clears her throat. "I really appreciate it."

"I'm glad to help. I'll bring Ruby, okay?" As soon as he says it, he wishes he hadn't, but he doesn't want to complicate matters by taking it back. Besides, Ruby will take care of Nelson, which Daniel cannot really manage. And Kate will never know.

I love you, Iris mouths.

He presses his hand to his heart, as if he has been stabbed.

"Ruby?" he says. "Would you like to go to Nelson's for the first part of the morning?"

Iris doesn't have time to drive back to her house, she doesn't even have time to transfer Nelson's car seat to Daniel's car, and she certainly has no time to jolly Nelson out of his annoyance that he is not going to be spending the morning with his mother after all. Daniel makes his way to Juniper Street with the kids in his backseat, Ruby snugly strapped in, while Nelson, as if to announce his policy of total noncooperation with Daniel, refuses to keep his seat belt on. Each time Daniel glances into the rearview mirror, he sees Nelson glowering at him, and before long the boy's antipathy becomes so wounding and, frankly, so irritating that Daniel feels it might be an appropriate act of discipline to slam his foot on the brake and send the boy pitching forward.

Mrs. Davis, a thin, tired-looking fifty-year-old black woman, is waiting nervously by the front door. She is so fretful that she doesn't even inquire as to why Daniel is coming there to look after Hampton, though she has never seen Daniel before. Perhaps his being with Nelson proves his legitimacy. She gives Daniel no instructions, nor does she offer any explanations or apologies. In fact, all she says is a quick hello to Nelson, and "Now I'm really late" to Daniel, and then she puts a tan ski jacket over her uniform, though it is at least seventy degrees outside.

"Mrs. Davis!" Daniel calls out, when she is nearly out the door. "Wait!"

She turns toward him with a practiced, opaque expression, unapproachable. "Yes," she says in a tone that says no.

He doesn't know exactly what to say, but he is suddenly afraid to be in charge. "Is there anything I need to know here?"

"When's Mrs. Welles coming home?" Mrs. Davis asks.

"In about an hour and a half."

"That man ain't going nowhere in the next ninety minutes," she says, moving past Daniel and out onto the porch. An old Ford Taurus is at the curb, with an immense kid of about eighteen at the wheel, wearing a sleeveless shirt. The car rattles as it idles, inky exhaust pours out of the tailpipe. Daniel stands on the porch and watches Mrs. Davis hurry toward the waiting car—had it been there all along? The driver starts to get out but she waves him back in; she goes to the passenger side and lets herself in, and a moment later the Taurus pulls away with an unmuffled roar.

Daniel goes back into the house and as soon as he is inside he can tell by the quality of the silence that the children are no longer there. He goes to the kitchen and looks into the backyard. An olive-green tent has been pitched between two hemlocks; Nelson is standing next to the flap while Ruby crawls in, and then he crawls in himself. Daniel wonders for a moment whether he ought to go out and show the flag of adult supervision, but then he thinks it would be pointless.

He wanders through the house, looking for a spot where he can unobtrusively sit while the time passes. What had seemed at first like a favor he was capable of doing for Iris seems now perilous, foolish, and strange. The entire success of the gesture hinges on Hampton staying asleep, and though Daniel is still enough of an optimist to believe that Hampton will not awaken before Iris's return, now that he is in the house—with its signs of suffering everywhere, a cane in the corner, a table filled with amber medicine bottles, brightly colored plastic baskets filled with laundry, piles of blankets for the frequent house guests, the loving family who come when they can to share the burden of Hampton's affliction—now that he is breathing the Lysol-tinged heat of this airless, sunny room, Daniel realizes not only that he is perched on the precipice of disaster but that he has been on this increasingly exhausting edge for months now.

He sits on the sofa facing the empty fireplace. Next to it is a large wicker basket filled with mail. Idly, Daniel looks in and sees that it is all for Hampton. Daniel scoops his hand into the pile, lets them fall; it's like a write-in campaign, an appeal to the governor for neurological clemency. Free the Hampton One, let him come back to renew his sub- scriptions, make his donations, place his order, balance his checking ac- counts, look after his investments, go to Bermuda.

Scarecrow comes waddling down the stairs, roused from her spot next to Hampton's bed. She seems to have aged years in the past six months. Her rump is massive now, her gait slow and uncertain, her brown eye is alert, but her blue eye, once keen and electric, is now milky and opaque. She moves toward Daniel, lowers her snout, and pushes the top of her head against his legs. He strokes her silky ears, and she emits a deep, mellow groan of pleasure.

"Oh, Scarecrow, Scarecrow, what in the world are we going to do?" Daniel says, in that plaintive murmur people sink into when they are opening their heart to an animal. The old shepherd raises her snout, looks up and her tongue unfurls from her mouth, lands on Daniel's chin, and then sweeps up over his lips. "What are we going to do, Scarecrow? What's going to happen to us? It's pretty messed up, isn't it, Scarecrow? How did everything get to be so broken?"

Daniel slumps back in the chair, continues to pet the dog. He closes his eyes and is about to sink into sleep when he is startled and revived by the sound of footsteps directly overhead. Hampton is awake, awake and moving. His first impulse is to hide; he stands up and his legs tremble for want of flight, his good eye looks for the quickest way out of the room. He tries to calm himself by thinking that perhaps it is someone other than Hampton upstairs, or even if it is Hampton, then he may not be coming down—he is going to get a drink of water, or take a leak, or maybe he has heard the children in the backyard and he is going to a window to gaze out at them. But no: this is merely a story Daniel is telling himself, a little explanatory fable that will allow him to believe that the worst is not about to happen.

Now the footsteps are on the stairs, coming down, and Daniel has not run, he has not hidden. He sits down. He will seem less threatening, less intrusive, seated. He crosses his legs, left to right, then right to left, and then leaves them uncrossed, the knees slightly parted, his clammy hands folded between them. He ransacks his mind for something to say, an explanation for why he is here, an apology, a bit of small talk, and then he remembers what should have been impossible to forget—Hampton cannot understand a word, not spoken or written, and all Hampton himself can say is that single stunned syllable: da. Da Da Da.

How strange, then, to finally see him, this strong, beautiful man whose throat was pierced by a rocket, this ruined prince who has lost everything. He is dressed in copper-colored pajamas, with white piping around the pockets and down the leg. The top buttons of his shirt are open, the scar just below the Adam's apple looks like a wad of chewed-up gum, and someone has spread talcum powder on his throat all the way down to the chest. He is freshly shaved but his eyeglasses have been snapped in two and then repaired with tape á la Ferguson Richmond. It seems unthinkable that Hampton would be wearing broken glasses, it is, for the moment, the saddest thing in the world. Sadder than his slack mouth, the corner of which is yanked down and to the side, sadder than his dull, unblinking eyes, sadder than the cologne Mrs. Davis has splashed on him, and sadder, even, than the fact that he is wearing his wristwatch, with its lizard-skin band and nineteen jewels, its expensive Swiss nervous system, its mini-clocks at the bottom giving the time in London and Tokyo.

"Hello, Hampton," Daniel says. He knows he cannot be understood, yet he can't simply stand there and say nothing. And even if the words are gibberish to Hampton, even if to his bombed-out brain the sounds Daniel makes are no more decipherable than the chattering of a monkey, perhaps the context will do, the logic of the moment, the gesturing hand, the smiling mouth, the deferential little bow.

"Da," Hampton whispers. He shuffles forward a step. He hasn't noticed that Scarecrow is underfoot now and on his second step he catches the dog's paw beneath his foot. She lets out a high, piercing yelp. Hampton is startled. His eyes widen, his mouth opens—his expressions are guileless and large. His personality, no longer projected through the scrim of language, has now an intolerable purity. He looks down at the dog and smiles. At first it seems to Daniel that there is some cruelty here, but then Hampton pats the dog's head with a wooden herky-jerky movement, and Daniel realizes that the smile was one of recognition: Scarecrow's cry has made more sense to Hampton than Daniel's hello.

When he has comforted Scarecrow, made his amends, Hampton straightens up again, looks at Daniel, taking him in in a long, silent gaze.

Daniel feels he must somehow communicate, but the only sign language he can think of is gestures of supplication. He folds his hands, lowers his head, and sorrowfully shakes his head. Yet even this does not seem enough—what could be? He wants Hampton to be restored. Short of that, he wants to be forgiven, he wants Hampton to give that to him, to lift him off the hook and set him free, to place an exonerating hand on Daniel's shoulder and admit to the idea—submit to it, if that's what it takes—that what happened in those woods was a fluke and had nothing to do with Daniel and Iris. Daniel will not allow himself to beg for mercy, he will not try to urge Hampton to see that the two of them are simply men who have been caught in the Rube Goldberg machinery of life.

Then, for no particular reason, he has a fleeting thought: Ruby. How long have those two been out there? A half hour? More?

But the thought evaporates because Hampton is crying. He is drumming his long fingers against his head—shaved by Mrs. Davis, nicked here and there, the cuts left to dry in the air—and he is shaking his head, more vociferously than a simple no, he is shaking it to clear it, to dispel some merciless, obliterating beast that lives within, eating his words. Tears as thick as glycerine streak down his cheeks, and his mouth is twisted into a scowl of grief. Daniel's heart, in a convulsion of empathy, leaps, as if to its own annihilation.

Inside Nelson's tent, the sunlight, filtered through the nylon, is pale green. The unmoving air smells of dirt, candy, and child. Nelson and Ruby sit on two beige bath towels that serve as the floor in Nelson's hideaway. Between them is a Styrofoam cooler that Nelson uses as a receptacle for his playhouse provisions. The lid is off and he is showing Ruby his treasures one by one, some of them his, some of them appropriated. A bottle of Elmer's glue, a manicure set in a leather case, a half-eaten PowerBar, an eyecup, a flashlight, several batteries, loose kitchen matches, a hand puppet of some kind of American Indian princess, a block of baking chocolate, and a gun, given to Hampton by his own father for the safety of the house, stored and then half forgotten in the drawer of his night table, on hand in case a robber should enter the house, or some vicious white kids looking for a little racial adventure, a gun sneaked out of the house by Nelson several days ago, which has gone unmissed, a pistol that has seen its better days, the front sight chipped, the blacking on the trigger guard and the barrel peeling off, but with an aroma Nelson finds entrancing, narcotic, a mixture of old steel and oil. He picks it up, careful to keep the barrel pointed toward the ground, and bends his head ceremonially over it, breathes in the blunt, manly bouquet, and then he lays the pistol in both his hands and holds it out there for Ruby to take her turn.

Hampton walks across the room and sits on the sofa Daniel has occupied. He covers his face with his hands, his feet move up and down as if he were walking. There is room on the sofa, but Daniel cannot sit there. Instead, he kneels in front of Hampton. Hampton uncovers his face, and tentatively, as if he and Daniel were creatures, different species, he offers his hand. And Daniel, upon taking it, and feeling the cool weight of it, the simple skin and bone of it, realizes in a grievous instant what he has at once known and prevented himself from knowing all along, the knowledge he has carried in his belly and denied: they are all of them ruined, Iris, Hampton, and himself, ruined.

"Oh, Hampton," Daniel says.

Hampton looks away, a sheen of dullness shrink-wrapped onto his eyes. "Da, da," he says, barely audibly.

"I'm sorry," Daniel says, knowing it cannot be understood. But maybe God is listening. "I'm so sorry."

"Da."

"Do you want anything? Something to drink or eat? Anything. Is there anything I can do?"

"Da." Hampton turns further on the sofa, twisting his body, almost looking behind himself now. The fabric stretches between the buttons of his copper pajamas. His feet continue to pump up and down, his legs waggle, he is squirming like a child desperate to relieve himself.

The children have a gun. The gun is loaded. The safety is disengaged. And when the gun fires the sound is so far removed from Daniel's expectations and so divorced from his experience of life that at first he barely reacts to it. A truck's backfire, a sonic boom. But Hampton responds immediately. He leaps off the sofa, runs across the living room toward the kitchen and the back door, and Daniel, awakened to reality by Hampton's response, follows, and now he knows that what he has heard is a gunshot.

Hampton and then Scarecrow and then Daniel race across the backyard. Daniel is shouting now; he can't really understand what has happened. In the few seconds it takes to get from the back porch to the tent, Daniel has two thoughts. Only one shot was fired, is the first thought, and let it be Ruby who is unhurt, is the second.

Hampton, in his rush, has lost his slippers. Daniel, who must wait for Hampton to crawl in before he himself can enter the tent, shouts out Ruby's name, but there is no answer, and then he calls for Nelson and is likewise met with silence.

Finally, Hampton is in the tent and Daniel follows, and the children are there, Ruby a frieze of fear, Nelson cool, a blank, but it's clear in his slightly narrowed eyes and the stubborn, impervious set of his mouth that he is ready to deny everything. The bullet has gone through the side of the tent about a foot above Ruby's head, and a brilliant, slow-turning rod of light shines through the hole. Daniel stares at it for a moment as if it were the presence of God.

The tent is too small for the adults to stand up. Daniel rises into a simian stoop and gathers Ruby into his arms. The feel of her, the comfort of her heft, causes him to straighten, and the pressure of his head against the top of the tent unfastens it from its pegs. The center pole wobbles and a moment later the entire tent deflates, tips over.

"You're wrecking it!" Nelson screams.

"Where's the gun, Nelson?" Daniel says. His voice is calm, gentle. The children are alive, unhurt, the anger is gone. Life is so precious, time is so short, we're all in it together . . .

"You're wrecking the tent!" Nelson continues to shout.

"Da da da," Hampton says, sobbing, the tears coursing down his stricken face. He places his hands on Nelson's shoulders, pulls him close. "Da," he cries. And then, lifting his face, he shouts it out again, toward heaven.

"Where's the gun, Ruby?" Daniel murmurs into her ear, and she points to the Styrofoam cooler, which is now partly concealed by the collapsed tent. Daniel places her on the ground—her frightened little hands grip his trousers—and he pulls the green nylon off the cooler's lid, opens it up, and there, on top of Nelson's heap of treasures, lies the pistol.

"Okay, please, everybody stand away," Daniel says, retrieving the gun. But Hampton cannot understand what Daniel is asking, and Nelson is staying with his father, and Ruby adheres to Daniel. He picks the gun up, careful to keep his hand as far as possible from the trigger, pointing the barrel straight down at the ground. He backs away, moving as if afraid the gun might spontaneously fire again. Hampton, Nelson, Scarecrow, and Ruby follow him, and now he stands in the middle of the backyard, holding the gun and trying to resist the impulse to heave it into the trees.

And now he is pounding his heel into the ground, digging out a hole so that he might bury the gun, but after a few moments the madness of this is apparent and he stops.

Hampton presses his hands on Nelson's shoulders, instructing him to stay exactly where he is, and then he walks over to Daniel and reaches for the gun. "Da," he says softly, in a somehow reassuring way. Daniel, at a loss, anxious to be rid of the gun, relinquishes his awkward possession of the pistol, and then steps back, gathers Ruby in. *What did I just do?* he wonders, as he imagines Hampton firing the gun. But Hampton puts the safety lock on, and then flicks the magazine catch, which is right behind the trigger guard, and then slides the magazine case open at the base of the grip and empties out three cartridges. He puts the cartridges into the pocket of his pajama bottoms and hands the empty gun to Daniel.

They walk toward the house, just as Iris is coming through the back door and stepping out onto the porch. Her initial frown of bewilderment is quickly supplanted by alarm. To see her lover, her husband, two children, and a gun is more than can be understood, but it can surely be evaluated.

"Daniel, Jesus Christ, what is going on here?"

"Da da da," Hampton says, excited to see her.

"Did you know there's a gun in your house?" Daniel says.

"Da da da . . ."

"Tell me what's happening?"

The terror of the gunshot is just catching up to Daniel, like those near misses on the highway that take a minute or two to rattle us, to make hands shake and hearts race. "Did you know there's a fucking gun in your house?" he says, his voice rising. "Did you know that?"

"Yes. Sort of. It's not something I think about."

"Da da . . ."

"It's not something you think about? Well, your son does. Your *son* . . ." His voice curdles around the word. He hears it himself, wonders for a moment at the ugliness with which he has infused it, and then he sees Iris's suddenly steely gaze. *Fuck it.* Yet even the phrase, and the way it stiff-arms his feelings, the way it pushes him out of love and into the emptiness and foreverness of his own solitude cannot stop the anger that is enveloping him like a trance, and when Nelson walks past him, Daniel is astonished by his own sudden desire to throttle the boy.

"Da da da da da da."

"What is he doing down here?" Iris asks.

"He got up, he came down. What was I supposed to do?"

"Oh Jesus," says Iris, while making a series of comforting gestures toward Hampton. *Easy now, it's okay, I'm here, easy, easy* . . . Nelson is next to her now, pressing his forehead into her stomach. She staggers back a step, touches him, holds him.

"What in the fuck are you people doing with a gun in your house?" Daniel says.

"You people?" Iris asks. "I don't believe what I'm hearing."

"You know what I'm saying, don't try to turn this into something else."

"Well, *we people* don't always feel safe when we're living in a house surrounded by *you people*."

"Da! Da!"

"All right, Iris." He feels tugging at his shirt and looks down at Ruby. Her face is flush, her eyes immense and glittering.

"Why is he saying that, Daniel?"

"It's okay, honey. We're going to leave now."

"But why is he saying that over and over?"

"He's not feeling well, baby."

"He's not feeling well?" Iris says.

"All right," says Daniel. "You supply the answer. Your kid just fired a bullet two inches over her head, so I'm sure this would be the right time to fill her in on all the neurological details."

Daniel lifts Ruby off the ground. "Sorry," he says. "There's something about a kid getting a bullet in the head that puts me a little on edge."

"I didn't do it," Nelson whimpers, looking imploringly up at Iris.

"Shh," she says, soothing his forehead. Then, to Daniel, "No one was hurt. The only person hurt around here is Hampton."

"Thanks to me."

"Okay, if that's how you want it."

Hampton, walking now toward the porch, toward his family, bumps into Daniel, and Daniel, with a vivid surge of temper, grabs the gun out of Hampton's hand. He doesn't know what he will do with it—he thinks again of simply heaving it—but he is certain that it must no longer be in Hampton's possession, nor with any of them. He will take it to the river. Or to the police. Yes, the police . . .

The police the police . . . He thinks it over and over, incorporating the unfamiliar idea into his little corner of consciousness. And then he turns and sees the police have indeed arrived—Derek Pabst and Jeff Crane. They enter Hampton and Iris's backyard, exuding confidence and implacability with every long stride. Their service revolvers are still holstered. They hold their caps in their hands, like country folk calling on neighbors.

"Da da da da . . ."

Crane, boyish at forty, with neatly combed reddish hair and a prim, self-righteous mouth, sees that Daniel is holding a gun. Hampton and Iris stand together on the porch.

"You want to place that weapon on the ground, Dan," Crane says.

Daniel does as he is told, immediately.

"We got a call about someone doing some shooting around here," Derek says.

"My fault," Daniel says, knowing he must, knowing any other answer will cause more trouble than his taking the blame.

Crane picks up the pistol, checks to see if there are any cartridges. Daniel watches him, wonders if Crane knows how far his daughter, Mercy, has gone to escape his world.

"Da da da da da da da da da da da da da da . . ."

"What the hell is he saying?" Crane asks.

"He's all right," Derek says. "Don't worry about that." Then, to Daniel: "Whose gun is this?"

"Mine."

"Yours?" Derek tucks his chin in, shakes his head. "Why'd you fire it?"

"Derek, come on. Obviously it was an accident."

"That's a hell of an accident, man."

"Was anyone hurt? Did it hit anything?"

"Scared the hell out of at least two people. Enough to call." Daniel sees it playing out. Derek does not believe him, he knows Daniel hasn't brought a concealed weapon to this house, but he's going to let it pass.

"Is this weapon registered in your name?" Crane asks.

"Yes, it is."

"Mind if we take a look?"

"I don't have it with me," Daniel says. He turns away from Crane, directs his request to Derek. "How about I bring in the paperwork a little later on?"

Derek looks at Iris, Hampton, and Nelson on the porch, and the three of them are silent, their faces blank, their gazes slightly averted, as his eyes carefully move over them. Satisfied, Derek turns back toward Daniel and, indicating Ruby, he says, "You're carrying pretty precious cargo there, buddy."

"I know, Derek. I know."

"It would be a hell of a thing."

"I know."

"Kate know you're here?"

"No."

Derek nods, his lower lip slightly extended. After a silence that seems to go on and on, he asks, "You all right?"

"Me?" asks Daniel.

"Yeah."

"I'm fine, Derek. Just a stupid mistake."

Derek gestures to Crane, time to leave. Crane hands the pistol back to Daniel.

"You okay?" Derek asks Ruby.

"I'm fine," she says. "It was stupid."

While they are talking, Iris, Hampton, and Nelson go inside their house. Daniel doesn't notice until he hears the door close behind them.

He only wants to go home, but he drives to his office instead. He can no longer afford to pay Sheila Alvarez's salary—nor can he bear her occasional disdain—and he has cut her hours to two half days a week. When he lets himself into the office he is surprised to see her there. She is at her desk, behind a pile of what looks like at least a hundred files.

"What are you doing here, Sheila?"

"I've been going through the files. There's a lot of people who owe you money, did you know that?"

He shakes his head no.

She looks at him and then she, too, shakes her head. "You poor thing," she says. "Just look at you." She swivels her chair, puts her back to him, and resumes entering numbers on a calculator. "Your parents were here about twenty minutes ago," she says. "They dropped an envelope on your desk."

He goes into his office. He and Iris cleared off his desk last time they made love here, and now the only things that are on it are his telephone and the envelope left by Carl and Julia. He opens it.

Dear Dan,

You're going to think we've gone senile, but we've decided not to change our wills, after all. The Raptor Center can do without us, and we're going to keep things the way they were.

Much love,
Mother and Dad

He stares at the words on the page until they blur and swim away. So the birds won't be getting his parents' money after all. He buries his face in his hands. Was this why he'd come all this way? Had he just been given what he had been seeking all along, this small, glancing caress?

He is exhausted, he feels unequal to the task of his life. He is not put together for such difficulties.

Three hours later, at two in the afternoon, Daniel is in his house, drinking a warm beer, staring out his small living room window at what he can see of the white oak in front, he is crouched deep down into the cellar of himself, waiting for the storm to pass. He does his best to speak kindly and rationally to himself, but he is inconsolable. He thinks of the tone of Iris's voice as she spoke to him from her porch, the distance, the contempt. As soon as there was anger she spoke to him as if he were, first and foremost, a white man. What happened to love bringing history to its knees? How could all those old adversities be having their way?

He weeps. Stops. Drinks. Belches. Stares. Weeps. Weeps. Tries to talk himself down, as if his life were a drug, a bad, a terrible, a most powerful and devastating drug that he must survive while it works its way through his system.

He has lost everything, and there is nothing he can say to himself that can change that.

Kate will never trust him with Ruby again.

Recoil. Try to think of something else.

Hampton. No. Not now. Something else.

Monkey mind swings from branch to branch.

A perfect, pulverizing memory of falling down those stairs.

My God, there is no safe thought, nothing in his mind that is not lethal.

Ruby's hands. Kate's kiss.

Those boys in their masks.

That rocket's fire in the deep wooded night.

And then, most terribly of all, wherever the monkey swings there is Iris. Her shoes. The smell of her scalp, her breath. The ten thousand details of her life fill the tree and then fly off, a terrifying flutter of wings. Cut the tree down, pull out the roots, and a river takes its place. And in that river she is there. Her hands, the taste of her, her hair, her darkness, her car, her keys, what she might say next.

The phone is on his lap, but it does not ring, nor can he dial it. He cannot hear her voice, not that voice from the porch. *If that's how you want it.*

Hours pass. Darkness bleeds across the floor, he pushes his chair back, afraid to have it touch him.

Then, at last, the phone rings, but he does not answer. It chirps in his lap, the machine comes on, he hears his own terrible voice, and then a dial tone. Night fills the room like floodwater. He lifts his feet, tucks them beneath him.

At eight o'clock, Iris arrives. He first sees her headlights flare against his windows, then he hears her footsteps. She lets herself in without knocking.

"Daniel?" she says softly, into the darkness.

He clears his throat, afraid of his own voice. "Right here," he says.

She fumbles for a lamp, turns it on, the bulb dull, quite helpless against the night. She is wearing a red T-shirt, baggy shorts, sandals. She is holding a clear blue plastic container of food.

"What are you doing?" she asks.

He can tell by her face what he must look like. There's nothing to do about that now.

"Thinking."

She sighs. She understands what that means.

"That was so terrible, Daniel. I'm sorry."

"*You're* sorry? Oh my God, Iris. I don't even know what to say."

"There's nothing to say. Look." She holds the plastic container higher. "I made some rice and beans. Are you hungry?"

"I don't know."

She takes his hand, pulls him out of his chair, and leads him to the relative neutrality of the kitchen. She seats him at the table, opens the container, and then finds a fork in the silverware drawer. She sits across from him, gestures for him to eat.

"I put a little extra hot sauce in it," she says. "The way you like it."

He tastes it. Its hotness feels cleansing.

"And hardly any salt," she says. "I've noticed you never salt your food."

He takes another bite. He hasn't eaten since yesterday. He sees her glancing quickly at her watch.

"You have to leave?" he asks.

"No. Well, actually, soon." She gets up, carries her chair next to his, and sits again. She runs her fingers through his hair.

"Who's home?" he asks.

"I've got somebody new, a really sweet Jamaican lady named Sandra." She crosses her fingers. "Want to see something?" She stands, lifts her T-shirt, exposing her belly. "Look how fat I'm getting."

"I don't see it. You look the same."

"Are you kidding? Look!" She grabs an inch of skin, shakes it. "I might be pregnant."

Daniel struggles to keep his expression detached. But he thinks *if only*. He takes another mouthful of her food.

"That would be all we need, wouldn't it?" says Iris.

"Do you really think you might be?"

"I don't know. I sure feel bloated. Who knows? Maybe we can be one of those couples who think they can solve the world's problems by creating a new race, or a non-race, or whatever."

"That might be a good idea."

She smiles, shakes her head. "I actually have to go. I told Sandra I'd be right back."

"How's Hampton? Nelson?"

"Let's not even talk about them. Can you do that?"

"I don't know."

"I have to leave, honey. I'm sorry."

"Thanks for the food."

"You were starved."

"It's good. Soul food."

"Not really. There's no ham hocks or any of that old-timey crap."

"It's still soul food."

Iris kisses his forehead, strokes his hair again.

"Do you still love me?"

"Yes," Daniel says.

"This is so hard."

"I know."

"Don't you sometimes wish . . . ?"

He reaches for her. "No," he says. "It's too late for that. There's no turning back."